FIRST CONTACT, SECOND CHANCES

THE SHANTIVIRA BOOK THREE

FAY ABERNETHY

First published in 2025 by
Fay Abernethy
c/o RA Matutis
Berliner Straße 57, 14467 Potsdam, Germany
www.fayabernethy.com

Text copyright © 2025 Fay Abernethy
This work is registered with the UK Copyright Service: Registration No.
284758296

German National Library Cataloguing in Publication Data
A catalogue record for this book is available from the German National
Library (*Deutsche Nationalbibliothek*). More details available at http://
dnb.d-nb.de.

Cover design and illustration © Patrick Knowles www.patrickknowles
design.com
Formatting by BB eBooks Co., Ltd. www.bbebooksthailand.com

ISBN: 978-3-949516-078 (ebook)
ISBN: 978-3-949516-085 (paperback)
ISBN: 978-3-949516-092 (hardcover)
ISBN: 978-3-949516-122 (audiobook, coming 2025/26)

Paperback edition

This book is dedicated to all those who, for whatever reason, have left the country of their birth and made their home elsewhere.

FREE NOVELLA

PART ONE

1. KIDNAP
JOE, JANUARY 2016

JOE SAT AT his regular table in the corner of the *Cath Palug*, nursing a pint of Brains and listening to *Life on Mars*. The radio was playing Bowie song after Bowie song in honour of the musician's death a few days ago. The lyrics had an ironic relevance, in the circumstances.

He rotated his glass on its beer mat, watching the pub fill with locals coming for Sunday lunch, cheerfully shedding their coats, hats and scarves and hanging them on the hooks by the door. Wooden chairs scraped across the flagstones and the white noise of chatter bounced off the low ceiling, making it hard to distinguish individual voices. A couple of familiar faces smiled and waved at him.

As he returned their greeting, his mouth went dry at the enormity of what he was about to attempt. He and his team had planned every detail, considered every possibility. He'd thought the isolated pub would be the perfect location but now, looking round at his fellow patrons, he suddenly doubted his decision. These people knew him. They trusted him and Kitty. What if someone got hurt?

Well, he'd just have to make sure nobody did, wouldn't he? There was no going back. If he wanted to protect humanity – not just from alien invasion, but from itself, too – this operation was necessary.

He twisted in his seat to glance through the window behind him, checking the weather one more time. The winter sky was still white: blank and boring. No wind, no sun, no rain. No snow, either. As good a day as you could hope for, for a military operation in Snowdonia National Park. They must have arrived by now.

Joe took a swig of beer and reached out with his mind to Kitty, who was currently a raven perched atop the pub's slate roof.

Report, babe? he asked, in Welsh.

They're getting into position. Very quick and quiet. There's a sniper with some serious kit along the roof from me, and the pub's surrounded, although you can't see them. There's a Land Rover and three vans: one for the soldiers, one's packed with electronics, the other looks like prisoner transport. I'm assuming that one's for you.

They wish. Joe projected all the confidence he could muster into his telepathic voice. *They've picked the wrong person to put pressure on.* Privately, he shivered, imagining himself being bundled into the van and driven to a secret location for interrogation by government agencies. They'd never get that far. Kitty would make sure they didn't.

They mean business, Joe. Are you sure you want to do this?

We need a back channel to the British Government, Cath. *The UN communication route is too slow. And we need to show them they're not in charge.*

What if they don't send your friend?

They will. Joe prayed he was right. *He's the biggest lever they've got.*

There's someone coming out of the middle van. Is that him?

Joe looked through Kitty's corvid eyes, momentarily disoriented by her present shape's near all-round vision. He pulled his attention away from the encircling mountains and focused on the man in hiking clothes descending from the vehicle. Relief surged through Joe's veins.

That's him. Major Robert Morgan.

He's radiating a strong electromagnetic signal. I think he's covered in surveillance kit.

As expected. Stick to the plan. Now get back down here before he comes in.

Kitty materialised beside him in domestic cat form. He stroked her back, then she jumped down to hide under the bench, awaiting her moment.

Angharad, the *Cath Palug's* landlady, brought over his lunch: steak and kidney pie with hand-made chips.

'Is everything all right, Joe?' she asked, as she placed the plate in front of him. 'You look kind of serious.'

'You know that thing we talked about?' he murmured. 'It's today.'

Angharad's eyes widened. 'Oh. Right. Well, they'd better not upset our customers.'

During their preparations, Joe and Kitty had decided that if they acted fast, they wouldn't need to evacuate the pub. He opened his mouth to explain, but it was too late. A figure appeared behind her: one he'd not seen for half a lifetime, but familiar all the same. Robert Morgan.

'*Barney!*' Rob exclaimed, 'What are you doing here?'

Joe gritted his teeth. No one called him 'Barney' anymore. '*Rob, mêt! Ti'n iawn?*' he replied, pressuring his former NCO to speak Welsh. Something he knew Rob wasn't used to.

'*Iawn, diolch*,' said Rob and slung his rucksack onto the chair opposite Joe. 'I just climbed *Moel Hebog* and I've worked up quite an appetite. Are you alone? May I join you?'

Joe flourished his hand in an expansive 'be my guest' gesture. 'Grab yourself a pint and order some food,' he said.

Rob grinned and stepped away to talk to Angharad's husband, Ianto, at the bar.

That mud on his boots is too dry to have got there today, muttered Kitty silently in Joe's head. *Does he really think you'll fall for his 'I was out walking and happened to bump into you' routine?*

These are the first steps of a dance, cariad. *Let him take them.*

Rob returned and set his brimming glass down carefully on a beer mat. Joe picked it up again, while lifting his own half-full pint. Rob stared at him, confused.

Now, Cath!

Strong fingers gripped Joe's ankle. He closed his eyes to prevent the nausea as his ears rushed with the diving-into-a-swimming-pool noise which accompanied teleportation. Sensing they'd arrived, he opened them to see Rob wild-eyed and hyperventilating on Joe's brown leather sofa.

He's gonna pop, Cath, *can you pass him the bin*?

Syenitian-shaped Kitty did so, while Joe put their beers on the dining table. Not a drop spilled, he noted with satisfaction.

6

When he turned back to the sofa, Major Morgan was puking his guts up into Joe's bronze waste paper basket.

'Sorry, Rob,' he said, passing him a cloth to wipe his mouth. 'If I'd told you to shut your eyes, you'd have known something was up.'

Rob darted a terrified glance at Kitty, who smiled at him, flaunting her over-sized canines. 'Get . . . her . . . away from me!'

Kitty retreated, busying herself by placing the pint glasses on coasters to protect the wooden surface.

Joe sat on the sofa and rested a reassuring hand on his friend's shoulder. 'Rob. You're safe here. Definitely safer than in a building surrounded by the military.'

'*Where* is here?'

Time to hit him with the truth. 'On *The Pride of Essoona*, my live-aboard spacecraft. We're in Docking Bay 3 of the *Shantivira* space station, 300 000 kilometres above the Earth.'

'You're having me on.'

Joe issued a brief command in Syenitian. The opposite wall became transparent, revealing the *Koppakuoria*, the *Shantivira's* beetle-shaped cargo ship, and the giant magnetically shielded opening into space. The Earth hung before them like a suspended marble, adorned with swirls of blue, green and white.

Rob made a choking sound of disbelief.

'Rob, we don't have much time,' Joe said urgently. 'Your team'll be wondering why they've lost the signal. I don't want them storming the pub and causing chaos. Take off your top.'

'*What?*' said Rob, tearing himself away from the view.

'You're recording as well as broadcasting, right? I need to tell them what's going to happen next.'

'How did you know I'm . . . ? Aargh!'

His voice became muffled as Kitty pulled his shirt off over his head. Rob's torso was plastered with surgical tape and electronics.

Joe chuckled. 'Proper prior preparation prevents piss-poor performance, Rob. You taught me that.'

Kitty began ripping off the tape and Rob yelped with pain. Joe emptied the glass fruit bowl and placed the recording equipment in it, item by item. He handed Rob his top and Rob struggled back into it, scowling.

Joe picked up a gadget with a microphone and a small memory block attached. 'This one, right?'

Rob said nothing, ignoring Joe to gaze at the Earth. Kitty nodded.

Here goes nothing, he said to her privately, holding the microphone to his mouth. Out loud, he said, 'This is a message from Joe Llewellyn, Captain of the *Shantivira* Earth Defence Facility and Galaksi Alliance Representative for Earth.'

'My boss doesn't speak Welsh,' Rob interrupted.

'I know,' said Joe. 'He'll have to get an interpreter, won't he?' He took a breath and continued. 'Major Morgan is safe and well. I understand Her Majesty's Government has many questions about my space station and my employers, but I'm not prepared to sacrifice my liberty to answer them. Major Morgan will be my guest on the *Shantivira* for the next twenty-four hours. He'll see everything I'm authorised to show him. I'll return him tomorrow,' he broke off and addressed Rob, 'where shall we drop you off?'

'I have a choice? Army HQ in Andover. That's where they'll want to debrief me.'

'OK,' said Joe, hoping they wouldn't take Rob straight over to Porton Down to do experiments on him. 'He'll be outside the Army HQ in Andover at midday. My proposal is that,' he looked at Rob, 'with his permission, Major Morgan becomes an unofficial back channel between the British Government and the *Shantivira*.'

Rob opened his mouth to speak, but Joe held up his hand.

'I can't always be waiting for the UN to schedule meetings. I need alternative paths to disseminate information.' Joe met Rob's eyes. 'I suggest Major Morgan visits us every few weeks to facilitate two-way communication. If you abuse this privilege by applying pressure on friends or relatives of *Shantivira* employees, the arrangement will cease immediately.'

He switched to English, the better to bring across the most important and urgent part of his message. 'If you inconvenience the pub's staff or customers in any way, then you can kiss your fancy equipment goodbye. Your attempt to abduct me has displeased my bodyguard and she's itching to throw it in the lake. I'm sure you've seen the video of our visit to the UN General Assembly and are aware of her . . . special abilities. She regards protecting the people of Wales as a sacred duty.' Joe paused, giving his future listeners a chance to picture a furious red dragon flying off with their taxpayer-funded vehicles and dropping them into nearby Lake Llywelyn.

'I've asked her to deliver this message and take any

action she deems necessary. If you want to interview the publicans, Ianto and Angharad, then order lunch and act like normal customers. The tip-off they gave you – that I was a regular – was at my request. I wanted to arrange a meeting on neutral ground. It's disappointing you came prepared to take me hostage, but not unexpected.'

Joe offered the microphone to Rob. 'Say something, mate. Let them know you're OK.'

Rob's nostrils flared. 'Am I OK? Sitting here on your sofa in outer bloody space?' He put a hand on his stomach. 'I still feel a bit sick from the teleporting.'

Joe suppressed a frown, reminding himself how scary this must be for him. 'I think we're treating you a little better than your lot would've treated me.'

Rob sighed. 'I guess you heard all that, guys. I'm fine. Looks like I'll be having an interesting day up here. Word to the wise: if anyone ever tries to teleport you, be sure to shut your eyes first. See you at HQ tomorrow, 12:00 hours.'

He returned the microphone to Joe, who said, 'That's it for now. Behave yourselves and the UK will benefit from a unique opportunity. Increased prestige on the global stage guaranteed. Rob will be back soon with lots to tell you.'

Kitty held out the bottle-green bowl full of Rob's electronics. In the meantime, she'd added some *omena* fruit and decorated the edge with pretty blue spring stars: a bloom native to the forests of Syenitia, but which also grew in abundance in the *Shantivira's* temperate biome. They were a traditional symbol of friendship, not that Rob's team would understand their significance. Joe placed his recording on top.

Good luck, he said, silently.

Thanks, she said and glanced at Rob, who'd got up and was staring out of the window at the *Koppakuoria*. *Will you be all right on your own with him?*

Of course. Rob might be angry and frightened, but Joe didn't think he'd become violent. *Will you bring our lunch back? I hope Angharad put my pie back in the oven to keep warm.*

Sure. See you soon.

She turned and disappeared. Joe picked up the drinks and crossed the room, handing Rob's still full pint back to him, hoping he wouldn't throw it straight into his face.

'Let's start again,' he said, raising his glass. '*Iechyd da* and welcome to the *Shantivira*. Despite . . . everything,' he made an all-encompassing gesture, 'it's great to see you.'

Rob took several thirsty gulps of his bitter. He wiped his mouth on the back of his hand and, to Joe's surprise, started laughing.

'We've been preparing this operation for *months*. They've been wanting to get you alone in an interview room ever since your appearance at the UN.'

'The *Saeson* have got you doing their dirty work, haven't they?'

'Not just the English. Our cousins, too. Lucrative promises were made to powerful people. I seem to be the only person who knows you who doesn't have diplomatic immunity. So *I've* been the one getting endless hours of grilling. Despite having had zero contact with you since you left the army.' Rob paused, then said, 'Are you aware your mother has disappeared?'

Joe's expression remained Sphinx-like.

Rob tried again. 'The last time we spoke – that phone call after your leaving party – was it *her* you were talking about?' He jerked his head at the spot where Kitty had stood.

Joe endeavoured to maintain his inscrutable act and failed. His face crinkled into a grin. 'Yeah. My life hasn't been the same since. Want to sit down?' He pointed at the table. 'She'll be back with our lunch soon.'

Rob took a seat, still looking out at the docking bay. Joe sipped his beer, watching him quietly. After the initial shock, he seemed to be taking it quite well. He studied his friend's profile. Almost two decades had passed since they'd last met. Rob's fair skin had become lined and weatherbeaten, his mousy hair receding at the temples. Neither of them was in their twenties anymore. Joe's own hair had begun turning grey.

He should have made more effort to stay in touch. Any effort at all would have been something. But in 1997 he'd walked away from his Earth life without a backward glance, entirely focused on new horizons and new friendships. He'd always been a live-in-the-present sort of guy. Later, he'd followed Rob's career with detached interest: with an almost academic curiosity about the path his own life might have taken, had he stayed.

Now, with the wisdom of middle age, he was beginning to understand he'd neglected something precious. True friendships were so rare, they deserved to be treasured. They required nurturing. Maintenance. He hoped it wasn't too late. He'd no idea what kind of a person Rob had become in the intervening years. Did they still share the same values?

'You OK, mate?' he asked.

No answer. Joe spoke a command, making the wall opaque again. Rob glared at him, waiting for an explanation.

'It's distracting you,' Joe said. 'Believe me, I get it. I'll show you everything later.'

In a dreamy voice, Rob said, 'We're so small, aren't we? Does anything we do even matter?'

'Yes, it bloody well does,' said Joe. What was the point, otherwise? 'What did you order?'

'The steak.' Rob remembered his beer and lifted it to his lips.

'Mmm.' Joe's mouth watered. 'Can I snaffle a couple of your onion rings when it comes? Angharad's onion rings are *the best*.'

'I don't know, Barney. I'm still annoyed at how you set us up.'

'Standard procedure for dealing with the *Saeson*. It's easier to get what you want if they think they have the upper hand.'

Rob gave a little shriek as Kitty materialised next to him, holding two plates.

'Careful, they're hot,' she said, putting them on the table. Reunited with his steak and kidney pie, Joe sighed with satisfaction.

Cheers, babe. How'd it go?

As well as could be expected. They didn't take me seriously to start with.

Joe imagined Kitty appearing from the tangled forest which surrounded the *Cath Palug*, with her cascading raven tresses and medieval-style red dress, holding the dish like some barefoot beauty in a John William Waterhouse painting.

I can imagine, he said.

In the end, I turned into Y Ddraig Goch *and roared at them from the pub roof to prove my point.*

No flames, I hope?

Course not. Although I dislodged a few slates when I took off for my flyover.

How did they take that? asked Joe, envisaging the Welsh dragon swooping low over the military vehicles, exposing her pale belly. *They didn't try to shoot you?*

No. Rob's boss didn't look best pleased, but the troops were delighted. They clapped; can you believe it?

I can. It's a peaceful, magical place, that clearing. You fit in there better than a bunch of guys with vans and guns. I'm sure they felt that.

Perhaps. Kitty picked up the empty pint glasses.

You going back?

Yeah. I don't trust them. They've gone into the pub for food. I'm going to stick around until they pack up and go home. Maybe I can fix the roof before Ianto notices I broke it.

Righto. Laters, then.

She patted him on the shoulder and disappeared.

'Doesn't talk much, does she?' said Rob, who was already well into his steak and potatoes. Joe noticed the fluency returning to his Welsh, which had been rusty from lack of use.

'She's the strong and silent type,' he replied, not trusting Rob enough yet to tell him about their private telepathic connection. 'So, are you going to give me an onion ring?'

2. AN AGREEMENT
JOE

'AND THIS IS Docking Bay 1,' said Joe. The quadrant-shaped hall was filling rapidly with spiky green *Tumbas*, entering through the gigantic opening in the outer wall. 'The ships coming in are our one-person fighters. They've been out disposing of space debris, to prevent damage to the terrestrial satellites and space stations.'

'They're like enormous conkers!' exclaimed Rob, stepping back as one landed in front of them.

Joe smiled. He'd been in this business so long that, to him, horse chestnut seeds always seemed like miniature *Tumbas*. 'They're grown from the seeds of the *Kastanja* tree. Once they're big enough, they're fitted with the electronics and power system, but they're still essentially a living organism. They have distinct personalities, so you need to get to know the individual craft to get the best out of it.'

'Can we go in one?' Rob approached the little ship, examining the organic pattern of veins running across the shell.

'You can take a peek when the pilot comes out. But they're tiny inside. If you want, I'll take you on a tour of the solar system in the *Pride* tomorrow morning.'

Rob turned to look at him. 'Seriously? Your fancy dragonfly spaceship?' Rob had blinked in disbelief when he'd seen *The Pride of Essoona* from the outside just now. With six legs, a shimmering blue-green hull and translucent latticed wings, it did look exactly like a mechanical dragonfly. But with heavy-duty weaponry when you needed it.

'Sure,' said Joe, keeping his tone casual.

The door of the *Tumba* before them opened downwards with a pneumatic hiss. Hanna descended the steps, pulling off her helmet and fluffing up her afro. 'Hi, Joe,' she said, eyeing Rob with curiosity, 'All set for Friday?'

'Yes, of course. I'm a witness, like you. William helped me prepare my statement and I've been practising.'

Friday was the day of Hassan's trial at the main court in central Essoona. He was facing charges of taking a vessel without consent, misapplying Alliance property, disobeying lawful commands, and obstructing operations. If found guilty, he could be exiled from all Galaksi Alliance planets and his promising career on the *Shantivira* would be over before it started. Until the trial, he was banned from the *Shantivira* and from using the teleport to Essoona. At present, he was staying at the *Shantivira's* language school in London, with the latest intake of first-year students.

Hanna, his loyal girlfriend, had been supporting him in every way she could, including making sure there'd be plenty of friendly faces from the *Shantivira* in the courtroom.

'I'm doing everything I can for him, Hanna. He's one

of my best pilots. We need him back here, where he belongs.' Joe remembered his manners and touched Rob on the arm. 'This is Rob, by the way. My former unit leader when I was in the army. He's here on behalf of the British government. I'm giving him the tour.'

Hanna held out her hand. 'Hi, Rob. Welcome to the *Shantivira*,' she said, switching to English. 'I'm Hanna.'

'Pleased to meet you,' said Rob, shaking her hand. 'How long have you worked for Barney?'

Hanna's face clouded with confusion. 'Barney?'

Rob attempted to explain. 'Barney was his army nickname. Because he looks like Barney Rubble?'

'Who's Barney Rubble?' she replied, still mystified.

'From *The Flintstones*?'

Hanna raised her eyebrows at Joe in a silent appeal for help. He shook his head in a don't-worry-about-it gesture, saying, 'Hanna, can we take a quick look inside your *Tumba*?'

'Of course,' she said. 'I'm off to the canteen. Bye, Rob.'

They climbed the steps and Rob inspected the dimly lit pod: a 270° screen, a huge bank of controls and a single, saddle-like seat at the centre.

In a low voice, Joe said, 'Not everyone here grew up watching American cartoons, Rob. Not everyone here grew up with a television. Don't make assumptions like that out loud or you'll piss off my crew.'

'Sorry,' said Rob.

Might as well say it, while they had some privacy. It would only keep irritating him otherwise. 'Also, I'd prefer it if you called me Joe. I left Barney behind a long time ago.'

'Sorry,' said Rob again. 'That's just how I think of you. Seeing you again: it's like time travel. I have all these memories bubbling up that I haven't thought of in years.'

Joe softened. 'Same here.' He smiled as a long-buried memory flashed into his head. 'Do you remember when you taught me to iron? How I tried to do my underpants and they melted?'

Rob bent double with laughter. 'I do now!' he managed to say between gasps. 'The way they shrivelled up into nothing! Oh God, your face, Joe. You couldn't understand what had happened.'

'I always bought natural fibres after that,' said Joe, deadpan. Not that he'd ever ironed an item of underwear since.

Gradually, Rob recovered enough to stand up straight again, holding on to Joe's shoulder for support. Not letting go, he said, 'We have a *lot* of catching up to do.'

Joe grinned and gripped Rob's shoulder in return. 'If you become our go-between, we'll have plenty of time to do it in. Come on, let me show you a biome.'

They left the *Tumba* and watched the steps rise, fitting neatly back into the hull. Rob nodded at the spot where Hanna had stood. 'What language were you speaking with the pilot?'

'Kawaida. The interstellar lingua franca.' Joe waved a hand at the docking bay, now packed with recharging *Tumbas*. 'Half our crew don't speak English, so we use it as the *Shantivira's* official language.'

Crossing the fields beyond the farmyard, Joe explained about the gravity generators and the magnetic shielding protecting the biomes from the harsh realities of space. He talked about the purpose of the biomes – to provide air as well as most of their fresh food – and the white cones which the *Shantivira* needed for propulsion and positioning, like the spikes on a *Tumba*. He neglected to tell Rob they also formed part of the weapons system: so far, he'd skilfully avoided all his friend's questions on that topic.

'Does your mother live up here?'

Joe scoffed. 'Not bloody likely! You know we've never got on. I couldn't have her on board, criticising my every decision.' He bristled. 'Is that one of your mission parameters? To track down my mam so your lot can take her hostage?'

He wasn't about to say she'd run away to Argentina with one of Kitty's ex-lovers: a man Joe suspected was responsible for the attempt on his life at the UN General Assembly last year. Apart from the security aspect, it was embarrassing. The idea of Grace dancing the tango with that creep made him cringe.

Rob looked sheepish. 'I have my orders.'

'Yeah,' said Joe. 'And I have mine. We'll have to find a middle way. Please, let's not talk about Mam.'

They entered the wild zone at the heart of the temperate biome, an ancient forest bursting with life, thick with layers of luscious greenery. Rich, organic fragrances filled Joe's nostrils, calming him.

Rob gazed around. Moss grew on every surface; glossy ivy enveloped tree trunks. 'What *is* this place?'

'The biodiversity zone. Our crops would die without it.'

'Why can't we see the *Shantivira* from Earth? It's huge!'

Joe pulled a bramble to one side, allowing Rob to pass him on the overgrown path. 'We're cloaked. The space station and all our spacecraft. Otherwise, they'd have spotted us years ago.'

They picked their way through the ferns, heading for the clearing with the beehives. Joe said, 'I suggest you come here for two days a fortnight. Bring a list of questions and I'll answer what I can in a two-hour session. I'll have queries and requests for you to pass on, too. The rest of the time you can spend getting to know the *Shantivira* and the crew. You can help out in the biomes and the kitchen, have a Kawaida lesson, wander about and chat with people, that sort of thing.'

'Unsupervised?'

Joe heard the surprise in Rob's voice and grinned. 'We'll notice if you start trying to reverse engineer spacecraft. You'll have to leave your phone with me so you're not taking unauthorised pictures. Standard stuff. But yeah, you'll have the freedom of the space station.'

'Cool,' said Rob, but Joe couldn't tell what he was thinking. They reached the clearing and sat on the fallen tree trunk the Shantivirans used as a bench.

'Will your family mind? Being away so often?' Joe knew Rob was married with two children: a six-year-old daughter and a four-year-old son.

Rob shrugged. 'They're used to it. It's the job. I haven't seen them since New Year's Day, due to the preparations for this mission.'

'A fortnight?' Joe was horrified. 'Man, I'm so glad I left the army when I did.' He considered for a moment. 'OK. I was going to suggest we go out in Essoona tonight—'

'—Essoona?'

'The capital of Syenitia, on the other side of the galaxy.'

'On the other side of the *galaxy*?' Rob echoed in disbelief. 'Just for an *evening*? Is your ship that fast?'

Joe shook his head. 'Nobody's ship is that fast. We have a point-to-point teleport on board which takes us straight to Essoona.'

Rob grimaced. '*More* teleporting?'

'It's more comfortable than travelling freestyle with Kitty, I promise.' Joe waved his hand at the trees surrounding the clearing, but meaning the entire space station. 'The Syenitians are the aliens running the *Shantivira* project, the ones paying for all of this. You know that, right? I've explained it to the UN often enough.'

Rob nodded and Joe continued, 'But we can do that next time. There will be a next time? You'll be our back channel?'

'Do you trust me?'

Joe rubbed his Sunday stubble. 'Honestly? I'm not sure, Rob. I *want* to trust you. I think we just need to get to know each other again and it'll follow naturally. Do you trust *me*?'

'I'm not sure,' said Rob, echoing Joe. 'Yet. I think we have a starting point to build on. Yes, I'll be your back channel, if my bosses allow it.'

Joe smiled with relief. Thank God for that. He didn't have a plan B handy if Rob had turned him down. 'Thank you, Rob.'

They shook hands formally and fell into a contemplative silence, watching the bees coming and going. Apart from Delius, the *Shantivira's* main computer, they were probably the hardest workers on the whole space station, Joe thought.

From nowhere, a muscular black jaguar sprang into the gap between them, her head level with their own.

'Aargh!' Rob shattered the peace with a shocked yell and jumped to his feet.

Joe put his arm across her shoulders and pulled Kitty in for a hug, kissing the top of her furry head.

Hey, you, he said silently.

Hey, she replied.

Rob said yes, he said, wanting to share his news immediately.

Good. Then today's been worthwhile.

Everything OK at the pub?

I think so. They packed up and went home. I watched until they were on the motorway.

'Jesus!' said Rob. 'I nearly had a heart attack!'

Joe threw his head back and laughed. 'You two haven't been formally introduced, have you? Rob, I'd like you to meet my wife – Kitty, the Red Dragon of the Britons.'

Kitty shifted into her Syenitian form and held out a pale, black-nailed hand. 'Pleased to meet you, Rob.'

Wide-eyed, Rob stepped back, arms limp against his sides. He took in Kitty's pointed ears and her reptilian eyes, which glittered an unearthly shade of green in the sunlight.

'—H-how?' he stammered. 'I mean, I saw it in that video of you at the UN, but close up . . . it's a whole different thing.'

Kitty lowered her hand. 'Shape-shifting? I just can.'

Joe said, 'Rob, mate, you're being rude. Sit down.'

Rob sat, keeping a cautious distance of several feet from Kitty and Joe, who put his arm around Kitty's waist. Shock was switching to fascination.

'Will you show me *Y Ddraig Goch*?'

'This clearing's not big enough for a dragon,' she said in her low, melodic voice. 'Also, that form takes more energy than this one. I only use it when I need it.'

Joe decided it wasn't the right moment to explain that space demons fed by absorbing the life energy of other beings. As a half Syenitian, Kitty had been brought up believing all life was sacred. She wouldn't waste precious energy on showing off. OK, he admitted to himself, not true. Sometimes she did. But not often. And, clearly, not today.

'Wait a minute.' Another penny had dropped for Rob. 'Your *wife*?'

Joe pulled Kitty closer. 'Yeah.'

'But she's an alien! How does that even work?'

Kitty put her hand to her mouth, covering a giggle.

'It works,' said Joe. '*Not* that it's any of your business. Anyway. We were talking about this evening.'

'And not going out in . . . where was it again?'

'Essoona. Would you prefer to go home instead? Kitty can drop you off and pick you up tomorrow morning. Then you can eat with your family and do bedtime stories or whatever.'

'Seriously?' Rob looked at Kitty.

'That's all right, *cariad*, isn't it?' asked Joe. 'He hasn't seen them for two weeks.'

'Because you were plotting to kidnap my husband?' Kitty teased. 'Promise never to do that again and I'd be happy to take you.'

Rob still wasn't sure. 'The same way you brought me here?'

'Close your eyes this time. Then you won't get sick,' Joe reassured him.

Rob gulped. 'Um . . . OK. When?'

Joe checked his watch. 'I've shown you everything I planned for today. How about now?'

'Now? Right. Um . . .' He glanced shyly at Kitty. 'So . . . we live in a village called—'

'We know where you live, Rob,' interrupted Kitty. 'You're by Danebury Ring.'

Joe smiled. Kitty probably knew the location of every Bronze Age and Iron Age fort in Britain. Hell, she could still remember some of the names of the people who'd lived in them, centuries before the Romans arrived.

They stood. Rob stared up at Kitty; she was at least a foot taller than him.

Gently, she took his hands. 'Ready?' she said.

'As I'll ever be.'

'Close your eyes.'

And they were gone.

Joe walked back to the farm, reaching out with his mind to talk privately to Kitty.

You don't need to stay and watch him, Cath. *I'll ask Delius to monitor his communications.* He still wasn't sure how far he trusted Rob. Tonight would be a test. If he contacted his superiors instead of just enjoying the unexpected time with his family, Joe would have to rethink their plans.

OK. Joe? Tomorrow, I'll go early and speak to the wife. He'll need her support.

Good idea. Try not to scare the crap out of her.

Joe felt Kitty smile. *I'll do my best*, she said.

A thought occurred to him. *Will you check on Mam later?* he asked. *They've been trying to locate her. I want to know she's still OK and that con artist Nestor hasn't sold out on her yet.*

Will do.

Cheers, babe, you're a star.

✦　✦　✦

THE NEXT DAY, Rob and Kitty appeared in the *Pride's* living area, just as Joe was finishing his second mug of tea. He always needed at least two to get going in the morning.

Rob was spitting with rage. 'How bloody dare you!' he yelled at Kitty, then turned to Joe. 'Did you put her up to that? Talking to my wife and children behind my back?'

He was in the shower when I rang the doorbell, explained Kitty silently. *The wife already had her suspicions. When that video of us at the UN did the rounds, he said he knew you. Then he never mentioned you again, even though the clip kept popping up in his search history. I didn't have to introduce myself; she recognised me.*

That's good. Joe's mind flashed back to their dramatic departure from the UN General Assembly Hall. Before teleporting him away, Kitty had shifted into her dragon form and he'd jumped onto her back. The few seconds they'd flown above a sea of upturned, open-mouthed faces had been the greatest rush ever.

I gave her your number, like you asked me to. Kitty pulled out a chair and sat next to him at the table. *Their kids are sweet. We played Lego. Then Rob came down and blew a gasket.*

'Barney?' said Rob. 'Answer me.'

Barney again, Joe noted with an inward sigh. 'She needs to know, Rob.'

'No. She mustn't. It's top secret.'

'I know *you* can't tell her,' said Joe. 'But Kitty hasn't signed the Official Secrets Act. Cup of tea?' He waggled his empty mug in invitation.

'No.'

'Sit down, then.'

Reluctantly, Rob sat.

'Look,' said Joe, 'I know how mind-blowing this stuff is. You need somebody you trust to share it with. It's too much for one person to keep secret.'

'But—'

Joe held up his hand. 'I don't have your faith in the State, Rob. I need someone who'll let us know if you disappear inexplicably.'

Rob frowned. 'You think that might happen?'

'I don't know. I hope not.' Joe turned his mug on its coaster. 'It depends how big the gap is between what you report to them and what they want to hear. I intend to be prepared in case we have to pull you out of trouble.'

Rob fell quiet. Joe took his breakfast things to the sink and washed them up.

'My kids never heard me speak Welsh before,' Rob broke the silence, his tone sad rather than angry. 'When I started shouting at Kitty, they goggled at me like *I* was the alien, not her.'

'Perhaps it's time to teach them,' said Kitty mildly. 'If you don't show them that part of you, they'll never fully understand who you are.'

Joe returned to the table, placing an mp3-player in front of Rob. 'This is for you. It's a copy of the audio language course we've created for Kawaida. The UN are turning it into an app, but this works fine. Share it with whoever you like. Upload it to the internet, whatever. But start doing it yourself, two lessons a week at least.'

Rob picked it up and turned it over in his hands. 'Two lessons a week,' he confirmed.

'The instructions are all on there in the first file,' Joe continued. 'Next time you come, one of our language teachers will have a session with you and we'll see how far you've got. The more you learn, the more you'll get out of your visits.'

Rob slipped it into the pocket of his hiking trousers. 'Thanks. So, what's on the programme this morning?'

'We've got a few hours,' said Joe. 'I promised you a tour of the solar system. Are you still up for it? Or would you prefer to take the teleport to Syenitia?'

'I want to see space.' Rob's eyes flashed with anticipation. 'I want to see what your ship can do.'

Joe gave a wide smile. 'Then you shall.'

Kitty shifted into her black jaguar form and sprang onto the sofa in a fluid bound. The leather creaked as she settled down for a nap.

Rob stared at her. 'I'm not going to get used to that.'

'You will,' said Joe. 'Come with me.' He took Rob to

the cockpit. Taking the central seat, he requested Delius to thin the shields enough for them to leave the docking bay. He initiated his preprogrammed autopilot solar system tour, which he occasionally used for guests. It meant he could focus on his passengers without risking any embarrassing in-flight mishaps.

Rob gazed at the stars, taking it all in. The spherical transparent cockpit which formed the dragonfly's 'head' gave them a virtually all-round panorama, emphasising the emptiness of space.

Joe watched him, trying to remember his own first trip around the solar system. Not in a *Tumba*. Rohini, who'd been the *Shantivira's* captain when Joe had done his pilot training, would never have permitted the space station's resources to be squandered on joyrides. Rohini was an old lady now, as formidable as ever, with arthritis and a clutch of great-grandchildren. How time passed. He made a mental note to visit her in Kolkata soon: to update her on the latest developments and get her advice on all the dreaded PR activities looming on his horizon. Her years of experience made her an invaluable sounding board. Unlike Aldeman, Joe's Syenitian boss and brother-in-law, she could be relied upon to view matters from a human perspective.

January in Earth's northern hemisphere was so de-pressing. Some Indian sunshine would do him good, he thought, already looking forward to it. Plus, Rohini's daughter-in-law was an excellent cook.

Next to him, Rob exclaimed, 'The colour! It's so beau-tiful, it makes me want to cry.'

'That's Neptune,' said Joe, as they passed the turquoise

planet. 'Like a jewel, isn't it?'

'I could look at it all day,' said Rob and fell silent again.

Joe returned to his daydreaming. Where was he? His very first trip around the solar system. Of course! 2003. When he'd brought the *Pride of Essoona* back from Syenitia, before he'd started work as Aldeman's personal pilot.

The *Pride* was a *Korento* class ship, a similar model to those used by the Syenitian diplomatic corps. His brother-in-law had given it to him as a wedding present, along with a job offer. Keeping it in Docking Bay 3 was cheaper and safer than paying for a berth in Essoona's overpriced spaceport.

It also meant he and Kitty had a private space in which to spend time together. Kitty couldn't stay away from the Earth for too long or all the *Shantivira's* point-to-point teleports stopped functioning, inconveniencing crew members who used them to commute. So Joe returned to the *Shantivira* for weekends and holidays, travelling back and forth to Syenitia via the Dunia House teleport.

He'd spent most of his adult life on the *Shantivira*. It was his home: the place he could genuinely be himself. All his friends were here, or often passed through. He pictured his mother's little house at the foot of the Bannau Brycheiniog, where he was, in fact, still registered to vote. He'd never left the UK, officially. But he didn't belong there; he could never go back. It would be like having to travel by *Tumba* after years of flying *Korentos*. No thanks.

They approached Jupiter's marbled cloud layers. Rob had relaxed a little now, but was still absorbing everything he could. Truly, it was a once in a lifetime opportunity. Only very special guests got offered this trip.

'Would you like a cup of tea, Rob? Or a beer?'

Rob glanced at Joe. 'I'd kill for a coffee. And have you got something to eat? I didn't have breakfast.'

Joe grinned. 'Kitty could probably do you some toast. Let's ask her.' He put the request through on the intercom, still unwilling to reveal their telepathic link. He was hyper-aware that everything he told Rob would go straight back to the British Government.

'Is there anything you'd like to ask me before you go back? Now's your chance.'

'Right,' said Rob, refocussing on his mission with visible mental effort. 'Good point.' He fumbled in his pocket, pulling out a paper notebook and pen. 'I wrote a list.'

He fired off question after question, which Joe did his best to answer or avoid, depending on the topic. Rob jotted down notes in handwriting so appalling that Joe wondered if they'd be any use at all. Not his problem. Still, he was relieved when Kitty arrived with the food.

You took your time, he said to her privately.

Third attempt, said Kitty, putting her tray down on the pop-up table between his seat and Rob's. *I know you say the toast needs to go in one and a half times, but I always thought you were joking. Either it's still white or it comes out black and smoking! I scraped the worst bits off. It's just brown now. Looks OK to me.*

Joe smirked, but didn't comment. 'Thanks, love,' he said out loud, picking up the mug of tea she'd brought for him.

Rob took a long draught of caffeine. 'Just what I needed. Thank you, Kitty. You make a great cup of coffee.'

Kitty acknowledged the praise with a regal nod. 'Enjoy your food,' she said, and left the cockpit.

'I have a colleague, Shakila, who's very particular about coffee,' Joe explained. 'She made me get rid of my jar of instant and get one of those glass jugs with a plunger, you know?'

'Mmm.' Rob took a bite of toast and screwed up his face.

'You don't have to eat it,' Joe said sympathetically. As Kitty didn't eat food herself, anything she prepared was a hit and miss affair.

Rob put the charred triangle back on his plate. 'I'll be fine with just the coffee,' he said.

AT LAST, THEY reached Mercury. 'Wow, the sun's huge from here,' said Rob.

'Yeah,' agreed Joe. 'And hot.' He checked the clock on the control panel. 'We should head back. Can't risk you being late.'

Rob groaned. 'They're going to grill me like a kipper.'

'At least you have plenty to tell. More than if you'd been successful with *your* plan.'

'I'll keep pointing that out. Joe?'

Joe raised his eyebrows. Was Rob finally going to stop using that stupid nickname?

'What?'

'How will I contact you?'

'You won't,' said Joe, matter-of-factly. 'Fortnightly

face-to-face contact only, up here. Don't bother with bugging equipment. Kitty and the *Shantivira's* computers can sense electromagnetic signals.'

Joe flew into Docking Bay 3, setting the spacecraft down neatly on its six legs. He folded the solar wings back along the dragonfly's spine and shut down the controls. In the darkened cockpit, he turned to face Rob.

'Just in case, your wife has my number. Don't use it unless you need it. Don't tell your bosses you have it. You'll be safer if they think you can't talk to me outside our meetings.'

In the living area, Kitty was waiting for them in humanoid form, a map of Andover projected on the wall.

Joe took a banana from the fruit bowl on the table and tossed it to Rob.

'I've scouted it out,' Kitty said. 'They're on high alert.'

'No surprise there,' said Rob, slipping the banana into his pocket.

Kitty stepped in front of the projector, her pale skin overlaid with Ordnance Survey graphics. She pointed at a patch of trees just south of the Army HQ. 'I'll drop you off here. You'll have to make your way to the Monxton Road entrance on foot. OK?'

'No problem.' Rob took a deep breath. 'It's been great to see you again, Joe. Thank you for showing me so much. And thank you, Kitty, for taking me home last night.'

'My pleasure,' she said.

'Mine, too,' said Joe, shaking Rob's hand and giving him a friendly slap on the shoulder. 'Tell them: they get one shot. This level of access is a huge and enviable privilege, which I will revoke the minute I smell any funny business.'

'Understood.'

'Good luck, mate. See you in a couple of weeks.'

'Ready?' said Kitty, holding out her hand.

Rob took it, closing his eyes. 'Ready,' he said, and they vanished.

3. THE TRIAL
HANNA

HANNA SHIFTED TO the edge of her hard wooden seat so her feet touched the terracotta tiles, easing the pressure on her buttocks. The Essoona law courts were built for Syenitians, and Hanna felt like a small child in a grown-up's chair. A child sitting in a forest clearing, because the walls and ceiling were covered in rich murals of plants and trees.

She glanced at Kia, next to her. Her teenage sister had kicked off her shoes and sat cross-legged, playing a game on her *zana*, which rested on her now-conspicuous bump. At least she was wearing her headphones.

On her other side, Lucy said, 'Look, they're coming in.'

A group of people entered through a door behind the podium, taking their places on the semi-circle design incorporated in the floor, facing the courtroom.

Hassan wore the dark suit they'd bought in the sales on Oxford Street last weekend. The trouser legs were wide enough to cover his black and silver boots, making them look like smart, if unusual, shoes. His orange shirt set off his complexion perfectly and Hanna hoped he felt as confident as he looked. William, a fellow *Shantivira* pilot and now Hassan's human lawyer, had also dressed for the occasion, wearing a miniature version of formal Syenitian robes. Woven through with silver and emerald thread, they glittered as he moved.

She nudged Kia. 'Put that away now,' she whispered, pointing at Kia's *zana*. 'It's disrespectful, otherwise.'

Kia made a face, but took off her headphones.

Hassan stood on the right end, next to William. Then came seven jury members of various species – Syenitian, Sayari, Wadudu, Tarumbet – and, on the far left, opposite Hassan, the judge. Hassan and William were the only humans.

The judge crossed to the centre of the semi-circle – marked by a black spot – picking up the waiting microphone and turning her back to the audience. The screen above the podium flickered to life and Hanna saw her face – the thin, creased skin and steel-grey hair indicating the Syenitian was coming to the end of her long life. Hanna thought of Eyvindran, the very first captain of the *Shantivira*, who still visited them occasionally. He looked about sixty, but he was almost two thousand years old. The judge appeared to be even older than him.

Beyond her, they could see the audience; what there was of it. Kia, Lucy and herself, a few dozen of Hassan's other friends and colleagues from the *Shantivira* – including Joe and Delius who, like Hanna, would be making a statement. Plus Hanna's best friend Farida, who'd left the *Shantivira* to study Syenitian Mathematics at Essoona University, and Aneira, their Amranese friend from last year's training at the Essoona Pilots' Academy. There were also a few unknown Syenitians.

Hanna almost yelped as Lucy nudged her in the ribs.

'See the female at the back with the plaited white hair?' Lucy hissed in an awed whisper. 'That's Dalian, the defence minister. What's *she* doing here?'

So that was Dalian. She'd heard of the councillor who believed the *Shantivira* project was a waste of Syenitian resources and should be shut down, but she'd never seen her in person before. Hanna put her hand to her throat, fingering her locket for reassurance.

'Ladies and gentlemen of the jury, we are here to evaluate the case of Hassan Nhial, a Dunian pilot on the Galaksi Alliance space station, the *Shantivira*. The *Shantivira* protects a developing planet called Dunia, in the Yerik'eti sector.'

The judge spoke directly to the jury, ignoring the audience behind her. But, thanks to the screen and the loudspeakers, Hanna could see her face and hear every word.

'Pilot Nhial is charged with taking a vessel without consent, misapplying Alliance property, disobeying lawful commands and obstructing operations, thirty revolutions before the autumnal equinox last year. He is represented by Commander Westwood, a fellow Dunian and a senior officer on the *Shantivira*. Commander Westwood?'

William stepped out of the semi-circle and crossed the floor to the centre. The judge returned to her place.

'Thank you, Judge Nurilan.'

Speaking fluently, William presented Hassan's case: Hassan had taken the *Shantivira's* cargo ship for a two-hour period, to deliver food and medical supplies to a remote refugee camp which had been cut off by severe flooding, in his home country of South Sudan.

'They don't have any papers or notes?' whispered Lucy.

Hanna, who'd learnt more than she wanted about the Syenitian legal system lately, shook her head. 'It's not allowed. Oral evidence only. The video is the official documentation. Everyone invited to the trial prepares a statement explaining their viewpoint. That's why there's a single microphone – so only one person speaks at a time.' Hanna prayed silently that, when her turn came, she wouldn't forget her lines or freeze with fear. Unlike the other witnesses, she had zero experience of public speaking.

William continued, 'At no point did the *Koppakuoria* permit non-Shantivirans to board, with two exceptions: the aid agency representative who provided the supplies and the young lady sitting in the front row, for whom there are extenuating circumstances. We will be hearing from her later.'

William pointed at Kia, who sat up a little straighter. Her Kawaida was good enough now to follow the gist of his speech.

'Pilot Nhial was aided in this mission by the *Shantivira's* main computer, Delius, who will face his own trial in due course. As you know, cybernetic life forms like Delius are programmed to protect life, in line with the Code of Harmony. Both Delius and Pilot Nhial chose to disobey lawful commands in order to save lives. Nhial had recently visited South Sudan, his place of birth, after many years away in the service of the Alliance. He was shocked at the situation of his countrypeople and vowed to help them however he could.'

The Wadudu juror put up one of his four hands. William gave him the microphone and vacated the speaker's spot.

'Judge Nurilan said Dunia is a developing planet. What does that mean, exactly?'

The insect-like life form returned to his place and William spoke again. 'Until last year, Dunia had no official contact with intelligent life beyond our planet. The *Shantivira's* captain initiated first contact with Dunia's authorities on behalf of the Galaksi Alliance some time before Pilot Nhial and Delius undertook their mission. I now invite Delius to make his statement.'

William watched the kindly giant make his way to the front, then returned to stand by Hassan. As tall as a Syenitian but twice as wide, the formidable cyborg had made no concession to the formality of the occasion, except to trim his beard. He wore the same plain tunic and trousers as always, his dark hair brushing his shoulders. In this strange place, he was something solid and familiar Hanna could hold on to.

'Good morning,' boomed Delius, his deep voice resonating across the room. 'When Hassan explained the urgency of the situation to me, I did my own research and concluded it was my duty to help. As I am senior to Hassan on the *Shantivira*, the charge of taking a vessel without consent applies solely to me. It is I who took the *Koppakuoria* without the knowledge or consent of my captain. I did so after judging that the benefit to life outweighed any negative consequences.

'The refugee camp was so remote and so lacking in

infrastructure, its communications were easy to block. There was no digital evidence of our visit. The ship was not at risk of being hijacked, nor was I in danger of being captured for disassembly and study. I suspect the residents believed the *Koppakuoria* was a form of aircraft. The presence of the aid agency representative, whom they knew, and Hassan, who speaks the local language, reassured them all was well.'

Delius paused, looking at each jury member in turn. 'Our visit made the difference between starvation and survival. There was no sign of panic: their focus was on the food we were delivering. This was a beneficial application of underused equipment. We deploy our cargo ship twice annually, to bring supplies from Syenitia. Operations were not obstructed. My colleague covered my shift and we returned within three hours.'

The Tarumbet juror asked him some technical questions and, once they were satisfied, Delius left the podium.

William said, 'I invite Joseph Llewellyn, Captain of the *Shantivira*, to make his statement.'

Hanna observed her boss approaching. His formal Syenitian clothing was less ornate than William's: a pale embroidered tunic over simple leggings and soft leather boots. She'd seen this outfit before – on the days Joe had to speak to the Syenitian Council. As always on official occasions, Joe wore his antique torc of Welsh gold.

'Good morning, Judge Nurilan, ladies and gentlemen of the jury, Commander Westwood, Pilot Nhial,' said Joe, making eye contact with each person in the semi-circle. 'At the time of the incident, I had already revealed the existence of the *Shantivira* to Dunia's authorities, but this knowledge had not been disseminated to the wider population. I was initially furious that so much patient negotiating had potentially been for nothing – and fearful my pilot's intervention would initiate a mass panic.

'However. News of the incident remained localised and, with no hard evidence, the story was not widely believed. At the same time, Dunia's authorities were compelled to treat the matter of first contact with greater urgency and I received permission to speak to the planet's senior representatives. Since then, negotiations have been progressing in leaps and bounds.' Joe shifted his stance to stand squarely with his feet apart: as if bracing himself against a strong wind. On the screen, Hanna watched him draw breath before continuing with his statement.

'The *Shantivira* has protected Dunia in secret for decades, but the time for openness has arrived. My mission, given to me by the Syenitian Council and the Galaksi Alliance, is to help Dunia transition to a spacefaring society: successfully and peacefully.

'Acting on his own intrinsic sense of the Code of Harmony, Pilot Nhial has measurably furthered that objective. With the agreement of Dunia's authorities, we will soon be using our cargo ship for regular aid deliveries, in return for biological waste we can use as fuel. This will save us at least one expensive supply run to Syenitia each year. Everybody benefits. My wish is for Pilot Nhial to be reinstated on the *Shantivira* with immediate effect. That is all I have to say.' Joe gave the jury a respectful nod and went back to his seat.

'We shall have a short break,' said the judge. 'Please return in half an hour.'

The room filled with the sound of murmuring voices and movement. Kia rose, saying, 'Where's the toilet? I have to go again.'

Hanna stood up too, her gaze fixed on Hassan. He caught her eye and gave her a little wave. She responded with a thumbs up, then he and William disappeared through the door at the back of the room. Too much to hope they'd be able to see them for the break. Never mind.

She and Lucy left Kia in the queue for the bathroom and bought themselves a cup of *saiju* each. Aneira and Farida joined them and there were hugs all round. Not letting go, Hanna buried her face in Farida's lilac headscarf. 'I miss you. *Zana* calls aren't the same.' Hanna hadn't seen her since December.

Farida stroked her back. 'I know. This last month must have been so tough for you. How do you think it's going?'

Hanna pulled away, wiping the unexpected moistness from her eyes. 'The trial? No idea.'

Lucy said, 'It isn't what I expected. He didn't even plead guilty or not guilty.'

'That's not how they do it here,' said Farida. 'The jury just try to understand what happened. The process and the verdict are guided by their consciences rather than a rigid application of the law.'

Aneira wasn't interested in the Syenitian legal system. 'How are your new *Tumbas*?' she asked.

Lucy brightened. Her second favourite thing after flying was talking about flying. 'The operational craft are way more powerful than our training *Tumbas*.'

'Mine's fast,' said Hanna, 'but we don't get on as well as I did with my school *Tumba*.'

'What about you, Aneira?' asked Lucy. 'Did you decide what you're going to do?'

Aneira's planet, Amra, had been destroyed by the Ranglatiri last November, and she hadn't heard from her extended family there since. Unsurprisingly, she'd been so distraught, she'd failed her exams at the Essoona Pilots' Academy.

'I'm retaking the year,' Aneira answered. 'I need to qualify so I can get my revenge on the Ranglatiri one day.'

Lucy patted her arm. 'Yeah. And I'll be with you when you do. Those fuckers won't know what's hit them.'

Aneira smiled weakly, then more widely as Kia rejoined them.

'Hi, Kia. You're getting big!'

Kia greeted her with a hug. 'Not done yet. I'm fed up with needing the toilet every five minutes.'

'You two are up next, aren't you, Hanna?' said Lucy. 'Are you nervous?'

'Terrified,' Hanna admitted. 'Although I feel better now I've seen how it works. We've practised my statement over and over.'

A bell chimed and they filed back into the courtroom. Hassan, William and the jury were already waiting on the tiled semi-circle; the judge stood at the centre. Hanna hoped Hassan had been able to sit down for a while. Even reunited with his black and silver boots – which were more comfortable than his terrestrial prosthetics – he'd be finding it hard. Syenitians could stand happily for hours. Still, she consoled herself, whichever way this went, she'd be on hand to massage his stumps later.

The judge said, 'Hanna and Kia Abebe, please present your statement.'

4. THE VERDICT
HANNA

HERE GOES NOTHING, thought Hanna, holding Kia's hand for reassurance. For hers or Kia's? She wasn't sure. They made their way to the podium and Hanna accepted the microphone.

Her mouth suddenly dry, she swallowed and said, 'Um. Hello, everyone. My name is Hanna Abebe, I'm a trainee pilot on the *Shantivira*, and this is Kia, my younger sister. Kia's still learning Kawaida, so I'll be speaking on her behalf today.'

Hanna focused on the ten people before her, trying to forget the audience and her thumping heart. What were the four points she needed to make? Mentally, she counted them on her fingers.

'So, the first thing to say is that Hassan, I mean Pilot Nhial, kept his plans absolutely secret. Only Delius, and Gambrinus, the *Shantivira's* backup computer had any idea. I'm his girlfriend and I sensed something was wrong, but he didn't say a word. I thought he wanted to break up with me!' A little giggle escaped her, and she clamped her hand over her mouth. Deep breath. Hand down. Do Point Two, she told herself.

'Pilot Nhial's home territory borders the place I grew

up in. It's a region abundant with nature, culture and resources, but economically impoverished. War, famine and natural disasters drive people from their homes. After my parents died, my siblings and I became separated.' Hanna fought to keep her voice steady, refusing to let the memories of that time overwhelm her. 'My three brothers are dead, but I have an older sister and a younger sister who has not yet reached adulthood.'

Kia squeezed her hand in an invisible gesture of encouragement and Hanna continued.

'When Pilot Nhial came to the refugee camp, he saw a girl who looked like me. He discovered she was my missing younger sister, so he brought her to me. It wasn't until much later that we realised she was with child.'

There was a little intake of breath from the jury. Hadn't they realised? Or did they think Kia was just fat?

One of the Syenitian jurors raised her hand. As she'd been instructed to do, Hanna passed her the microphone and stepped to one side so the juror could take the speaking spot.

'I am confused,' she said. 'I understood your sister is still a child and requires your care. So how can she become a parent herself?'

How could she explain *that*? Panicking, Hanna scanned the podium for help and caught William's eye. He raised his hand for the microphone and the juror gave it to him.

He said, 'You are aware that, compared to Syenitians, Dunians have extremely short lifespans?'

The jurors nodded. That had been in their information packs.

'Our lives are compressed, as it were,' William continued. 'A Dunian reaches reproductive maturity earlier than we achieve emotional and intellectual maturity. Lacking supervision, a sexually mature child may initiate reproduction without considering the consequences.'

He noticed the juror's questioning expression and elaborated, 'Dunian infants require a complex support system to be raised successfully to adulthood: a community, emotional support, financial support, adequate food and healthcare. As an orphan in a refugee camp, Kia could provide almost none of these things.'

He handed the microphone back to Hanna, who'd composed herself and knew what she wanted to say.

'Unfortunately, the baby's father left the camp before Kia, unaware she was pregnant. We have no way of contacting him. Without Pilot Nhial's intervention, my sister would have given birth while lacking the resources to provide for a child. It's possible both would have died. I'm so grateful to Pilot Nhial for finding her so I can help look after the baby.'

Hanna looked up at the jury. 'There are many people in Kia's situation, all over my planet. I know we can't help them all. But I can and will help my sister. Thank you for listening.'

Thank God that was over with, she thought, as she and Kia returned to their seats. But would her words help Hassan?

Kia took her hand and whispered, 'Well done, big sis. Do you really think I might have died?'

Hanna hadn't told Kia about her own almost-fatal miscarriage, or that she'd once been homeless and alone in one of the world's richest cities. Perhaps it was time. Kia was already further along in her pregnancy than Hanna herself had managed. Hanna was determined *this* baby would have the best possible start in life. 'Let's talk about it later.'

William said, 'I invite Dalian, the Syenitian defence minister, to make her statement.'

Heads turned as Dalian made her way forwards, her heavy cobalt robes sweeping the terracotta tiles in the central aisle. A scent lingered in the air after she passed Hanna's row, fresh and floral, with overtones of cinnamon. She mounted the podium and, as Hanna watched the minister's solemn face appear on the screen, she realised Dalian had once been beautiful. But her features had hardened into the grim expression of someone who'd long since forgotten how to feel joy.

'Good morning, Judge Nurilan, jury members, Commander Westwood, Pilot Nhial.' Her voice rang out, clear and cold like a hammer on ice. 'Trainee Pilot Abebe said there are many on Dunia in her sister's position and we can't help them all. I concur with that statement.'

Back on her hard chair, Hanna's spine stiffened. Where was this going?

'The Syenitian Council has agreed to offer technical support to Dunia's authorities. But this is a classic case of mission creep. If Dunia cannot care for its own citizens, how is that our concern? Only, perhaps, as evidence Dunia does not deserve our help. We must not get involved in local matters. Once you start with these backwater planets, it never stops. They always want more. We must remain firm in all our dealings with them.'

A jury member – the Sayari – put his hand up. Dalian stepped aside to let him speak. He reminded Hanna of Irion: his hair was the same shade of neon green as her adoptive mother's. A little bit of home. She willed him to say something nice.

'Defence Minister,' he said with a little bow. 'Forgive me, but your opposition to the *Shantivira* project is well documented. Surely, if Captain Llewellyn is to achieve the objective the Syenitian Council has given him, he must win the Dunians' trust? Was this incident not a positive step along that path?'

Dalian's wide sleeves swayed as she took the microphone again. 'Perhaps,' she admitted. 'My opposition to the *Shantivira* project has nothing to do with this particular case. Although it is only a nine-series facility, in view of the growing Ranglatiri threat I believe the space station would be better deployed defending an Alliance member planet, such as Sayari.' She shook her head, rippling her snowy braids. 'I bear the Dunians no ill will. But Llewellyn's pilot took Alliance property for what was essentially a personal errand.'

Here she looked straight at Hassan and Hanna winced on his behalf. 'If you were under my command, you would have been exiled at once for this blatant breach of discipline. I question Llewellyn's judgement in requesting your return. That is all I have to say.'

Dalian strode over to William and thrust the microphone at him, not bothering to bend down so he was forced to reach up for it. Hanna's nostrils flared in silent outrage. Just because William had dwarfism, there was no need to be rude.

Dalian's robes swirled as she spun on her heel and made her way back to her seat. William passed the microphone to Hassan, who took his place on the speaker's spot. Hanna touched the locket he'd given her, praying his statement would go well.

'Good morning, Judge Nurilan and members of the jury,' said Hassan, making eye contact with them in the same way Joe had. 'When I decided to take the *Koppakuoria* to aid my people, I knew I would be caught. I also knew that, if I'd asked first, I would have been refused permission.'

He went on to explain the context of his actions: how, last summer, he'd returned for the first time to the place he'd left as a ten-year-old orphan. The grinding poverty and the lack of opportunities for his compatriots had horrified him.

'I knew I must do something to help, even if it cost me my career and perhaps my freedom. I don't understand why Dunians are unable to provide this aid themselves. But the fact is, they haven't. If I'd not taken the action I did, people would have died, including many children.'

Hassan shifted, glancing briefly at his feet before standing up straight.

'I agree with Defence Minister Dalian, we can't help everyone. But does that mean we should help no one?' He looked at each jury member in turn, his defiant expression challenging them to disagree. After a moment's silence, Hassan continued. 'I believe it is against the Code of Harmony to stand by and watch people suffer. The question is what help and how much of it to offer. That's always a balancing act. My actions won't change the structural inequality on Dunia. Only Dunians can do that. But the people in that camp are grateful to us for getting them the supplies to survive the rainy season.'

He lifted his hand and pressed its splayed fingers to his chest.

'Ultimately, I did what I did because I could not do otherwise without damaging my own soul health. You might call me selfish for that. But I have no regrets. And I believe it was the will of the universe for me to help reunite Kia and Hanna.' He bowed to the semi-circle. 'Thank you for taking the time to assess my case today. I humbly accept whatever punishment Judge Nurilan decides upon. I will not be making an appeal.'

Hanna saw William flinch. That hadn't been part of the statement they'd practised. Lucy hissed in her ear, 'Is he nuts? What if they send him to live on Grooka or something?'

William summarised everything that had been said, repeatedly emphasising the Code of Harmony angle. Syenitians prioritised the Code of Harmony above all their written laws, and Hanna prayed this would make Hassan's sentence more lenient.

Finally, he passed the microphone to the judge. She said, 'We shall adjourn for our deliberation period. Please return in three hours for the verdict and sentencing.'

Hassan looked straight at Hanna. She blew him a kiss before he and William exited through the podium door. Everyone else was standing up to leave.

'I'm starving,' said Kia. 'Where will we have lunch? Must we hang around in town for three whole hours?'

Hanna, Kia and Lucy filed out of the hall, waiting at

the door for their friends. Together, they left the building via a high-ceilinged corridor which hummed with the voices of those attending the hearing. Even here, the Syenitians found it impossible to leave their surfaces unadorned. Glossy green tiles broke the monotony of the utilitarian cream walls, protecting the paintwork from the hallway's heavy traffic. The top row displayed a repeating pattern of jade-coloured fish and creamy, waterlily-like flowers against a swirling background of khaki curves.

They pushed their way through the double-height doors and spilled out onto Kalakaivo Square. Kia crossed the pale flagstones, heading for the stone fountain at its centre. The intricately carved pillar of glistening fish and other sea creatures, all spraying water out of their mouths, fascinated her each time she came here. As water covered ninety per cent of their planet, Syenitians had a close relationship with the ocean.

Hanna and her friends – Lucy, Farida, Aneira, Felix, Saïd, Nikolai and Roberto – joined her. Lucy sat on the edge of the fountain, looking back at the *maalaus* graffiti panels which flanked the base of the Law Court building they'd just left. Scattered throughout Essoona, *maalaus* were artworks created by members of the public for their fellow citizens. Hanna had helped paint several herself. But here, in one of the city's two main squares, they generally had a political flavour. Many were vocal criticisms of the Galaksi Alliance's lack of action to help the devastated Amra; Hanna knew one was the work of Aneira and her Syenitian boyfriend Elian.

She studied them in turn, trying to figure out which. Most were text-based: petitions for government support and aid donations. One stood out, the entire six square metres covered in vivid orange flames, with the Kawaida words for 'Who's next?' in black capitals in the centre. Hanna thought she recognised Aneira's writing. A black Ranglatiri battle frigate was depicted in each of the top corners, as if flying out of the picture to attack. Even as a painting, the hideous ships filled her with fear. Hanna shivered, remembering the terrible day one had clashed with the *Shantivira*. So much damage, caused by a single vessel.

Amra didn't belong to the Alliance, so the Alliance had no obligation to provide military support. However, there was a growing sense that a Ranglatiri attack on an Alliance planet was becoming inevitable. Some argued a pre-emptive strike would be justified. But the Syenitians and many other Alliance members abhorred violence and would put off direct action for as long as possible. Which, no doubt, the Ranglatiri were aware of.

'I'm soo hungry,' said Felix, echoing Kia. 'Where shall we eat?'

Saïd took Farida's hand and pointed towards a gap at the corner of the square. 'Ruokakuja's closest. Let's go down there.'

They descended the steps to the narrow alley next to the River Soon, the exotic cooking odours assaulting Hanna's sense of smell before they were half-way down. She hoped they wouldn't make Kia sick, although her all-day 'morning' sickness had eased off in recent weeks. The street was crammed with food stalls and tiny restaurants, all offering something different.

After some discussion, they agreed on a place specialising in fish soup and dumplings. This was the first time Farida and Aneira had seen the others since before the holidays, and Farida wanted to hear about Nikolai and Roberto's trip to Russia.

Nikolai had recently discovered that his mother – a former *Shantivira* pilot who'd been absent during his childhood – ran a clandestine research facility in Yakutsk, developing weapons to protect the Earth against alien invasion. Kitty was secretly funding her operation without telling the Galaksi Alliance, or even Joe.

Last year, some alien refugees had given Lucy and Nikolai a working example of their micro-fusion reactor plus an electrolyser for generating the necessary hydrogen. Nikolai had taken them to Svetlana for her to reverse engineer.

Nikolai glanced at the crowded street behind them. 'We can't talk about it here. But she was pleased.'

Lucy asked, 'How did Svetlana take your coming out?'

A broad grin spread across Nikolai's pale face. 'She already knew. She just hugged us and said she hoped we'd be very happy together.'

'Yeah,' said Roberto, 'Niko made her sound so scary, but she was brilliant.'

Nikolai said, 'They have an awesome punk scene there. We went to this crazy concert – it was *packed*.'

'It was the only time I was properly warm all week,' added Roberto.

'Was it very cold?' asked Hanna.

'Cold isn't the word. In Siberia, the air attacks you, like needles in your face, in your lungs. We didn't stay outside for more than ten minutes at a time.'

Nikolai wrapped his arm around Roberto and squeezed. 'We warmed up once we got to Brazil though, didn't we?'

Roberto grinned. 'My family adopted him like a pet,' he said. 'Mom made him fresh *pão de queijo* every morning.' He kissed Nikolai on the cheek. 'I told you they'd love you.'

When they'd finished eating, Lucy checked her *zana*. 'Two hours to go. What shall we do?'

Hanna felt like sitting quietly in the *Ohimo* and praying for Hassan. But she couldn't see the others wanting to, and this was a welcome chance to catch up with Farida and Aneira.

'Let's go for a walk,' suggested Felix. 'I need to digest those dumplings.'

Kia groaned. 'I'm not walking anywhere,' she said.

Farida looked at Hanna. 'How about we have a session in the bathhouse? Then we needn't walk at all. The boys can do what they like.'

A good compromise, thought Hanna. Peace to gather herself for the verdict and a chance to talk, too. 'Sure,' she said.

'Fine by me,' Kia agreed.

They climbed the steps back to the square and stood outside the public baths: an imposing structure split into symmetrical halves. Each bore a colossal relief of a naked Syenitian – one female, one male – the white marble contrasting starkly with the building's polished black stone. Hanna remembered being rather shocked the first time she'd seen it. A long time ago. She'd been here so often, she barely glanced at it anymore.

'Keep an eye on the time, won't you?' Lucy reminded Felix. Her happy-go-lucky boyfriend had never managed to live up to the German reputation for punctuality. Spontaneous and sociable, he was likely to get talking to someone and forget his next appointment.

'You too!' he replied, grinning.

The women entered the female half of the baths via the grand door, which almost reached the sculpture's knees. They passed through the different stages at a leisurely pace: showering first, then bathing in meditative silence in pools of varying temperatures.

At last, they arrived at the final stage – the large, open-air bath on the rooftop, where socialising was permitted. Hanna gazed across the city to the sea as the steaming green water loosened the knot between her shoulders.

Kia was floating, eyes closed. Lucy was interviewing Farida about her first weeks back at university and the new second years living at Dunia house. Hanna listened in for a while, then noticed Aneira's absent expression.

'Aneira?' she said, 'You OK?' The effervescent Amranese she'd met last year had withdrawn into her own private misery.

Aneira shrugged.

'I really appreciate you coming today,' persevered Hanna. 'How's Elian?'

'Good, thanks. He's joined the Syenitian Planetary Defence Service. He's a proper pilot now. Like I should be.' She stared at the horizon, not meeting Hanna's eye.

'It's not your fault, Aneira. You'll pass this time and then you can do the same.' Hanna paused. 'If that's what you want.'

'We'll see. I'm going to use this year to keep up my protests to the Council.' Only then did she turn to face Hanna. 'You saw our *maalaus*?'

Hanna nodded. 'The one with the flames?' she confirmed. 'It was the best by far. It really stands out.'

'Thanks.' Aneira's expression tightened, controlled rage churning close beneath the surface. 'I can't believe the Alliance has done nothing to help. There's so few of us left to raise awareness.' Underwater, she wrapped her arms around her chest in a protective self-hug. 'It's like, the Syenitians were shocked initially, but now they've put it out of their minds so they don't feel uncomfortable. But the problem hasn't gone away.'

Hanna said, 'I think Dalian's taking the Ranglatiri seriously, judging by what she said. I bet there's high-level stuff going on behind the scenes that they can't make public.'

'I hope so.' Aneira frowned. 'If there's no retaliation, the Ranglatiri will dare to go further. Which planet will be next? Sayari? Tarumbet?'

'They'll pick off non-Alliance planets first,' said Hanna with a certainty she didn't feel.

'Like yours?'

Cold dread spread through Hanna's stomach. It didn't bear thinking about. 'No one's ever heard of our planet. And we have the *Shantivira* to defend us.'

'Yeah,' said Aneira darkly. 'You're lucky.'

✦   ✦   ✦

AN HOUR LATER, they were back in the courtroom, waiting

restlessly. 'What will you do if they exile him?' whispered Kia. 'Will we go and live with him?'

'William said it probably wouldn't come to that,' said Hanna, surreptitiously digging her nails into her palms. 'Eat when the food is ready and speak when the time is right, Kia. There's no need to decide anything until we know what'll happen to him.'

They wouldn't exile him, would they? Not when Joe had said he wanted Hassan back on the *Shantivira*?

The door behind the podium opened and the participants took their places on the semi-circle. Hanna tried to catch Hassan's eye, but he was staring at a fixed point on the opposite wall.

The room hushed and the central juror, a male Syenitian, took the speaker's spot, facing Hassan.

'Hassan Nhial, this jury finds you guilty of disobeying lawful commands. We do not find you guilty of misapplying Alliance property, obstructing operations, or taking a vessel without consent. We believe it was the will of the universe that you acted as you did.'

Hanna murmured to Lucy, 'That's good, right?'

Lucy squeezed her hand, but said nothing.

'Judge Nurilan, I invite you to pronounce your sentence.'

The judge came forward and took the proffered microphone. She, too, addressed Hassan directly, so Hanna could only see her right profile on the screen. Her grey hair was braided simply, revealing a slightly pointed ear – the only obvious physical difference between humans and Syenitians apart from their height.

To Hanna's astonishment, she was smiling. Positively

twinkling, in fact.

'Hassan Nhial, your punishment is as follows: your mandatory *Shantivira* service period has been extended by five years. You will forego your five-year bonus. In addition to your defence pilot duties, you will fly the upcoming aid deliveries as agreed by Dunia's authorities, for no additional payment.'

On the podium, Hassan and William caught each other's eye and beamed. This was the best outcome they could have hoped for.

'No Cylf shall travel to Dunia's surface again,' the judge continued. 'You and three volunteer colleagues will undergo training to fly the *Shantivira's* cargo craft unassisted. If you feel the urge to break the rules again, young man, resist it. Next time we will not be so lenient.'

Relief coursed through Hanna's veins. They could be together again. Every day. She bit the inside of her cheek, trying not to release an inappropriate shriek of joy. Kia had no such reservations and stood up, cheering. Within seconds the rest of the room had joined her, clapping and whistling, Hanna included.

There'd be a party on the *Shantivira* tonight, she was sure of it.

5. A NEW START
DAN, FEBRUARY 2016

DAN SAT IN the waiting room, tapping his foot impatiently, his heart swollen with a mixture of pride and relief. He was bursting to tell Afra about the message he'd just received, but her physiotherapy session wouldn't finish for another twenty minutes. Her broken arm had healed nicely, but the Ranglatiri secret police's metal club had damaged her left knee for good.

Since their escape from Amra and their arrival in Aldina, Syenitia's second city, Afra had had two operations and weeks of physio. She'd probably walk with a stick for the rest of her life.

Dan's injuries were psychological. He still had nightmares about the claret-coloured Ranglatiri blood all over his hands: that it flowed unstoppably up his arm and into his mouth, drowning him. He regularly woke up bathed in sweat, gasping for air.

Strangely, he never dreamt about Bellyn's death. The police had torn him limb from limb and eaten him directly; the standard penalty for a Ranglatiri regarded as a traitor to their species. Instead, a stony nugget of fury had lodged in Dan's stomach, cold and hard. He swore the Ranglatiri authorities would pay for their treatment of his friend and mentor, starting with the reactivation of the contraceptive smuggling operation Bellyn had risked everything to build: the reason the secret police had come after them in the first place.

When Dan and Afra saw the newsfeeds and realised Amra had been stripped of its resources and the population enslaved and transported, they'd been stricken with guilt. Afra had cried for weeks and Dan had slumped into what he suspected was borderline depression.

Eventually the fog in his head cleared and he told himself – and Afra – get mad, not sad. They could have predicted the destruction of the pharmaceutical factory and their own treatment, but the Ranglatiri's response was excessive, even by their standards. Either there was some other agenda or they were concerned that providing Ranglatiri males with access to contraception would bring their whole society crashing down. Afra and Dan were not responsible for the razing of Amra. And if their smuggling business could, in a small way, contribute to social attitudes on Ranglatiri becoming more progressive, that was fine by him.

The door opened and Afra came out, her features tight with exhaustion. Her silver skin still had a dull sheen from the hardships of the past months. The attractive Sayari physiotherapist followed her, smiling and chatting, radiating vitality. Dan didn't like him. Afra always spoke Sayari with him and Dan couldn't understand more than one word in fifty.

Dan and Afra left the practice, making their way slowly along the wide sidewalk to the tram stop on the corner. Dan found life on Syenitia almost too easy. Free, efficient public transport, clean streets, friendly people and elegant architecture. Everything just . . . worked. That said, the composting toilets had taken some getting used to.

Despite being the planet's principal spaceport, Aldina felt very safe. He walked home each day from his course at the interstellar pilot training centre. Gradually, he was getting to know the city. The six-storey houses were organised in blocks around what were effectively village squares, all offering different amenities: bathhouses, schools, libraries, religious buildings, sports centres. Individual, street-level shops provided for the residents' daily needs.

He hadn't seen a single shopping mall. Or, indeed, any kind of personal transport – apart from the ubiquitous bicycles, which travelled at alarming speeds along a dedicated track parallel to the sidewalk, and the overpriced pods which you could hire like a taxi.

Of course, looking like a local helped. Although his shoulders were untypically broad for a Syenitian, his hair covered his ears and nobody on the street gave him a second glance. If they deemed him on the short side at only 6'4", they were too polite to say so.

The one thing that confused him was the money. He couldn't understand why they had so many different currencies. In addition to the Alliance *fedha* there was the Aldina dinar, which only worked here in town, and the Syenitian shilling, which was legal tender across the planet. The shops accepted all three currencies, but things were always cheapest if you bought them with dinar.

He wondered how much it would cost to rent an apartment. It was the most civilised place he'd ever been –

including Boston, the hometown he'd probably never see again, which until now had been his benchmark. Maybe one day, when he and Afra had made enough to retire on, they could return here and settle down.

They took the lift up to the tram platform. The flying trams travelled on three levels, criss-crossing the city like a tightly woven nest of airborne snakes. Air traffic control regulations meant all spacecraft had to stay at the spaceport and could not be used for local personal transport. Intercity travel was possible, but apparently involved a considerable amount of paperwork. The Syenitians preferred to keep their spacecraft for space travel.

The Number Seven arrived to return them to the spaceport, where they were living aboard the *Gezi Urdina*, Afra's streamlined, sapphire-coloured ship. Once they'd found seats and he'd made sure Afra was comfortable, Dan said, 'So . . . I passed.'

Afra's face lit up. 'You got your results? You have your pilot's licence?'

Dan nodded, beaming, and Afra threw her arms around his neck, her electric-blue hair soft on his cheeks. He closed his eyes and inhaled the scent of it, thinking about taking her to bed the moment they got back.

✦ ✦ ✦

AFTERWARDS, THEY SAT companionably in the mess room, discussing their next steps over lunch. Dan's news seemed to have ignited a spark in Afra and she'd regained some of her old fire. He realised she'd been longing to get back into deep space and had only been waiting for a qualified co-pilot to replace Bellyn.

She'd already organised as much as she could from Aldina. While Dan was at school, she'd used their remaining funds to fit the *Gezi Urdina* with a hyperdrive, and had been in frequent contact with the other factory, launching production of the contraceptive pills. She'd also hunted high and low for the tracking beacon she suspected the secret police had attached to her ship. Finding nothing, she'd fitted a transmission detector to alert her if the *Gezi Urdina* started sending out signals she didn't know about.

Bellyn's backup facility was on Oso-Urrun, at the outer edge of the galaxy. That was why they needed the hyperdrive, and why they'd originally based their operation on Amra, which was located at the intersection of several trade routes.

'So, before we make the trip, we need a customer for our product,' she said, looking at him meaningfully. 'Are you sure you want to be the one to make contact?'

Dan gulped. They'd discussed the best way to handle their approach to the Ranglatiri pirates for weeks on end, but talking about it and doing it were two different things.

'It has to be me. They'll be as jumpy as hell and they won't trust a female. They want someone they can look down on. Someone they can easily dispose of without consequences. They've never seen you, but they all think I was Bellyn's slave. Henning's the best choice. He knows me already and he's a cocky bastard. I reckon I can appeal to his vanity.'

Afra squeezed his hand. 'Bellyn would've been so proud of you.'

'Yeah, well. I'm doing this for him as much as for us. What about your physio sessions? Don't you have a few more weeks to go?'

'Fuck it.' Afra's jawline hardened as she came to a decision. 'My leg's not going to get a lot better than it is now. I know what exercises I'm supposed to do.' Her ears waggled: the Sayari expression of mirth. '*You'll* have to make sure I do them. The longer we leave it, the harder we'll have to work to get the business up and running again.'

Dan took a swig of his *saiju*. 'OK. I'll need the communicator in Bellyn's mask to make the call.'

'Did you remove its oxygen reduction system?'

'Of course.'

LATER THAT AFTERNOON, Dan stood alone in the empty storage bay where Bellyn had taught him to fight with a *stakarh* – the combat staff the Ranglatiri used to settle disputes. Dan kept up his training as a way to stay fit, appreciating the meditative aspect of the now-instinctive moves. He'd just completed a session, aiming to clear his mind and reinhabit the headspace of a Ranglatiri slave. He focused on the two-inch circle tattoo on the inside of his right wrist. His slave marking. Life insurance, Bellyn had called it. He was about to test that theory to breaking point.

There was no precedent for what he was about to do. He hoped that, as effective outcasts from their society, the pirates would be willing to deviate from the Ranglatiri's strict code of conduct concerning other species.

As he systematically recalled everything he'd learnt about correct slave behaviour, his mental state shifted and he bowed his head automatically. It was time.

He put on his dead friend's mask and issued the command to connect.

'Yess?' said Henning in strongly accented Kawaida. 'The owner of that communicator is dead. Who are you and what do you want?'

Henning was suspicious, and with good reason. He and his crewmates would be acutely aware of what had happened to Amra and why.

'S–Sir,' Dan stammered, the tremor of fear in his voice absolutely genuine. 'Bellyn was my master. Perhaps you remember me? The primitive he found in Laro?'

'The Ssyenitian lookalike? You escaped? Or did you trade your master's life for your own, you miserable worm? How dare you approach me, sslave, with your master's own mask?' Henning's voice became high-pitched with outrage.

'My escape – and the pilots' – was part of my master's plan, sir. We'd *never* betray him. He knew the authorities would catch him one day and he prepared us for it. My orders are to continue his legacy, sir.'

'How? They burnt down the factory and ate all the sscientists.'

'My master was wise, sir. He set up a separate manufacturing plant in a distant sector. On his instructions, the pilot activated it after his death and it is producing the pills as we speak.'

There was silence at the other end of the line as Henning digested this news. Dan imagined dollar signs in the pink eyes behind the mask. He pressed his advantage, laying it on thick.

'My master always held you in such high esteem, sir. He told me if they came for him, we should keep the operation going for as long as we could, to help his brothers on Ranglatiri. He said I should approach you first for an exclusive deal, because you were his best and most reliable customer.'

More silence. Dan waited.

'I must consult with my captain. I will call you back, Sslave-Bellyn.' The line went dead.

Dan removed the mask and leaned against the wall, taking deliberately deep breaths to slow his racing pulse. Hard to say how that had gone. Time would tell. He picked up the quarterstaff again and spun it in a rapid figure-of-eight, waiting for Henning.

Almost an hour passed before the little red light in the mask began to flash. Hurriedly, Dan put it on to accept the call.

'Sslave-Bellyn?' said Henning's voice.

'Yes, sir. I'm here.'

'Come to Mwongo to discuss terms.' Henning gave him a date and coordinates. 'My captain wishes to meet you in person. We also need a sample of the product for analysis.'

The planet Mwongo? Please no, thought Dan. Its slippery, eponymous inhabitants could be found right across the galaxy, generally in pursuit of a fast and easy buck. Dan had met several and they gave him the creeps. Lord knew what their home planet was like. Then again, they could hardly meet somewhere reputable. At least the

Mwongo could be paid to keep quiet. Out loud, he said, 'Yes, sir. Um . . . the sample is a little problematic. The facility is so far away, the pilot says the logistical costs are too high to make the trip unless we already have a customer and an agreed price. Even with a hyperdrive, we'd only be able to make two shipments a year.

'I humbly suggest we use our meeting to negotiate a price and terms of business. Then the pilot and I will collect the shipment and bring it to you. No payment will be due until the product passes your tests. We are confident it will.'

'Two shipments a year? Iss that all? How will you make a profit?'

Dan flushed. 'We . . . er . . . we'll have to put our prices up, sir.' Before Henning could object, he added, 'Remember, sir, you would be the exclusive supplier, so you can charge your end customers whatever you like.'

'Hmm. Then we will ssee whether we can come to an agreement.'

'It would be an honour to do business with you, sir.'

6. A MOTORISED HAMSTER WHEEL
JOE

KILOMETRES OUT OF his comfort zone, Joe shifted position on the TV studio's unforgiving guest sofa. The heat from the artificial lights was making him sweat. The Graham Norton Show last week had been a lot more fun than this. *And* he'd got to meet PJ and Duncan – some actual pop stars from back in the day. Apparently, they were famous for something else now. How should *he* know? He didn't have time to watch television, except for the rugby.

These media types found it hilarious that his knowledge of popular culture ended in 1997 and he'd never heard of Julianne Moore, the other guest. An Oscar winner, by all accounts. She'd been very nice about it. He'd put watching *The Big Lebowski* on his mental to-do list. Delius would be bound to have it in the *Shantivira's* archives.

'Captain Llewellyn?' said the interviewer, a grey man in a grey suit. 'What is your view on the Transatlantic Trade and Investment Partnership currently under negotiation between Europe and the United States?' His tone suggested it wasn't the first time he'd asked.

Whoops! Drifted off there for a moment. Joe's brain

scrambled to rerun the last few minutes of discussion with the other guest. 'TTIP?' he said, playing for time. 'Well, I'm no economist. I guess you have to ask, who's it really for? Will it improve the lives of citizens on both continents, or will it just make it easier for money to flow between corporations?' The expression on the interviewer's face told him that was the wrong answer.

The other guest – who *was* an economist – became visibly agitated. 'Our economies will be boosted by hundreds of billions. GDP can only go up!'

'I don't care about GDP,' said Joe, no doubt branding himself an ignorant heretic in the eyes of the business community. 'It doesn't measure what's important. I care about people's lives. Any economic system which doesn't enable *all* its citizens to flourish isn't doing its job, in my book.' He shrugged. 'But like I said, I'm no expert. I came here to talk about aliens.'

'You did,' agreed the interviewer. He thanked the other guest, who stood up and left rather gruffly, then summarised for the audience who Joe was and why he was on the programme.

'—and we'd also like to welcome Gerhard Stadler, Captain of the *Monte Maria* container ship.' A tall white man in his late fifties entered the studio and took the empty space on the sofa. His well-cut, pinstriped suit gave him the air of a bank manager.

Joe's heart sank as he recognised the name of the ship. Fuckity *fuck*. Everything came back to bite you in the end, didn't it? He arranged his face into a polite smile and studied Gerhard's patrician features. It was the first time he'd seen him close up.

The presenter jumped straight in. 'Herr Stadler, you allege a spacecraft shaped like a gigantic beetle once landed on your vessel in the North Pacific Ocean and stole twelve thousand metric tonnes of fish.'

Gerhard leaned back in his seat, crossing his long legs. His shoes were black leather lace-ups, Joe noticed, with an expensive sheen. 'I know it sounds crazy. However, sources at the UN have confirmed what we saw is identical to the *Shantivira* space station's cargo ship.' He turned his head and looked Joe in the eye. 'So I want know, was it you, and if so, what the hell do you think you were doing? You scared us senseless!'

Joe took a deep, slow breath. At least they weren't talking about trade agreements anymore. He might as well come clean and tell the whole story. He held Gerhard's gaze and gave him a disarming smile. 'I'm sorry we frightened you. I think that was unavoidable in the circumstances.'

'—You *admit* it then?' interrupted the monochrome interviewer, more animated than Joe had seen him all morning.

Joe ignored him. 'As I recall, the crew were asleep. Only you and the Officer of the Watch were on the bridge that night. We took the fish, yes, but all accounts were settled. We paid for every last flippin' kipper. It was an emergency.'

Gerhard's eyes widened. 'You were there in person? Was it *you* on that cable?'

Joe grinned, despite himself. 'We picked a ship going through a storm to reduce the risk of confrontation, but man, I got so wet! I don't know how you do it, working in those conditions.'

The interviewer frowned. 'What kind of an emergency needs twelve thousand tonnes of fish?' he said, leaning forward.

'An invading fleet of a hundred thousand starving human-sized octopuses.' said Joe, willing the invisible future audience to understand, to be sympathetic. Was he about to go viral? Again? Or would the show's producers cut this bit out before broadcasting? 'They were refugees planning to settle in our oceans, as their own planet had been destroyed.'

'That was careless of them, letting their planet get destroyed.'

Joe stared at the interviewer, resisting the urge to punch the idiot on his smug, grey chin. Deep breath, Joe. And release. And repeat. He forced himself to smile, although it felt more like a grimace. 'Well, unlike some species I could think of, they didn't manage to do it all by themselves.'

He explained about the Ranglatiri; how government-sponsored pirates would invade planets more bountiful than their own and strip their resources, leaving dusty wastelands in their wake. Any intelligent life they found would be enslaved or eaten. 'Ranglatiri are carnivorous cannibals,' said Joe, speaking directly to the camera. 'Life isn't sacred to them. They'll happily eat each other, too, they're not fussy.'

'But your space station can protect us from them, right?' said the presenter. Finally, the man was taking him seriously.

'We're working hard to make sure they remain una-ware of the Earth and all its riches. If it came to a full-on assault – I honestly don't know. But the *Shantivira* is the Earth's best hope. Without us, Earth's an all-you-can-loot buffet.'

Joe rubbed his jaw, wondering how much more he ought to say. In for a penny, in for a pound, he decided. There was no going back now. This was a golden opportunity to speak frankly to the general public. He might not get another one. 'The Ranglatiri have some new shield tech,' he continued. 'Ten of our pilots lost their lives in a battle with a single frigate. The Syenitians are currently working on ways to penetrate it. We managed to destroy the enemy ship – as far as we know, the Ranglatiri still don't know what's here.'

The interviewer leaned back in his seat. 'Star Wars on our doorstep? How do we know you're not making all this up to justify your operation?'

Unable to contain himself, Joe leapt to his feet. 'Did you not hear me? I lost ten pilots that day. Ten! Colleagues in my care, who died to protect our planet.' He bent over, jabbing a finger in the interviewer's chest. 'Don't you *dare* demean their sacrifice. You haven't a clue what you're talking about.' In the corner of his eye, Joe noticed two security guards moving his way. He stepped back and sat down again. 'Apologies. It's just—there's a lot going on up there. People down here have no idea.'

'What about the octopuses?' said Gerhard. 'What happened to them? They're not still here, are they?'

Joe smiled at him, grateful for the change of tack. 'No. The Syenitians agreed to give the Pweza a home. Like us, they have large oceans. And thanks to your fish, Gerhard, the Pweza were able to continue the journey in their own spacecraft.'

'Tell us about these Syenitians,' said the presenter, his composure recovered. 'Why would they fund your operation? What's in it for them?'

'Everyone asks me that,' said Joe. He settled back in his seat, relaxing into familiar territory. 'Syenitians live for thousands of years, so they take the long view. They believe all life is sacred – especially intelligent life. All their actions must comply with their moral framework, the Code of Harmony.'

Gerhard and the presenter studied him, saying nothing. Joe suspected they were thinking the Syenitians sounded like a bunch of Buddhist monks. If only. Dalian and her machinations to remove Aldeman from the Council proved Syenitians could be as Machiavellian as any human. Still, with their joint undercover operation on Ranglatiri in full swing, Dalian's and Aldeman's objectives were aligned, for now.

Joe gathered his thoughts and continued. 'Syenitia is a founder member of the Galaksi Alliance: a union of intelligent life from thirty-three different planets in this galaxy, promoting peace, trade and the exchange of ideas. The *Shantivira* is one of several Alliance projects to safeguard the development of what they see as still-primitive civilisations, in the hope they will ultimately contribute to a peaceful galaxy. The *Shantivira* is managed by the Syenitian Council, so I report to them – other Alliance governments run other projects.'

Gerhard folded his arms. 'When will they come here?' he asked.

'They won't,' said Joe. 'Not to settle. They tried, about twenty thousand years ago when sea levels were lower, but their island colony was a failure.' Kitty had told him the settlers were unable to breed, despite their planets' superficial similarities. Their long lives meant Syenitians weren't particularly fertile, even on their home world, and the Earth's extra gravity had been an insurmountable barrier to embryo development.

'They left bits of their language behind and feature in a few of our myths and legends, but that's it,' Joe said. 'You might get the occasional visiting dignitary at some point, or unofficial tourists. They won't be competing for our resources, if that's what you're worried about.'

'What do you mean, feature in our myths and legends?' said the interviewer. 'Like your bodyguard who turned into a dragon in front of the UN General Assembly?' He looked around, suddenly nervous. 'Where is she today?'

Joe laughed. 'On call if I need her. Kitty's only half Syenitian and arrived here long after the destruction of the settlement. But she's very old and has her own place in Celtic folklore. Normal Syenitians can't shapeshift.'

Gerhard's eyebrows shot up. 'Hold on a minute. Destruction of the island settlement? And they came when sea levels were lower? You're talking about the Lost City of Atlantis, aren't you?'

'You might think so,' twinkled Joe. 'I couldn't possibly comment.'

+ + +

SHAKILA, WHO'D BEEN working flat-out behind the scenes to organise Joe's charm offensive/PR campaign, was predictably furious. 'Mark my words, Joe, that interview will have diplomatic repercussions. Let's hope speaking about the Ranglatiri so openly doesn't trigger an anti-alien backlash. I thought we agreed you'd take things slowly?'

'Sorry,' said Joe, unrepentant. 'At least I didn't call the interviewer an ignorant fuckwit. I nearly did. And worse.'

He looked up at the *Koppakuoria*, towering above them, his mind already on the next task. 'How did the first fuel pickup go, do you know?'

Professional as always, Shakila dropped her anger and moved on. She shook her expensive haircut. 'No. I've been babysitting our honoured guest engineers in the conference room.'

That was today, was it? Oh hell. Joe ran his fingers through his hair. 'I'd forgotten about them,' he admitted.

Her mouth gave an amused twitch, but she was kind enough not to comment.

'I'll go down to say hello in a minute,' Joe said. 'What are Dipesh and Oksana teaching them?'

'Magnetic shielding 101 this week,' said Shakila, not even having to check her clipboard. 'They've finished translating the specs into English and Russian. The Chinese and Japanese versions should be ready next month.'

'Good,' said Joe. 'Remind me, who is it today?' He should definitely know this already, but his memory was drawing a blank.

'ISRO,' came the reply. 'Rohini insisted we get the Indians in first.'

Of course she had. Now he thought about it, he could vaguely recall that conversation. 'That was it. Thanks for arranging everything, Shakila.'

'What would you do without me?' she teased.

'Get into even more trouble, probably,' he said, his face crinkling into a boyish grin. 'See you in a bit; I need to talk to Delius first.'

He left her and strode to the circular control room at the apex of the docking bay quadrant. Delius had seen him coming and was waiting. Something in the way he stood suggested he was worried about something – as far as it was possible to guess at a Cylf's mental state. It couldn't be his trial, that had gone as expected. No more illicit trips to undeveloped planets and a two-year ban from visiting the Essoona Library in person. Plus they'd extended his *Shantivira* service period by another twenty years, which had delighted Delius and the rest of the crew.

'Hello, Delius, what's up? How did the fuel pickup go?'

'The biological waste transport went smoothly, Captain, thank you for asking.' Delius' tone indicated that something else hadn't.

Joe raised a questioning eyebrow. 'But . . . ?'

'There is a quality issue, sir. The level of contaminants is too high for our digesting bacteria to handle.' Joe detected a tinge of disgust in his gravelly voice. 'It contains pesticides, hormones, pharmaceutical products, microplastics, endocrine disruptors, excess nitrogen and phosphorus, as well as fats which will clog up our pipes.'

Shit. Literally. 'Do we have to take it back?' Even Joe knew that would be a public relations disaster.

'We can use this batch,' said Delius, 'if we dilute it with our existing supplies. But we can't keep using it, sir, or our engines will sustain damage.'

Joe rubbed his eyes. One bloody problem after another. 'I thought the sample we took was OK?'

'It was, sir. Perhaps it wasn't big enough. Perhaps the contaminants weren't mixed homogeneously.'

'Where did it come from?' asked Joe. Something else he should probably already know. There was so much going on these days, it was getting impossible to stay on top of all the details.

'A wastewater treatment plant for an urban area in Brazil.'

Joe leaned against the control room's central pillar, conscious that all the *Shantivira's* organic waste and sewage flowed through it behind him, en route to the main generator.

'So filling the *Koppakuoria's* tank in one go from an industrialised population isn't going to fly. We need quality crap. Organic ordure. From somewhere where people don't perpetually pop pills or spray pesticides.' He closed his eyes, letting his thoughts settle, like sediment in a septic tank. A septic tank! That was it!

'People in rural areas mostly have septic tanks, don't they, Delius? And getting them pumped out can be a right hassle.'

Delius understood where Joe was headed. 'Most efficient would be for us to access remote settlements with dense populations, Captain. Such as refugee camps.'

Refugee camps. *Of course.* Why hadn't they thought of that in the first place?

'Brainwave!' said Joe. 'High five, Delius!' he cried, adding, 'Gently!' when he remembered Delius' valkoinium chassis. Too late. Massaging his wrist, he said, 'When we send Hassan's team with supplies, they can pump out the local septic tanks at the same time. I'll get Shakila to coordinate with UNHCR.'

Delius gave a slow nod, still thinking. 'We'll need to take samples first. But that could be done on the spot. The smaller volumes will ensure the result is more reliable.'

'When are the aid deliveries scheduled to start?'

'Next month, Captain.'

'Good.' Joe stood up straight and headed for the door. 'Well, I'd better say hi to our visitors before Aldeman turns up. Honestly, I feel like I'm on a motorised hamster wheel these days. It never stops.'

But Delius wasn't finished. 'One more thing, sir—'

'—what?' Joe spun on his heel to face him, releasing the door handle.

'I just received an alert from the database in Aldina.'

Aldina? 'Yes?' said Joe, scrabbling to remember why that might be significant.

'Dan Simpson has qualified as an interstellar pilot there.'

That was it! Aldina was where the ex-NASA astronaut and his Sayari girlfriend had fled after the Ranglatiri attack on Amra. Joe beamed. 'Looks like he was right when he said he'd be fine and we shouldn't contact him again. That's great news. One less thing to worry about. Thanks, Delius.' He exited the room whistling a cheery sea shanty.

+   +   +

ON THE *PRIDE of Essoona*, Joe slumped thankfully on his sofa, cursing as tea sloshed out of his mug and onto the well-worn leather. As he mopped at it with his handker-chief, he heard someone on the steps outside, which he left down during the day as part of his open-door manage-ment policy.

Aldeman's head appeared in the doorway to the living area. 'Am I too early?'

Joe raised his mug in a mock salute. 'Yes! This is the first breather I've had all day. Will you join me for a cuppa? I've got biscuits in the cupboard.'

'With pleasure. Don't get up.'

Familiar with Joe's galley kitchen, Aldeman Var-pushaukka, Leader of the Syenitian Council and Syenitian Representative to the Galaksi Alliance, busied himself with the kettle. Then he kicked off his boots and sat cross-legged on the sofa next to Joe. Unusually, his waist-length black hair was loose, reminding Joe of Kitty. There was a certain resemblance: like her, Aldeman was descended from the former Syenitian royal family, who had abdicated power millennia ago, allowing the planet to become a republic.

In a practised movement, Aldeman scooped it over his right shoulder to prevent it getting stuck between his back and the sofa. 'Where's Mrs Llewellyn today?' he asked.

'Argentina, watching over Mam. She's been keeping me updated on your marriage problems.'

Aldeman inclined his head, understanding. 'Your marriage problems' was a code they'd agreed to refer to the activities of Aldeman's wife, Kitty's sister Rowan, the only other shape-shifting space demon in the galaxy.

After the destruction of Amra, Aldeman had sent her on a secret mission to Ranglatiri: to embed herself there as one of them and work her way into the Ranglatiri government, with the intention of bringing it down from the inside. To be fair, the whole crazy plan was Rowan's idea. As it was utterly illegal, just five people knew about the operation: Rowan, Aldeman, Dalian, Kitty and Joe.

Dalian – the Syenitian defence minister and a long-term opponent of the Shantivira project – had argued strenuously against Joe being informed, but she was too late. The sisters told each other everything via their space demons' telepathic connection. Rowan and Aldeman could talk to each other privately, wherever they were, in the same way Joe and Kitty did.

The sisters felt Aldeman would need Joe's emotional support over the coming months, or possibly years, so he should be told the truth. The cover story was that Aldeman's and Rowan's marriage had foundered and they were having a period of separation in an attempt to fix it. As Aldeman's brother-in-law and best friend, Joe was the obvious person for him to turn to. They'd decided they'd be less likely to be spied upon if Aldeman came to the *Shantivira* more often, instead of meeting at the baths as they usually did.

For security reasons, they never spoke of the matter out loud. But both knew the other knew, and Joe hoped that comforted Aldeman. He was lonely without his wife and concerned for her mental health – living a lie amongst those barbarians. At the same time, he and Dalian were using Syenitia's most effective weapon to prevent other planets ending up like Amra and Pweza.

As they drank their tea, Joe did the weekly update: everything he'd been doing to make first contact a success, the non-fuel-grade sewage, and that Dan Simpson was on

Syenitia, up the coast from Essoona in Aldina. He also texted Yisheng, asking him to meet them in the memorial orchard. Now Joe was occupied with what he secretly thought of as 'PR bullshit', Yisheng and Kazembi were organising the routine space station tasks: staff rotas, space debris dematerialisation, training plans, maintenance and the monitoring of food supplies. Sometimes these repetitive jobs had bored Joe; now he missed them.

Once they'd finished, they left their mugs in the sink and headed to the temperate biome for their orchard meeting. They found Rob digging up carrots in the neighbouring field. This was only his third visit to the *Shantivira*, but he was settling in well. He'd befriended the temperate biome managers and thrown himself into farmwork. In the mornings, he had a Kawaida lesson with Kia and Irion, who came from London twice a week to teach Kia.

'*Ti'n iawn, Rob, mêt?*' Joe called.

Rob stood up and rubbed his back. '*Shwmae, Joe. Iawn, diolch.*'

'There's someone I'd like you to meet,' said Joe, switching to English. Rob approached them, wiping his muddy hands on his jeans. 'This is Aldeman, my boss.'

In greeting, Aldeman held his arms at ninety degrees to his body, his palms facing Rob. Rob mirrored the pose intuitively and performed his first Syenitian hand press as if it were the most natural thing in the world. Joe experienced a small surge of pride on his behalf.

'Welcome, Major Morgan,' said Aldeman. 'It is a pleasure to meet you. I hope you are finding your time with us beneficial?'

'Very, thank you.' After learning to conjugate verbs

with Irion, a silver-skinned Sayari, meeting a Syenitian was less of a hurdle than it might have been six weeks ago. Rob hesitated, then said, 'Are you . . . like Kitty, sir?'

Inwardly, Joe cursed himself. He should have explained the difference between Kitty and normal Syenitians more clearly. Was Rob reporting back to his superiors that every Syenitian could teleport and shape-shift? That wouldn't do at all.

Aldeman's glacier-blue eyes gleamed with amusement. 'No, Major Morgan. I am a humble mortal, like yourself. Mrs Llewellyn is only half Syenitian. Her mother was an ancestor of mine, but her father was an ancient space spirit from the dawn of the universe. She inherited her . . . abilities from him.'

Joe saw Yisheng approaching: time for their walk-and-talk meeting. 'We'll do our session tomorrow, Rob,' he said. 'OK?'

'Sure. Looking forward to it.'

✦   ✦   ✦

AFTER DINNER, JOE returned to the *Pride of Essoona* and poured himself two fingers of whisky. What a day. Where was Kitty? She should be back by now. He reached out with his mind.

Babe? Where are you? Did Rob get back alright?

Yes, of course, that only took five minutes. Joe, I need to stay with Grace tonight. She might say something that puts her in danger.

Suddenly, Joe was on full alert. *What's happened?*

Are you sitting comfortably? I mean, are you alone and

do you have time?

Joe put down his glass. *Yes. Tell me.*

OK. So. Nestor had a visitor today. And we know him.

Who? said Joe.

Your excitable Argentinian friend from the UN with the species summaries, remember? In Vienna?

Joe did remember. The elderly gentlemen's unprovoked aggression had been distinctly unsettling. But, what with everything else that had happened that day, the Argentinian delegate had slipped entirely from his mind. Until now.

Jorge Mendez? he said, astonished he hadn't forgotten the name.

Mmm-hmm, confirmed Kitty.

That's not a total surprise is it, that they know each other?

No. Get Delius to see if there's a provable link between them. Nestor called him Pedro.

Will do. Joe picked up his glass again, cradling it against his chest and inhaling the sharp, peaty fumes.

There's more, Kitty continued. *They talked. Nestor doesn't realise how hard Grace has been working on her Spanish, so he was less guarded than he should have been. She was in the kitchen, but she heard every word and understood the gist of what they were saying. I saw her face afterwards; Joe, I don't know how long she'll be able to contain herself. We both heard it; I was a gecko on the ceiling. Poor Grace – her world's been turned upside-down.*

Heard what? he demanded. In his mind's eye, he saw his mother standing frozen with shock, a red-chequered tea-towel hanging limply from her hands.

It was *Nestor who tried to kill you. He organised the whole thing, with Mendez's help. I don't have a recording, but it's certain, Joe. It was him.*

Joe took a large slug of whisky. Bastard. Fucking bastard. I'll have your miserable head on a plate, Nestor, if it's the last thing I do, he swore to himself. Then he blinked. Get a grip, Joe. He suppressed the volcano threatening to erupt inside him, resisting the urge to throw his glass against the wall. Funny, the difference between suspecting something strongly and knowing it for sure. His strength of emotion alarmed him.

OK, he said to Kitty, taking a deep breath and releasing it slowly. He couldn't afford to lose his temper. If she realised how upset he was, she might launch some spontaneous, rage-fuelled revenge mission, which wouldn't help his mother. Keep it cool, Joe. *Well*, he said. *We were pretty sure already.*

The situation's changed, though. Kitty's voice had an uncharacteristic urgency. *Grace knows and I can't predict how she'll react. What do you want to do? Pull her out? Start criminal proceedings? Confront him?*

Joe pictured his mother's expression as she stood motionless in that strange kitchen. One part fury. Two parts terror. He could see it quite clearly. Just like in the old days, when his father had been around. He shivered, swatting the memory away before it could start gnawing at his peace of mind.

Joe? said Kitty, waiting for his answer.

I don't know, love. You should stay with Mam until we decide. If he realises she knows the truth . . . Joe didn't want to finish that sentence. *I have to think.*

7. A COMPLICATION
HANNA

H ANNA SLIPPED HER hand into Hassan's as he pressed the doorbell of his former home in Kampala. Since his return to the *Shantivira*, they were spending all their spare time together and Hassan had decided it was time to introduce her to his foster parents.

'What if they don't like me?' Hanna said in a small voice. She'd always been in awe of them: they both worked at Makerere University, which meant they must be impossibly intelligent. And rich. The house where Hassan had grown up was a solid, comfortable bungalow with a garden full of vegetables, and pretty pot plants by the front door. It was a different world to the mud hut she'd lived in until her parents died.

Hassan looked down at her, smiling. 'How could they not like you? They're going to love you.'

They heard rapid footsteps and a voice singing, 'Morris! They're here!' before the door opened. Hanna braced herself. Too late to run away now.

A statuesque woman, dressed in a brightly patterned skirt and matching blouse, emerged onto the porch. She flung out her arms, embracing Hassan. 'My boy, it's wonderful to see you!' She released him and held out her hand for Hanna to shake.

'You must be Hanna. My, you're as pretty as a picture!'

'It's a pleasure to meet you, Mrs Rukundo,' said Hanna.

'Call me Rose, dear.' Rose gestured towards the interior of the house. 'Please, come in.'

Behind her, a man appeared: shorter and wider than his wife. He welcomed Hassan with a prolonged handshake, then extended his hand to Hanna. She gave him a respectful nod and placed her left hand on her right forearm as an added courtesy.

'Welcome, Hanna!' he boomed cheerfully. 'I'm Morris. It's great to meet you at last.'

Hanna smiled shyly, taking in the cramped hallway. Thick, fraying rugs on terracotta tiles, faded floral wallpaper and bookcases, double-stacked and piled high with books. More pot plants jostled for space: on the shelves, on the floor, even hanging from the ceiling. The overall effect was pleasantly chaotic.

'You have a beautiful home,' she said.

'Thank you,' said Rose. 'Will you help me in the kitchen while the others lay the table?'

The fitted kitchen was newer than Mary and Irion's 1980's antique, but not so modern as to be intimidating. Rose passed her an apron. 'Put that on over your smart skirt, dear. Is it your own design? Hassan told me you enjoy sewing.'

Hanna nodded, happy she'd made the effort to dress up. 'This one's my favourite.'

'Would you make me one, if you have time? I'm so

tall, I find it hard to get skirts the right length.'

'I'd love to,' said Hanna, chopping onions, already considering which colours would suit Rose best. A bold geometric pattern, she thought. Or maybe big, splashy flowers? 'I'll take your measurements before I go. Although,' she hesitated, 'I don't know when I'll have it done. My sister's having a baby soon.'

Rose's eyes sparkled. 'Hassan told us,' she said, patting Hanna's hand. 'There's no hurry. A little one will certainly keep you busy.' She poured cooking oil into a large pot and turned on the heat, adding Hanna's onions bit by bit, along with a generous helping of pre-chopped garlic. 'I've started the knitting: I'm doing everything in yellow as we don't know if it's a boy or a girl yet.'

Hanna's eyes blurred, no doubt due to the onions. Everyone was being so sweet about Kia. At Dunia House, Mrs Park had already crocheted an entire blanket and was as excited as any grandmother-to-be. According to Irion, Mary had a whole stack of babygrows in all different sizes, ready and waiting for the day the baby came. And now Rose, whom she'd never even met.

'Thank you,' she said.

'My pleasure,' said Rose. 'I'll show you after lunch.'

They ate outside on the veranda, surrounded by more verdant pot plants. Hanna recognised a few, but felt ignorant for not knowing their names. With Hanna's assistance, Rose had made Kikalayi and bean stew, serving up the fried pork on a large handmade platter.

'So, Hassan,' said Rose. 'How was your first official trip in the *Koppakuoria*?'

'Brazil, wasn't it?' added Morris.

Hanna glanced at Hassan, surprised at how well-informed his foster parents were. Then again, he did call them faithfully each weekend.

'It all went smoothly,' said Hassan. He grinned mischievously. 'I didn't crash.'

Hanna nibbled her pork, the rich flavours warm and comforting, listening to the conversation without being part of it.

Rose said, 'Remind me, who are your co-pilots?'

'Gildas was with me that day. Gaositwe and Ginika have also done the training so they can take it in turns to come with me,' Hassan explained.

'Ginika?' said Morris. 'I haven't heard that name before.'

'She's in my year. An Igbo, from Nigeria.'

'No Ozzy?' Rose said.

Hassan scooped up more stew with his chapati. 'He wanted to do the training, but we decided we should be an all-African team, seeing as most of the camps we'll be visiting are here. Ozzy's going to do extra *Tumba* shifts for me, so I get some time to spend with Hanna.' He winked at her and Hanna smiled back silently, her cheeks bulging with beans.

'Where will the next trip be?' asked Morris. 'Back to Brazil?'

Hassan shook his head. 'Too many chemicals in the slurry. We're going to empty the septic tanks at the camps we go to instead.'

'What about you, Hanna, dear?' said Rose, changing the subject. 'How are you settling in?'

Hanna swallowed her mouthful and dabbed at her lips

with her napkin. 'I love it,' she said. 'No more commuting on packed trams, no exams and I already know everyone.' Her face split into a wide grin. 'And I see Hassan every day!'

They laughed and Hassan squeezed her hand.

Hanna continued, 'I'm looking forward to qualifying. Then I can contribute properly at last, as thanks for all the training they've given me.'

'What about your sister? asked Morris. 'How's *she* finding life on the *Shantivira*?'

'Kia prefers it to Dunia House. She likes the village atmosphere and that most of the crew are human.' Hanna took a sip of her banana smoothie, savouring the fruit's full flavour. 'She'd much rather live on the Earth, though.' She sighed as she placed her glass on the table. 'But that's just not practical at the moment. Kia hasn't grasped how much a baby's going to change her life.'

Rose patted her arm. 'Nobody ever does. That's normal.'

Hanna disagreed. Now Hassan's trial was over, most of her spare mental energy went on researching how to care for a newborn baby. The more she learned, the more terrified and excited she became. Kia wasn't doing any reading at all, saying she'd work it out when the baby arrived.

Hassan said, 'Hanna's teaching Kia to swim.'

'Like you taught me,' said Hanna, her mouth curving into a smile as she enjoyed a brief flashback of her swimming lessons with Hassan. So long ago now. 'It's one of the few things we can do together, now Kia's so far along in her pregnancy.'

THE NEXT MORNING, Hanna was back at work, flying a standard tour to dematerialise space debris which risked entering the orbits of the terrestrial satellites. She still hadn't really gelled with Urca, her new *Tumba*, and found herself making unfavourable comparisons with her former school *Tumba*, who'd felt more like a friend.

Still, today's task was undemanding and she and Lucy chatted on a private channel as they flew and fired. Hanna related the details of her trip to Uganda and Lucy spoke about her own weekend. She'd gone home to Devon to tell her parents about her role on the *Shantivira*.

Joe had asked them all to inform their families if they hadn't already done so. He was arranging for a group of journalists to visit the space station and it was possible the crew members' identities would be revealed. 'It's better they hear it from you than finding out some other way,' he'd said.

'How did they take it?' asked Hanna, relieved she'd not had to go through the same ordeal herself.

'First time I've seen my mother speechless,' said Lucy, grinning.

Having met Lucy's parents the previous Christmas, Hanna could imagine. 'What about your dad?' she said, calmly obliterating a jagged, football-sized piece of wreckage. Wouldn't want *that* crashing into a satellite. She watched her fuel gauge twitch a notch upwards, due to the energy her dematerialisation beam had extracted from the debris.

Lucy took a sip from her water bottle. 'I think he was rather proud of me. You know he was in the Royal Air Force?'

'As a pilot? You mentioned it.' Hanna smiled to herself. Several times, in fact. Not that she'd ever embarrass her friend by saying so.

'Yeah, so, he understood why I wanted to do this. And why I hadn't told them earlier: military secrecy and so on.'

Hanna said, 'Did you tell them about David Wang and getting kidnapped by Nestor?'

Lucy chuckled. 'No way. That's not something they ever need to know.'

They both fell silent, remembering. They did an entire orbit of the Earth before Lucy spoke again. 'Nikolai told his dad, did you hear?'

'Just about himself, not about his mum, right?' said Hanna.

'Just about himself,' confirmed Lucy. 'He took Roberto with him and came out at the same time.' Hanna heard the amusement in Lucy's voice. 'I think that was enough new information for his dad to take on board in one go.'

'I can imagine,' said Hanna, feeling sorry for the much-lied-to Mr Poroshkin.

'I'll tell you what Roberto told me, though,' Lucy continued, firing on a drifting piece of sheet metal until it glowed and vanished. 'Svetlana's leaving Yakutsk.'

Hanna blinked. That was unexpected. 'She is?'

'She's going to buy a DSV she can run her operation from.'

'A DSV?' Hanna frowned. 'What's that?'

'Sorry,' said Lucy. 'I spent too much time with Björn last year. A Diving Support Vessel.'

The penny dropped. 'She needs access to seawater so she can use the Pweza's technology,' said Hanna. A statement, not a question. 'Has she found a way of scaling it up?'

'Looks like it,' said Lucy.

Hanna shivered. She wasn't sure how she felt about anti-spacecraft weapons being located down on the planet. What if someone unfriendly got hold of them and aimed them at the *Shantivira*?

Still, if Kitty was funding it, she must think it necessary. And Svetlana was an ex-Shantiviran, not an alien-hating nutter like Nestor. Every so often, she wondered what had happened to him. His young assistant, Matthew, too. Were they biding their time somewhere, preparing to make trouble again? Surely Kitty would have dealt with them both, one way or the other?

Their shift over, they returned to Docking Bay 1. Lucy was already waiting when Hanna climbed out of her *Tumba*.

Hanna said, 'I'm looking forward to a hot shower.'

'Space is cold,' agreed Lucy, stretching her stiff muscles. 'Routine missions don't keep you as warm as a training flight.' Her *zana* bleeped: she glanced at it and groaned. 'Damn and blast. I completely forgot.'

'Forgot what?' asked Hanna.

Lucy made a face. 'Dad's been on at me for ages to set up a pension. Now he knows how much I'm earning, he says I should be squirreling it away for the future.'

'Saving up for your retirement?' Hanna giggled. 'Lucy, you're only twenty-nine!'

Lucy tapped at her *zana*. 'I've got an appointment with a financial advisor, an hour from now, in London.'

'Better get your skates on, then.'

Together, they headed for the cylindrical lift at the apex of the docking bay. Before they were halfway there, Joe's camouflage-clad friend Rob came running around the central column from the direction of Docking Bay 3. His legs were so long, he reminded Hanna of a galloping giraffe. She smirked inwardly at the image.

To her surprise, he came to a breathless halt in front of her.

'Hanna!' he said. 'Thank God you're back. Kia's in the sick bay. Can you come?'

Sick bay? She looked at Lucy, half hoping she'd ditch her appointment and come with her. She didn't want to admit it, but Hanna was a little shy of Joe's former boss.

'Go,' ordered Lucy. 'I'll catch up with you later.'

Hanna swallowed her disappointment and followed Rob, hurrying to keep up. 'What's happened?' she asked. 'Is the baby coming?' Stress pitched her voice higher than usual. 'It's too early!'

He glanced back at her and slowed his stride. 'She's OK. The baby's not coming yet. Sorry if I scared you. I just know she'd prefer to have you with her rather than me.'

They reached the row of chairs outside the sick bay which served as a waiting area. Through the glass, Hanna saw Kia sitting on the examination table with her feet up. Hagar was nearby, preparing a syringe. Kia gave Hanna a cheerful wave. She looked fine. Panic over.

Hagar turned and seeing them, pointed at the seats, mouthing 'Wait there.'

'What's happened?' repeated Hanna as she and Rob sat.

'You know how Irion makes us walk round the biomes for our Kawaida lessons?'

'Yes?' said Hanna, wondering what that had to do with anything.

Rob ran a hand through his thinning brown hair. 'She says it helps us remember vocabulary, but I think she just likes visiting the forest when she's here. Not much of *that* in central London.'

Get to the point, man, Hanna thought, but said nothing.

'Kia started complaining about an ache in her calf. I looked and the skin there was hot and tender. So I got her to sit down and wait while I fetched Hagar.'

'And what did Hagar say?' asked Hanna, thinking it sounded like Rob was making a fuss about nothing.

'What I thought. Deep vein thrombosis.' Rob glanced over his shoulder at the two figures on the other side of the window. 'We brought her back here for tests and Hagar said she has everything she needs to treat it.'

'Deep vein thrombosis? What's that?' As she spoke, a faint recollection nudged her memory. Wasn't that what people got on long bus journeys? Or long-haul flights?

'A blood clot,' said Rob. 'Dangerous, but not immediately life-threatening, as long as it doesn't break free and block the blood flow to somewhere important.'

There was a rap on the glass and Hanna saw Hagar beckoning them to come in.

Hanna rushed to Kia and took her hand. 'You OK?' she asked.

'I'm fine,' said Kia. 'They've all been looking after me. Especially Rob.' Her expression changed to one of distaste. 'Hagar says I need injections until after the baby comes.'

Hagar touched Hanna's shoulder. 'Kia has a blood

clot, Hanna. It's a serious pregnancy complication, but we've caught it in time. I'm treating her with heparin. In due course, her body should be able to dissolve it.'

'Will the medication hurt the baby?' asked Hanna urgently.

'No. What's important is that Kia gets regular, gentle exercise, every day.' Hagar handed Hanna a leaflet, written in English, entitled 'Deep Vein Thrombosis and Pulmonary Embolism in Pregnancy'.

Pulmonary embolism? That sounded scary.

Hagar said, 'Read that and come back to me if you have questions.'

Hanna looked at Hagar. 'Thank you. For everything.'

'Thank Rob, for noticing it in time.' Hagar's mouth formed a crooked smile. 'The symptoms are easy to ignore, if you don't know what to look for. Once it's too late, well . . .' She didn't finish her sentence.

Hanna turned to Rob, who was leaning against the doorframe behind them, keeping his distance. 'Thank you, Rob.'

'Yes, thank you, Rob,' echoed Kia.

He gave them a little bow. 'My pleasure, ladies.'

Kia cleared her throat. 'I think you were right, Hanna.'

'Right?' Hanna raised her eyebrows. 'About what?'

'I *should* stay up here until the baby's born.' She waved her arm at her surroundings. 'The clinic at the camp didn't have all this equipment. I don't think they'd have been able to treat me there, even if I'd realised something was wrong.'

Hanna squeezed Kia's hand, unable to get any words past the knot in her throat.

'You're better off with us,' said Hagar matter-of-factly, helping Kia down from the table. 'We'll look after you and your baby.'

8. NOTHING WORTHWHILE IS EASY
JOE, MARCH 2016

J OE WRAPPED HIS legs more tightly round horse-Kitty's flanks to prevent himself slipping. Riding bareback was trickiest when climbing hills, and this path was steep. He wound his fingers into her flowing black mane and looked about with interest. This was his first visit to Argentina.

Beyond the green strip of the Chubut Valley, the hillside was an almost-desert: an unforgiving scrubland of rock and dust. What plants there were had to fight stubbornly to survive. But survive they did. Like the people, Joe thought. They'd carved themselves out a home here in this harsh environment, their lives sustained by the river. Respect to them. It was the very opposite of Wales, where luscious vegetation abounded. And yet the locals there complained constantly about the rain.

It was only mid-morning, but the late-summer air was hot and dry in his throat. Joe wished he'd remembered to bring a water bottle. He pushed the thought away, turning his mind back to what they'd found out about Pedro Mendez. According to the *Shantivira's* archives, he'd attended an assessment day in 1973 but had failed the flight test. Kitty, of course, had been kicking herself that she hadn't recognised him. 'I *knew* there was something familiar about him,' she'd said. 'Jorge Mendez my arse!'

No doubt he'd spent the intervening decades harbouring a grudge against the *Shantivira* and its then-captain, Eyvindran, who'd rejected him and, by association, Syenitians in general. Delius had traced his records to the *Universidad de Buenos Aires*, where he'd studied Economics. That must have been where he'd met Nestor, who'd been studying engineering there at the same time. A match made in heaven – or hell.

He had to get his mother away from Nestor, immediately. If Nestor realised she knew what he and Mendez had attempted, there was no telling what he'd do. The problem was, Joe still had no idea what to say. The last time he'd tried being honest with her had been an utter disaster.

Are you sure about this, Cath?

This is the best chance we've had all week. Nestor's at work with his assistant, Matthew. Grace is alone; she obviously came up here to think. It's your birthday – maybe she's even thinking about you. We can't wait any longer.

Yeah, sighed Joe. *I know.*

They crested the hill and found Grace sitting on a bench, facing away from them, taking in the view over the small town of Gaiman. A pleasant breeze cooled Joe's sweaty forehead, making the heat more bearable. He slid off Kitty's back and patted her neck.

Stay here for a minute, will you? We don't want to overwhelm her again.

Sure.

He approached the bench cautiously. '*Helo*, Mam, may I join you?'

Grace's jaw dropped. 'Joe! What are you doing here?'

'Came to see if you're OK. Can I sit down?' As always, they spoke Welsh.

Grace gestured to the empty seat beside her. 'Go ahead.'

Joe sat and for a moment they were both silent. His brain whirred frantically. Somehow, he had to persuade her to come with him, for her own safety. But after her reaction in September, when they'd parted on the worst of terms, he'd no idea how to approach the topic.

'I saw you on the telly,' said Grace. 'Quite the celebrity, you've become.' She returned her focus to the vista below them.

'It's my job, Mam.' He smiled thinly. 'I must make sure people aren't scared of us. That they want us to carry on with our work.'

Another beat of awkward silence. The metal bench beneath his buttocks was hard and unyielding. He perched on the edge of it, his spine stiff and straight.

'Happy birthday,' she muttered, still not looking at him.

So she had remembered. 'Thanks,' he replied, only slightly gruffly.

She stared resolutely at a satellite mast on the horizon. 'Doing anything special?'

'Thought I'd come and see me Mam.'

She sniffed. 'If you'd said you were coming, I might have got you a present.'

'I couldn't though, could I?' Joe leaned forward and rested his elbows on his knees. 'There's no telling what Nestor might have done.'

Grace puckered her lips into a small rosette, the wrinkles from a lifetime of smoking deepening into little crevices around it. Finally, she turned to confront him.

'You knew, didn't you?' she said. 'That he tried to kill you?'

'I only found out for certain last week,' said Joe. He sat up and studied his mother's face. She was more suntanned than he'd ever seen her. Her eyes had developed laughter lines he didn't remember.

Unflinching, Grace returned his gaze. 'I've been a hostage all these months, haven't I? Without even knowing it.' Her nostrils flared with disdain. 'He only befriended me to get to you. Why didn't you tell me? I feel like such a fool.'

'*How?*' he said. 'You made it clear you wanted nothing to do with me and *Cath.*'

Grace's shoulders tensed visibly as she scanned their surroundings. 'I presume she's nearby?'

There was a little miaow and a small black cat jumped onto the bench. Grace relaxed and responded automatically, stroking its back. 'Hello Blackie, how did you get up here?' The cat arched its spine against her hand and purred. 'Wait a minute!' Her head snapped round to face Joe. 'It's *her*, isn't it? This stray I've been confiding in for months.' Quickly, she pulled her hand away.

Kitty shifted into her Syenitian form and sat on the bench next to her. 'Sorry Grace. Joe insisted I watch over you. Well done with your Spanish learning, by the way.'

Grace's posture became more upright. 'Thank you,' she said primly. She paused, then said, 'I was unforgivably rude the last time we spoke. I apologise.'

!!! said Joe, privately.

Kitty replied, *Shut up, Joe. This is big.*

Kitty took Grace's hand in hers and smiled, carefully keeping her teeth hidden. 'Apology accepted.'

Grace appeared a little starstruck. 'You're really *Y Ddraig Goch*?'

'I really am.'

Gently, but politely, Grace withdrew her hand from Kitty's. 'And you've been looking after my boy, all these years?'

Kitty gave a snort of laughter. 'As much as he'll let me! You know how stubborn he is.'

It was Grace's turn to smile. 'I do. He was a terrible toddler. Wore me right out.'

This was getting out of hand. They'd be ganging up on him next. 'Hey!' interrupted Joe. 'I'm sitting right here. *And* it's my birthday.'

Calm yourself, honey bunny, retorted Kitty silently, winking at him. *We're just bonding.* Her expression became more serious as she turned back to his mother.

'Grace,' she said, her tone earnest. 'You're not safe here. However good an actress you are, at some point, Nestor will realise you know. That you know he doesn't care about you and that he wants to harm your son.'

Grace frowned. 'I still don't understand,' she said, folding her arms. '*Why* does he want Joe dead? What has Joe ever done to him?'

'It's my fault,' admitted Kitty, tucking a dark strand of hair behind her ear as she lowered her gaze to study the dusty gravel at their feet. 'A long story. He hates me because of something that happened before Joe was born, but he's too scared of me to attack directly.'

Joe interrupted to prevent her from going into more detail. 'The point is, Mam, you need to leave this place, and soon.' He looked her in the eye, willing her to understand the urgency of the situation. 'If you like, we can take you with us right now.'

'No thank you, Joe,' said Grace formally. 'I know I must go, but I'll make my own way home. I got young Matthew to book me the flights on the Interweb, for Tuesday. One of my chapel chums will take me to the airport.' Her voice hardened. 'I came up here to work out how to tell Nestor I'm leaving.'

'Matthew?' chorused Kitty and Joe.

'Nestor's colleague. The English boy. He's none too happy either. Apparently, they were in Switzerland before, with a whole team who spoke English.' Grace tilted her head in sympathy. 'He's lonely here, with only Nestor and me to talk to. I suspect Nestor is rather a hard taskmaster. Matthew says he doesn't even have time to learn Spanish.' At this, an edge of disapproval crept into her voice.

'And you trust him not to tell Nestor?' said Joe, trying not to sound overtly sceptical. As far as he understood, the apprentice was utterly faithful to his master.

'Doesn't matter if he does.' Grace shrugged, unconcerned. 'I had fun when I first came here, but the novelty's worn off. I was wanting to go home anyway.' Her lips thinned. 'Nestor spends most of his time working on . . . whatever it is they do. They're very secretive. Do you think it's something illegal?'

It was Joe's turn to shrug. 'I don't know,' Mam,' he said. Developing weapons for use against extra-terrestrials in space was probably a grey area as far as the law was

FAY ABERNETHY

concerned. He certainly didn't want to discuss it with his mother.

'What if Nestor tries to stop you?' he asked.

Grace jutted her chin. 'He wouldn't dare!'

'He might, Grace,' said Kitty gently. 'You haven't seen his nasty side. Would you mind if I stuck around to see you get off safely?'

'As Blackie?' said Grace.

Kitty's expression flickered. 'If you like. But I can be even more discreet.'

'All right. If you feel it's necessary.' Grace unbent enough to pat Kitty on the knee. 'Thank you, dear.'

'What will you tell him, Mam?' asked Joe.

Grace's posture stiffened again. 'That I feel like our relationship has come to its natural end. I've already stayed far longer than I intended. Thank you for having me to stay; it was fun while it lasted.' She spread her hands in her lap and examined her fingernails. 'But it's spring in Wales and my garden needs me. And I want to be at home to take part in the June referendum. Helping reclaim our sovereignty is my patriotic duty as a British citizen.'

Joe's eyebrows gave an involuntary twitch of surprise. It wasn't like his mam to be up to date with current events. Was the UK government actually going ahead with that then? He'd always thought they'd reverse-ferret out of it, if things got that far. Surely leaving the EU wasn't in their best interests?

They'd give her a postal vote, wouldn't they? Kitty asked Joe privately.

I expect so, he replied. *But I'm not sure Mam knows that.*

SHAKILA WAS WAITING for him when Kitty dropped him back on the *Shantivira*. 'Have you got a minute, Joe?'

He suppressed a sigh. It never bloody stopped, did it? He kissed Kitty briefly on the mouth and she disappeared, returning to Argentina straight away. She wouldn't leave Grace until his mam was on the plane home.

'Sure,' he said, lowering the steps to the *Pride*. 'Come on up.'

Once aboard, Joe went straight to the kitchen for a large glass of water, which he gulped down thirstily. That was better. Then he busied himself making coffee, extra strong, the way Shakila liked it. He wondered what she was about to hit him with now.

Shakila sat at the end of his dining table, unpacking her sleek leather briefcase, methodically laying out papers and pulling up files on her *zana*. 'It's starting,' she said, her diamond ring flashing rainbows as she accepted the coffee. 'Just like we thought it would.'

Joe pulled out the chair next to her and sat, cupping his hands around his mug. 'Go on,' he said.

'Now the technology transfer sessions for the shields and gravity generators are underway – and the participants have communicated their value to their respective governments – the powers that be are making noises about accessing more Alliance technology.'

'Ah,' said Joe, taking a swig of the bitter liquid.

'That interview where you talked openly about the Ranglatiri seems to have focused a few minds in high places,' Shakila continued. 'They're beginning to take us seriously.'

'Which is good,' said Joe. It was high time they did,

after all their months of work.

Shakila crossed her legs, the black fabric of her wide-legged trousers draping elegantly over her ankle. She was the only person Joe knew who actually enjoyed wearing high heels.

'Of course it is.' She sat up a little straighter. 'But this is where our *real* mission starts. And they're not going to like it.'

Joe took another gulp of coffee. 'Restructuring the Earth's globalised society away from the single-minded pursuit of profit, you mean? Nope. They're not going to like it one little bit.'

A wry smile flitted across Shakila's lips.

'This is the part I've been dreading all along,' Joe admitted, putting his mug on the table. He'd let it cool off before having any more. 'If we get it wrong, Dalian will ensure our funding is cancelled and shut the *Shantivira* project down forever. Aldeman's position on the Council has been weakened due to his perceived separation from Rowan; I don't think he'd be able to help much.'

Shakila's response surprised him. 'I agree with Dalian, in this instance. We get one shot at this. We have a decade, maybe two, to turn things around.' Her tone toughened. 'If we don't act right now, global heating will soon threaten our entire civilisation. We're dangerously close to multiple tipping points. If we *can't* act, well, I'm not sure we deserve outside help.'

Joe dragged his palms down his face. She was right, of course. He just didn't want to go there.

'We have to be strategic, Joe,' said Shakila. 'We've shown them the carrot. You've talked about the stick.'

'The Ranglatiri?'

She nodded, her mouth a determined line. 'Now we need a step-by-step plan to help them transition without plunging the world into chaos. Access to useful alien technology will be strictly tied to milestones on that journey.'

'Any ideas on where to start?' said Joe. 'I'm feeling rather overwhelmed, to be honest.'

With thoughtful precision, Shakila replaced her coffee cup in its saucer. 'I've been talking with Delius and Aldeman. The Syenitians have been through this process with a number of planets. They weren't always successful, but they have a structured approach we can tailor to the Earth's specific situation.'

'What if they don't go for it, Shakila?' said Joe, trying to think of the worst-case scenario. 'What if they say, "Sod you, we'll carry on with business as usual, thank you very much"?'

Shakila shook her head in rebuttal, rippling her dark curls. 'We're fighting for the *Earth*, Joe. For humanity's very existence. I'm not ready to give up at the first sign of resistance.' Her jaw tightened. 'My country's been all but destroyed thanks to the fossil fuel industry. I'm going to take those bastards down, and *you* are going to help me.' She jabbed a finger in the direction of his chest.

Joe grinned, invigorated by her ferocity. 'Yes, Ma'am.'

'The first step is to share the Syenitians' records about the history of planets which failed to evolve sustainably,' she said.

Joe tilted his head, trying to understand what she meant. 'Like The Ghost of Christmas Yet to Come?'

'From Dickens?' Shakila's eyes sparked with recognition. 'Yes. Exactly. Scare the crap out of them.' She picked up her cup again and drained the remaining liquid. 'Delius has pictures, video testimonies from the inhabitants and so on. "If only we'd acted before it was too late", that sort of thing.'

Joe nodded. Breaking the huge impossible task down into smaller possible ones made him feel more optimistic. 'I can do that. Then what?'

'Delius will brief you in detail about his analysis of human systems,' said Shakila. 'The most urgent priority is changing the underlying legal structure of all companies away from pure profit maximisation.'

'What's a business for, if not to make a profit?' said Joe, confused.

Shakila frowned. 'True, legitimate businesses are there to fulfil the needs of citizens, Joe. Otherwise, there is no reason for their existence. We propose reconfiguring the legal definition of an enterprise so its objectives are weighted equally between all interested parties.'

'Interested parties?' said Joe. 'What, like the shareholders? Or do you mean the workers?'

'Everyone who contributes to or benefits from the business.'

'Like a cooperative?'

'Not really. It wouldn't have members, as such. The company would have decision makers representing different groups, to ensure everyone involved is treated fairly. The shareholders and the employees, yes, but also, for example, suppliers, customers, the local community and the environment.'

'The environment, too?' said Joe. It sounded a bit airy-fairy, pie-in-the-sky to him.

Shakila smiled at his scepticism. 'Hard-nosed regenerative economics, Joe. You can't make anything without extracting resources from the ecosystem. Finite or slowly replenishing resources.'

Joe still wasn't convinced. 'I just can't see a business like that being able to compete,' he said. 'Not in today's global markets.'

'Well, no,' said Shakila. 'That's why we need to roll it out everywhere at once – to make it the standard way of doing business. Of course investors need to make some kind of profit. But their concerns must not override those of the other stakeholders like they do in most corporations at the moment. Balance is everything.'

It sounded good, Joe had to admit. Revolutionary, in fact. But he could see change on that scale going down like a lead balloon. Sure, entire populations would benefit, but a small group of ultra-wealthy people would lose a lot of money and influence. They'd need to be approached individually to persuade them cooperation was in their best interests. Perhaps Kitty could remind them that the best things in life cost nothing. Things like human contact and the natural world. Or, if they remained obstructive, the simple pleasures of free movement or, indeed, breathing.

Shakila wasn't finished. 'The next-most urgent priority, is to dismantle the international Investor-State Dispute Settlement system—'

'—the *what?*' Shakila had pronounced the words fluently, but to Joe it sounded like a particularly evil tongue twister.

'The global system which enables corporations to sue countries for billions if their governments introduce policies which negatively impact their profits,' she explained. 'Like environmental legislation, or renationalising industries, for example.'

'Never heard of it.'

'Hardly anyone has. In recent years, it's become an entire industry. An investment vehicle with a guaranteed return.'

Making money out of obstructing progress? 'That's *perverse*,' said Joe.

Shakila's lip curled as she nodded in agreement. 'It's one big reason why politicians are no longer able to improve the lives of their countries' citizens,' she said. 'They're paralysed by this system, which is rigged in favour of the already powerful.' She uncrossed her legs and placed both feet firmly on the floor. 'If we can remove it, we give governments the power to rein in corporations and make decisions in the interests of their voters – without risking a crippling lawsuit.'

If, thought Joe. To him, it felt like yet another many-headed monster to battle.

Shakila noted his disheartened expression. 'I see what you're thinking, Joe. I know they won't go down without a fight,' she said. 'But if we can make those two changes, the rest will follow.'

'I don't get it,' he replied, brows furrowed. 'Shouldn't we be prioritising shutting down the fossil fuel industry?' He picked up his mug again. 'At least stopping their subsidies?'

'As much as I hate the trouble it's caused, the fossil fuel industry isn't the real problem, Joe.' Shakila placed her palms on the table, scrutinizing her black nail polish with a critical eye. In a clear, deliberate voice, she said, 'The root cause is that most corporations have a legal obligation to maximise profits or "shareholder value" at the expense of all else. From what I've heard, even the people running them feel trapped and helpless.' She sniffed. 'They fear the climate crisis as much as we do, but they're so embedded in the system, they can't see there's a different way to run things.'

Joe sipped his lukewarm coffee, considering this. 'I suppose, if we could get them to do what you said, the fossil fuel industry would shrink naturally. If it's forced to consider the human costs – and the environmental ones – it won't have a leg to stand on.' He put down his mug and looked at Shakila. 'Coal mining killed my father; did I ever tell you?'

Her eyes widened. 'An accident?'

Joe shook his head. 'Emphysema. His health was collateral damage in the industry's pursuit of profits.'

Shakila laid a warm hand on his. 'Like the destruction of Iraq, and so many other places. We can stop it, Joe, with the Alliance's support.' Her hand squeezed his. 'If we achieve one thing in our lives, let it be this.'

'Nothing worthwhile is easy, right?' Joe smiled thinly, leaning back in his chair.

Shakila said, 'I'll work out the details with Delius and Aldeman. Then we'll present it all to the appropriate people. OK?'

'OK,' he said, exhaling.

'There's something else,' said Shakila, her eyes sparkling with unexpected mischief.

'Yes?' Joe said, intrigued.

'The Earth's financial community is up in arms at the moment.'

'About what?' In view of what he'd just learned about the Investor-State whatsit system, Joe found himself strangely unable to care about the Earth's financial community.

'According to my contacts, some strange banking errors have been happening to billionaires' fortunes.' There was a definite note of amusement in her voice.

Joe raised a lone eyebrow. 'Only billionaires?'

'Only billionaires. Some high-profile figures,' Shakila said. 'The value of their personal holdings keeps resetting to a hundred million US dollars, without there being a transaction to make it happen.'

Joe snorted with laughter. 'Down to their last hundred million? My heart bleeds.'

'The money doesn't go anywhere,' continued Shakila. 'It's not being stolen. It's a mystery. The banks correct the error, then a few weeks later, it happens again.' Her nostrils flickered with suppressed mirth.

That was the funniest thing he'd heard all day. Joe said, 'Almost as if someone's trying to tell them they have too much money.'

'Almost.' She fluttered her long eyelashes in simulated innocence.

Joe considered for a moment, allowing his imagination to come up with potential implications. Hilarity aside, there could be serious repercussions to this. He said, 'You think it's Delius taking matters into his own hands, don't you?'

She inclined her head in the barest of acknowledgements. 'Should we do anything?' she asked.

'I think I really don't want to know,' Joe said, resisting the urge to stick his fingers in his ears and sing la-la-la. 'If it *is* him, he won't leave a trail they can follow.' And *I* certainly won't go looking for it, he thought to himself. He wasn't sure if he should be angry with Delius or proud of him. *If* it was him. Or Gambrinus. Or both of them, pooling their considerable processing power. Best not to think about it. 'No one's blaming aliens yet, are they?'

'No.'

'Then we wait until it starts to smell,' he said.

Shakila's eyes twinkled. 'Aye aye, Captain.'

9. *YOU'RE* THE ALIEN
JOE

THE FOLLOWING TUESDAY, Joe escorted Rob to Essoona via the *Shantivira's* direct teleport to Dunia House. The soap-opera music drifting up the stairs told him Mrs Park was working alone this morning. He led Rob into the kitchen to say hi.

'Song-yi!' He strode across the stone floor and kissed the elderly housekeeper on the cheek. Her clean skin smelled of lavender.

'Joe! What a pleasant surprise!' Mrs Park reached for the remote and turned down the volume. On the TV screen, a Korean couple in Joseon-era clothing were staring dreamily into each other's eyes. The man's translucent black hat was excessively tall, Joe thought. He must have to duck every time he went through a doorway.

'This is my friend Rob, Song-yi,' he said in Kawaida. 'We're having lunch with Aldeman later, but I wanted to show him Dunia House first.'

'Good morning, Rob,' she said, with a respectful bow. 'It's an honour to meet any friend of Joe's.'

Rob swiftly retracted the hand he'd extended in anticipation of a handshake and bowed back. 'Good morning, Song-yi.'

Mrs Park's wrinkles deepened into a smile. 'Have you eaten?' she asked, as Joe had known she would. She gestured to the scrubbed wooden table that took up most of the room. 'Please, take a seat.'

'Actually, I've already had breakfast,' said Rob, looking at Joe for guidance.

Behind Mrs Park, Joe shook his head vigorously and mimed slashing his throat. 'Sit down and eat what you're given,' he insisted in Welsh.

Rob sat. Joe, who'd had nothing that morning in hopeful expectation of this precise scenario, sat beside him and picked up a pair of chopsticks. Mrs Park ladled the contents of various pots bubbling on the stove into porcelain bowls. Rice and a sauce Joe knew would clear his nostrils for the whole day.

'Can I help you carry something?' Rob offered politely. His Kawaida stumbled slightly, but it was a respectable effort.

'Sit!' was Mrs Park's fierce response. She placed the bowls on the table, along with two empty plates so they could serve themselves. 'Eat!' she said, more gently. 'Enjoy.' Then she bustled to the fridge and extracted a bowl of salad, cold dumplings and a plate of baked fish.

'Thanks, Song-yi,' said Joe and got to work.

While they ate, Joe explained the role of Dunia House: providing accommodation for the *Shantivira's* second-year human trainees, as well as acting as an unofficial embassy for humans on Syenitia.

Mrs Park made a pot of tea and sat with them, wanting the latest on Kia's pregnancy. Joe did his best. He knew she was due soon, but couldn't remember the exact date.

Rob could. 'April 22,' he said confidently. 'We've talked about it in our Kawaida lessons.'

Minutes later, Rob was being interviewed on the subject of his own children, Joe helping him with unfamiliar vocabulary. They should make a move before Mrs Park brought out the items she'd crocheted for the baby, otherwise they'd be here all day.

He stood up and cleared away the dishes. That was the deal: Mrs Park insisted on serving the food, but, once she sat down, she'd accept all help with tidying up. 'Where's Min-joon today, Song-yi?' Joe asked. 'Rob should meet him too.'

'On the allotment,' she said. 'Will you take him his mid-morning snack for me?'

'Sure.'

ROB'S EYES LIT up when he saw the allotment.

Joe laughed. 'You've caught the gardening bug, haven't you?'

Rob gazed at the fruit trees, the neat rows of cabbages and trellises of runner beans. 'I wish I had a plot like this. So many possibilities. But it'd be too much work to dump on Sarah when I'm away for months at a time. On top of her job and the kids, you know? It wouldn't be fair.'

Joe nodded. He'd never envied army wives and all they had to put up with. 'Sacrifices of army life?' he said.

Rob narrowed his lips in tacit agreement. 'Sacrifices of army life,' he said.

An elderly Korean gentleman was making his way towards them from the other end of the garden. His outdoor complexion belied his age and the sprightly figure under the thick, hand-knitted jumper and patched-up trousers was surprisingly skinny for someone married to Song-yi Park.

'This is Min-joon Park,' Joe said to Rob. 'Dunia House's caretaker and gardener. Song-yi's spent the last forty years trying and failing to fatten him up.'

Joe introduced Rob, who bowed promptly. With Joe's help, he asked a multitude of questions about what produce they grew and the work involved.

Vegetable vocabulary exhausted, they still had plenty of time, so Joe decided to walk into town. A stroll would help them digest their enormous breakfast. Rob was stunned by the sheer quantity of greenery the Syenitians packed into their capital city: the mature trees, the living walls on the middle storeys of the buildings, the allotments, the secluded gardens reserved for each pair of U-shaped housing blocks. Thick safety strips of tall grasses and wild flowers separated the pavements, cycle lanes and roads.

Like every human visiting for the first time, the level of public luxury Essoona offered its inhabitants fascinated Rob. Free transport, high-quality, rent-controlled accommodation, enviable community facilities. He found the flying trams thrilling and he made Joe promise to take him on one before they returned to the *Shantivira*.

They reached the main squares and Joe pointed out the classic landmarks: the baths, the Law Courts, the *Ohimo*, the Council Chambers, and across to the Library, the Planetary Museum of Syenitia and the *Laulaahaalia* building.

Then he ducked down an alleyway leading to the oldest part of town: a maze of tiny streets which was home to the Nakymaton bar, where they were meeting Aldeman. At this time of day, the bar was practically empty – just a couple of Wadudu near the entrance, talking in their language of clicks and whistles, plus a group of furry green Grookas, eating noisily.

Fine by Joe. Fewer people to observe them. It was almost as dark as in the evenings, the light from the small windows barely reaching the back of the room where they had their regular table.

'I hope you've worked up an appetite again,' he said to Rob.

Rob grimaced. 'Not really.'

Aldeman was already waiting for them. He stood up, greeting them both with a formal hand press. They sat and a Sayari waiter appeared with menus. When he'd gone, Rob glanced around, taking in the low ceiling, the plain wooden furniture and rustic paper lanterns. Not to mention the other clientele. Syenitians didn't tend to hang out here, which was the chief reason Joe and Aldeman liked it. Much easier to have an uninterrupted conversation if you're not constantly bumping into people you know.

'No offence, sir,' Rob murmured to Aldeman, 'but this isn't the sort of place I'd expect to see you in. Is it safe?'

Aldeman caught Joe's eye in a sidelong glance and Joe tried not to smirk.

'Safe enough,' Aldeman replied. 'The food here is excellent. I recommend the seafood noodles.'

Joe helped Rob choose a small portion and ordered

beers all round. He didn't usually drink at lunchtime, but he was a little on edge, waiting for news about his mother. She was supposed to be flying home today, if everything went to plan.

'I hear you are staying on the *Shantivira* tonight, Rob,' said Aldeman. 'Is that the first time?'

'That's right, sir,' Rob replied. 'It's the Easter holidays. My wife has taken the children to visit her father in Edinburgh.'

Aldeman glanced at Joe. 'Edinburgh? Is that north of Wales or south of Wales?'

'North,' said Joe, amused and pleased by Aldeman's baseline reference for UK geography. 'It's the capital of Scotland.'

Rob continued. 'He's getting rather frail now. She doesn't see him as often as she'd like.'

The food arrived and, as he ate, Rob fizzed with questions about the city and how its splendid facilities were funded. Aldeman explained Syenitia's bottom-up system of government, where decisions were taken at the lowest possible level with active involvement from citizens. They discussed how most Syenitians spent significant periods volunteering, and the comparatively few hours' labour the planet's economy required of its workforce.

By the time they'd finished eating, Rob had had a crash course in Syenitian social policy and economics. The only questions Aldeman hadn't answered were about the Syenitians' power sources. But he'd side-stepped these so elegantly, Joe hoped Rob might not have noticed. Eventually, their time ran out and Aldeman had to return to the Council Chambers.

As promised, Joe took Rob back to Dunia House on the flying tram. They had to wait a while at the third storey tram stop, exposed to an icy sea breeze. Despite his warm, full belly, Joe felt a chill settle on his shoulders. Spring took a long time to come in Essoona, zigzagging without warning between the tantalising promise of summer and the winter everyone had already had enough of.

Once they were safely on board, Rob stared out of the window at the city flashing by, mesmerised by the new perspective.

Joe said, 'You haven't been to a bathhouse yet.'

'What?' Rob turned to look at him. 'Sorry, mate, my head's still spinning from all the input. I must make some notes.'

'You can do that back on the *Shantivira*,' Joe said. Having had the idea, the anticipated sensation of soaking in hot water until his bones warmed through again was too tempting to resist. 'I want a bath first.'

'A bath?' Rob said, mystified. 'Isn't there a shower on your ship?'

Joe chuckled. 'You'll see. We still need to do our official fortnightly communication session. A bathhouse is ideal for that.'

The bathhouse in the square behind Dunia House wasn't as grand as the one in town, but it was less crowded. There were no other humans to overhear them: the second-year *Shantivira* trainees were still at flight school and wouldn't return until the evening.

Rob was somewhat perturbed when he realised he'd have to strip naked in front of what he called 'a bunch of aliens'.

Joe laughed. '*You're* the alien, Rob. Seriously, mate, no one cares what you look like. This bathhouse is used to humans,' he said, unbuttoning his shirt and stuffing it into a locker. 'You won't be a novelty. Anyway, you're not as hairy as me. Once you're in the water you could almost pass for a local.'

They worked their way through the different-temperature pools and Joe relaxed. If all went well, Kitty would be home soon and they'd be able to spend some time together. He'd missed her these past days while she'd been in Argentina.

They'd agreed that, with Rob's visits to the *Shantivira*, it should be safe for Grace to stay in her cottage in Brecon. Now they were on speaking terms, Kitty would check in on her regularly, helping with heavy lifting in the garden and generally making herself useful. If Nestor came after Grace, which Joe doubted, they'd be ready for him.

Now they were on speaking terms. Joe thought that applied more to Kitty than it did to him. With her constant guardian presence, his wife had managed to build some bridges to his mam that weren't open to him yet.

He thought back to his birthday trip to Gaiman. There had been a definite defrosting on both sides but, if he was honest, only from solid ice to just above zero. The soil was still too cold to plant anything in. And that was fine. Their relationship was too broken to expect more. He wasn't sure they'd ever be able to fix it. He hadn't even realised he wanted to until she'd been kidnapped.

He sighed inwardly and lowered his head beneath the water's surface, washing the thoughts away. Some problems were unsolvable, no matter how much you turned them over in your mind. Kitty kept saying he should give Grace time. Himself too. Perhaps she was right.

At last they reached the final pool, where people socialised with their fellow bathers. The other pools were small and dimly lit, with an unofficial code of silence which turned the experience into a meditative ritual. This one was large and light, with potted plants around the edges. It had a retractable glass roof, enabling the bathers to see clouds scudding across the spring sky. In mild weather, they opened it all the way and you could stargaze while floating on your back in perfectly warm water.

Mid-afternoon, it was almost empty. Good, thought Joe, pleased. Not that anyone was likely to eavesdrop on a conversation in an obscure alien language like Welsh. But years of working with Aldeman meant his habit of discretion was deeply ingrained. The fewer people who saw Rob here, the better.

Joe sat on the underwater bench which ran along one side of the pool, pulling his knees up to his chest. 'Where do you want to start?' he asked.

'With the official information exchange?' Rob asked, taking a seat beside him.

'That's right,' said Joe.

'Dan Simpson. I passed on your news about his pilot's qualification and I have a message from his parents.'

'Yes?' said Joe, wondering what NASA would make of the official notification that their former astronaut was exploring space in ways they could only dream about. No doubt they were already preparing a million experiments to do on him, should Dan ever return home. To be performed with or without his consent.

They'd argue he was still an employee because his resignation letter (hand-delivered anonymously by Kitty) was invalid without a full debriefing. After all, he'd been absent without leave for months before they'd received it. Joe hoped Dan had the sense to stay away from the Earth for another decade or two at least.

'Just "thank you" and "it's a relief to know he's OK,"' said Rob.

'Good,' said Joe. Thinking about it, it was unlikely Dan would come back anytime soon. Judging from Kitty's report, his Sayari partner didn't exactly move in the same rarified social circles as Dan's staunchly Republican family. In fact, Kitty suspected her of criminal activity. Even without the small matter of her silver skin and blue hair, she wasn't the respectable sort of girl Dan could safely introduce to his parents.

Rob continued, 'And I've persuaded more people to try the audio language course you gave us.'

'Good,' said Joe again. Growing the number of Kawai-da speakers on the planet was a critical part of their strategy. Apart from acquiring the skills to access the wealth of knowledge available in Kawaida, learning a language promoted the first tender shoots of intercultural understanding. People became familiar with previously alien concepts and, as a consequence, more open to them. Less frightened of the unknown. Less likely to do something stupid.

Widespread automated machine translation had its place, but Joe knew from his years working as Aldeman's personal pilot that it was virtually useless without genuine linguistic expertise on hand to quality-control its output. This meant the interstellar community considered proficiency in Kawaida an essential prerequisite for interacting with each other. If Earth's population was to have any hope of avoiding diplomatic incidents while fending for itself in the wider galaxy, as many people as possible needed to become fluent.

'All the space agencies are using it already,' Rob said. 'The Foreign Office will roll it out as standard training next month.'

'What about you? How are you getting on, yourself?' Joe asked. 'Will we be able to have these sessions in Kawaida soon, instead of in Welsh?'

'I wouldn't go that far,' said Rob with a bashful grin. 'It'll be a while before I catch up with young Kia, but I'm making progress.'

Joe stretched his legs below the surface, scissoring them a few times back and forth. 'Thanks for your help with her recently. Your swift reaction made all the difference.'

Rob frowned, remembering. 'Poor kid. I'm glad I could help. Sarah's first pregnancy was bloody difficult.' He hugged his knees. 'In the end they had to do an emergency caesarean and we nearly lost her. I'll never forget the terrifying sensation of powerlessness. That's why I'm so clued up about pregnancy complications; learning about what could go wrong was my way of trying to stay in control.' He smiled ruefully. 'Trying and failing.'

'I'm sorry.' Joe slid further into the warm water, so only his head was above the surface. 'Kia will be OK. We'll make sure of that.'

'No sign of the father?' Rob said.

'No. It's not his fault: he has no idea she's pregnant,' Joe replied. 'We'll have to wait until he tries to get in touch with her at the refugee camp.'

For a moment they were silent. Then Joe remembered what he wanted to tell Rob.

'When you go back, I have some material for you to take. I'll be giving it to my UN contacts, but it would be helpful if you could disseminate it too.'

Rob released his knees and extended his legs alongside Joe's. 'What is it?' he asked, no doubt anticipating some prestigious nuggets of information which would delight his superior officers.

'Translated histories and documentation about planets which failed to evolve sustainably. It's bleak reading, but the Earth governments need to know you're currently on a path which leads to a dead end.' Joe gave a thin, mirth-free smile. 'Dead being the operative word.'

'Thanks. I think.' Rob's expression was that of a man who'd been told he'd won an all-expenses-paid holiday, only to realise it was a week's camping in Mordor.

'The Alliance has a plan, Rob,' Joe tried to reassure him. 'A proven road map for change. We can save the Earth, but it involves fundamentally changing the way the planet's economy is run.'

Rob scoffed: an involuntary bark of shocked, cynical laughter. 'Good luck with that, mate.'

'Thanks.' Joe persevered. 'We'll need it. Powerful people will fight tooth and nail to cling on to their riches. We've got to persuade them that hiding in a remote bunker surrounded by armed guards won't save them from climate breakdown.'

He picked at the cuticle on his right thumb, almost talking to himself now. 'We need them on our side. We need to give them hope that collapse isn't inevitable. Help them understand that they can be a big part of the solution. And that we know what needs to be done.' He looked up at Rob, who was staring blankly at the steam rising in front of them. 'These documents I'm giving you are the first step in that process.'

Rob didn't turn his head. In a dreamy voice, he said, 'They say people find it easier to imagine the end of the world than the end of capitalism.'

'There's a crisis of imagination, Rob,' said Joe, touching his friend's arm underwater, breaking his trance. 'We need to inspire people to think differently, mate, or the end of the world won't be something they have to imagine.'

They fell silent, lost in their own thoughts. A waterjet spurted into life behind Joe and he massaged a spot on his lower back which had been troubling him.

As he did so, he felt a nudging at the edge of his consciousness. Kitty. At last.

Hey, Cath, *how's it going?* he asked her silently.

It's done. Grace is home safely. She just walked through her front door.

Joe exhaled. That was a relief. *Good. Thanks for watching out for her. Does that mean we'll sleep in the same bed tonight?*

He could feel Kitty smile. *Looking forward to it*, cariad, she replied. *You're in Essoona?*

Yeah, he said. *I'll be back soon.*

See you on the sofa.

Joe grinned. *Laters, babe.* Out loud, he said, 'Rob?'

Rob was low in the water, eyes closed, pummelling his shoulders with one of the jets.

'Hmm?'

'Sit up and look at me, mate. I have something else to tell you.'

'What?' Rob's forehead creased in response to Joe's abrupt tone. He sat up, giving Joe his full attention.

Joe scratched his chin, trying to find the right words. He'd shaved that morning, but his beard was already breaking through. He said, 'You know you kept asking about my mam, when we first met again?'

'And you refused to say where she was?' Rob answered. 'In the interests of transparency, I can say my bosses believe she's in Argentina, although her exact whereabouts are unknown.' He gave Joe a lop-sided grin. 'I didn't suggest they searched in the Welsh-speaking areas.'

So they'd been through the airline records. Made sense. 'Don't tell me,' Joe said, suppressing an urge to chuckle. 'Your English bosses didn't know there were any?'

Rob lifted his eyebrows in silent acknowledgment.

'Thanks,' said Joe. 'I appreciate it. She *was* in Argentina,' he admitted. 'But she's home again now. No doubt your lot already know, if they're monitoring flights.'

'Why are you telling me, then?' said Rob.

Joe held his gaze, trying to impress the importance of his message on Rob with a single look. 'To remind you she's out of bounds. If your . . . colleagues approach her, if anything happens to her, this back-channel arrangement is over. No more one-to-one meetings with me, no more trips to the *Shantivira*, no more visiting Syenitia. Do I make myself clear?'

'Crystal, mate,' Rob said. 'Don't worry. The great and the good in London are enjoying the resurrection of the "special relationship" too much to jeopardise it. Grace is safe from us.'

Joe smiled. At least *something* was going according to plan.

10. A MEETING

DAN

D AN SET DOWN the *Gezi Urdina* with practised ease and peered out of the windscreen. The early morning light was cold and half-hearted; wisps of mist rose from the water-filled potholes which dotted the surface of their landing bay and the road beyond. So this was Mwongo.

'Looks lovely,' he said sarcastically.

'I'm glad it's still quiet,' said Afra. 'Normally I wouldn't go out on Mwongo without a couple of blasters handy. I don't like it that you're going unarmed. Be careful, Dan.'

'I'll be OK once I have my costume on, at least to get over to their ship. No one will touch me then.'

They'd agreed Dan should wear Bellyn's old clothes and mask. He looked so like a Syenitian, suspicions would be aroused if he boarded the Ranglatiri vessel undisguised. There was nothing a Mwongo liked more than juicy information to sell to the highest bidder. They also didn't want the Ranglatiri connected with the *Gezi Urdina*, so he'd take his stuff with him and find a place to get changed.

Afra reached into her pocket and pulled out a donut-

127

shaped blue stone, about an inch across. It was looped into a leather thong, so it could be worn as a necklace.

'This is for you,' she said. 'It'll bring you luck.'

'What is it?' asked Dan, holding it up. The polished surface glinted in the light.

'Touch your finger and thumb through the hole and think of our first date.'

He did so and the stone began to glow. A small projection of him opening the door of his old flat in Laro appeared above his hand – how Afra must have seen him. Suddenly, he could smell the goulash bubbling on the stove behind him and once again felt the rush of hope and excitement he'd experienced that day. Woah.

'It's a Sayari memory stone,' she explained. 'Bioenergy powered. I put my memories of our special moments on it; there's plenty of space for you to add yours.'

She showed him how to record a memory: by closing his fist around it and consciously reliving a particular experience in his mind. Then she carefully fastened it around his neck.

Wonderstruck, Dan fingered the warm ring at his throat. 'Like a psychic photo album. Thank you, Afra. What a present. I'll treasure it forever.'

He stood up and swung his pack onto his shoulder.

'Bay 66, you said?'

'That's right,' said Afra, pulling up a map on the head-up display to show him his route.

'OK. I'll find it.' He kissed her – a few brief seconds of intense connection – then broke away. He had to do this now, before his courage failed him.

'Good luck!' Afra called after him, but he was already so focused on the task in hand, he barely registered her.

Outside, the air was cool, with a slight tang of sulphur. Quickly, he strode in the opposite direction to his intended destination, in case someone was watching. He didn't see a soul; at this hour he appeared to be the only person on the move. Apart from the non-local spacecraft – some of which were so luxurious, they reminded him of the Yacht Haven marina in Boston – the spaceport had an atmosphere of neglect. The Mwongo evidently weren't big on maintenance.

He ducked down a deserted alleyway and, a little way along, found a derelict shed. That would do. Quickly, he got changed and left his human clothes bundled under a dusty tarpaulin. Thinking it would be inappropriate, he'd chosen not to wear Bellyn's formal white battledress, just his everyday black tunic and leggings beneath his heavy grey cloak. Dan fitted the mask and pulled up the hood. Now only a Ranglatiri would be able to tell he wasn't one of them, and only once he was in range of their empathic field.

Trying to walk like a Ranglatiri – upright, ghostly, and with the supreme confidence of a creature at the top of the food chain – he took a roundabout route to Bay 66. The pirate ship was a smaller version of the near-indestructible frigate he'd seen doing battle with the *Shantivira*. That had been a prototype, testing new shields using a superconducting mineral called *kahack*.

He craned his neck at the dull black hulk. What now? How was he going to get in? Did it have a door bell? Should he call Henning to say he'd arrived? Before he had a chance to issue the command, a ramp lowered and four guards marched out.

'Come with uss,' one said.

He followed the first two; the other pair brought up the rear. Inside, the walls and floor were coated in grime and there was a gag-inducing smell of unwashed flesh and raw meat. Trying not to be sick, Dan breathed through his mouth. Into the belly of the beast, he thought.

They led him to a hall filled with tables and chairs. Their canteen? He tried not to imagine it packed with ravenous carnivores. Waiting for him in a clear space at the front were two Ranglatiri in pristine white battledress: elaborate breastplates and long, pleated, skirts. 'Strip him and ssearch him for weapons,' said one, and Dan recognised Henning's voice.

The guards pulled off Dan's cloak and mask, along with his top, leaving him standing bare-chested in his leggings and boots. Heart thumping, he knelt quickly and bowed his head. At least the smell wasn't as bad in here.

He took two slow, calming breaths, then said, 'Sir, you of course understand, I only wore my master's clothes to protect you. Looking the way I do, a disguise was necessary.'

'Indeed.' Henning stepped closer. 'What's thiss?' he said, a snow-white hand fingering Dan's memory stone.

Shit! He'd forgotten to take it off when he'd got changed. With a flash of inspiration, he said, 'It's the sign I belong to the pilot now.' Bellyn had once said Ranglatiri were so ignorant of other species, you could tell them almost anything as long as it fitted with their worldview.

'Hmm,' said Henning, letting the necklace go. 'Sslave-

Bellyn, this is my captain. It is he you will be negotiating with today.'

The second Ranglatiri stepped forward. 'Explain yourself, Sslave. How do you dare to come before us?'

'My master saved me when I was lost and starving. I loved him like a father, I mean, like an uncle,' said Dan, adapting his words to Ranglatiri family relationships just in time. 'I know you can't sense my feelings like you can for each other, but be assured, I mourn him deeply and intend to uphold his legacy. And ... um ... my new owner, the pilot, wishes to continue making a healthy profit.'

This released the tension and both the Ranglatiri laughed.

'Of course she does. Don't we all? What are her terms?'

'A forty percent increase over what you were paying before.'

Roars of laughter.

'Remember, this is for exclusive access to the product,' persisted Dan. 'Due to the distances involved, we can only make two shipments a year, which would both be to you. You will have a monopoly. A licence to generate credits.'

Dan and Afra had discussed their business strategy exhaustively. They didn't have the capacity to serve multiple customers and, anyway, the extra risk wasn't worth it. Afra believed Henning had as much to lose as they did, so he could be relied upon to be cautious. Dan hoped she was right.

The captain shook his head.

'You are a crew member down. You have fewer

mouths to feed and, as I hear it, your kind eats no meat. The sservice you offer is inferior to what Bellyn provided. We require a forty percent disscount to even consider doing business with you.'

A forty percent discount? They were kidding, right?

'Circumstances have changed, sir. The risk is much higher now,' Dan argued.

'I agree,' said the captain. 'You and your pilot are on the Ranglatiri police's Wanted lisst. I am endangering my entire operation just by talking to you.'

Henning interrupted. 'How about we ssolve this disagreement in the traditional way, ssir?'

The captain tilted his head, evaluating Henning's idea.

'If the primitive wins, he getss a twenty per cent increase, if we win, we get a twenty per cent discount,' Henning continued. He switched to Ranglatiri, saying, 'And if it doesn't work out, we'll hand him and his pilot over and collect the reward. We can't lose, sir.'

Still on his knees, Dan studied the floor, not showing he'd understood this last bit.

The captain addressed Dan. 'Do you know what a *stakarh* fight is, Sslave?'

In Dan's head, Bellyn's voice said, 'No messing about. Kill, or be killed. Outworlders don't call us "the walking death" for nothing.' The memory was so strong, so clear, Dan could draw strength from it.

'My master mentioned it, sir,' he said.

'Good. We will deliver your corpse to your ship, as a message for your pilot. Then we will negotiate with her directly.'

With reverence, one of the guards passed the captain a

staff decorated with geometric patterns. The captain began spinning it flashily, showing off his skill. Another guard tossed a much plainer version in front of Dan.

Dan grabbed it before it came to rest, simultaneously bringing one foot up onto the ground and, with lightning speed, drove the end of the staff forwards and upwards, under his opponent's *stakarh*. The captain's head whiplashed as the staff made contact. He staggered back and fell to the floor with a groan.

Dan jumped up, his ears filling with a fearsome, primal roar as he closed in for the kill. With all his strength, he slammed the end of his staff into the exposed sliver of skin between the breastplate and the mask. There was a satisfying crunch as the captain's spine snapped, and blood pooled beneath his neck. The roaring ceased; Dan realised the sound had been coming from him.

There was a moment of absolute silence, then, as one, the four guards stepped forward. Dan took up a defensive pose, his staff centred and ready to strike. He couldn't take them all. They had blasters. He'd never leave this room alive.

Henning laughed and the guards stopped, looking to him for orders. A hand signal told them to stand down and in Ranglatiri he said, 'This isn't over, lads. I'll be the one to break his neck as vengeance for our captain, the moment he outlives his usefulness. For now, we let him go.'

Henning switched to Kawaida. 'You just got me a promotion, Sslave-Bellyn. I have been second-in-command for too long. The twenty per cent price increase is yours. Don't forget we will need to test a sample before making payment.' He gestured towards the captain's corpse. 'Would you care to join us feeding?'

Dan bowed low. 'Thank you, sir, but as you know, I am a vegetarian,' he lied.

One guard waited impatiently while Dan put his Ranglatiri disguise back on. The rest started stripping the dead body with practised efficiency. The armour clattered on the floor as they tossed it to one side. Then they removed their masks to bite into the still-warm flesh.

Under his breath, Dan muttered, 'Goodbye gentleman, it was a pleasure doing business with you.' He was glad none of them turned around.

The guard escorted him to the exit. Dan's knees almost buckled with relief when they reached the fresh air. The guard hurried back inside to join the feeding frenzy, not staying to watch Dan leave.

PART TWO

11. YONAS

HANNA, APRIL 2016

'NOW, KIA! PUSH!' Kia crushed Hanna's hand in hers and groaned: a primeval, animal bellow.

'I can see the head!' cried Hagar, 'Keep going, Kia, almost there.'

Kia stared at nothing, totally focused on the next wave building inside her. Hanna watched her fill her lungs with air, like a diver about to jump, and strain with everything she had.

'Head's through! One more push.'

Eighteen hours had passed since Kia's waters had broken and Hanna had brought her down to the sick bay. Their world had shrunk to the walls of this room and part of her felt they'd be here for all eternity.

The worst of it had been the contractions to dilate the cervix. Kia coped well with the first few, but they'd gone on and on. She became exhausted and wild-eyed with the pain and, between contractions, the fear of the next one. Then Hagar's team gave her an epidural and, as the drugs took effect, Hanna watched her sister return to herself, like magic. Kia had smiled for the first time in hours and asked for something to drink.

She'd said, 'I can still feel them, but it's like they're happening at a distance, you know?'

Hanna didn't, but was overjoyed to have Kia back. Watching her writhe and sob in agony had been unbearable. Hagar had warned her that the younger the mother, the more dangerous the labour, and doom-laden scenarios marched in a constant procession through Hanna's head. She couldn't face losing her sister again.

'That's it!' Hagar yelled, triumphant. There was a cry – a roar almost as loud as one of Kia's – as the baby took its first breath. Hagar picked up the slimy bundle and placed it on Kia's chest, saying, 'Congratulations, it's a boy!'

Kia wrapped her arms around him, holding him tight. 'Hello, Yonas,' she whispered. The crying stopped and the baby snuffled his way across her torso. He found a breast and latched on. Kia squeaked. 'Ow!'

Hagar laughed. 'He knows what *he* wants.' She activated the electric motor to raise Kia to a sitting position.

Hanna's bottom lip trembled as complex, unexpected emotions bubbled up inside her. She knew with a bright, pure certainty that she would do anything for this child. Moral, immoral, legal, illegal. It didn't matter. Whatever she had to do to protect him.

They watched Yonas feed, the only sound his tiny, cute little snuffles. Kia's expression was beatific: love, enchantment and new-found strength, all directed at the dark little head bobbing under her chin.

Hagar said to Hanna, 'That's a good sign. Not every baby manages to feed well straight off.'

'What's that white stuff?' Hanna whispered. 'It's all over his hands and feet.'

'It's called *vernix caseosa*,' said Hagar. 'Perfectly normal, but he doesn't need it anymore. You can wash it off in a minute, after you've cut the cord.'

'Cut the cord? Me?' exclaimed Hanna. Her hand flew to her throat; Hassan's golden locket was warm and smooth, grounding her. 'I don't know how. What if I do it wrong?'

'It's easy,' Hagar said. 'I'll show you. After you've bathed him, we'll check him over and weigh him.'

Kia's body gave a little shudder and the placenta slithered out onto the examination table.

'Ah!' said Hagar. '*That's* what we were waiting for.' She picked it up and examined it carefully, turning it over in her hands. 'We must ensure it's in one piece,' she explained. 'If there's a bit missing, it's still inside Kia and we'd have to extract it before she haemorrhages or gets an infection. But this seems fine.' She looked at Kia. 'You haven't changed your mind? You don't want to keep it?'

Kia shook her head. 'No! Get rid of it. It's gross!'

'No problem,' Hagar chuckled. 'All those stem cells will run the *Shantivira's* generator for days. Right then, time to cut the cord.' She turned Yonas gently on his side, then fixed a clamp close to his belly button and another a few centimetres away. She passed Hanna a pair of surgical scissors and a piece of sterile gauze.

'Hold the gauze below the cord and cut between the clamps.'

Hanna did. As soon as he could, Yonas began suckling again. The whole operation hadn't bothered him one bit.

Hagar put the placenta and cord in a metal tray and took it away. Then she filled the sink with warm water.

'Bathtime,' she called. 'Will you bring him over, Hanna?'

Hanna's heart lurched with irrational panic. Pick him up? What if she dropped him?

Her uncertainty must have shown on her face because Hagar said, 'You'll be fine, Hanna. Just make sure you support his head the entire time.'

Hanna summoned her courage and took her nephew in her arms. Blood and goo smeared her blouse and she didn't care at all. 'Hello, little man,' she said, entranced by the miniature face so close to hers. 'I'm your Auntie Hanna. Welcome to the world.'

She lowered him into the water and rubbed him clean, keeping one hand under his head.

'That's it, Hanna,' said Hagar. 'Great job. Right, here's a towel. Dry him off and we'll see how much he weighs.'

Hagar took the naked baby and placed him on the scales. 'Almost three kilos. That's fine.' She picked him up and put a tiny nappy on him before handing him back to Kia. Yonas latched straight back onto her nipple. Kia's jaw tensed, but if it hurt, she didn't complain.

✦   ✦   ✦

DAYS PASSED. NIGHTS passed. Hanna and Kia could barely tell the difference. Yonas was on a two-hour rhythm: wake up crying, fill his nappy with a preposterous quantity of tan-coloured slurry, be sweet and playful for half an hour after getting cleaned up, start crying again, feed for forty minutes, vomit up the excess milk, sleep for forty minutes. Repeat.

Joe gave Hanna a month's leave, saying she was such a

good pilot already, he'd no doubt she'd still be able to qualify with the others in June. She moved out of the cabin she shared with Hassan and into Kia's. Hagar supplied Kia with a breast pump so they could share the night-time feeds, permitting them each an aspirational four hours' unbroken slumber. It didn't always work, but it helped.

Hanna started taking strolls around the *Shantivira*, trying to get Yonas to sleep without disturbing Kia. He had a fancy pram, but hated it, preferring to be carried wrapped warm and snug in a sling; his little head close enough to kiss whenever she wanted.

The space station rotated on a cycle simulating night and day in the biomes, which meant she could always find daylight and company if she wanted. Mostly, though, she couldn't be bothered to trek to the other end of the *Shantivira* and access the tropical biome. Instead, she would put on her wellies and winter coat and steal across the accommodation deck to the temperate biome.

In the small hours, the biome often faced away from the sun, forcing her to navigate by starlight. The stars were abundant, as clear and sharp as when she was flying her *Tumba*. But now she had time to look at them: to absorb their cool beauty.

She developed the habit of taking Yonas to his cousin's tree, located in a clearing at the heart of the ancient forest. The first time she'd dared thread her way through the silent trees in the dark, her body had thrilled with a primordial fear of the shadows. But she knew the way so well, was so familiar with every tree and bush, she soon relished the nocturnal solitude.

Occasionally, jaguar-Kitty joined her, a comforting

black shape in the darkness, reminding Hanna of her first grief-filled weeks on the *Shantivira*, mourning the loss of Samuel. They never spoke. They just were.

Once Yonas dropped off and she could return him to his cot, Hanna still couldn't relax entirely: she'd read so much about Sudden Infant Death Syndrome, she felt a frequent compulsion to check he was still breathing.

Their days were punctuated by visitors: people knocking on the door with gifts, wanting to see the new arrival, or coming up to them in the canteen, offering help. But lack of sleep had reduced Hanna and Kia's world to surviving the next hour and the one after that. Hanna didn't have the mental capacity to organise a babysitting roster. Instead, she found herself refusing, saying, 'We're fine for now, thanks. Kia's doing really well.'

Now they weren't working together or sleeping in the same room, she hardly saw Hassan. For his part, he was flat out doing one and a half jobs. The others were already making plans for when they qualified in two months' time and took their long leave. Hanna didn't intend to go travelling: she'd stay on the *Shantivira* with Kia, Yonas and Hassan. She couldn't abandon them now, just to go on holiday.

Hanna's birthday came and went. Lucy wanted to organise her a party, but Hanna was too tired to celebrate. As an alternative, Lucy volunteered to do a nightshift with Yonas and Kia so Hanna could spend a romantic weekend with Hassan.

Hanna didn't feel comfortable leaving the *Shantivira* for more than a few hours, so they ate at a favourite restaurant in Essoona and returned to Hassan's cabin for an early night. Full of good food and an unaccustomed beer, she just had time to remove her shoes before passing out on the bed and sleeping for twelve hours straight.

12. HYDROGEN AND HYDRANGEAS
JOE

J OE STOOD NEXT to Shakila and jaguar-Kitty in Docking Bay 3, watching the *Koppakuoria* grow from a black speck into a towering spacecraft, its six legs already extended for landing. Hassan had taken a delegation of journalists and photographers on his latest refugee camp delivery and organic waste pickup trip, and now they'd come for a guided tour of the *Shantivira*.

He wasn't nervous, he told himself. He'd given a million tours over the years. But it was the first time actual *reporters* had come. Taking pictures of his crew, his ships, the whole space station. Lord knew what the unintended consequences of today would be. But it was necessary. People on the planet couldn't be expected to trust them if they didn't know who they were.

Hassan set the *Koppakuoria* down gently. Clearly, he'd been practising. Joe remembered Hassan's disastrous initial attempt, where he'd nearly smashed the *Pride of Essoona's* bulbous cockpit. He could smile about it now, but at the time, he'd been almost as furious as on the day Hassan had first 'borrowed' the *Koppakuoria*.

Hassan lowered the ramp and a group of people filed out, headed by Susan Omondi, Director of the United

Nations Office for Outer Space Affairs. Hassan remained onboard, transmatting the contents of the containers in the hold to the *Shantivira's* fuel tank.

Joe strode over to greet Susan. 'Susan! Great to have you back on board!'

Her face split into a grin. 'Hello, Joe,' she said, shaking his hand with genuine warmth. 'We're making history again today, wouldn't you say?'

'I would,' he said, acknowledging the private joke with a wink.

Susan crouched to make a fuss of Kitty, who allowed herself to be stroked under the chin, closing her eyes with pleasure. The other visitors hung back, alarmed by the proximity of the black jaguar and unsure what to make of the enormous docking bay.

'Don't be shy,' called Joe. 'Welcome to the *Shantivira!*' To keep things fair, they'd agreed on one journalist and photographer for each continent, from countries without big space agencies.

They shook hands and he introduced Shakila, who'd organised the whole event, and referred to the silent Kitty as his bodyguard. One journalist, bold enough to try and pet her, withdrew his hand quickly when she growled at him.

Joe laughed. 'Let her get to know you first. You have to earn her trust.'

Joe, said Kitty in his head. *Stop that photographer.*

Joe turned to see a photographer raising his camera to take a picture of the *Pride of Essoona*. 'Hey,' he called, 'That's a private individual's vessel. No photos, please.' This was going to be a day of herding cats. Great.

'What *can* we take pictures of, then?' said another photographer, an undertone of frustration in her voice.

'Most things,' said Joe. 'But I'd prefer it if you asked first. This *is* a military facility, although we're more relaxed than your terrestrial equivalents. When photographing people, you must ask the person concerned for their permission.' To the journalists he said, 'Of course you can *talk* to anyone you like. Adults only, though. Not the kids.'

'There are *children* on board?' said the reporter from Bolivia.

'We're a family-friendly organisation,' said Joe, trying to reassure her. 'In fact, our newest resident was born here, just a fortnight ago.'

'Can we interview the mother?' asked the South African journalist.

Damn, he'd walked straight into that one. 'I'd rather you didn't. We must respect her right to privacy.'

Joe led them out of Docking Bay 3 and into Docking Bay 2. 'These are our one-person fighters,' he said, waving an arm at the *Tumbas*. 'Take all the pictures you like. We have a hundred craft here, and another hundred in Docking Bay 1.'

Shakila took over, providing more detailed information and opening the door of one so they could peer inside. Joe stayed back to talk to Susan.

'How are you, Susan? Did you have a good trip?'

'I'm very well, thank you, Joe,' she said. 'The trip was fine. I thought I might have trouble getting to the pickup point, but it all went smoothly.'

'Trouble?' he enquired.

Susan removed her glasses and cleaned them on the edge of her blouse.

'There's a global problem with private jets at the moment. They're getting grounded by mysterious electronic faults. Or Air Traffic Control won't give them take-off clearance because their computer can't find them in the system.' She replaced her glasses, pushing them up the bridge of her nose with her forefinger. 'It's strange: governments and official bodies like the UN don't seem to be affected – just planes belonging to corporations and ultra-high-net-worth individuals.'

Joe rubbed his face. He had a distinct suspicion this could be another form of direct action by Delius. Was the *Shantivira's* computer going rogue?

'That's weird. Are commercial flights affected?' he asked.

Susan shook her head. 'Not at all.'

'Perhaps they have better maintenance.'

They toured both biomes, stopping to interview crew members and take photos. The guests were impressed by the *Shantivira's* attempts at self-sufficiency and suitably amazed by the view of the Earth, which captivated every first-time visitor.

In between presenting the space station, Joe was enjoying the chance to talk to Susan without either of them having to rush off to another meeting. With jaguar-Kitty padding at their heels, they discussed the Syenitian documents about failed alien civilisations and their common thread: that, at some point, the resources a society needed to keep existing were greater than the available supply. Alternatively, the pursuit of those

147

resources resulted in ecological breakdown and the collapse of all systems dependant on the planet's biosphere – including civilisation itself.

'It's all rather depressing,' said Susan in her understated way. 'Don't you have any examples of planets which were able to change the way they did things?'

'Shakila's plan was to give you the bad news first, as a wake-up call. The success stories will come next,' Joe replied. 'But there aren't many of them, I'm afraid. Generally, civilisations either work out a way to live sustainably long before the planetary boundaries are exceeded, or they fail, like the Maya, or the Roman Empire.' He crouched down and used a stray leaf to rescue an earthworm which had found its way onto the dry path. Carefully, he transferred it to the safety of a patch of soil and stood up again. 'Last-minute handbrake turns like we're going to have to pull off are extremely rare.'

Susan watched the worm burrow into the soil. 'But not impossible?'

'But not impossible.' Joe's face crinkled into a grin. 'I'm not giving up hope just yet.'

They continued walking, the main group now some way ahead of them. Susan said, 'Do *you* think we ought to make the information public? Publish it on the IPCC website?' She folded her arms. 'Everyone I speak to in the diplomatic community is in favour of suppressing it. But I can't believe that's the right path.'

Joe studied Susan's profile. Her steel-grey curls were a softer, paler shade at her temple, like a winter's sky. 'They're frightened,' he said simply. 'And they bloody should be. They're being told: change or perish. But change itself seems impossible and terrifying. They don't know where or how to start. To them, the ostrich approach to problem-solving is a natural response right now.'

Susan smiled, despite herself.

Joe continued, 'Based on their millennia of experience, the Syenitians have put together a road map for civilisations to transition from an exploitative model to a durable one.' He thought of all the work Shakila and Delius had put in over recent months, transforming that precious information into bite-size packages they could disseminate to humanity via the UN. 'We can offer the Earth authorities proven solutions, a path to safety, if they'll listen.'

'If they'll listen.' Susan's long years of working for government bodies had made her cynical.

'Baby steps, Susan. First we show them where they're headed and give them time to digest that knowledge, then we explain what they must do to avoid that fate.' Joe shoved his fists into the front pockets of his jeans. 'If they don't go public and start implementing the solutions once they have them, I'll leak the information to the news agencies,' he added.

For their lunch in the canteen – Thai green curry with tofu and rice – Shakila had seated the members of the press with *Shantivira* personnel from their own countries. This was inspired: the animated conversations along the table made Joe feel the journalists were connecting with his crew on a level unachievable in a formal interview setting. Kitty shifted to her Syenitian form and worked her way around the guests, allowing each reporter to ask her questions.

Shakila hadn't arranged activities for the afternoon session. She planned to let these arise naturally from the discussions between compatriots.

Maneewan took the Asian representatives from Thailand under her wing. She offered them an exclusive interview with her and her Indian husband Vijay, plus a guided tour of the *Shantivira's* catering facilities.

The Canadians went off to play on the flight simulators and the Italians to explore the maintenance deck. The Bolivians and Australians returned to the biomes to learn about agriculture in space, and Nkosi and Kazembi each took a South African for a ride in a *Tumba*. Officially only for one person, the little fighters had an extra fold-down seat in the back wall, for training and emergencies.

As the table emptied, Joe leaned back in his chair with satisfaction. 'Well done, Shakila. I don't think that could've gone any better.'

Susan agreed. 'Yes. Thank you, Shakila. I appreciate the effort you must have put in before today.'

Shakila bowed her head in gracious acknowledgement. 'It was worth it. We'll have six different stories instead of one, which can all be translated and published globally.'

Joe remembered something. 'There's another story on the horizon.'

Susan and Shakila looked at him enquiringly.

Addressing Susan, he said, 'You remember the Pweza I told you about?'

'The refugee octopuses, now living on Syenitia?'

'That's them,' Joe said. 'They're sending some ships back to look for survivors and they'll stop here on the way.'

Susan arched an eyebrow. 'Are you asking me or telling me?'

'Well,' said Joe, feeling awkward. 'Telling. This is the only point on their route where they can replenish their supplies. And we promised we'd help. We can do it discreetly, but it shouldn't be a secret this time.'

Shakila said, 'We won't need to steal any fish. We have enough notice to organise it in advance.'

Joe nodded. 'Exactly. But they'll have to enter the upper atmosphere to reoxygenate their tanks.' To Susan he said, 'In the interests of transparency, we could provide a live video feed so governments can see what's going on.'

She frowned. 'When would this be?'

'They've just left Syenitia, so two months from now, or thereabouts,' he replied.

'June, then.' Susan made a note on her phone. 'I'll bend a few ears and smooth the path for you. Let's not tell the journalists about it for now.'

✦ ✦ ✦

THE FOLLOWING MORNING, Joe made his way down to the *Shantivira's* conference room. Björn's contract working underwater with the Pweza on Syenitia had ended at the spring equinox. He'd returned to the Earth and, after a holiday, had thrown himself into setting up a new venture, funded by a Syenitian development grant. They'd agreed he'd update Joe on his progress each month. Joe would include the information in his regular reports to Aldeman.

Björn was already waiting for him as Joe stopped on the threshold to remove his shoes. The blond giant jumped to his feet and enveloped Joe in a bear hug.

'It's great to see you again, my friend!' he boomed.

'It's been too long, mate,' said Joe. 'How've you been?'

'Good, thanks,' said Björn. 'I hear the *Shantivira* has a new crew member?'

For a moment, Joe's mind went blank. It did? Then he realised Björn was talking about Yonas.

'I remember when Sören was born,' Björn continued, sitting back down on the tatami mat floor. 'Hagar did a fantastic job looking after Tima when he arrived early.'

Joe joined him, sitting on one of the conference room's hard little cushions and folding his legs into a relaxed lotus position. He had a flashback to the day when, a week before her scheduled maternity leave, Tima's waters had broken while she'd been instructing a group on the *Shantivira's* simulators. Unlike Yonas, Joe's godson had been born seven weeks premature after a labour the others referred to as 'difficult' and Joe privately thought of as 'hellish'.

Kitty had taken the blue-lipped bundle in her arms, flooding Sören with life energy until his skin flushed pink and he finally took his first breath. Joe's eyes pricked with tears as he relived the emotions of that day. Now that baby had just celebrated his eighth birthday. Where did the time go?

Björn noticed. 'Getting broody, mate?'

Joe shook his head, recovering quickly. 'No point, is there? I'd love to be a dad. I've seen the joy your three bring you and Tima. But it's never going to happen. If Kitty could have children, surely she'd have some already? It's not something we ever talk about.'

His friend studied his face and Joe decided to deflect him before he probed any deeper. 'How was your holiday?'

Björn allowed his attention to be redirected. 'Good. But—'

'What?'

'I revisited some favourite dive sites.' Björn said, picking absently at a small hole in his sock. 'They're not the same as they were twenty or even ten years ago.'

Joe waited for him to continue.

'The coral's bleaching. The fish are smaller and fewer.' Björn looked up at him. 'Earth's oceans are dying in front of our eyes, Joe. It's terrifying.'

Joe lowered his head in silent acknowledgement. He'd been hearing the same from Kitty for years. There were no comforting words to make the problem go away.

Björn ran a hand through his hair. It was as thick and plentiful as it had always been, but Joe noticed that, in places, the gold was turning to silver. 'But that's why I'm here, right?' Björn said, becoming more business-like.

'Is it done?' Joe asked.

'Signed and sealed.' Björn grinned. 'You're looking at the proud owner of an oil company with some aging infrastructure in the North Sea.'

'What happens now?'

'I sacked the board of directors and the share price is nose-diving.' Björn placed his *zana* on the floor and searched for a file. 'This is part of the speech I made to the employees last week. I already told them I'm one of them: that I spent my career as a saturation diver repairing oil pipelines.'

An image of Björn standing on a dais in a conference

hall appeared between them. Despite the corporate setting, he wore his usual jeans and white T-shirt, revealing his colourful sleeve tattoos of sea creatures.

'I've ordered pumping to stop,' said the mini-Björn. 'I've revoked existing supply contracts and paid the refunds and fines. We're free from all customer commitments and ready for a change in direction. This company is no longer an oil company.'

Murmurs of shock and disbelief rippled round the hall.

'The share price will fall to nothing. But as I now own most of the shares, the share price is irrelevant. I believe the true value of this company lies in *you*, the employees – your knowledge, your creativity, your personal connections and your hard work.' He pointed at them with his index finger. '*You* are this company's most precious resource. Not its equipment and facilities and certainly not the rights to drill for a substance which must stay in the ground if we want to avoid climate breakdown.

'There will be no redundancies. Some of you will be needed for decommissioning the oil operation. Some of you will be working on a new project, proving a concept to generate industrial quantities of hydrogen from seawater.'

More murmurs. 'What about the rest of us?' called a voice in the audience.

'The company will continue paying your current salaries for the next ten years – on one condition.' Björn raised his voice to a level guaranteed to reach every corner of the auditorium. 'I want you to use your skills and creativity to start a renewable energy cooperative in your home community, or someplace else people know you.

Renewable energy works best in small, decentralised operations. Resistance to new projects falls dramatically if the people living there have a stake in them themselves.

'These projects just need someone to get them started – that can be you. Get involved in local government. Try to make your community energy self-sufficient. *That's* how we can help stop the climate crisis. There are thousands of us. Imagine what a difference we could make.'

'Will you be doing the same in your own home town?' called another voice.

Björn laughed. 'I'm from Malmö, in Sweden. They're doing fine without me. No, I'll be working my ass off on the hydrogen generation project. I should add, this company will have no rights regarding anything you set up. This isn't going to be one big "renewable energy" company,' he said, making air quotes with his fingers. 'Whatever you create will belong to the people directly involved in it.

'Of course, you're welcome to piss off to another oil corporation, if that's where you see your future. But I'd be delighted if you stayed with us to help improve the energy security of your friends and neighbours.'

He paused briefly, standing with his feet apart and his hands behind his back. He looked out across the crowded hall, letting his message sink in.

'So, have a holiday, take some time to think about how best to apply your skills. Return home and find out what your community is already doing. You have six months from today to come up with a plan and present it to the team I'm setting up. Their job will be to ensure your project is viable and to provide advice and small-scale grants.'

'Where's the money coming from?' shouted a man in the front row.

'The company's capital to start with,' said Björn. 'And I have a wealthy, independent backer for the rest. They're not willing to reveal their identity at this stage. Money isn't the big issue here. My backer's priority is preventing further breakdown of our planet's ecosystems and to help us transition to a low-carbon economy. They take the long view.'

Björn stopped the video.

Joe said, 'Can you send Aldeman a copy?'

'Already have.'

'What are your next steps?'

'Find people to oversee the community renewable energy projects and do the payroll administration,' Björn said matter-of-factly. 'I'll keep on most of the HR department, but they'll need some retraining.'

'You mean you need people to ensure your employees aren't just sitting at home on their arses, pocketing your cash?'

Björn snorted with laughter. 'You've been spending too much time with politicians, Joe,' he said. 'Real people aren't like that. Give them an opportunity to do something meaningful with their lives and they'll grab it with both hands. Sure, there'll be a few freeloaders, but they'll be a minority. Others might have caring responsibilities preventing them from contributing as much as they'd like. My team will evaluate each individual situation on its merits.' He rested his hands on his knees. 'I'm building a body of advocates, like the Galaksi Alliance does with former Shantivirans.'

Joe hoped it would work. 'But the community projects are just a side-show, right?' he said. 'It's great you're keeping on the workforce, but they aren't the main reason you got Aldeman to buy you a bunch of ancient oil rigs?'

'No,' said Björn, pressing his palms together. 'The real job is to build a team of engineers who can help me scale up the Pweza's micro-fusion reactors and electrolysers.' He touched his fingertips to his chin, as if in prayer. 'Everything depends on getting them working well. The octopuses regard hydrogen as a waste product. Their ships vent it into space for propulsion. But we can repurpose the oil rigs to compress it and store it underground, where the oil used to be.'

Joe nodded. 'And flood the market with cheap, green hydrogen?' he confirmed. That had always been Björn's ambition, ever since he'd helped the Pweza build their subsea refugee accommodation on Syenitia last year. 'You're going to annoy some powerful people.'

'We've a way to go before we get that far. What is it you always say?' Björn's cornflower eyes sparkled, mirroring Joe's own. 'No risk, no fun.'

+ + +

THE NEXT DAY was a Sunday. Instead of having lunch at the *Cath Palug*, Joe had arranged to go to Brecon to see how his mother was settling in back home. He and Kitty materialised in their customary spot on the hillside behind Grace's cottage and strolled down towards the garden gate.

It was a perfect spring day, full of light and promise. The sun on Joe's cheek had a real warmth to it and, all around them, the Beacons were bursting with new life: fresh greens dotted with tiny pink and yellow flowers. He breathed deeply, inhaling the familiar scent of the ferns as his legs brushed past their fronds. High above in the cloudless sky, the piercing song of a skylark announced winter was officially over.

You're not shifting? he asked Kitty, who'd retained her Syenitian form. Unusually for her, she wore jeans and a checkered shirt.

Grace is used to seeing me like this now. The jaguar still freaks her out a bit.

Oh, said Joe, disappointed. In this place, he expected and wanted the big cat by his side. That was how it had always been, since they'd first met. He took Kitty's hand.

Nervous? she asked.

Just remembering the last time we came, he said. That day was seared onto his cerebrum for all eternity. The latest addition to a lifetime's collection of traumatic memories associated with this place.

She's changed, Joe. Kitty gave his hand a supportive squeeze. *Nestor broadened her horizons. And she's grateful for all my work in the garden.*

I didn't know you were into gardening, he said. It seemed incongruous, somehow. Kitty belonged in wild places. Unstructured. Unconstrained. Untamed. Like the Bannau Brycheiniog. Or Eryri.

Kitty's smile flickered, as if she guessed what he was thinking. *You asked me to win her trust*, she said. *Grace's heart is in her garden.*

They reached the dry stone wall which separated Grace's plot from the open moor. A row of blackthorns grew in front of it, their branches covered in delicate white blossom.

Kitty opened the creaking wooden gate and strode through, calling, 'Grace, we're here!'

His mother appeared at the French windows and came out to greet them. 'Good morning!'

No hugging or touching. That would be going too far.

She said, 'It's such a lovely day, I thought we could have a picnic. What do you think? Joe?'

Joe wasn't listening. He stood and stared at the house he'd grown up in. For the first time in his life, he had a clear view of the stonework.

'What happened to your wisteria, Mam?'

'Kitty helped me get rid of it. I hated it once it took over, but I never felt up to doing something about it,' Grace admitted. 'Too big a problem to tackle by myself.'

'But you always said it was so pretty in summer!' Not that he'd ever particularly liked it. But the change would take getting used to.

'I was making the best of things. Actually, it made me feel like I was in prison. I had to fight with it just to open the windows.'

'Oh,' said Joe. 'OK.'

Grace glanced at Kitty and gave her a distinctly conspiratorial smile. 'That wife of yours is a marvel,' she said. 'I'm saving a fortune on weedkiller.'

'Grace has green fingers; I have brown fingers,' joked Kitty.

How did you do it? Joe asked Kitty privately. *It covered the whole bloody house!*

I put my hand on the trunk and took its life energy. Once it was dead, it was easy to break it up into bits.

You have been busy, he said. *Are you two besties now or what?*

Kitty glanced at Grace, who was still looking back at her cottage. *We have more in common than you might think.*

Like what? Joe couldn't imagine.

Kitty smirked. *The same taste in men, for starters.*

Time to change the subject. 'Did you say something about a picnic, Mam?' Joe said out loud. 'Can we help you carry anything?'

Grace gave them jobs: Joe spreading blankets and cushions under the shade of the blossoming cherry tree, Kitty carrying a tray loaded with crockery, cutlery and drinks. Grace herself brought out the food, apparently not trusting either of her guests with the responsibility.

Fair play to her, she'd done them proud. Pork pies, a steaming pot of cawl, cheese, coleslaw, salad and freshly baked bread. A feast. Kitty sat cross-legged beside them, pouring tea for Grace and opening a bottle of local cider for him.

Eagerly, Joe filled his bowl with stew. It smelled exactly like the cawl his Nan had made when he was a boy – served in the very same earthenware pot – when they'd lived in Blaenavon and only visited Grace's mother during the holidays. He took a spoonful and let the flavours unfurl on his tongue. Mmm. Tasted the same too. It was definitely best with bacon.

'The cawl's good, Mam.'

Grace grunted, gruffly acknowledging his statement of the obvious. Wordlessly, she passed him a hunk of bread and cheese to go with it.

'Thanks,' he said. 'I see your hydrangeas are out already,' he persevered, trying to start a conversation. Surely the garden was a safe topic? 'And the tulips are looking great.'

'They're just the leftovers from last year,' Grace scoffed. 'Normally I'd plant fresh bulbs for a proper display, but I missed a whole planting season, what with being in Argentina and all.'

Whoops.

'The daffodils and crocuses were lovely this spring,' she continued. 'They're over now, of course, but my peonies'll be out soon.'

Kitty sat up straighter. 'Grace has been teaching me to sow seeds in trays and plant them out when they're big enough.'

'Oh, yes?' said Joe. Kitty knew he wasn't interested in gardening. But she sounded genuinely enthusiastic. Was *she* catching the bug?

Grace said, 'Kitty has a natural talent for getting things to grow.'

Well, duh. That was just channelling life energy. She did it every day.

'I just need to teach her the difference between plants and weeds and she'll be a great gardener.'

Joe smiled inwardly. He could quite imagine Kitty strongly disagreeing with Grace's views on which plants were permitted to live and which had to die. Kitty believed all life deserved a chance, as long as it wasn't hurting other life forms.

'What've you planted so far, *Cath*?' said Joe, his curiosity now growing beyond 'polite conversation' level.

'Vegetables mostly,' said Kitty, jerking her head at the greenhouse and raised beds at the other side of the garden. 'Leeks, parsnips, carrots and potatoes. What comes next, Grace?'

Grace rubbed her chin, a genetic replica of the mannerism Joe himself made when he was considering something. Except Grace didn't have stubble to rub. Still. It was weird.

'Tomatoes and cucumbers,' said Grace, decisively. 'Onions. And hollyhocks.'

The women started discussing plant varieties and went on to prioritise upcoming jobs. Amused, but feeling a little left out, Joe concentrated on his food.

After a while, they fell into a companionable silence. Grace continued eating; Kitty idly observed a stag beetle – a miniature *Koppakuoria* – making its way laboriously through the grass stems between them. High on the chimney stack, a blackbird sang an intricate melody, pausing only for the answering song from a friend further down the valley.

Joe leaned back on his elbows and groaned with satisfaction. He couldn't eat or drink another thing.

'Thanks, Mam, that was champion.'

'Call it a belated birthday present,' said Grace. 'So much has happened, I thought we deserved a fresh start.'

'You haven't heard from Nestor?' he said. Now was as good a time to ask as any.

'Not a peep. Long may it last.' Grace concentrated on

spreading home-made raspberry jam onto a Welsh Cake. 'Kitty told me why he wanted to kill you,' she said.

Joe raised his eyebrows. What was this? Confessions of a space demon? 'The whole sorry story?'

'The whole sorry story,' Kitty confirmed, not looking up from her beetle studies.

Grace bit into her Welsh Cake and chewed. 'The thing is,' she said, swallowing, 'I can see why he was so upset.' She patted Kitty's knee. 'And I also see you meant him no harm, dear. It was all a terrible misunderstanding.'

A terrible misunderstanding? Joe couldn't believe what he was hearing. Whose side was she on? 'Mam, he tried to shoot me! He kidnapped my staff! And you!'

'I'm not making excuses for him. Of course what he did was wrong.' Grace turned to Kitty. 'You need to go and see him. Face-to-face, to talk about what happened. Give him the chance to forgive you. Give yourself the chance to forgive him.'

'You've changed your tune!' said Joe. 'We never talked about the hard stuff when I was growing up.'

'And look at where it got us!' Her voice was higher-pitched than usual. 'I wish you'd told me about your life years ago. But I understand now, I never created the conditions for you to be able to.'

That was quite an admission, Joe thought, saying nothing. He didn't know what *to* say. Perhaps Kitty was right. Perhaps she *had* changed.

Kitty frowned. 'Do you think I should?' she said. Joe watched her push her fingertips into the lawn, as if she found touching the soil reassuring. 'I've wanted to, a million times, but I'm worried I might tip him over the edge and make him do something terrible.'

Grace snorted. 'More terrible than murdering your husband?'

Kitty's tone was calm and firm. 'He *didn't* murder my husband.'

'Not for want of trying,' replied Grace. 'Go and see him, love. You both need closure. He's not in a position to cause trouble anymore. Not to you.' She took another bite of her Welsh Cake. 'What's the worst that could happen?'

Joe caught Kitty's eye. What *was* the worst that could happen? She winked at him, clearly less concerned than he was.

'Grace is right,' she said. 'This has gone on long enough. I'll do it.'

13. A SPONTANEOUS SPACEWALK
DAN

'WE CAN'T TRUST them,' said Dan, thinking about Henning and his crew as he watched the planet Tarumbet shrink on the rear monitor. They'd just stocked up on supplies and were headed to a spot beyond the asteroid belt where it would be safe to make the jump to hyperspace. They'd done a few short hops to test the new hyperdrive, but this would be their first ever hyper-long-distance voyage.

'Duh. Of course not.'

'Are you sure about this, Afra?' A surge of existential doubt welled up within him, unaccustomed and unwelcome. 'We could walk away now and do something else with our lives.'

'Do you want to?' Afra turned in the pilot's seat, challenging him.

Dan rubbed his neck. 'No. Yes. No. I feel like I owe Bellyn. But if you wanted to pull out, I'd understand.'

'We're not pulling out,' she said with a fierceness that surprised him. 'Bellyn was like a father to me. I promised him we'd keep going. If the backup factory is destroyed, I'll consider stopping. Not before.'

'You mean if another whole planet gets destroyed because of us?'

'It wasn't our fault, Dan,' she insisted, not for the first time. Dan wondered who she was trying to convince. Him? Or herself? 'Where we're going is so small and far away, they probably wouldn't bother with the actual planet,' she said. 'It's more likely they'd just find us and kill us.'

Dan winced. Sometimes Afra's straight talking was a bit too straight. 'And you're OK with that?'

Afra frowned. 'Everyone dies, Dan. I made my peace with not growing old a long time ago. This isn't just about keeping a promise. It's the right thing to do.' Her spine stiffened and she jutted her silver chin: a picture of determination. 'If we can help trigger social change on Ranglatiri, we'll be doing the whole galaxy a favour.'

'I didn't realise you were so *committed*,' said Dan, taken aback by her strength of feeling.

She studied him, eyes narrowed. 'If you're not up for this, we'll turn round and I'll drop you off on Tarumbet.'

Dan shook his head. 'You're not doing this by yourself, Afra. No way. Maybe I don't feel as passionately about the cause itself, but I'm with *you*. All the way.' He reached across the cockpit and squeezed her hand. 'Where you go, I go.'

'To the end?' Her brown eyes moistened, glittering like wet stones under the harsh electric light.

'To the end,' he said.

They flew on in a companionable silence. Eventually, Dan broke it.

'So . . . I have a question. I always meant to ask Bellyn, but . . . then it was too late.'

Afra gave him a sidelong glance and continued edging

her way past the asteroid field.

'On a Ranglatiri wedding night, the female eats the father as soon as he's fertilised her eggs. That's why the uncles bring up the kids. Right?'

'Right,' she said.

'So why bother taking a contraceptive pill?' Dan had never quite understood the demand for their product. 'I mean, if you're going to die anyway? To save your brother from a life of domestic drudgery? I didn't think Ranglatiri were so self-sacrificing.' He wouldn't do it for *his* brother, Dan realised, but then again, they'd never got on.

Afra shook her head, her cobalt hair rippling on her shoulders. 'It doesn't work like that. The female can smell when the male is fertile. She won't mate with him otherwise. By taking our pills, the males are ensuring a marriage can't take place at all.'

'Oh.' Dan digested this. 'And you don't think the females will have noticed a drop in male fertility over recent years?'

'I think they *have* noticed,' said Afra. 'If they'd just been after Bellyn, they wouldn't have razed Amra the way they did. We're hitting them where it hurts, Dan.' She stopped talking briefly to navigate around a jagged piece of blackened rock. 'I doubt Henning and friends have realised though, or they wouldn't consider doing business with us.'

Dan disagreed. Henning was vain and greedy, but he wasn't stupid. 'They just want to make some cash before they sell us out. There's a reward out for the *Gezi Urdina*, did you know?'

'Only among the Ranglatiri.' Afra shrugged, as if that

didn't count. 'I reckon we can still distribute enough pills to ensure a population blip. Enough to shift the power balance in the males' direction. To make life fairer for them.' Her mouth became a thin, wistful line. 'That's all Bellyn ever wanted.'

They stared into space for a while. In due course, they cleared the asteroid belt and Dan guessed it must be nearly time to enter hyperspace. A blue light on the control panel began to flash. 'Is that the signal the trip calculations are done?'

Afra's eyes widened. 'Shit!'

'What's the matter?'

'It's the transmission detector.' Hastily, she initiated a program which displayed a 3D image of the *Gezi Urdina*. A blue circle flashed at a point above the co-pilot's seat. Dan's seat. He glanced up, but could see nothing.

Afra said, 'So they *did* attach a tracking beacon. It must be on the hull.'

'Who activated it?' said Dan. 'I thought we killed everyone who could've known about it.'

'Maybe it triggered automatically, as soon as we came in range of . . . I don't know.'

'Maybe it was on a timer,' he said, thinking fast. 'Waiting for us to forget about it, to lull us into a false sense of security, you know?'

'That's possible.' Afra inclined her head. 'Maybe the timer was triggered by proximity to the Ranglatiri ship when we were on Mwongo. It doesn't matter. We must get rid of it now, before we enter hyperspace.' Dan could hear the tension in her voice. 'We can't risk going back to the planet either, we'd be putting the Tarumbets in danger.

We have to jettison it in deep space.' Afra looked at Dan. 'Are you up for a spacewalk? I'd do it myself, but I can't with this leg.'

Dan gulped.

'You told me you've done loads of spacewalks,' she said accusingly.

He *had* said that, hadn't he? Did two count as 'loads'? He'd certainly never mentioned the months of EVA training in a swimming pool for the minutely planned scenarios which had, regrettably, not included unsticking tracking beacons.

'Have you got a suit for me?' he asked, stalling for time.

'Bellyn's will fit you,' she said with certainty. 'You're broader across the shoulders, but he was taller.' She patted him on the hand. 'It shouldn't take too long. We know where it is now. You just need to detach it and chuck it into space.'

HALF AN HOUR later, Dan was suited up and standing on the wrong side of the airlock. The last time he'd done anything like this, he'd been able to see the Earth and had had a whole support team telling him precisely what to do.

Tarumbet was a pinprick behind the already-distant asteroid belt and there was nothing except him and the blue hull of the *Gezi Urdina*. After helping him into his spacesuit and explaining how it worked, his 'support team' had said, 'Don't come back in until you've found it,' and gone back to reading her book, as relaxed as a cat on holiday.

He took a few experimental steps with his electromagnetic shoes, operating them with the controls on his walking frame. The walker – to which his suit was attached via two sturdy cables – ensured he always had two magnetic anchor points on the hull, even when one foot was detached to take a step. To be fair, it felt pretty safe.

Cautiously, he shuffled his way forwards along the convex roof of the spacecraft, an intergalactic geriatric on a mission. His stretchy compression suit was less bulky than a NASA spacesuit and more comfortable. No Maximum Absorbency Garment though, so whatever Afra said, he'd be coming back in if he needed the bathroom.

He arrived at the front of the ship and studied the hull in the region above his seat. Nothing obvious. He crouched for a better look, activating his magnetic knee pads so he could kneel. He lowered his head to the surface as far as his helmet would allow – and then he spotted it. A tiny raised circle, not much bigger than a quarter dollar coin, exactly the same shade of blue as the hull. No wonder they hadn't noticed it until it started transmitting.

He tried to get a grip on it, but his gloves were too thick and his fingers kept slipping off the edge. Damn. It must be superglued on. That made sense: a magnet would disrupt the signal. He'd have to use brute force.

He drew the chisel from his tool belt and tried to get underneath the disc. He put his whole strength behind it until his knee pads skidded. The chisel slipped and made an ugly gash in the *Gezi Urdina's* paintwork. Oh no, thought Dan, as he extended a hand to stop himself landing on his chin. Afra'll kill me if she sees that. Dan pulled the floating chisel back by its cord and returned it to its holster. A different approach was required. He unsheathed his knife.

He got down on his elbows and placed the point at the base of the tracker, trying to wangle his knife between it and the hull. He worked his way around until, finally, the tip slid in, just a fraction of an inch. Bingo. He pushed harder, wiggling the blade from side to side, and pressing the handle down towards the curving surface of the spacecraft. Twenty minutes passed. He persisted with dogged patience, entirely focused on the task at hand.

The tracker separated from the hull abruptly, a checkers piece catapulted noiselessly into space. How might it have sounded, if he'd been working in an atmosphere? Dan leaned back on his heels and watched it spin away, relieved and somewhat surprised he'd managed to shift it. Then he stood, slowly and painfully, his joints cramped from the long period kneeling. Gripping his walker, he shuffled back to the airlock.

Afra was waiting for him. 'You did it!' she cried, flinging her arms round his neck and kissing him enthusiastically. The transmission detector on the control panel must have stopped flashing. He hugged her back, suspecting her earlier nonchalance had been an act. She *had* been worried about him after all.

'Help me out of this suit,' he said. 'I gotta pee.'

14. CEREBRAL HAEMORRHAGE
NESTOR, MAY 2016

NESTOR STUDIED THE output of his painstakingly written program, not wanting to believe what it was telling him. There was no getting past it. Without a more intensive energy source, he'd never be able to scale up his mini-satellites into a weapon capable of worse than tickling a space demon, let alone deter potential alien invaders.

Without access to depleted uranium or other, equally hard-to-come-by substances, all his efforts were for nothing. He looked around his workshop, remembering the happy days in Switzerland when money had been no object and David Wang, his traitorous partner, had had the connections to get them anything they needed.

Funding and connections which were abruptly severed the day he shot the bastard. Not the high point of his career, but he'd do it again if he had to. His nostrils flared in disgust at the notion of that *monster* bankrolling all the progress they'd made. Did she think she had a right to his inventions, just because she'd paid for them?

There was a knock at the workshop door. '¡*Adelante!*' he called in an imperious tone, wondering who it could be. Not Matthew, who had his own key. Although he'd been acting strangely since Grace had left.

The door opened and *she* walked in, wearing the same flowing red dress she had that night in Buenos Aires. He stood up hastily, backing away from the computer terminal. His heart pounded: no doubt his blood pressure was shooting up again. The demon in human form raised its hand in a gesture intended to reassure. He wasn't falling for that.

'Nestor! I'm not here to hurt you. I just want to talk.'

'How did you find me?'

The devil-in-disguise merely twitched her ruby lips.

'I came to apologise.'

He was so surprised, he laughed out loud. 'Forty-seven years late?'

She held out her hands. 'Better late than never. So here it is: I'm sorry I seduced you, Nestor. I'm sorry you saw what I really look like without being prepared for it. I'm sorry you still feel you sold your soul for a single night of passion. I'm sorry you think I'm the Devil. I'm sorry I didn't discover you were an irrational, xenophobic, controlling, grudge-bearing psychopath before sleeping with you.'

Irrational? Xenophobic? *Him?* He knew lots of foreigners. He even still worked with one. But the creature was in full flow now. There was no stopping her to ask what she was talking about.

'I'm sorry you've spent your entire life blaming me for all your failures. I'm sorry you never learnt how to love. I'm sorry for the choices you've made. I'm sorry your beauty faded with every evil deed. I'm sorry I secretly funded your operation in the hope something good might come from it.'

She had a bloody cheek. Red-hot rage boiled inside him, lava seeking its way to the surface. Was the bitch ever going to shut the fuck up?

'I'm sorry you kidnapped my friends and my mother-in-law. I'm sorry you murdered David and tried to kill my husband. I'm sorry you've made your life into a crusade against all extra-terrestrials because you had one negative experience with me. I'm sorry you've lived your life in fear.' Finally, the mocking voice ceased. His turn.

'Have you quite finished?' His legs were trembling but he'd never get another chance like this. From a safe distance, he jabbed an aggressive finger at her. 'You are an abomination. You should not exist.' He straightened his tie, trying to project a confidence he didn't feel. 'And yet I am grateful you helped me find my vocation.'

'Your vocation?' She arched a supercilious charcoal eyebrow.

'Protecting the Earth from unnatural creatures like you.'

The witch threw back her head and laughed, revealing her predator's teeth. They were yellowish, like those of a wild beast. Disgusting. 'We'll never agree on the best way to protect the Earth, will we?' she said. 'But I've been doing it a lot longer than you, kid. I like to think I'm making a better job of it.'

She closed the distance between them in two swift steps, placing a black-nailed hand on his sternum. Nestor tried to back away, but found he couldn't move a muscle.

'If you ever approach Grace or Joe again, I *will* kill you,' she said matter-of-factly. 'It'll feel like this.'

A deathly chill spread outwards from Nestor's heart;

in vain, he fought for breath as his lungs stopped working. His eyes bulged as panic overwhelmed him.

It stopped as quickly as it had started. Warmth from her hand flowed into him, making him feel stronger and more alive than he had in decades. Euphoric, almost. She released her supernatural hold on him and he staggered away from her, sucking in lungfuls of precious air.

'I regret how I treated you, Nestor, but your decisions and your actions have been your own. That was your very last warning.' She spun away from him in a swirl of black hair and red velvet, slamming the door behind her as she left the workshop.

Weak with relief, Nestor slumped in a chair. The relief switched to anger. How *dare* she come here, threatening him? And who was she calling a kid? He was sixty-six years old! He'd given Grace the time of her life. They should be grateful to him. He hadn't been able to prevent her sudden departure without blowing his cover but, as he'd long since tired of her company, he'd decided to just let her go. He scowled. It must have been Grace who'd informed the enchantress of his location. *La batidora.*

He reached for his desk drawer and pulled out a bottle of Fernet. He needed a drink to soothe his nerves. He sipped the bitter liquid, thinking. Grace hadn't mentioned wanting to leave until her chapel friends were waiting outside in their car, beeping their horn.

The woman he'd brought to Gaiman wouldn't have been able to organise an intercontinental trip alone. She must have had help. Why had she kept her plans to herself? Did she suspect something? Had someone warned her about him?

He jumped as the workshop door opened, then relaxed. It was just Matthew. Why did he have a suitcase with him? Was *he* leaving, too?

Matthew left his luggage by the door and made his way to Nestor's desk. If only the boy would stand up straight, he'd cut a more impressive figure. Nestor refilled his glass.

'Nestor?'

Here we go, he thought, but said nothing.

'I'm sorry,' said Matthew. 'I've had enough. This isn't working out. I'm going home.'

Nestor stood, still holding the Fernet bottle. 'Going home? Just like that?'

'The taxi to the airport will come in half an hour,' the boy mumbled. 'I wanted to say goodbye first. To thank you for everything I've learnt from you.'

'You didn't want to discuss this with me first, before booking your flight?' Nestor waved the bottle at the workshop. 'How am I supposed to get anything done here, if I must do everything myself?'

Matthew gave an awkward shuffle. 'I'm frightened of you. Frightened of your temper. Once Grace left, I realised I could too.'

Nestor's eyes narrowed. 'You helped her. You booked her flight.'

'Yes,' Matthew admitted, studying the concrete floor.

'Why?'

'She asked me to.'

Nestor groaned. The idiot child. 'You never understood who Grace was, did you?'

'Who?' Matthew looked up again, his eyes wide with

curiosity.

'Llewellyn's mother. She was our *security*, Matthew,' Nestor emphasised. 'As long as we held her here, in secret, they couldn't act against us. Do you think I'd have put up with that whinging cow for so long otherwise?'

Matthew's jaw dropped. 'You mean she was a hostage?'

'*She* didn't know that. She believed I cared for her.' Nestor allowed himself a small, inward smile. 'But now she's gone, she's told the enemy where we are. I just had a visit from the demon, threatening me.'

'The demon?' The young man's Adam's apple bobbed up and down with alarm. 'It knows where we are?'

'Everyone betrays me,' said Nestor, almost to himself.

Matthew straightened up and took a deep breath, as if plucking up his courage. 'I'm going to wait outside for my taxi. Goodbye, Nestor.' He turned to head for the door.

Fury flooded Nestor's body, making him strong. 'Don't you dare leave me, boy!' He raised the Fernet bottle and brought it down hard on the back of Matthew's head. Amazingly, it didn't shatter. Matthew's knees folded and he crumpled to the ground with a little sigh.

Nestor stood over him, triumphant. He lifted his leg, ready to give his unconscious assistant the kicking he deserved, when a stabbing, blinding pain in his head made him cry out. Literally blinding: his vision blurred and suddenly he couldn't see at all.

He dropped the bottle and clutched his skull in anguish. The bottle smashed on the floor, the brown liquid releasing a bitter, complex odour. Overcome by a wave of nausea and dizziness, he fell to his knees. What was happening to him? He vomited, retching desperately on all fours. The pain! Oh, the pain!

His arm crumpled beneath him and Nestor slumped onto the cold, rough concrete. The power of thought slithered away from him into the darkness, like a snake.

Then, nothing.

15. MY HOVERCRAFT IS FULL OF EELS
HANNA, JUNE 2016

'HANNA, YOU CAN'T go on like this.' Hassan stood next to her *Tumba*, helmet under his arm. They'd just returned from a space debris dematerialisation mission and, as was so often the case since she'd returned to work, Hanna had not been on top form. Yonas had had a temperature last night and she was almost floating with lack of sleep. Frankly, she was amazed she'd been able to fly at all. Her brain revolved around fantasies of curling up under a thick blanket and succumbing to oblivion. But she soldiered on.

'Your flying was all over the place today. *And* you missed those simple shots.' He grimaced. 'I can't keep covering for you, Hanna. One day something will happen. Something you could have prevented if you'd been your usual self.'

Hanna shrugged. Hassan had no idea what it was like, caring for a newborn. It wasn't his fault; he was already spread thinly – flying the *Koppakuoria* missions in addition to his regular shifts. But there was no way Kia could manage alone. A least the two-hour cycle had become a four-hour cycle now. They were getting more sleep than when Yonas had first arrived. Last night had

179

been a one-off, that was all.

'Let people *help*, Hanna. It's not all on you. I'm sure there are plenty of experienced parents you could ask. What about Maneewan and Vijay? Or Kazembi and Nkosi? Kia doesn't have to do everything by herself. Then we could spend more time together too. I miss you.'

Ah. So *that's* what this was about. Hassan was feeling neglected. Didn't he understand, your whole life went on the back-burner when you had a baby to look after? She didn't have time to go on dates right now. It was an achievement just finding a moment to wash her hair.

'I miss you, too,' she mumbled and looked up at him. She really did. Hassan *and* the life of freedom they'd had before. 'It's not forever. Things'll get easier in a couple of months. But night-shifts are hard to delegate. I'll think about who to ask.'

Hassan enfolded her in his long arms and she rested her head against his chest, closing her eyes and breathing in his warm, comforting scent. 'Good,' he said, kissing the top of her head. 'Now get yourself back to your cabin and have a nap.'

+   +   +

HANNA SURFACED FROM a deep sleep, like a diver kicking her way up from the darkness into the colourful world of shallower water. She was still groggy, but full consciousness was within reach. Her empty stomach rumbled. She pulled her *zana* towards her and checked the time. Wow. She'd slept the entire afternoon and it was time for dinner.

She sat up, rubbing her eyes. God, she'd needed that.

Sleeping when you were tired was one of life's greatest and most basic pleasures, along with eating when you were hungry and drinking when you were thirsty.

She made her way down to the canteen, queuing at the hatch for a plate of red-lentil dhal and cauliflower curry. Tima and Björn were ahead of her, holding hands like teenagers. How had they managed it? Three children and still smiling.

They greeted her warmly. 'How are you doing, Hanna? How's Kia?' said Tima.

Hanna blinked. 'Oh, you know. Surviving one day at a time.'

Björn laughed, his deep voice booming across the canteen. 'The zombie phase. I'll never forget it.'

They took their plates over to the tables to eat together. Hanna sat with her back to the window: the view of the Milky Way felt too overwhelming for her right now.

'Seriously, though, Hanna, I've never seen you looking so exhausted. Are you and Kia getting enough help?' Tima asked. 'There are plenty of us here who'd love the chance to spend a few hours with little Yonas.'

'Even at four in the morning?' Hanna was sceptical.

'Even at four in the morning,' insisted Tima. 'We could set up a rota.'

A rota. That would involve talking to people. Organising. And . . . handing Yonas over to someone who wasn't her or Kia. She wasn't sure she could.

'I don't know, Tima. It's a good idea, but I should talk to Kia.'

She patted the back of Hanna's hand. 'You do that. Don't suffer in silence.'

'What about you, Björn?' said Hanna in an attempt to change the subject. 'How's your new project going?'

'Great, thanks,' he said, swallowing his mouthful. 'When the Pweza come by to reoxygenate next week, they'll also deliver the first batch of self-powering electrolysers they've been making for me. Cephalo, their chief engineer, and a couple of his team will stay behind to help me get them running.'

Hanna's eyes widened. 'The Pweza are coming?' she said, wondering why nobody had told her. She was so out of touch with events. Looking after Yonas was making her feel isolated, she realised. 'I hadn't heard.'

'You will.' Björn ate another forkful of curry. 'It's a rescue party, going back to their planet to look for survivors. They've been travelling for weeks already and they'll need to restock their supplies by the time they reach us.'

'So will your visitors stay until their fleet returns?' asked Hanna.

'No, Kitty's promised to teleport them back to Syenitia when we're done,' Björn replied. 'We needed a spacecraft to transport the electrolysers, and they were coming anyway. We'll send the *Koppakuoria* for the next batch.'

'Where will they sleep?' said Hanna, remembering the swaying underwater towers she'd seen while snorkelling on Syenitia's west coast last year.

Björn put down his fork. 'They'll have to stay in the open sea,' he said, his expression clouding with uncertainty. 'We can drop some rudimentary sleeping quarters down for them, but I'm a bit concerned. Will they find enough to eat? What if the current washes them away and they get lost? What if some fishing boat captures them in their nets? We'll have our first interstellar diplomatic incident.'

Tima said, 'I thought you were going to prevent access for all unauthorised craft within a five-mile radius while they're here?'

'We will. Doesn't stop me worrying though.'

Hanna jumped as a plate slammed onto the table. Lucy slumped into the chair beside her. 'Did you hear?' she said to the little group, not even saying hello. Her tone was belligerent but her expression made Hanna think her friend was on the verge of tears.

'Hear what?' said Hanna, imagining terrible things.

'They've only voted to leave.' Lucy saw Hanna's confusion and added, 'The EU. The UK has voted to leave the EU.'

Is that all? Hanna managed not to say out loud. Even out of the EU, Lucy's UK passport still gave her more freedom than Hanna's Ethiopian one. Then she remembered the nightmare she'd had trying to get a Schengen visa and felt a twinge of sympathy.

Björn and Tima both exclaimed in disbelief and disappointment, and Lucy sniffed and dabbed her eyes as they offered words of comfort. It seemed this was a big deal after all. Joe arrived at the table and set his plate down next to Lucy's. 'You've seen the news?' he said, pulling out a chair. Lucy looked at him and nodded, distraught.

'Try not to take it too hard. It'll never happen for real.'

Lucy's moist eyes glinted in the light. 'You think so?' she said hopefully.

Joe shook his head. 'The vote was only advisory. Nothing will change. Whatever you might think of the Conservatives, they're not going to wilfully wreck the economy.' He picked up his fork and began shovelling down his dhal.

'I'm upset so many people voted the way they did,' said Lucy, her voice stretched thin. 'Don't they understand what a privilege it is to be in the EU? The benefits it gives us? The opportunities? Don't they *want* to be part of something bigger?'

'Perhaps they don't,' said Joe. 'I think lots of folks just took the chance to give that smug git and his mates a kicking after all their cuts to public services.' He skewered a piece of cauliflower with uncharacteristic aggression. 'Like I said, it's only advisory. You watch, Lucy. They'll start back-pedalling any day now. They can't put a hard border between Ireland and Northern Ireland without throwing the Good Friday Agreement under a bus. Breaking an international treaty would trash Britain's reputation. They're not that stupid.'

Hanna ate in silence, listening. It sounded like a big old storm in a tea-cup compared to the other things happening at the moment. Like official, undeniable first contact with aliens. Alien octopuses who were about to drop by to use the Earth as a motorway service station. Ongoing wars in, for example, Syria or, until recently, South Sudan. The refugee crises. She didn't understand why Lucy was so emotionally discombobulated by what was essentially just politics – nothing to do with real life at all.

Tima and Björn got up to go. Their places were promptly reoccupied by Kia and Rob, who arrived at the table laughing like old friends. Kia put down her plate and sat opposite Hanna.

'Guess what? I can speak Welsh!'

Hanna raised a quizzical eyebrow.

Kia looked at Rob, who made an encouraging gesture. She paused and concentrated, frowning with the effort. *'Mae fy hofrenfad yn llawn llyswennod.'*

Joe guffawed, slapping his hand on the table.

'What does it mean?' said Hanna.

'My hovercraft is full of eels,' said Joe. 'From Monty Python.'

That meant nothing to Hanna, but Lucy smiled for the first time since she'd sat down.

'Where's Yonas?' Hanna asked Kia.

'Irion's giving him a bottle. Did you sleep well?'

'Yes thanks,' said Hanna. 'Did you come back to our cabin? I didn't notice.'

Kia smirked. 'You were snoring your head off, so we left you to it.'

+ + +

ANTICIPATING THE CAPTAIN'S briefing, Hanna stood ramrod straight in the third row of pilots. They all wore their navy-blue flight suits, ready to go. To avoid getting distracted, she focused on the person in front of her and the silver design on his back: two fish, one dark, one pale, swimming head-to-tail in a circle – the emblem of the Galaksi Alliance.

Docking Bay 1 crackled with anticipation: the rest of the crew milled around, waiting to see them off. An undercurrent of excitement was buzzing through Hanna's classmates. If everything went well, this would be the mission where they qualified as *Shantivira* pilots. A pay rise and a long holiday beckoned.

Joe paced slowly along the front row, hands behind his back. 'This isn't a difficult job, but it's an important one,' he said, loud enough for them all to hear. 'We'll be flying uncloaked and the *Koppakuoria* will transmit a live video-feed to the UN. The world is watching folks, so no fuck-ups.'

He gestured towards Gambrinus, who stood at the end of the first row. 'Gambrinus and I will be in the *Koppakuoria*. We'll transmat the fish and the minerals the Pweza need to each spacecraft individually. There are only fifty ships: each gets an escort of two *Tumbas*. We'll split them into groups of ten. Group 1 will get their fish first. The others will enter the Earth's upper atmosphere one group at a time with their *Tumba* escorts to pump in the air they need.'

He reached the end of the row and turned, making his way back again.

'We have permission from the UN for ten Pweza ships and twenty *Tumbas* to enter the Earth's atmosphere at once, as long as we stay at an altitude higher than 90 kilometres,' he continued. 'You're there to ensure the Pweza don't go lower, or wander off. It should take about half an hour per group.'

'What about Björn's delivery, Captain? And the visiting Pweza engineering team?' Hassan asked. 'How will that work?'

Joe acknowledged the questions with a brief nod. He

stopped his pacing and said, 'We'll transmat the electrolysers to the *Koppakuoria* once we're done with the fish, and deliver them personally tomorrow, cloaked. Kitty will teleport Cephalo and his colleagues to the habitats Björn has set up at the base of the rig. No one on Earth will know about them, or the electrolysers. They'll be safer that way. Any other questions?'

Qingqing, Yisheng's grown-up daughter, put up her hand. 'Will we have a party after they've gone, like last time?'

Joe grinned, his shoulders loosening. 'I haven't actually thought that far ahead, Qingqing.' He glanced at the crowd behind them and exchanged a look with someone not visible to Hanna. 'I think Maneewan and Vijay might have something up their sleeves. Let's do our job first, yeah? Then we'll see. Right. Get yourselves to your ships, and good luck to us all.'

Hanna headed for Urca, turning back to face the docking bay once she'd reached her *Tumba's* lowered steps. She scanned the crowd: Kia was next to Maneewan, jiggling Yonas on her hip and waving her a cheerful goodbye. Yesterday, Hanna had explained to her how significant this mission was, and Kia had volunteered to do the whole night shift. So Hanna had spent the night in Hassan's cabin, catching up on sleep. Just as well; it was going to be a long day.

Hanna clamped on her helmet and climbed into the cockpit, sinking gratefully onto the saddle as the door closed and sealed behind her. She was looking forward to getting on with the task in hand, free from all distractions and interruptions. A task well within her abilities. She found herself smiling.

'Right Urca,' she said. 'Let's do this. Today's the day you help me qualify.'

She ran through her pre-flight checks: Mervatius, the maintenance Cylf, had made sure everything was ready. Fuel tank full, weapons charged (not that they'd need them, all being well) and coordinates set for the rendez-vous in the Earth's upper atmosphere.

In front her, the *Tumbas* were leaving the docking bay, row after row. She lifted off; hovering for a moment before heading for the opening. Twenty-one circular video feeds appeared down the side of her screen: Delius in the *Shantivira's* control room, Joe and Gambrinus in the *Koppakuoria*, and nineteen of her colleagues under the label 'Group 2'. Ooh, did that mean they'd be first into Earth's atmosphere?

The Group 2 escorts included many familiar faces. Kazembi, their leader, Lucy, Felix and Saïd from her year, Hassan, Aussie Ozzy, Emanuela and Ginika from the year above, plus some more experienced pilots she recognised too: Junko, Enrique, Qingqing, Nader and Thammanoon.

Out in space, the Pweza ships were already waiting, colossal silver sausages with a transparent dome at the front end. When Hanna zoomed in her camera, she saw human-sized blue octopuses swimming about inside. Cool.

As the *Tumbas* gathered, the ships shifted position, arranging themselves into five groups of ten. The *Koppakuoria* flew over Hanna's head and one group peeled away from the others to encircle the cargo ship. In the moonlight, they looked like shiny garden slugs surrounding a stag beetle. She'd never thought of the *Koppakuoria* as small before. The slugs had plasma guns tacked to their bellies; the *Koppakuoria* had no weapons to speak of. Joe and Delius were taking a lot on trust.

'Follow me,' said Kazembi in Hanna's earpiece, and they fell into line behind her. As they flew towards the Pweza craft closest to the Earth, Kazembi listed who'd pair up with whom. Hanna prayed to be with Hassan or Lucy, but Kazembi put the less-experienced pilots with the old hands. Hanna was with Nader, a grizzled Tunisian in his late fifties. She knew him by sight, but had never had a conversation with him. Her instinctive shyness made her feel a little awkward now.

Two by two, they flanked each of the ten cylindrical vessels, Hanna on the starboard side of the eighth craft, Nader on the port side. With Kazembi and Ginika leading the way, they headed in a line towards the Earth.

'Move to the front of your ships, people,' called Kazembi as they approached close enough for the Earth to fill Hanna's screen: a glowing blue strip of atmosphere above a sea of cloud.

'Our shields are stronger than theirs. We can give them some heat protection during atmospheric entry and reduce drag at the same time.'

Hanna tipped her saddle forwards in response, until she was a safe distance ahead of the ship's dome, side-by-side with Nader. She prayed she wouldn't mess this up.

Kazembi's voice came again in her headset. 'Now spread out so we have plenty of room. The Pweza craft will follow your lead. Take it slow: we don't want any plasma forming. Fly in long, shallow S-curves to dissipate the heat.

If you feel yourself skipping, increase your angle of descent, but watch your thermometer.'

'You OK, Hanna?' said Nader on their private channel. His fatherly smile made her suddenly glad to be with such a veteran.

'I've never entered Earth's atmosphere before,' she said.

'I know.' His moustache twitched. 'But you must have re-entered Syenitia's atmosphere a hundred times or more last year.'

'Of course.'

'This feels the same. You can do this, Hanna.' The moustache twitched again: a friendly black caterpillar with a life of its own. 'The only thing different is we have a great big space cigar to guide in.'

'And stronger gravity,' added Hanna.

'Not much stronger,' Nader reassured her in a kindly voice. 'I'm communicating with the ship behind us; it's called the *Sedna*, by the way.'

Hanna looked down at the Earth. 'You can do this,' she told herself. 'You can do this.'

They watched the seven groups ahead of them edge their way one-by-one into the fuzzy band of atmosphere, like divers descending into the blue. Then it was their turn. Sticking close to Nader, Hanna wove her way downwards, conscious of the less manoeuvrable craft following in their wake. Apart from the view, it was all rather unspectacular. An alarm bleeped: they were 92 kilometres above sea level and five minutes from the rendezvous point. The sky above was still black; below them, where the air was thicker, it had become an azure arc.

'Good,' said Nader. 'That's the hard part done.'

She saw the others ahead: seven smooth cylinders each accompanied by two prickly green spheres. They joined the row and watched as the final two Pweza craft descended to join them. 'Now we wait for them to do their thing,' said Nader.

Hanna waited. She couldn't remember the last time she'd just sat, doing nothing. Her heartbeat slowed and, bit by bit, she relaxed, staring at the blue below and remembering her snorkelling excursions at the Pweza's settlement on Syenitia. She hoped they'd find some survivors to rescue.

Ranglatiri were land-dwellers and hadn't exploited the oceans. But stripping the Pweza's planet of vegetation meant the seas became uninhabitable too. This was why the Pweza had evacuated, in a desperate dash across the galaxy. They were returning as soon as they could, but it was a race against time.

At least some of them had escaped. Unlike the Amranese, she thought, before her mind swerved away from the topic. There was nothing she could do about it. There was no point in dwelling helplessly on the horrors Aneira's people must be facing.

Her headset pinged, drawing her back to the here and now. In Hanna's ear, Kazembi said, 'They're all done; we can head back. We'll take a much steeper angle this time. Our *Tumbas* know the amount of power needed to achieve escape velocity.'

Hanna stuck to Nader's side like a burr as they rose up

through the thinning layers of gas. With her back to her planet, it felt exactly like taking off from the flight school in Essoona for training in a low Syenitia orbit. Familiar. Routine. She relaxed a little. They arrived back at the rendezvous and Group 3 peeled away to make their descent. The *Koppakuoria* was still surrounded by Group 1: it seemed the transmatting was the bottleneck in the process. They waited. Ten minutes. Twenty. Then the circle around the beetle broke up and returned to the rows of silver ships. Kazembi said, 'Right, Group 2, our turn. Flank your Pweza craft while they get their fish.'

They approached the *Koppakuoria*: so close that, when Joe threw back his head and laughed, Hanna could see the movement in the beetle's transparent cockpit. She remained starboard of the *Sedna* and waited, debating whether to open a private channel with Hassan for a chat. She decided against it. She didn't want to get him into trouble or jeopardise her chances of qualifying.

Her stomach rumbled and she eyed her bag on the floor. It was early for lunch, but nobody would mind if she ate now, would they? Judging by Group 1, she'd be waiting here for nearly an hour.

'Urca? I'm getting my bag, OK?' She unfastened her harness and retrieved it before returning to her seat as quickly as she could, checking to see Urca hadn't moved. The saddle-joysticks used to steer the *Tumbas* were highly responsive. Just getting on and off could move the craft if you weren't careful.

Tulu, her training *Tumba*, would have held still automatically, but Urca wasn't as perceptive. She was faster and more powerful, but less in tune with her pilot. Where

Tulu would seize the initiative, instinctively knowing what Hanna wanted, Urca required clear instructions. Hanna hadn't quite mastered the art of giving them.

She opened the metal box, curious to see what Maneewan's team had prepared for the pilots. Rolex with spinach, tomato and red onions. Excellent. She hadn't eaten Ugandan rolex since her trip to meet Hassan's foster parents. The omelette was cooked perfectly, the chapati soft and fresh. She bit into the street food, catching the excess moisture with her napkin.

She ate the first two halves, promising herself she'd save the second two for later. Then she ate those as well. Mmm. She was just unscrewing the lid of her bottle, when Nader said in her headset, 'How are you doing, Hanna? Did you enjoy your meal?'

'Yes thanks,' she said, realising that of course everyone on her screen had seen her eat. But she'd been hungry. 'Do you think they'll be much longer?' she asked.

'The *Sedna* has received its load. Two more ships to go, then we're done.'

Hanna sipped her water and waited. At last, Kazembi announced the transmat operation was complete. 'Return to your original positions and wait for the other ships to finish. It'll be at least another three hours before they're ready for their onward journey. I hope you all brought something to read!'

Hanna had plenty of books, music and videos on her *zana*. But once they were back in the row of waiting ships, she found the novelty of peaceful, uninterrupted head-space a greater temptation. She ate the chocolate brownie they'd been given for dessert. And the apple to clean her teeth, wishing she had a flask of coffee to wash it all down. But they weren't allowed hot drinks in their *Tumbas*.

Now the others were all concentrating on their own food, Hanna took the opportunity to relieve herself. The cockpit camera was trained on the pilot's face, so nobody could see if you were weeing. Still, she preferred to do it while the rest of the group were distracted.

She unzipped her flight suit and pressed the button under her seat to extend the sanitary funnel, shuffling forward to put it in place. She watched with satisfaction as the pointer on Urca's fuel gauge swung further into the green. Ah. That was better.

Hanna dimmed the interior lights and leaned against her backrest. Warm and comfortable, she let her mind wander. She thought of last night with Hassan, and the restorative powers of a good night's sleep. He was right. She should get her act together and organise more night-time help for Yonas. They couldn't carry on as they were. As much as she loved him, he was Kia's baby, not hers. She needed to take a step back.

Anyway, now she was about to qualify, she ought to take the chance to recharge her batteries before fully committing to her *Shantivira* duties. She'd been neglecting them lately, but Joe had been very understanding, bless him.

So. A holiday. Kia would be fine on the *Shantivira* if she and Hassan went away for a long weekend. A week, even, perhaps . . . Somewhere warm, relaxed and easy to reach from London. She'd love to visit the Caribbean. Bit far though. Unless – brainwave – would Kitty give them a lift and save them a long-haul flight? Just this once? She imagined herself walking along a palm-fringed beach, hand-in-hand with Hassan. She closed her eyes, the better to focus on the pictures forming in her mind.

+ + +

'HANNA!'
'BEEP!'
'HANNA!'
'BEEP!'
'HANNA!'
'BEEP!'
'*HANNA!*'

Hanna woke with a jump. The proximity alarm on the control panel was beeping and flashing red, and the faces on her screen were all yelling at her. She could see their mouths moving, but it was only Kazembi's voice in her headset. That was loud enough.

She glanced at the rest of the screen, confused because it had gone blank. Normally it went black when it was off. Why was it grey? Oh *SHIT*. She was so close to the *Sedna*; it was all she could see!

Instinctively, she flung herself away from the Pwezan ship, her heart pounding as it grew smaller. That had been a close one. Surely Urca's shields would have prevented the *Tumba* damaging the *Sedna's* hull if they'd come too near?

'What the actual *fuck*, Hanna?' yelled Kazembi. 'You fell asleep without telling your *Tumba* to hold position?'

A sudden lump of emotion in Hanna's throat made it hard to speak. 'I—I must have done. I must have tipped the seat and started drifting.' She blinked away tears, resisting the urge to drag the back of her hand across her face. 'Sorry,' she added in a small voice. 'I was tireder than I thought.'

Kazembi's tone softened. 'At least we managed to wake you in time. I have to warn you though: Joe's furious. You're lucky the *Sedna*'s between you and the camera on the *Koppakuoria*: no one on Earth will realise we nearly had an avoidable crash. Otherwise, they'd never take Joe or the *Shantivira* seriously. And why should they? Honestly, Hanna. What were you *thinking*?'

Hanna said nothing. There was nothing *to* say. She hung her head, fuming at Urca for not having the sense to hold position. Tulu would have. Stupid Urca. Stupid. Stupid. Stupid Hanna. It was her own fault. Her responsibility. Not Urca's, for responding to the slight movement of the saddle. Stupid Urca. Stupid Hanna. Stupid.

Finally, the hour to return to the *Shantivira* came. Simultaneously relieved and apprehensive, Hanna flew Urca into Docking Bay 1 and set her down on her fuelling port. When she descended the steps, Hassan was already waiting for her. He said nothing, just enfolded her in his long, strong arms while she sobbed into his navy-blue flight suit.

At last, she came up for air and looked around. The other groups had landed and the pilots were milling about, shaking hands and hugging each other. The rest of her year had gathered in a circle to celebrate qualifying as *Shantivira* pilots by dancing the Hokey-Cokey with much laughter and cheering. Hanna couldn't bear to face them.

Gambrinus approached. From his demeanour, Hanna

could tell he already knew of her shame. Soon everyone would.

'Hanna?' he said. 'Joe wants to see you in Docking Bay 3.'

Oh no. Hanna dipped her head in meek acknowledgment, struggling silently with her surging anxiety. Best get this over with before it paralysed her completely. She started to move.

Hassan grabbed her arm. 'Do you want me to come with you?'

Hanna considered briefly. 'No. Thanks.' She rearranged her expression to simulate resolute courage. 'I have to do this by myself.'

She turned her back on him and headed for the apex of the hall, her body suddenly heavy, as if it were trying to slow her down. Her pulse thundered in her ears and Hanna prayed she wouldn't faint. She rounded the cylindrical control room and walked towards the *Pride of Essoona*, where Joe was waiting for her, sitting on the lowered steps, his arm across jaguar-Kitty's back. He stood as Hanna approached, a complicated expression on his face.

'Hello, Hanna,' he said. 'You fell *asleep*. On *DUTY*.'

'Yes,' she croaked, unable to meet his eye. She bowed her head. 'I'm sorry, Joe.'

'I cannot *begin* to tell you how disappointed I am. This was a super easy way to qualify.' He folded his arms. 'And you of all people, messed it up!'

'I know,' she whispered. If only she could run away and hide in a deep, dark hole until the end of time. 'I'm sorry.'

'You're bloody lucky the incident wasn't caught on camera for all the journalists to see. We'd never have lived it down.' He shook his head in bewilderment. 'Months – years – of work down the drain all because *you* haven't been looking after yourself. I'd have had to sack you.' He smiled faintly. 'And I really don't want to.'

So he *wasn't* going to sack her? A butterfly of hope fluttered in Hanna's belly. Beside her, jaguar-Kitty's head pushed up under her hand, renewing her strength.

'So—what happens now?' she asked.

'You get your life in order, Hanna,' Joe said sternly. 'Accept the help people are offering you and Kia. Stop trying to do it all yourself.' He threw his hands in the air in exasperation. 'Or *do* it all yourself, if that's what you want, but give up any notion of working as a pilot at the same time. It won't work. You can't do both. Adjust your expectations. Yonas isn't a newborn anymore. Life moves on.'

She nodded, still staring at her boots and the white floor. But the tightness in her chest had eased. Surreptitiously, she stroked the fur on jaguar-Kitty's head. She was going to be OK.

'I need to be sure of your full commitment, Hanna,' Joe insisted. 'Otherwise, I'm putting the rest of the crew at risk. If you don't do better on your next mission, you're out, do you understand?'

'I understand,' she murmured. Jaguar-Kitty left her side and padded back to Joe.

'Now, get to your cabin,' Joe said. 'I don't want to see you again until I've calmed down.'

16. AN INDECENT PROPOSAL
DAN

'THAT'S THE LAST box,' said Dan, passing it to Afra who was carefully arranging their precious cargo in the hold. To make the trip worthwhile, they had to cram the *Gezi Urdina* with as many pills as they could carry. Millions and millions of them. Even his *stakarh* training area had been pressed into service. He'd have to be careful not to damage the stacks of crates during his daily practice.

'Thanks,' she said, slotting it into place. She picked up her stick again, taking the weight off her bad leg while she stood back to admire her handiwork. 'I hope we'll have enough room for our own supplies. Will you do the shopping after lunch?'

'Tomorrow, before we go. I have a little treat planned first.'

Like Earth and Syenitia – and unlike Sayari – Oso-Urrun was an ocean-dominated planet. In Aldina, Dan had watched the boats crossing the harbour with longing. He'd wanted to share the sheer joy of being out on the water with Afra, but she hadn't been fit enough, so he'd said nothing.

Afra arched a curious eyebrow.

'We deserve a break. I'm taking you sailing.'

'*What?*' Afra looked doubtful.

'I've rented a boat.'

The pharmaceutical factory was on the edge of a small tourist town next to a large salt-water lagoon. Dan had done his research during the week they'd been there. There were pretty islands, no tides and a light but steady wind. A safe place to take a first-timer.

Consequently, the boat rental shop had been – in Dan's opinion – extremely relaxed about his sailing credentials, which he'd been unable to prove. Then again, they'd assumed he was Syenitian and had grown up by the water. Which he had, of course: just in Boston, Massachusetts.

'A *boat*?' she echoed. 'Sailing? That's . . . without an engine, right?'

'Right. I've made us a picnic.'

Her eyes sparkled. 'You're full of surprises, aren't you?'

'I hope so,' said Dan. It was all part of his Big Romantic Plan.

AN HOUR LATER they parked the bikes they'd borrowed from Afra's factory contact next to a boardwalk landing stage. The boat Dan had rented was waiting for them. The *Boeng Kai* was twenty feet long and six feet wide, the wooden hull painted with pea-green fish scales and a pair of eyes at the front. Afra's ears waggled with delight and she clambered aboard eagerly.

There were three turquoise sails: a jib, a mainsail and a

mizzen at the back. No boom, but that was OK. Dan wasn't planning on sailing close to the wind today. A liftable centreboard meant they wouldn't run aground in the shallow parts of the lagoon. He slung the food into the locker under the seat and pulled out two life vests. He passed the blue one to Afra, who wrinkled her nose. 'It smells of mildew.'

'Put it on,' he said in a no-nonsense voice. 'It'll keep you afloat if you fall in.'

'Aye-aye, Captain,' she replied in a sarcastic tone, but complied good-naturedly.

Dan fumbled with the sails, working out what went where. 'I'm a bit rusty,' he admitted, 'but it's like riding a bike.'

Bemused, Afra studied the centreboard casing with the oars neatly stowed on either side. 'Why? Does it have pedals?'

Soon they were cutting along nicely, sails full. The breeze was a little stronger than in the forecast and the sensation of speed so close to the water thrilled Afra. Dan put her at the front, in charge of the jib, and explained how to tack: travelling against the wind in a leisurely zig-zag. He didn't know any sailing vocabulary in Kawaida, so he taught her the terms in English.

She quickly learnt to prepare the sail to switch sides in response to his call of 'Ready about' and to trim it after they'd changed direction. Dan relaxed and began enjoying himself: one hand on the tiller, the other fingering the small box in his pocket. It held the ring he'd been carrying since they'd left Syenitia, patiently waiting for him to find the right moment and work up sufficient courage.

He'd found it in a second-hand store and known instantly it was perfect: a sparkling blue gem set in a glistening white valkoinium band. It had cost him four thousand Aldina dinar – everything he'd managed to save while working aboard the *Gezi Urdina*. He was sure it would be worth every cent.

The island ahead grew. What had been fuzzy strips of green and gold crystalised into individual trees and bushes bordering a deserted beach. That was their picnic spot. 'Afra? Keep an eye out for underwater rocks. We're stopping for lunch.'

'OK.' She leaned over the bow, her blue braids cascading over her shoulder.

Dan let the wind out of the mainsail and pulled up the centreboard. The little boat beached and he jumped out, tugging it further up and attaching a line round a tree stump so it wouldn't drift away without them. He helped Afra disembark and returned for the food and wine.

He unfolded the picnic blanket with a flourish and unpacked his wares. Afra squealed with pleasure as he brought out treat after treat: as many of her favourites as he'd been able to find on the remote planet. The water lapping the shore was like the sound of breathing, rhythmic and calming. He could do this. No need to be nervous. The *Boeng Kai's* port-side eye seemed to stare at him and he imagined it winking, sharing his secret.

Afra had eagerly scoffed half a wheel of soft cheese before he had time to pour the wine. Real glasses. No need to drop standards.

'It's fizzy!' she exclaimed. 'Are we celebrating something?'

Dan twinkled at her. 'Maybe. Eat your lunch.' He bit into his steak and radish sandwich. Man, that was good. They ate everything, including the *embwaki* fruit pastries Dan had brought for dessert, and finished the wine. Replete and a little drunk, they lay back on the blanket and watched the clouds scudding across the sky.

Afra turned on her side to face him, her intelligent brown eyes studying his. She reached out and stroked his cheek affectionately. 'Tell me then, Dan. What's all this in aid of?'

Dan pressed her fingers to his lips and got up on one knee. This was it. The moment he'd waited months for. How would she react? Would she be head-over-heels-delighted? Or just cautiously pleased? Heart thumping, he pulled the box out of his pocket and passed it to her. 'This is for you.'

She opened it and her brow furrowed with confusion. 'It's lovely, Dan. But you know I don't wear rings. They get in the way when I'm fixing machinery.'

'You don't have to wear it when you're working. I'm asking you to marry me, Afra. Will you be my wife?'

A hand flew to her mouth. Oh no. Had he embarrassed her?

'You're serious, aren't you?' she said, studying his expression. She sat up abruptly. 'While I was in hospital, I read everything I could find about Dunians in the Syenitian archives.' She spoke slowly, choosing her words with care. 'As I understand it, marriage – in your culture – publicly signifies the ownership of a female of childbearing age passing from her father to her husband. That's slavery, Dan.'

Dan shook his head. 'Maybe in the olden days. Not anymore.'

She pulled away from him and stood. 'Perhaps not officially. But I read that, on your planet, females in formal partnerships perform most of the domestic tasks in addition to their paid work.'

Dan stood too. 'Hey! *I* do all the housework. You don't even *notice* what needs doing. Why would that change if we were married?' He heard Bellyn's voice in his head: the time he'd said, 'Afra's a typical female. She keeps the ship running beautifully, but I sswear she thinks the cooking and cleaning and shopping happen all by themselves.'

They glared at each other over the remains of their picnic. In a frosty tone, Afra said, 'I researched *your* customs. Did you research *mine*?'

Dan studied the sand at his feet. 'No.'

'Sayari don't marry publicly like Dunians, Dan. We pair for life, but the commitment we make is to each other. Morally binding, but not legally binding. If you truly loved me, you'd have found that out already. You ignorant, patriarchal *primitive*!' She threw the ring box back at him in fury and frustration, then turned and limped away from him, head held high. She'd left her walking stick in the boat, of course.

He ran after her. 'Afra! Wait! I just want to spend my life with you.'

'You *are* spending your life with me! I gave you a *memory stone*, dammit! Didn't you understand what that *meant*? What more of a commitment do you *want*?'

A moist splat hit Dan's cheek and he reached up to

touch it. What? The sky had darkened to a lowering steel-grey mass, directly overhead. That wasn't supposed to happen. They'd been sheltered by the island but, with the wind coming from behind it, he hadn't noticed the approaching storm. Now it was too late. They were going to get wet.

'Afra!' he called again. 'We have to go!'

She heard the change in his voice, stopped and turned.

He pointed at the sky. 'Before it gets too bad.' Not waiting for her, he ran back and scooped up their lunch things. He threw the bag into the boat and helped Afra aboard before untying the line from the stump. He pressed his spine against the bow and dug his feet into the sand, pushing with all his might. Finally, the keel slid away from him. He shoved the boat until it floated freely, then splashed into the water, soaking his shoes and trousers. One athletic leap had him back on board.

'Life vest,' he barked at Afra, as he zipped up his own and grabbed the oars. Years of childhood practice were coming back to him and his muscles knew exactly what to do. Skilfully he swung the *Boeng Kai* round and, with a few strong strokes, they were soon far enough from the beach to drop the centreboard and raise the sails.

Plop. Another spot of rain landed on his face, fatter and heavier this time. Plop. And another. Plop. Plop. Plop. Plop. It was officially raining. The drops became larger and closer together, splashing noisily as they hit the water, turning the smooth surface jagged as far as Dan could see. Which wasn't very far. The island had become a misty smudge behind the deluge.

He stowed the oars and took the tiller. Tacking

wouldn't be necessary – it was downwind all the way to the jetty. The poor visibility didn't perturb Dan. He'd brought a compass and had no problem sailing on a bearing.

He let the sails fill, skimming along as fast as he dared, racing the wind to the shore. The rain bucketed down and Afra huddled forlorn in the bow, knees to her chest, wet hair plastered in blue stripes across her silver face. It was impossible to tell if she was crying or just soaked.

What had happened? Dan asked himself. They should be laughing together, despite the awful weather. How had his plan gone so wrong?

His hand gripping the tiller was almost Ranglatiri-white with cold. Unwavering, he steered towards the land, hoping there wouldn't be a thunderstorm. Please not one with lightening.

How were they going to work together on the journey ahead? Weeks on end, unable to avoid each other? He prayed he hadn't lost her. If only Bellyn were here to mediate.

At last they reached the landing stage: a pair of washed-up, half-drowned rats. Dan sprang onto the jetty and made the little boat fast at bow and stern. He helped Afra off, longing to enfold her in his arms and bury his face in her hair, but didn't dare.

The wind dropped, but the rain still fell relentlessly, in straight, solid rods. He narrowed his eyes at the clouds above. Conditions weren't going to improve anytime soon. The bike ride home was going to be miserable.

Afra released his helping hand and said, 'Dan?'

'Yes?'

'Sleep in your own cabin tonight, please. I need to be alone. I need to think.'

'Sure,' said Dan, trying to sound nonchalant. 'If that's what you want.'

17. A TRIP DOWN THE M4
JOE, JULY 13, 2016

JOE WAS WALKING across Kalakaivo square in central Essoona, headed for the Council Chambers, when Kitty tapped at his consciousness.

Hey babe, what's up?

Joe?

Something in her voice made him stop and lift his head. *What?*

I'm at your house. Grace isn't here.

What do you mean?

I came to dig up the new potatoes for her. We agreed a time and everything. I'm sure I don't have the wrong day. Her handbag's still on the kitchen table.

Grace never went anywhere without her hideous red handbag. It was probably the most expensive thing she owned. *So where is she?* Joe said, puzzled.

I'm looking, said Kitty, scanning for Grace's biosignature. *She's on the M4, near Swindon. Travelling east, fast.*

Why would she be heading for London? *Something's up*, he said. *Go and check it out, love. Show me through your eyes, will you?*

Will do.

She cut the connection and was gone. Joe walked over

to the fountain and sat on the edge, facing the *Ohimo* at the far end of the square. Its roof tiles sparkled like emeralds in the bright sunshine. He checked the time on his *zana*: he had more than half an hour before his meeting started. He'd been intending to visit a few people in their offices for a chat first, but that could wait.

Kitty reconnected, filling his head with a live feed of what she saw. She was crouching on top of a black SUV, travelling on the motorway which sliced through the ancient chalk downs in a direct line to the capital. Through the sunroof, he could see his mother on the back seat, sandwiched between two bulky males in dark suits. She looked tiny and frightened.

What are you going to do? he asked.

Kitty deliberated. *If I teleport her out of there, I'll cause an accident. Other people will get hurt. Oh crap, they've seen me.*

Below, the men were pointing up at Kitty and shouting. The vehicle began swerving from side to side in an attempt to dislodge her. Inside the car, Grace screamed.

Idiots, Kitty muttered.

Joe's perspective changed and broadened as Kitty stood up and shifted. Now she was facing their direction of travel and they were lifting above the road, above the trees, higher. At the corner of his vision, he could see her leathery red wings beating steadily, straining to gain altitude while carrying two-and-a-half tonnes of vehicle. The downs unfurled beneath them, a green-brown patchwork of fields stretching as far as he could see. She peeled away from the motorway, heading for an oval formation on a hill to the south.

Hillfort? he asked.

Liddington Camp, she agreed. *Late bronze age. There was a big battle here once. We won.*

Dragon-Kitty set the SUV down gently in the centre of the earthworks and landed. The side windows had all shattered where her claws had gripped the roof. She shifted into her space demon form, extending red scaly arms to rip off the rear door. She tossed it away carelessly, like a litter lout chucking fast food packaging out of a moving car.

The men inside opened fire with semi-automatic pistols. Terrified, Grace shrank into her seat, hands over her ears. Kitty glanced at the cloud of lead slugs collecting in front of her chest then, when their magazines had emptied, swatted them dismissively to one side. They fell onto the grass with a dull rattle.

She reached into the vehicle and hauled the closest kidnapper out by the arm, throwing him easily towards the rampart encircling them. Joe winced as he heard the man thud to the ground with a shriek of pain. That had to hurt.

In Kitty reached again, this time for Grace. She shifted to her Syenitian form, the sleeves of her medieval dress trailing crimson inside the SUV's dark interior. 'Are you coming, Grace?'

His mam nodded, shuffling along the back bench to the opening, trying to avoid the tiny chunks of safety glass which, minutes ago, had been solid windows. The other man grabbed her arm, preventing her.

In English, Kitty growled, 'Let her go NOW, or I'll break your neck.'

The driver crunched the gears and revved the engine in a flurry of panic. Kitty flicked her wrist and before the car could move, it lifted off the ground, wheels spinning helplessly centimetres above the grass.

Kitty scowled. 'I'm not kidding. None of you are going anywhere until you give me back my mother-in-law. Come on, Grace.'

Grace took her hand and this time the guard didn't try to stop her. Kitty switched back to Welsh. 'That's it, nearly there.' When Grace's feet touched the turf, Kitty said, 'Now close your eyes.'

Grace obeyed. Joe didn't, hoping he'd see what Kitty saw when she teleported. He'd always been curious. Disappointingly, she severed their connection and he found himself back in the real world, staring down at the glinting white flagstones under his boots.

He waited, watching the passersby on Kalakaivo Square as they went about their business. Syenitians, Wadudu, Sayari, Grookas, Tarumbets, Mhasibu: a cosmopolitan cross-section of interstellar civilisation. Minutes passed and, finally, Kitty re-established contact.

Everything OK? he asked silently.

Sure. Your mum's waiting for you on the Pride, replied Kitty. *Go to your meeting, she'll be fine for a couple of hours.*

The idea of his mother unsupervised in his home unsettled Joe. *Can't you stay with her?* he asked, without much hope.

I'm after the kidnappers, explained Kitty. *They're trying to work out how to get out of the fort without landing upside-down in the ditch.* She giggled. *It's funny to watch.*

She shared what she was seeing and Joe couldn't help smiling. The top-heavy SUV hung precariously on the steep narrow track which was the fort's only exit point, and the three men inside were all shouting at each other. Their four-wheel drive would ensure they'd make it down eventually, but not without harming the ancient monument.

You going to take them all to your 'interview suite'? he asked.

Kitty's secret lair was deep inside a mountain, not far from the *Cath Palug*. Nobody got in – or out – without being teleported by the Lady of the Lake herself.

I'll take two, then I'll help the driver back on the road before he does any damage. He can go back with his tail between his legs and report to his masters.

And you'll be watching to see who that is?

Yup. See you back on the Pride, *cariad,* she said.

OK, Cath. *Have fun with your catch.* A note of caution entered Joe's voice. *Remember, you'll need to let them go in one piece after you've found out all you can.*

I know. But they don't know that, do they? Kitty gave a comedy-sinister laugh and cut the connection.

Those kidnappers were about to have a very bad day, thought Joe. Good.

✦   ✦   ✦

LATER, JOE RETURNED from Essoona to find his mother in his galley kitchen, making Welsh cakes on a bakestone he hadn't known he owned.

'Hello, Joe, how was your day?'

'Mam!' He dumped his bag on the table and crossed the room towards her. Then stopped. He wasn't ready to hug her yet. He wasn't sure how he felt about having her on the *Shantivira*. Let alone here, in his inner sanctum. He preferred her at a safe distance, separate to his real life. This was too close for comfort.

'Cup of tea?'

'Thanks,' he said. 'I see you've made yourself at home.'

'Might as well make myself useful.' She busied herself with the kettle. 'Nice place you've got here,' she said.

'Thanks.' He blobbed some jam onto a Welsh cake. 'Mmm. These are good!'

'They're always better when they're still warm.'

Joe pulled out a chair and sat at the table. 'Are you alright? Really?'

Grace placed a mug in front of him and sat down herself. 'It wasn't Nestor, was it?'

'I doubt it,' said Joe. 'Kitty warned him off pretty thoroughly after you left. We'll know more after she's interviewed your kidnappers.' He paused, wondering how much to say. 'I think the timing's significant.'

'Why?' Grace was mystified.

'Don't you listen to the news?' he said, taking a gulp of his tea and immediately wrinkling his nose in distaste. It wasn't strong enough. Grace had taken the teabag out too quickly. 'The UK's looking the other way today. The old prime minister's gone, the new one's just arrived. I can't believe either of them knew about this.' Joe replaced his mug on its coaster. He couldn't drink that milky dishwater. 'I suspect it's some darker agency behind the scenes, taking advantage of the distraction Brexit is causing. Don't you have the feeling nobody's in charge of the country at the moment?'

Grace shrugged. 'I don't follow politics. I'm just happy we got our sovereignty back,' she said, without a trace of irony. 'All that extra money for the NHS will do a world of good.'

Joe resisted the urge to bang his head on the table. Had she honestly fallen for those obvious lies?

Grace hadn't finished. Seeing his expression, she said, 'You don't live there. Britain doesn't work anymore. We don't have enough houses, or schools, or doctors to cope with all these foreigners coming in.' She sniffed. 'I've nothing against them personally, mind. But it's a small island with limited resources. Something had to change.'

'Yeah,' said Joe, gloomily, 'Change for the worse. Things can always get worse.'

They sat in silence. Grace drank her tea and Joe re-strained himself from voicing his own opinion – that the government had deliberately run public services into the ground so they could sell them off to their mates in the corporate sector. It wouldn't solve anything, and Grace had already had a rough day. He released a heartfelt sigh. 'I'm afraid you'll have to stay on the *Shantivira* until we get this sorted,' he said.

Grace groaned. 'Who'll water my plants? When can I go home?'

'I don't know, Mam.' Joe stood up. 'Come on. I'll show you around and we'll find you a cabin.'

After a lightning tour of Level Zero, Joe found Grace a berth close to the entrance to the temperate biome. He explained how the shower and toilet worked, competing for her attention with the view of Asia from the window. He said, 'If you make a list of what you need, Kitty can bring your stuff later.'

Grace sat on the bed. 'I'm dying for a ciggy, lad. Where I can get some?'

Uh oh. With everything that had happened today, he hadn't given a moment's thought to her long-standing addiction. She wasn't going to like this one bit. 'Um, so, the whole base is No Smoking, Mam,' he said.

'You're joking!' Her cheeks flushed. Joe could almost see the cogs in her brain turning as she contemplated getting through the coming weeks without nicotine.

'Sorry,' Joe continued. He wasn't really. 'You'll to have to do without. Someone might have some patches. I'll ask around.'

'Patches?' Her eyebrows shot up in almost-comical horror. 'But I don't want to give up smoking,' she said, her voice an octave higher than normal. 'I love smoking!'

'You can't smoke here, Mam,' Joe insisted. 'It messes up our filters. It's just until we know it's safe for you to go back to Brecon.'

'And how long'll *that* be?'

'Weeks? Months? I don't *know*, Mam.' Just then, he had a small brainwave. 'Wait here a sec, will you?'

Joe hurried out of the cabin and knocked on the neighbouring door. He returned a few minutes later with a plump Native American lady approximately the same age as Grace.

He said in English, 'This is Chooli, Mam. Chooli, this is my mother, Grace.'

Grace stood and Chooli shook her hand. 'Please to

215

meet, you, Ma'am.'

'Chooli's our Stores Manager,' Joe said. 'She's kindly agreed to look out for you while you're here. She'll show you round properly and introduce you to people. In return, perhaps you can help her with her work?'

'No problem,' said Grace. 'I prefer keeping busy. After all, the Devil finds work for idle hands, doesn't he?'

Chooli laughed, a warm, throaty expression of amusement. 'He don't get a look-in round here! We all have plenty to do. I'm happy for any assistance you can offer, Ma'am.'

'Grace, please,' said Grace. 'Where are you from, Chooli?'

'Gallup, New Mexico, originally. Uranium mining country. I've been up here for more than twenty years now, though.'

'Oh, really?' Grace's politeness turned to genuine interest. 'My late husband was a miner; did Joe ever tell you?'

Chooli gave Joe a penetrating stare. 'No, he did *not*. My late husband was a miner, too.'

Joe took a step back. 'Well, I'll let you two ladies get to know each other,' he said. 'I'll see you later, Mam.'

'Yes, dear. Thank you. And—I'd be grateful if you could track me down some of those patches.'

'I'll see what I can do.'

As he turned away, he heard Grace ask Chooli, 'Kitty told me you grow food up here. Outside? Would you show me? Joe doesn't have time to give me the full tour today.'

He stepped into the lift to return to the *Pride*. Kitty materialised next to him as the door closed, making him jump, then smile. He pulled her close and they enjoyed a brief snog before arriving at the docking bay.

How'd it go? he asked her silently as they walked arm-in-arm back to his ship.

I followed the driver to Thames House.

MI5, then? He'd suspected as much.

She nodded. *Looks like it. I didn't manage to touch him, so I won't be able to track him like the others.*

Did you find out his name?

Kitty made a face. *He stopped at Membury services and I eavesdropped on his calls. He used the name Norman Smith. Could've been an alias. He wanted to leave the SUV and get picked up, but they told him to bring it back to London. The police stopped him because of the missing rear door, but he flashed his ID card and they let him go. I couldn't glimpse it, unfortunately.*

Joe rubbed the stubble on his jaw, thinking. *You have the time and location. See if you can get Delius to trace the call. We need those phone numbers.*

Will do, Boss, said Kitty.

What about the other two? he asked.

I'm letting them stew in the dark. I'll go back after the bats have woken up.

Standard Kitty procedure. *OK,* Joe said. *If they're connected to the British government, we'll have to pause all the courses.*

That's the deal, Kitty agreed. *Any attacks on Shantivirans or their families and we withdraw all cooperation. The aid deliveries, too. We must show we mean it.*

Joe sighed. *Yep. I know.* Quickly, he assembled a mental to-do list. *We should warn Rob we'll probably be stopping his visits. Can you drop him home before you go back to Snowdonia?*

Sure. Will you inform the UN? Her expression said 'Joe, you *must* inform the UN.'

I will, Joe said. He wasn't looking forward to that job one bit. *And Aldeman*, he added. The shame Joe felt about the antics of his fellow humans made him even more reluctant to do that. He hated disappointing Aldeman. *But before I do anything, I want to know for sure who those goons in your cave are.*

✦   ✦   ✦

ALDEMAN FOLDED HIS arms behind his back and stared out to sea, the wind whipping strands of black hair across his face. Standing beside him, Joe fought the urge to lift a hand and brush them away, like he'd do for Kitty.

'*Perkele!*' Aldeman swore.

'I know,' said Joe. 'And things were going so well.'

'How is your mother?' said Aldeman, turning to face Joe. 'How did she take it?'

Joe thrust his hands deep into the pockets of his jeans. 'She was shocked, naturally. But she's changed. Opened up. I hate to admit it, but her time in Argentina did her good. She and Kitty have reached some kind of under-standing – to the point where I feel a bit excluded, to be honest. She's making friends on the *Shantivira*, getting stuck in to all the jobs that need doing.' Joe laughed at the ironies of life. 'She used to be terrified of anyone who looked different to her. People with dark skin. Young women wearing headscarves. Even people with disabilities.'

Aldeman pursed his lips. 'I can imagine, in the life she had before, she did not *know* many people who looked different to her.'

'Exactly. Now she's got to know some as individuals, she's realised humans all have the same hopes and dreams, wherever we come from.'

'All life forms fear the unknown. It is natural.' Aldeman placed a warm hand on Joe's arm. 'She is *your* mother, Joe. And *you* are the most open person I know. She always had it in her. She just needed the opportunity for a change of perspective.'

Joe grunted and studied the rolling waves to the east. The sun was still relatively high above the water, but he knew from experience the closer it sank to the horizon, the faster it seemed to move. They had perhaps an hour of daylight left.

'Let us walk,' said Aldeman, striding away along the beach towards the green-and-white lighthouse on the headland. Joe followed, trying to stay on the strip of sand which was compacted and easy to walk on, but not too wet.

After some time, Aldeman said, 'Tell me more about these kidnappers.'

'There's not much more to tell,' Joe said. 'When Kitty questioned them, they were blissfully ignorant of precisely who they were working for. Part of their contract, I'm sure. Ex-special forces, not currently employed by the British Government. We're watching their bank accounts, but I suspect they won't be getting paid.' He smiled grimly.

'They didn't finish the job, after all. Mam got away. Kitty delivered them to Swindon police station and Mam made a statement. There were plenty of witnesses on the motorway. Perhaps it'll come to something.'

'And the vehicle?'

'The vehicle's registered to the British Security Services. I've talked to the new prime minister and she's promised to make enquiries.' Joe stooped to pick up a perfect pink shell which fitted pleasingly in the palm of his hand. 'It looks like a set-up to me,' he continued. 'They want us to think it's the British Government so we don't look any further. But it's in chaos at the moment, because of that referendum I told you about.' He tucked the shell into his back pocket. 'I think whoever organised this seized the chance to make the most of that confusion for their own ends. Perhaps some low-profile organisation acting on behalf of the fossil fuel industry? Our demands for the Earth to change its economic system are a direct threat to established power structures. I've been expecting some kind of pushback for months.'

Aldeman prodded a dead, washed-up jellyfish disdainfully with the toe of his boot.

'It does not matter who sent them,' he said. 'The point is, Earth's authorities must understand the consequences. That the malevolent actions of one rogue group disadvantages them all. Then they will police themselves.'

'Yes,' said Joe. 'We've paused the whole knowledge transfer programme for all countries. Let them miss it for a while. Let resentment against the UK build. Once the governments involved recognise they can't manoeuvre in the shadows without everyone losing access, we should be able to restart them without endangering the families of *Shantivira* crew members.'

Joe gave a wry smile. 'The prime minister was pretty pissed off her government has lost their coveted back channel to the *Shantivira* the same day she started her new job – and that the international community already knows why. Not a good start, on top of all her other problems.'

'What does Major Morgan say?'

'Rob?' said Joe. Poor Rob. He'd gone completely white and collapsed into a chair when Joe had told him he couldn't visit the *Shantivira* again. Rob had been betrayed as much as the rest of them. 'He's gutted. Furious, too. Considering handing in his papers and getting another job. He reckons some high-ups in the army believe he's biased in our favour and wanted the cooperation stopped.'

'Is that likely?' Aldeman frowned.

Joe shrugged. 'Dunno. Like you said, the consequences are more important than who triggered them. There's always going to be someone out there with a grudge. They need to know it's not worth acting on, or the Shantivirans on Earth'll never be safe.'

They reached the end of the beach and climbed the rocks to the base of the lighthouse. Panting slightly from the effort, they rested against the sun-warmed wall and watched the day turn to twilight. There was a grinding, creaking noise behind them and a vibration in Joe's spine as the lighthouse began its nightshift.

'I heard Rowan's news,' said Joe, standing on a step so his head was level with Aldeman's. 'That's good, isn't it?'

According to Kitty, Rowan had infiltrated the Ranglatiri Council and become a minor member herself, going by the name of Reinecka. Thanks to the violent nature of Ranglatiri dispute resolution, she was hoping her promotion to the top table would be rapid.

'Hmm. Yes. I suppose so.' Aldeman turned to Joe and said quietly, 'I miss her. We have never been apart this long before. I worry about her constantly.'

Joe enfolded his friend in his arms and Aldeman responded by pressing his face into Joe's chest. Joe stroked his hair wordlessly as he watched a container ship coming in to dock.

The enormous vessel reminded him of his latest grounds for suspicion that Delius had become a clandestine environmental activist: cruise ships around the globe were suffering software problems, preventing them from leaving port. He considered telling Aldeman, but he had no proof. Better not attract attention to the issue. He'd continue turning a blind eye for as long as he could. He trusted Delius not to get caught.

By the time Aldeman pulled away, it was almost dark. 'Thank you,' he muttered. 'I was aching for physical contact with another being. That did me good.'

AFTER DINNER, JOE returned to the *Shantivira* for the night. He climbed the steps to the *Pride*, looking forward to a peaceful evening alone with Kitty. To his disappointment, he found *Pobol y Cwm* playing on the big screen and Grace on his sofa, stroking jaguar-Kitty's belly. He'd never seen them so relaxed together. Was this the result of all their gardening sessions?

'Room for one more?' he said, resigning himself to an

enforced catch-up on events in Cwmderi.

Kitty shifted to her Syenitian form, making space for him. He sunk gratefully onto the sofa. What a day. What a week.

How's Aldeman? she asked privately.

Lonely, said Joe. *I'm a bit worried about him, to be honest.*

The soap finished. Joe flicked off the screen and got up to pour himself a beer.

'What did you get up to today, Mam?'

'I helped Chooli on the storage level,' said Grace. 'She showed me the fuel tank. It's huge, isn't it?'

'Mmm,' said Joe. He sat down again and took a thirst-quenching gulp. That was better.

'She also told me how you rescued Yisheng's daughter from drowning in it.'

'That was years ago,' Joe said, dismissively, not wanting to talk about it.

'Brave of you, though,' Grace insisted.

Kitty snorted. 'Suicidal, more like! That was the first time we argued,' she told Grace. 'He should have called me for help. I nearly lost him, just when I'd found him again.'

Grace patted her on the knee. 'Stubborn, my boy. Just like his father.'

Time to change the subject. 'You're getting on well with Chooli, then?'

'Oh yes,' she said. 'The Navajo and the Welsh have plenty in common, you know.'

'We do?' said Joe, mystified. 'What?'

'Being a minority in a powerful country. Our language, our ancient culture, permanently under threat.

Having to sacrifice our landscape and the health of our menfolk to dig up minerals. Not for ourselves, but to make others rich.' Grace contemplated her teacup. 'She told me how her husband died. Lung cancer. He never smoked a cigarette in his life.'

'Nasty stuff, uranium,' agreed Joe.

Grace nodded. 'I'm glad my Gareth didn't suffer like that, at the end.'

'What do you mean?' said Joe, frowning. 'How do you know? I thought you never saw him again, after that day?'

The conspiratorial glance between Kitty and Grace was impossible to miss.

'*Cath?*'

Kitty also spoke out loud. 'Um. So. I took his life. When the time came.'

Rage and disbelief bubbled up in Joe, each fighting for the upper hand. 'You killed my Tad? And never mentioned it once, in all the years we've been together?'

'She cared for him for months, Joe,' said Grace, trying to explain. 'Did his shopping, his washing, cleaned his flat.'

'I told him the council had sent me,' said Kitty. 'He assumed I was human, at least to start with. Later he convinced himself I was one of the fair folk from *Annwfn*. He never saw me shapeshift. He didn't know I was your *Cath*.'

'The point is,' continued Grace, 'he didn't die alone. When his life became unbearable – when breathing got so difficult, he was drowning in his own body fluids – he begged her to release him and she did.'

Why didn't you heal him? Joe demanded privately.

Kitty studied her fingernails for a moment, then looked up at him, her expression fierce. *I chose not to, OK? I've never forgiven him for how he treated you and Grace. He ruined her life and would have killed you if I hadn't stopped him.*

I haven't forgotten. Joe's tone was icy.

If he'd been healthy, he might have tried to return. I couldn't risk that. He was a bad, weak man. But—she hesitated—*he had a certain . . . spark. And he was the spitting image of you. You were away with the army: visiting him in his grotty flat over a chip shop in Wrexham was a way of staying close to you.*

'Joe?' said Grace. 'Say something.'

He ignored her and drained his pint.

He called me his Angel of Death and welcomed me into his home, said Kitty, still trying to justify her actions. *He was ready to go, Joe. I just helped nature along.*

Don't, said Joe, holding up a hand.

He was so proud you joined the army, said Kitty. *He talked about you all the time.*

Joe stood up and pointed at the door. 'Get out, both of you. I want to be alone.'

18. THE SPIDER FROM MWONGO
HANNA

'OK, URCA, LET'S try again. Make sure you keep the turns on track this time.'

Hanna was alone in a medium Earth orbit, doggedly putting Urca through her paces, like a dressage champion schooling a horse. Since the Pweza's visit, Hanna had been volunteering for extra shifts and doing additional training, working hard on improving her bond with her *Tumba*. She should have done this months ago, when she'd first realised their partnership hadn't gelled properly.

Still, better late than never. Things were easier now she'd stepped back from hands-on childcare. Joe's mother had turned up at just the right moment and got stuck in, changing dirty nappies with a brisk efficiency Hanna herself had never achieved. Hanna wasn't sure she liked Grace, but Kia seemed to have taken to her. And Yonas' tiny face lit up the minute he heard her voice.

Communication between Kia and Grace was tricky, accomplished mostly through mime and the few Kawaida words Grace had picked up since she'd arrived. But, driven by necessity, they'd found a system which worked for them.

So now Hanna was sleeping in Hassan's cabin again,

only doing one night-shift a week with Yonas. She was getting enough sleep for the first time in months: it felt amazing. She was rejuvenated, brimming with energy and ambition. Which was just as well, because she needed to prove her commitment to the *Shantivira*. Joe might have given her a second chance, but there wouldn't be a third.

Hanna leaned forward to examine a fast-moving speck at the top of her screen. 'What's that? Zoom in on it, Urca, will you?'

It wasn't behaving like a satellite, or an asteroid. What was it?

'OK, we need to get closer. Pursuit mode, Urca. Hurry.'

Urca complied and Hanna watched the speck turn into a grey box with a yellow symbol she didn't recognise on the side. Hard to guess its size without anything to compare it against. She activated her link to the *Shantivira's* control room. 'Delius? Have you seen this?'

'Hello, Hanna. I detected a foreign object. Thank you for the close up.'

'Do you know what it is?'

'That script is Mwongo. Keep tailing it; find out where it's going. I'll get Joe.'

Mwongo? Not good. Mwongo had a reputation for being interstellar scammers and con artists, constantly out to make a profit for the least possible effort. Hanna accelerated, trying to close the gap between Urca and their quarry. Minutes later, she pulled up abruptly to avoid a collision: the box was hovering right above the International Space Station.

A hatch in the underside opened, ejecting a black,

cylindrical object like an ice hockey puck in the direction of the ISS. It extended eight spindly legs before landing on the surface and scuttling to the nearest antenna. Hanna watched in horrified fascination as it bedded in, attaching itself to the hull. Then the legs folded upwards towards the centre, like a sinister flower.

'Hanna?'

Hanna had never been so relieved to hear Joe's voice. 'Joe, did you see? What is it? What do I *do*?' Before she had time to answer, the grey box sped away into space. Shit!

Joe read her mind. 'Catch that box, Hanna. Hold it in your tractor beam outside your shields, in case it has a self-destruct.'

'I'm on it,' she said, flinging Urca away from the ISS. 'It won't get away.'

'Drop it off in Docking Bay 3. I want to see what it's carrying.'

'Aye, aye, Captain. What about that spider thing? Will the ISS crew have to do an emergency spacewalk?'

'Kitty's coming to prise it off before it does any damage,' said Joe. 'See you in Docking Bay 3.'

It didn't take Urca long to catch up with the cube. It was already in a low Earth orbit, heading for a large communications satellite. Carefully, Hanna deployed her *Tumba's* mini tractor beam. There was a brief tug of war as the box tried to pull away: then it appeared to shut down, offering no more resistance. Hanna returned to the *Shantivira* as fast as she could, holding it beyond Urca's shields as Joe had told her.

Kitty, Joe and Delius were waiting in Docking Bay 3.

Kitty held the mechanical spider at arm's length, its legs paddling feebly in the air. Hanna set down the box, then left again to land in Docking Bay 1, where Urca had her recharging station.

By the time she'd jogged back to Docking Bay 3, they had the cube upside down and the hatch open. There were another three spiders folded up inside. Kitty pressed the underside of the one she was holding and its legs retracted into the dormant position. She fitted it back into its slot, next to the others, and closed the hatch.

'Excellent work, Hanna,' said Joe. 'We were lucky you spotted it before it managed to deploy all four. Who knows where they'd have ended up?'

'What is it?' she asked again, approaching to examine it more closely. She knew not to try and touch it: fresh from space, it would freeze her fingers. She sniffed it experimentally, but smelt nothing.

'A set of Mwongo spy drones. The sharks are circling.'

Hanna shivered. 'What do they want with us? How do they even know about us?'

'The information's available to anyone able to access the Essoona Library archives. No doubt, they're trying to discover the best way to screw the planet out of some easy money.' Joe's eyes sparkled. 'But they didn't get past *you*, did they? You kept your head and responded swiftly and appropriately. In fact,' he held out his hand for her to shake, 'welcome to the crew.'

Hanna stared at him, uncomprehending.

'Congratulations. You've just qualified as a *Shantivira* pilot.'

Hanna blinked as she digested Joe's words. She wasn't

sure she believed them. 'I have?'

'On a solo mission, no less,' said Joe. 'I've been watching the effort you've put in over the last month. The changes you've made to turn things round. Well done.'

Joy swelled her heart until she felt like doing cartwheels. She pumped Joe's hand up and down vigorously, resisting the urge to hug him. 'Thank you. Really. Thank you.'

Kitty was not so restrained. She picked Hanna up and whirled her around, cheering. Hanna was quite dizzy when her feet touched the ground again. Delius offered her a formal Syenitian hand press. 'Congratulations, Pilot Abebe. I look forward to working with you.'

She beamed up at him. 'Me too. But what do we do with that?' She pointed at the box.

'Delius found their ship waiting behind Mars,' said Joe. 'I think we need to have a little chat with them. Then we'll escort them out of the solar system, to underline the message.' He turned and headed towards the control room at the quadrant's apex.

'I'll leave you to it,' called Kitty. Still walking away, Joe lifted a hand to acknowledge her.

Hanna put her hand on Kitty's arm. 'Is everything OK? This is the first time in weeks I've seen you two in the same place. Joe's mum mentioned there was some kind of argument?'

Kitty hunched her shoulders. 'I'm not his favourite person right now. For reasons. He'll get over it eventually. We still have to work together. Thanks for asking.'

'It's not like you to fall out.'

Kitty's head drooped, her hair swinging down to hide

her features like a black curtain. 'No. Joe doesn't usually stay angry this long.'

Hanna hugged her, pressing her face against the soft velvet of Kitty's dress. 'I hope you sort it out soon, whatever it is. Grace is worried it's her fault.'

'Oh, no.' Kitty smiled wistfully. 'It's mine. It's always my fault.'

WHEN HANNA ARRIVED in the control room, Joe was talking to the captain of the Mwongo ship, negotiating the return of their probes. The captain, whose name was Malwod, insisted he was part of a trade delegation, doing research on the best way to approach humanity for mutual benefit.

Hanna studied Malwod and what she could see of his ship with interest. She'd come across the occasional Mwongo in Essoona last year, but had always looked away, not wanting to attract their attention. Now her overall impression was: *slippery*.

Malwod wore drab tan robes with long sleeves hiding his hands. Did Mwongo have hands? She wasn't sure. His hairless skin was an earthy brown which glistened with a moist coating. A flexible trunk the length of Hanna's forearm hid his mouth from view. The most disconcerting thing about the Mwongo was his tiny black eyes. These were on the end of extendable, independent antennae, which could zoom in on things at any angle and retract just as suddenly.

The wall behind Malwod was also brown, flecked with an interesting variety of mould. There were actual mushrooms sprouting from a particularly damp spot near the ceiling. She wrinkled her nose, imagining how the Mwongo ship must smell.

Joe's polite smile was humour-free. 'My planet's not ready for interstellar trade on the open market. Take it from me, Malwod, the best way is not to approach at all. Mwongo are not welcome here. You never will be.'

THEY AGREED THE Mwongo spacecraft would stay where it was. Joe would deliver the cube using the *Koppakuoria*, transmatting it into their hold once they were close enough. To guarantee his safety and demonstrate their strength, a hundred *Tumbas* would escort him. These would then accompany the Mwongo ship to the edge of the solar system to ensure it left.

At last, Joe disconnected. 'Slimy git,' he said. 'Delius, inform the Docking Bay 2 crew we launch in fifteen minutes. I'll get the pallet truck and load the probe. Hanna?'

'Yes?'

'You've done enough for today. Take the rest of the day off.'

'Thanks!' Although how she'd relax knowing half the crew were out escorting an enemy ship, she didn't know. She turned to leave.

'Will you update Maneewan?' Joe called after her. 'I think we'll be hungry when we get back.'

After stopping by the canteen, Hanna returned to her cabin thinking vaguely about a shower. Hassan was out on a dematerialisation shift; Lucy and the others were still away on their long break. The urge to see Kia and Yonas was . . . resistible. This was *her* free time. A present from Joe. Then again, she needed to tell someone her news or she'd pop. What time was it in Essoona? She flicked the clock on her *zana*. Perhaps Farida would have a moment.

She sat in the centre of the double bed she shared with Hassan and initiated the call. Farida picked up almost immediately and Hanna saw the familiar surroundings of her friend's room at Dunia House.

'Hanna! Hold on, just let me sort myself out.'

The image blurred. Hanna caught a flash of ceiling and a glimpse of the trees outside. Then it settled to show Farida sitting on the patchwork bedspread Hanna had stitched for her, back in the days when she'd had free time.

'So, how've you been?'

Hanna couldn't hold back her grin any longer. 'I qualified!'

Farida screamed and clapped her hands. Once she'd calmed down, she said, 'Tell me.'

Hanna related the story of the cube, the spider and the Mwongo. 'All the work I've been putting in with Urca paid off today. She responded exactly as I would have wished; I didn't have to think about it. We're finally a partnership.'

'That's fantastic, Hanna. Well done.'

'What about you? No university?'

'First day of the summer break.'

'Of course. Sorry, I didn't think. So, what are your plans?'

'Saïd's coming for a few weeks and he's taking me rock climbing,' said Farida. 'I've booked a holiday cottage in the forest where they all used to climb last year.'

'He's been home in Grenoble, hasn't he?'

'That's right. He's looking forward to chilling in Essoona. Mrs Park can't wait to have him back. She's been interviewing me on his favourite foods.'

'Bless her.' Hanna smiled.

'And once he starts work again, I'm going to Palembang. See my parents and enjoy the rest of the dry season before uni begins.'

Hanna felt slightly envious. She'd had her own break already this year, but looking after a newborn Yonas hadn't exactly been a holiday. 'Have you heard from Aneira?' she asked, changing the subject.

Farida's face lit up. 'Yes! She took me to Aldina last month. I met her brothers. And her dad.'

'What are they like?'

'Nice. But, you know, still frantic and sad about all their relatives on Amra. And furious at the Galaksi Alliance's failure to act.' Farida examined her nails. Midnight blue this week, Hanna observed, with silver sparkles. 'It's a fair criticism, if you ask me. Just because Amra isn't an Alliance planet. The more planets the Ranglatiri destroy, the bolder they get.'

'I think they're testing to see how far they can push without any retaliation,' said Hanna. 'Sizing us up.'

Farida nodded. 'The Alliance should be taking preemptive action now,' she said. 'Otherwise, one day it *will* be an Alliance planet.'

'I worry about what'll happen if the Ranglatiri turn up *here* again,' said Hanna. 'Earth isn't an Alliance planet either. We escaped by the skin of our teeth last time.'

'The skin of Kitty's teeth you mean,' Farida replied.

'I'm not sure she'd be able to pull that trick twice. From what I heard, she nearly ate the whole *Shantivira* fleet by accident.'

Hanna grimaced, remembering. 'Kitty told me Nestor saved us all, that day. From her. I think she might have a soft spot for him.'

'Eew, Hanna, that's gross,' Farida made a disgusted face. 'Anyway, Aneira's doing OK now. She's determined to pass this year and sign up to the Syenitian Defence Service.'

'Where Elian is?' said Hanna. 'How's he getting on?'

'He's in the Quturjuuk system, on a fifteen-series space station. From what I hear, it makes the *Shantivira* sound like an antique.'

The *Shantivira was* an antique, Hanna knew. That didn't stop her loving it. Quite the opposite, in fact. Some of the trees in the biomes were over four hundred years old: living history. 'No teleporting though, I'd imagine.'

'Nope. No handy space demon for them,' said Farida. 'So they don't see each other much. But with luck, Aneira will join him next year.'

✦   ✦   ✦

LATER, HANNA SAT in the corner of the window seat with Hassan, looking out at the Milky Way. On the ceiling, the post-Mwongo party was in full swing: noisy and exuberant. Joe was at the heart of the action, dancing as only a white, middle-aged male can. *Appallingly.* Kitty was nowhere to be seen, which was unusual.

Hassan studied her with his soft brown eyes. 'I'm so

proud of you, Hanna. Not just for today. In general.'

Hanna's face creased into a smile. Her cheeks ached from constant beaming, but it felt wonderful. So many problems resolved, from a single afternoon's work. Things were finally slotting into place and the future – at least the next few years – was no longer filled with uncertainty. 'Thanks,' she said. 'I'm proud of you, too. But you know that.' She sighed. 'I wish the others were here to help us celebrate. It's not the same without them.'

'Did you get any replies to your messages?'

'Some. Lucy and Felix say hi. Not a peep out of Nikolai and Roberto.'

'It's hard to stay in touch when you're travelling. Your head's completely detached from normal life.'

'I remember,' said Hanna, thinking about last summer and the knots she'd tied herself in while Hassan had been away. She wouldn't make that mistake again.

Reflected in the glass, Hanna noticed Kia approaching with Yonas in her arms, accompanied by Grace and Grace's friend, Chooli.

'I'm going to dance,' said Kia. 'Do you want to come?'

'We're still digesting our food, Hanna replied. 'We're comfy here for now.'

'OK. Take Yonas, then.' It wasn't a request. She was already handing him over. Yonas gurgled and made a grab for Hanna's hair.

'Hello, my darling,' she cooed, rubbing her nose on his tummy and inhaling his gorgeous smell. Babies were so *yummy*. 'Come to Auntie Hanna.'

'See you later.' Grinning broadly, Kia took a running jump at the wall next to them and skipped her way up to the dance floor.

Grace's mouth fell open in astonishment and Hanna took pity on her. 'Gravity generators, Grace,' she said in English. 'You can walk on the walls and the ceiling. We don't generally, but it's handy if we need extra space.'

'Good heavens!' Grace said, craning her neck to watch Kia and noticing the dancers above her head for the first time.

'May we join you?' asked Chooli.

Hassan gestured at the long, deep bench. 'Plenty of room, ladies. Pull up a cushion.'

'It's moments like these where I crave a ciggy,' said Grace as she sat down and leaned back against the glass.

Chooli pouted disapproval, but Hanna remembered how Nikolai had struggled to give up when they'd first arrived at Dunia House. 'Do you think you'll be able to go home soon?'

'I don't know, love.' Grace's shoulders slumped. 'I think I'm going to miss the whole summer in my garden. Heaven knows what kind of a state it'll be in by the time I get back to it.'

'I thought Kitty was looking after it for you?' said Hassan.

'She's doing her best, but she doesn't have the knowledge or the patience. And she likes to let things grow wild.' Grace's lips puckered with disapproval. 'But she'll keep it alive. She's down there right now, actually. I asked her to bring us some raspberries.'

'Speak of the devil,' said Chooli, glancing up. Kitty approached them, carrying a large bowl of raspberries.

'Hi there,' she said, taking a chair from the nearby table and flipping it round to face them. She presented the

237

raspberries to Grace, saying 'I brought dessert.'

Grace studied the contents critically and gave a small nod of approval. She took a handful and passed the bowl to Chooli. 'Ripe but not squidgy.'

'I left the squidgy ones for the birds.' Hanna noticed Kitty's swift glance to the ceiling, where Joe was still dancing, oblivious. Then Kitty's focus returned to Grace. 'I have news,' she said in a low voice.

'News?'

'You had a visitor.'

Grace's eyes widened. 'Not more men from the Ministry?'

'Matthew.'

'*Matthew?*' There were sharp intakes of breath. They all knew who Matthew was.

'He nearly did a runner when he spotted me,' Kitty grinned, revealing her pointed canines. 'He'd come to apologise to you, Grace. He had no idea you were being held hostage.'

'Poor laddie,' Grace said, frowning. 'He didn't have much idea about anything except his computers.'

Kitty leaned forward, resting her hands on her knees. 'He also came to tell you: Nestor's dead.'

'Dead?' they chorused.

Grace eyed Kitty suspiciously. 'Do you have something to tell us, Kitty?'

'I didn't touch him!' she said, indignant. 'Well. I *hardly* touched him. He was fine when I left him. Apoplectic with rage, but that was normal for him, wasn't it?'

Hanna jiggled Yonas in her lap and looked at Hassan. Hassan picked up the bowl and ate some raspberries, then held it out to Hanna. This was more engrossing than an evening at the cinema.

'Matthew told him he was leaving,' Kitty continued. 'Right at the last moment, before departing for the airport. Nestor was so angry, he knocked Matthew out with a bottle. When Matthew came to, Nestor was lying in a pool of vomit, too cold and too pale to be alive. Certainly not breathing. Matthew panicked and fled to the airport without calling an ambulance, arriving just in time for his flight. He's been holed up in Wolverhampton ever since.'

'Goodness,' said Chooli.

'So why come to visit me now?' asked Grace.

'He's been tracking the police investigation,' said Kitty. 'He's quite the professional little hacker when he needs to be. He was worried they'd be searching for him: that there'd be traces of his blood or hair on the bottle, or they'd interview the taxi driver who took him to the airport.'

'And did they?' asked Hanna, enthralled by Kitty's story.

'Nope. Nestor's paranoid need for secrecy worked in Matthew's favour,' Kitty said. 'The workshop is isolated and it was a Sunday. The industrial estate was empty. They might have looked closer, but the post mortem said it was a cerebral haemorrhage resulting from a stroke, so they didn't bother.'

'Quick, then?' asked Chooli.

'Very,' said Kitty. 'Once they read his medical records, they closed the investigation. His blood pressure was sky high and he'd repeatedly refused medication for it. Matthew decided it was safe to come out of hiding and get on with his life.'

'Stubborn sod,' said Grace. 'I'm glad he didn't suffer, all the same.'

'Me too. Although you could argue he suffered his whole life.' Kitty's eyes darted to the ceiling again. 'I'd better tell Joe.' She didn't sound enthusiastic.

Grace said, 'Good luck. Give him time, love. He'll come round. You'll see. Thanks for the raspberries.'

Kitty said nothing. She gave them a sad smile and strolled up the wall to where Joe had stopped dancing to drink a bottle of beer.

Kia passed her on the way down. 'That was awesome,' she said in Nuer, plunging her hand into the bowl of berries. 'Mmm, they're yummy. Why are you all looking like that? Who's died?'

Hassan grinned, lightening the mood. 'No one you know. Don't worry about it.'

Kia didn't. 'OK. So. While I was dancing, I reached an important decision. I came down to tell you.'

'What decision?' said Hanna.

'Now you're qualified, you're going to be working up here for years, right?'

Hanna stole a glance at Hassan. 'That's the plan,' she said.

'Well. I'm not staying. I want to live down on the planet.' She lifted her palm to silence Hanna's protest. 'Not straight away. I'll stay until the end of the year. Perhaps a little longer. I need time to find somewhere. But I want to be settled by Yonas' first birthday. I don't want him growing up thinking the sky's black.'

Hanna had to admit she had a point. But she said

nothing, just clung to Yonas as if she were adrift and he was her only buoyancy aid.

The pitch of Kia's voice raised a notch. 'You'll help me, right? You said you'd support us whatever happens – and you have a proper job now, like you wanted all along.'

Hanna pulled herself together. 'Yes,' she croaked, a frog in her throat. Then, more strongly, 'Of course.'

'Great!' said Kia, all smiles again. 'Anyway. It's your turn to dance. Give me Yonas.' She stretched out her arms and Hanna handed him over reluctantly. Hassan squeezed her hand before unfolding his legs and slotting his stumps back into his black and silver boots.

'We're going to join the others,' he explained to Grace and Chooli in English, pointing at the ceiling. Hanna was glad they hadn't understood their exchange. She needed time to get her head round it before people started sticking their oar in with helpful suggestions.

'Have fun, dears,' said Chooli. 'We'll look after Kia and Yonas.'

Thankfully, the music had calmed down a little. Hanna put her arm around Hassan's waist and moved her hips to the rhythm. Behind him, she saw Joe frowning at Kitty. When she turned away to teleport, in the instant before she disappeared, the expression on her face was a complex mixture of sadness, anger and hurt. Mostly hurt, if Hanna was reading it correctly.

To Hassan's shoulder, she muttered, 'I wonder what it is Joe and Kitty have argued about. I've never seen him treat her so coldly.'

'I can tell you exactly what it is, Hanna,' said Hassan. 'It's none of our business. Keep out of it.'

Hanna sighed. He was probably right. But Kitty had been there for her when *she'd* felt desperate. She'd like to return the favour, if she could.

They let the music guide them, their bodies fitting together naturally. Familiar yet exciting. Hanna's head was still spinning from Kia's announcement. Would she be able to live with Kia and commute to the *Shantivira* via teleport, like Tima did? What about Hassan? Would he come with them? If he lived on Earth, he wouldn't be allowed to take his Syenitian prosthetics. That was a problem. Plus, Kia was a country girl and Hassan preferred big cities. Her mind circled uselessly.

'Hassan?' she said.

'What?' His eyes crinkled as he looked down at her.

'If I go to live with Kia and Yonas, will you come with us?'

'On Earth, you mean?' he said. 'Like Kia was saying before?'

'Yeah.'

'No,' said Hassan, in a flat tone which brooked no argument.

Hanna stopped dancing. '*What?!*' Her voice was near a shriek. She hadn't expected such a blunt response. She thought he loved her. That he'd do anything for her. Was she mistaken?

Hassan reached for her hands, taking them in his. 'I don't want to live on the Earth, Hanna. Holidays, yes, but my life is here, on the *Shantivira*. My *home* is here. Yours too, I thought. Was I wrong?'

Hanna gazed up at him, 'Yes. No. I mean, yes this is my home too. No, you're not wrong. I'm just trying to find a way for us all to be together.'

'Just because Kia wants to live on the planet, it doesn't mean you have to,' he said. 'You know that, right?'

Hanna nodded, numbly, not trusting herself to say any more. How could she keep Kia, Yonas and Hassan in her life at the same time if they weren't all in the same place? She didn't want to commute. She'd exhausted herself last year, splitting her time between Essoona and London. And it still hadn't been enough.

She couldn't live like that again. She wouldn't.

19. RECONCILIATION
DAN, AUGUST 2016

A FRA LANDED THE *Gezi Urdina* and taxied into the waiting hangar. They were meeting Henning on Vruxil: he'd rented a remote location where they could do the handover privately.

The journey from Oso-Urrun had been hell. Weeks in deep space, in a sour atmosphere of cool politeness. Dan didn't think he'd laughed once.

He and Afra had consistently done their jobs, making sure the trip ran smoothly and organising the delivery. They were a well-oiled team, even when they were barely speaking. Permanently professional. But outside work, they'd gone out of their way to avoid each other. It was as if their personal relationship had frozen, become so brittle it was liable to shatter if they dared to try and change its shape.

Dan spent the evenings alone in his cabin, playing his guitar, or down in the hold, practising the *stakarh*. He had no idea what Afra did in her free time. He'd never been so lonely – not even when Rowan had first exiled him on Amra, eighteen months and a lifetime ago. He hadn't a clue how to break the impasse. Or if Afra wanted him to. Every so often he got the sense she was about to say something not work-related, but then – nothing.

He kept wanting to throw himself at her feet and beg forgiveness for his ignorance and insensitivity, but somehow couldn't bring himself to do it. Pride? Shame? Fear of another rejection? Dan wasn't sure.

Perhaps neither of them wanted to risk damaging this fragile truce they'd constructed, because their survival depended on their being able to work with each other. But this delivery would test that truce to breaking point. If they were to get through it in one piece, they both had to keep a clear head.

Dan lowered the ramp and peered out. Henning and another Ranglatiri with a black case on wheels were already waiting. The hangar doors were rolling closed, blocking out the daylight. He stepped back and called to Afra, 'They're here!'

'OK!' she replied, and he heard the bolt slide across the cockpit door from the inside. They'd agreed Afra would stay out of sight and not get involved in the handover.

Normally they landed in public spaceports and, if something went wrong, the backup plan was a speedy departure. That would be difficult with the hangar doors shut. Afra would have to blast a hole in them first.

The giant doors shut with a grating crash, plunging them into darkness. Not a problem for Ranglatiri, a species which had evolved in deep, lightless caves – resulting in their albino appearance and, without their breathing masks, an inability to tolerate the oxygen levels most life forms preferred. Very much a problem for Dan, as the combination of darkness and a closing door could trigger the panic attacks which were a legacy of his slave training.

He touched the memory stone at his throat for courage and comfort, willing himself to channel the debilitating anxiety into subservience rather than a total loss of control. Deep slow breaths. And again. Don't let it overwhelm you. *Breathe*, Dan. In . . . two, three, hold . . . two, three, out . . . two, three. Stay focused.

The friendly yellow light from inside the *Gezi Urdina* spilled down the ramp, illuminating the approaching figures. Dan bowed low, keeping his eyes respectfully downcast. 'Welcome, sirs,' he heard himself say, his voice almost steady. 'Please follow me.'

He led them to the hold, where he'd set up a table for the Ranglatiri chemist to perform his quality control tests. Henning plunged his knife into random boxes, taking samples. Dan stood to one side with his hands behind his back, eyes on the metal floor, studying the regular bumps of its anti-slip pattern.

He prayed the Wadudu on Oso-Urrun had done their job properly. If not, he wouldn't leave this room alive. Not this time. His existence depended on his customers' satisfaction with the product. He shivered. Waited. Tried to watch what they were doing without lifting his head.

'Sslave-Bellyn?' said Henning's voice. 'The formula iss a match with your previous deliveries.' Dan's shoulders sagged with relief. 'You can sstart unloading the boxes.'

Woah, woah, woah, hang on a minute there, buddy, Dan thought. He lifted his head marginally. 'Sir, the agreement was to transfer payment once the product's quality has been confirmed. The pilot has closed the ramp from the sealed cockpit and won't open it until she's received the credits.'

Henning hissed, then shrugged. He spoke a Ranglatiri command into his mask, then said, 'Transfer in progress.'

They waited in silence. The chemist packed his case and stood beside the motionless Henning. Finally, Dan's communicator bleeped. He checked Afra's message.

Paid in full. Lowering the ramp now.

He bowed again. 'Thank you, gentlemen.' They ignored him and left the room. Seething, Dan loaded a box onto their only pallet truck and followed them. Were they going to make him unload the whole cargo by himself? In the dark? This was going to take hours.

When he reached the ramp, Henning and the chemist were waiting at the bottom, at the edge of the pool of light cast by the *Gezi Urdina*.

'Sslave-Bellyn,' Henning called, 'bring the cargo down the ramp and we'll do the rest.'

'Yes, sir,' said Dan with a subservient bow. Thank goodness for that. He trundled his truck down the slope, off-loaded the crate onto the floor and pushed the empty pallet truck back up the ramp. When he returned with the next load, the chemist was waiting in a forklift. He picked up the pallet and drove away into the black corners of the hangar.

Dan worked as fast as he could, hyperconscious of his customers' impatience. His muscles would pay for it tomorrow, he was sure. And no chance of a massage from Afra. Still, he strained every sinew, trying to keep up with the forklift which was always waiting for him, each time he got a new load down the ramp.

Finally, he delivered the last pallet. 'That's it, sir,' he

said to Henning, who'd stayed by the ramp, watching the whole operation impassively.

Henning inclined his head, ever so slightly. 'Until next time, Sslave-Bellyn. We'll be in touch.'

Dan bowed, saying nothing. To his relief, the hangar doors groaned and began to open, flooding the hangar with light. In the cockpit, Afra initiated the engine warm-up sequence. The *Gezi Urdina's* ramp started closing when Dan was only halfway up it. By the time he reached the now-unlocked cockpit she was already taxiing towards the take-off zone.

OUT IN THE safety of space, she switched to autopilot. To Dan's surprise, when she swung her seat round to confront him, there were tears in her eyes.

'Dan . . .'

He waited.

'I was watching, the whole time, on the cameras. The way they treat you – like you're *nothing*. I kept thinking they'd kill you and leave your body for me to find after they'd unloaded everything.'

Dan gave a weak smile. 'That crossed my mind, too. But then they'd have had to do the donkey work themselves. I'm more use to them alive. For now.'

Afra dragged the back of her hand across her eyes. 'And you worked so hard for them. They were so *rude* to you. They never treated Bellyn like that.'

'Of course they didn't. I'm the lowest of the low to them. It must really hurt their pride, having to do business with me.'

'I never realised how ... vulnerable you were with them. I don't know, Dan, maybe we should stop. Before something happens. I have a bad feeling.'

'That's not what you said before. You wanted to keep Bellyn's operation going for as long as possible, whatever happened. Because it was the right thing to do. "I made my peace with not growing old a long time ago," you said.'

'I *know*. I *said* that. But—it's more real now, somehow. Watching you today. I didn't understand how much I was asking of you.' Afra exhaled audibly. 'Bellyn sacrificed himself so we could live. He wouldn't have wanted either of us to die for his mission.'

'No,' agreed Dan. 'And yet. It *is* the right thing to do. You've brought me round to your way of thinking. We worked so hard to set this all up. I'm not ready to stop, Afra. Bellyn taught me well. I reckon we can pull this off a while longer.'

Afra rose to her feet with a swift, liquid grace. Guessing what might be coming, Dan stood up too. She wrapped her arms around his chest and kissed him full on the lips. He returned her embrace and they spent a few happy minutes reconnecting.

'Are we friends again, then?' he asked.

'We were never not friends, Dan. I'm sorry about the last couple of months. I was just so angry with you. And we had a job to do.'

He held her hands and studied her elegant face. 'Explain why you were angry with me, without getting angry. Help me understand.'

She sighed. 'For a Sayari, giving someone a memory stone is a promise of permanent commitment. Like you and your ring. I thought you understood that. I thought, by accepting it, you were agreeing to be with me forever. Then you pulled your stunt with your ring and I realised you didn't know what the memory stone signified and hadn't bothered researching Sayari customs at all. I was so disappointed.'

Dan tugged her back to his chest. 'I'm an idiot. We all know that.'

'And . . . I'm afraid of the open water,' Afra continued, speaking to his shirt. 'I was too embarrassed to tell you, when you'd gone to so much effort. So I was already in a bad mood. And then the weather changed so suddenly. It was like it was trying to tell me something.'

'It was just a storm, Afra. They blow over, you know?' Dan laughed. 'So all this time, you were angry with me because I was too dumb to understand you wanted to spend your life with me – and I was sad because I wanted to spend my life with you and believed you'd turned me down?'

Eyes wet again, Afra's ears waggled. 'Pretty much.'

'I love you, Afra.'

'I know.'

Dan reached into his pocket and pulled out the little box he always carried. Time for another go. 'Don't shout at me,' he said, opening the lid. He summoned all his courage. 'Dearest Afra Azu. Would you accept this humble token of my continued commitment to you? No ceremonies. No laws. No audience. Just you and me, together forever, as long as we both shall live.'

Afra took the ring and fitted it onto her slender finger. The stone matched her hair perfectly. Her eyes shone as she said, 'Yes, Dan. I accept.'

He picked her up and spun her around, making her squeal. 'With all your research you probably know that, in *my* culture, when two people agree to spend their lives together, it's traditional to have an exotic holiday.'

She grinned at him. 'There *is* somewhere I've always wanted to show you. Great beaches, fantastic food, right off the beaten track. We can afford a couple of weeks there before the next factory run.'

Dan glanced back at the control panel. 'The autopilot's good for a while, isn't it?'

Afra nodded, then shrieked as Dan swung her up into his arms.

'Let's go to your cabin. We have some catching up to do.'

20. PLAYING POLITICS
JOE, SEPTEMBER 2016

C ATH? *HELP.*

What is it? Joe felt Kitty frown in response to his urgent tone.

Just come, he pleaded. *Please?*

Syenitian-Kitty materialised next to the futon which, up until he'd discovered the truth about his father's death, had been their marital bed. He'd never been so relieved to see her.

What is it? she asked again.

Something's terribly wrong with my body, he said. *I think I might be dying.* Even his telepathic voice was a pitiful croak.

Dying? she repeated.

Joe closed his eyes again. That helped the headache. *Felt rough last night,* he explained. *Didn't drink any alcohol. Hoped an early night would sort it. Woke up and now my whole body hurts. I'm sweating and shivering at the same time.*

Kitty said nothing. He opened his eyes and saw her hiding her mouth behind her hand, eyes sparkling with amusement.

It's not funny, Cath! *The tech-transfer courses are all*

starting up again today. And I have that meeting in Washington DC this afternoon. He couldn't afford to cancel. It had taken Shakila weeks of persistence to get an audience with the POTUS. But he was so feeble, he didn't think he could stand. *What's wrong with me?*

Oh, Joe, she said. *You're not dying, love. You have the flu.*

Flu? he said, confused. *But I haven't been ill since I was in the army. Not so much as a sniffle. Why now?*

Why do you think? Kitty dropped her arm and looked down at him, her expression still inexplicably merry.

He thought. *Because you were boosting my life energy the whole time? But not recently, because I haven't let you near me in weeks?*

Mm-hmm, said Kitty, kneeling on the tatami mat floor at his bedside, her ruby dress flowing outwards in a warm, velvety pool. She extended her hand, her sleeve brushing his torso. *Peace offering?*

Joe took it and placed it on his chest. Immediately, the warmth flowed into him: spreading through his body, down his arms, his legs, chasing the aches and shivers away. His head cleared and the pain receded, before vanishing completely.

He beamed up at her. *Thank you.*

I'm sorry I didn't tell you about your dad, she said. She lowered her head and her hair tumbled down like a waterfall, tickling the back of his hand. *I was afraid how you'd take it.*

I might have overreacted a teeny bit, he admitted, absently twirling a lock of her hair in his fingers. *I hated the bastard, but if I'm honest, I'm glad you made his end easier.*

So, she said, *does that mean you forgive me?*

Joe pulled her onto him, swiftly rolling over so he was on top, straddling her hips. *God, I've missed you*, he said, studying the familiar curves of her face.

Kitty remained motionless. *Can I sleep here tonight, instead of in my tree in the tropical biome?* she asked, still unsure.

Joe kissed her: lips, cheeks, forehead, neck. *Please come back to me*, Cath. *I'm sorry it took so long. I backed myself into a corner and was too stubborn to come out.*

I understand, she said, returning his kisses. *You felt Grace and I were ganging up on you. But we really weren't.*

That's about the size of it. I'm an arse. I'm sorry.

I missed you, too, she said. Her emerald eyes welled with tears. *Staying professional at work while knowing you were angry with me was . . . horrible.*

Joe ran his fingers along her clavicle, feeling his penis harden between them. *All done now. How about some make-up sex to seal the deal?*

Kitty laughed and shifted to her space demon form. Her original form, that she rarely showed other people. The scarlet scales on her belly and chest were smooth beneath him, radiating heat. He traced his tongue from the curve of her stomach up to her throat, inhaling her intoxicating scent.

She shivered with pleasure. *Thought you'd never ask*, she said, twitching her sinuous tail.

✦　✦　✦

THE DELEGATION FROM the European Space Agency

trooped off the *Koppakuoria* with their suitcases, gazing round the docking bay in awe. Joe greeted them warmly then watched Shakila lead them down to the conference room to start their session with Dipesh, the *Shantivira's* head of maintenance.

After a six-week break, it was good to be kicking things off again. They'd proved their point by suspending the gravity generator and shield generator courses over the summer, without falling too far behind schedule. The UK was in the international space community doghouse and was unlikely to have another go at putting pressure on the *Shantivira*.

The attempted kidnap had so disillusioned Rob, he'd left the army and was taking a sabbatical. They'd agreed to stay in touch, discreetly, while he was working out what to do next.

Joe hoped Grace would be able to return home soon. Although improving, their relationship was too brittle for him to relax properly around her. Her endeavours to fit in were praiseworthy but, nevertheless, he still kept expecting jabs from the constant stream of barbed comments he'd grown up with.

To be fair, they'd only slipped out infrequently since her arrival on the *Shantivira*. She was clearly making a huge effort. Perhaps it was the company she was keeping: between helping Chooli in the stores and looking after Kia and Yonas, she'd also managed to find herself a new 'gentleman friend'.

Vadim, a senior pilot from Armenia, was nothing like Gareth or Nestor. He was kind and quietly spoken, with a bristly grey moustache and deep laughter lines. Born the same year as Grace, he'd joined the *Shantivira* in the 1990s, shortly after the collapse of the Soviet Union, and had lived aboard ever since.

It didn't appear to be a romantic relationship; they simply enjoyed each other's company. Vadim's poor English was the source of much amusement, but, despite the language barrier and their different backgrounds, a genuine friendship had kindled between them.

JOE RETURNED TO the *Pride* to wait for Shakila. He busied himself in the galley, making coffee. They were setting up a big visit of VIP guests in December; deciding who to invite – and who not to – was a diplomatic minefield. His appointment at the White House today was to invite the current US president in person. He experienced an unwelcome stab of adrenaline whenever he thought about it, so he was trying hard not to.

The kettle clicked off and in the ensuing silence came the unmistakable sound of Shakila's stilettos clacking across the docking bay. Seconds later, her head poked through the open doorway.

'Morning, boss!'

'Good morning to you, too, Shakila!' He held up the cafetière. 'I made us coffee. I think we're going to need it.'

Shakila slung her *zana* and the printed lists she liked to work with onto the table and sat down. 'I have a genius plan.'

Joe twitched his eyebrows as he set the table with cups, a milk jug and the sugar bowl. 'A genius plan, eh? Let's hear it.' He sat beside her and depressed the plunger on the cafetière, taking care not to spurt coffee all over Shakila's papers.

She leaned back, crossing her legs. 'You know how we were driving ourselves nuts, trying to decide which world leaders to invite and which to leave out, without causing a diplomatic incident?'

'I do,' he said, wondering where this was going.

'Forget the G7 and the G20. We want to show the *Shantivira* to a group of people representing as much of the planet as possible, don't we?'

'Yes,' said Joe. He spooned three sugars into his cup and stirred.

'So, we don't invite presidents of nation states if their country is part of a larger organisation.'

'What do you mean?'

'Forget Merkel, May and Hollande. Forget Putin and Modi.' Shakila smiled. 'We invite the leaders of all the continental unions.'

Joe frowned. 'The what?'

'You know, like the European Union, the African Union, ASEAN and the rest.' She pushed a list in front of him. It read:

Continental Unions

African Union: Chairperson – Idriss Déby, Chad

European Union: President of the European Council – Donald Tusk, Poland

Union of South American Nations / UNASUR: Secretary General – Ernesto Samper, Columbia

Association of Southeast Asian Nations / ASEAN: Chair – Thongloun Sisoulith, Laos

Gulf Cooperation Council: Secretary General – Abdullatif bin Rashid Al Zayani, Bahrain

Eurasian Economic Union: Chairman – Nursultan Nazarbayev, Kazakhstan

South Asian Association for Regional Cooperation / SAARC: Secretary General – Arjun Bahadur Thapa, Nepal

Pacific Islands Forum / PIF: Secretary General – Meg Taylor, Papua New Guinea

Plus

People's Republic of China: President – Xi Jinping

United States of America: President – Barack Obama

United Nations: Secretary General – Ban Ki-moon, South Korea

United Nations Office for Outer Space Affairs: Director – Susan Omondi, Kenya

What about Canada?!

'A dozen dignitaries,' said Joe slowly, considering the idea. This could work. It was certainly a better plan than anything they'd come up with so far. 'Plus journalists, I suppose. But manageable. You realise few of these people have any real power?'

'That's not the point though, is it?' said Shakila. 'They're representatives. This is the smallest group of people empowered to speak for the largest number of Earth's inhabitants.'

'Does it really cover everyone?' he asked. '"What about Canada?" Why did you write that?'

Shakila set down her cup. 'As far as I can see, it's the

only major economy not represented in some other way. Unless you count the Commonwealth. But we already have representatives for the other Commonwealth countries.'

Joe scratched the back of his neck. As much as he'd like to meet the Queen, he didn't think a royal visit would send the right message. In fact, it would be a terrible distraction. Surely a Canadian should represent Canada? 'If we invite it as a nation in its own right, the others might accuse us of bias,' he said thoughtfully. 'It's hardly equivalent to the PRC, or the US. Not economically, not in terms of population. Some – not me – will say the US could act on its behalf.'

'A diplomatic incident waiting to happen,' Shakila agreed.

Then again, the *Shantivira's* Canadians would give him no peace if their country went unrepresented. 'We invite them,' he said decisively. 'Better they're on board.'

Shakila bent her head, adding 'Prime Minister – Justin Trudeau' next to her handwritten note.

'Damn!' said Joe.

She looked up sharply. 'What?

'Now there's thirteen official guests.'

Shakila arched a charcoal eyebrow. 'Is that a problem?'

'Some say it's an unlucky number,' he mumbled, uncomfortable revealing his superstitious streak in front of his hyper-rational colleague.

She studied the list, unfazed. 'What if we leave Susan out? She's been up here plenty. Or Ban Ki-moon?'

'No.' Joe was emphatic. 'I need Susan. She's brilliant at the international leader chit-chat stuff. And in the eyes of

the Alliance, Ban Ki-moon is humanity's official representative. He *has* to come.' He gave himself a mental
shake. 'It's just a stupid superstition. What's the worst that
can happen? Maneewan putting too much chilli in the vol-
au-vents?'

Shakila chuckled. Maneewan had a reputation for
erring on the spicy side.

Joe said, 'I'm being silly. Let's invite the lot.'

AT LUNCH, JOE saw the newly qualified pilots had all
returned from their long break. Planning the duty roster
would be easier now. He put down his tray in front of
Lucy and Felix and sat beside Hanna and Hassan.
'Welcome back,' he said. 'What did you get up to on your
holibobs?'

Lucy launched into a blow-by-blow description of
their road trip starting from Nesselwang im Allgäu, where
Felix's parents had their sawmill. They'd driven through
the Alps to Lake Garda, across to Venice, and through
Tuscany to Rome. Then south to visit the Roman ruins at
Pompeii, before taking a ferry to Corsica. After a week,
they'd returned to Germany, stopping off in Como and
Switzerland. It sounded exhausting but, as Joe acknowledged privately to himself, his patience for overland travel
had been spoiled by years of teleporting with Kitty.

'It was so relaxing, not having to fly,' continued Lucy.
'Travelling slowly, you see how the different countries
blend into each other. The Alps are like their own separate
region, with a distinct architecture and culture.'

'Yes,' agreed Hanna, 'I had the same thought that time

we drove from Munich to Switzerland.' She fell abruptly silent, obviously remembering their failed attempt to rescue Lucy and Irion.

Joe said, 'What about you two, Hanna and Hassan? Isn't it time you took a break? We don't want you burning out. Now the others are back, we can spare you for a week or two.'

The couple looked at each other, as if they'd not considered it. Perhaps they hadn't.

'We could,' said Hanna, doubtfully.

'We should,' said Hassan. His face spilt into a broad grin. 'We will. Thanks, Joe.'

✦ ✦ ✦

JOE AND KITTY returned from the White House in time for dinner with the engineers from the European Space Agency. They were full of enthusiasm after their tour of the base, and brimming with anticipation about the knowledge they'd acquire in the coming weeks. Kitty felt she'd had enough human contact for one day and made herself scarce, leaving Joe and Shakila to play hosts.

The conversation turned to the upcoming US elections. The consensus was the Republicans couldn't possibly win with the candidate they'd chosen. Not wanting to show off, Joe decided against divulging where he'd spent the afternoon. He said, 'I didn't think the Brits would vote for Brexit. All bets are off, if you ask me.'

He instantly regretted the change of subject. His guests found the referendum result inexplicable and appeared to have a morbid fascination with the mysterious motivations of the British.

One German guy said, 'It's like—we thought we knew who you British were; we thought you were our friends. Now it turns out more than half of you want nothing to do with us. It's not our business what you do with your country, but I must say, you've hurt our collective feelings.'

'Imagine how it feels *inside* the UK,' said Joe, trying not to grit his teeth. 'People you've known your whole life: suddenly you realise their world view is entirely different to yours. It's like losing the ground under your feet. People defining themselves purely by the way they voted, irreconcilable differences in opinion splitting friends and families.'

Was he going to tell them his mother had voted enthusiastically for Brexit and remained convinced she'd been right to do so? And that *he* thought she'd been brainwashed by the right-wing press? No. He wasn't. That was between him and Grace. On top of all their other problems, somehow, they must find a way to forgive each other for their voting choices.

Instead, he said, 'The way I see it, there are many reasons people voted the way they did. I think,' he paused, searching for the right words, 'some voted Leave in desperation because they believed their lives couldn't get worse and hoped Brexit might change things. Others took what they were told at face value.' He shook his head ruefully. 'More money for the NHS, my *arse*.

'Some voted Leave because they assumed it would never happen. Either they wanted to punish the government for their cuts to public services,' Joe's mouth twisted with contempt, 'or they were so fucking *complacent*, they believed their actions would have no direct consequences. Still,' he said, trying to sound more positive, 'as long as the UK government doesn't trigger Article 50, there's plenty of time to work out the best way forward.'

Finally, the guests disappeared to their cabins and Joe's time was his own again. But his head was buzzing too much to go straight to bed. He needed to digest what he'd learnt today at the White House: to talk it over with someone neutral and allow his thoughts to crystallise. He flicked at his *zana* and put through a call to Björn.

'Björn, mate, are you still up? Fancy a bath?'

TO ENSURE THEIR meeting remained private, Kitty took them to a bathhouse in the old-town of Aldina: an establishment neither of them had visited before. Joe wondered fleetingly if they'd bump into Dan, but it was hardly likely.

They progressed wordlessly through the series of pools. Gradually, the tension ebbed from Joe's shoulders and stomach. His mind emptied, allowing the impressions of the day to bubble to the surface so he could examine them at leisure.

In due course, they climbed the stairs to the final pool which, like many baths in Essoona, was open to the night sky. Joe could taste the first hint of autumn in the cool air: a promise of ice and decay. They took a corner seat at the far end, away from the rest of the bathers. As usual, their tattoos attracted curious stares. Body art was an alien concept on Syenitia.

'You first,' said Joe. 'How are you getting on? Did Cephalo get home OK?'

Björn blinked. 'Yes, ages ago. Did Kitty not tell you?' When Joe said nothing, he continued. 'The reactors and electrolysers are running non-stop. Smooth as silk. We're pumping the hydrogen into the empty well for now. We're testing that's viable as a storage strategy.'

He dipped his hands into the warm water and splashed his face. 'We'll need a pipeline once we scale up. Or a fuel-cell-powered tanker ship.'

'Is there such a thing?' asked Joe.

'There will be. People are working on them. But it's early days.' He let out a sigh. 'It's easier to make the gas than to get it where it needs to go.'

'And the oxygen?'

'Less of a problem. For now, we're compressing it to a liquid, then shipping it out in standard cryogenic tanks. There's quite a market for industrial oxygen.'

'The steel industry,' said Joe, nodding. He'd read about that.

'That's right,' said Björn. 'Welding, sewage treatment. All kinds of things. We're also looking into using it to reoxygenate the sea in places suffering from anoxia.'

Suffering from *what*? Joe had never even heard that word before. 'Anoxia?' he repeated.

'Dead zones, where oxygen levels in the water are utterly depleted,' Björn explained. 'It's much worse in the Baltic than in the North Sea. Kitty's running experiments: taking gas cylinders to suitable locations and slow-releasing the oxygen. I got her a deep-water camera so she can take a photo each week for the next two years and document the changes.' Björn frowned. 'Didn't she tell you about this? She was thrilled by the camera; I would've thought she'd have at least mentioned it.'

'We had a massive row,' Joe admitted. 'Rare for us. We made up this morning, but we've a lot of catching up to do.'

'Marriage, eh?' said Björn sympathetically. 'Quite the roller coaster.'

You can say that again, thought Joe. 'You know me, mate. Sometimes I brood too much without saying anything. Then things get stuck, start to fester.'

Björn emitted a bark of laughter and squeezed Joe's shoulder. 'We all do that.'

Enough of the psychological insight. Joe said, 'Anything else to report, or can I use you as a sounding board?'

Björn stretched his legs, scissoring them underwater as he thought. 'The employees are coming back with their renewable community proposals, but I'll tell you about that another time. The deadline isn't until next month.' He retracted his limbs and sat cross-legged on the bench next to Joe. 'So, shoot,' he said with a friendly grin. 'What's on your mind?'

'OK. So.' Joe wondered where to start. 'Kitty took me to the White House today and I had a meeting with the US President.'

'As you do,' Björn twinkled.

It was Joe's turn to grin. 'As you do. I went to invite him to this VIP event we're organising for December.'

'And did he say yes?'

'Like a shot,' said Joe. 'I think he sees it as a last hurrah before his term ends.'

Björn nodded, understanding. 'Who else are you inviting?' he asked.

'President Xi's already agreed. I went with Yisheng for that one, last week. The UN Secretary General – and Susan Omondi, of course.' He told Björn about Shakila's plan with the continental unions. 'We'll start setting up the meetings next week. But that's not why I wanted to talk to you.'

Björn raised a questioning eyebrow.

'You remember I told you about the mysterious banking errors reducing billionaires' fortunes to a mere hundred million dollars?'

Björn smirked. 'I do.'

'While I was using the gents at the White House – in a cubicle, you understand, last night's curry – I overheard some people talking about it.' Joe paused for effect. 'There's been a development.'

'And?'

Joe failed to suppress a snigger as he thought about it. 'Now the missing money's being split between every single registered employee of the individual billionaire's companies, in an automatic payment.'

Björn guffawed, a sound combining shock and amusement.

'A nice windfall for most people,' Joe continued, still trying not to laugh. 'It's traceable: the money can be recovered, but—'

'—it's embarrassing to ask for it back,' said Björn.

'It's definitely highlighting the inequality built into their business model. So far, they've managed to keep the information from the press, but it's bound to get out in the end.' Underwater, Joe folded his arms and extended his legs. 'The guys in the men's room were terrified people'll rise up and demand a fairer share of profits in general. They were talking like it was the end of the world.'

Björn tilted his head in acknowledgement. 'It might be, for them. The end of the world as they know it, at least.' He was silent for several long seconds, then turned to look at Joe's face. 'And you think it's Delius and you're worried he'll trigger a revolution.' A statement of fact rather than a question.

'Or a violent government crackdown,' Joe agreed, quaking at the thought. That was far more probable than peaceful wealth redistribution. Revolutions were always messy. People generally died. 'Unintended consequences, certainly. Yeah.'

'Why not just ask him, straight out?' Björn challenged him.

'I'm scared he'll admit it,' said Joe. 'Then I'll have to *do* something, won't I?'

'Well, *don't* ask him.'

Joe buried his face in his hands. 'I don't know what to do, Björn.'

'I don't think there's much you *can* do,' said his friend. 'If you even hint the *Shantivira* is involved in some way, all your hard work will have been for nothing. The establishment will see you as a threat and act against all your people it can reach. Just hope it never, ever gets out.' Björn lowered himself in the water until his chin touched the surface. 'Keep schtum, mate, that's my advice. If it's Delius, he'll have weighed up the consequences and decided it's worth doing despite the risks.'

267

THE INVITATIONS WENT out to the heads of the continental unions the following week. The Secretary Generals of the Pacific Islands Forum, the Union of South American Nations and the Gulf Cooperation Council were the only people to accept immediately.

Days turned into weeks and there was still no answer from the others. Joe and Shakila visited them in person, but the only response was 'we'll get back to you'. At the same time, they were fending off a stream of approaches by US, European, Indian and Chinese corporations, think tanks and individual billionaires, who all wanted to come to the event in December. They seemed to believe they were as important as actual world leaders. Worse, in the current global economic system, they probably were.

After a great many phone calls and another round of visits, they eventually got positive replies from the African Union, the European Union and ASEAN. Now they were only waiting on the South Asian Association for Regional Cooperation and the Eurasian Economic Union, who were no longer picking up the phone.

Joe sat in the *Ohimo*, a simple structure in the temperate biome which served as the *Shantivira's* church/mosque/synagogue/temple for anyone who wanted to pray – or needed a bit of solitude. Cross-legged on the woven-grass matting, he closed his eyes, seeking inspiration from the tranquil surroundings. There had to be a way to break the impasse. But how?

He'd been contemplating the problem for a whole ten minutes when the sound of a screaming baby reached his ears, volume increasing by the second. His heart sank. That was that for the peace and quiet.

His mother appeared between the trees, pushing Yonas in his all-terrain pram. 'I know, I know, my darling,' she was saying in Welsh. 'We'll change your nappy as soon as we get to the clearing; then you'll feel much better, I promise.' She looked up and spotted Joe in the open-framed structure. 'Oh, *shwmae*, Joe. Not interrupting, are we? His Majesty's done a proper stinker.'

Joe bit back a sigh and jumped down to join them. '*Helo*, Mam. No, of course not. Can I help?'

'You're all right. I'll do the honours.'

He watched Grace lay out a towel on the springy turf next to Samuel Abebe's Wanza tree, pick up the howling child and place him on it. His arms and legs thrashed like furious windmills as she rummaged in her gigantic bag of baby paraphernalia. Kneeling beside him, she swiftly removed the dirty nappy, wiped the tiny bottom clean and dry, then fitted a fresh one.

'That was slick,' said Joe.

Grace sniffed dismissively. 'Practice.'

Realising the source of discomfort had vanished, Yonas' face broke into an angelic smile.

Grace beamed back at him. 'That's *better*, isn't it?' she said in the voice adults use with babies and pets. 'Yes, it *is*. Yes, it *is*.' She rubbed her nose on his tummy and he squealed with laughter, thrashing his arms and legs once more – joyfully this time.

When she sat up again, she said, 'You can give him his bottle, if you like.'

And so Joe found himself sitting barefoot on the grass, his back resting against the sun-warmed base of the *Ohimo*, with Yonas' head in the crook of his elbow. Joe had fed Sören a couple of times, but that was years ago now. He'd forgotten how babies lived absolutely in the moment. Yonas was intensely focused on getting the precious liquid out of the bottle, sucking, slurping and dribbling. It was compelling to watch. Calming, too.

He glanced up at his mother. She was sitting on a rock, determinedly making a daisy chain despite knuckles swollen with arthritis. He had to admit, things between them had got better since she'd been on the *Shantivira*. There were still plenty of topics they edged their way around – not to mention bloody Brexit – but, day-to-day, the negative emotions her presence usually triggered were gradually subsiding.

The omnibus edition of *Pobol y Cwm* had become a regular feature of their Sunday evenings, just before his update slot with Aldeman. Her mood had noticeably improved now Kitty was taking her and Vadim back to her cottage for gardening visits. Joe suspected she used the opportunity to sneak cigarettes. Vadim too, perhaps.

Vadim had always found the *Shantivira's* no-smoking policy a challenge. That was doubtless how he and Grace had first bonded, Joe realised in a moment of insight. He was due to retire next year and would probably rekindle the habit straight away.

Grace felt his gaze and looked over at him. 'So why are you here on your own, in the middle of the day? This is where people come to think, isn't it? Is there something on your mind, laddie?'

He weighed up how much to tell her. It was hardly a secret. 'It's this visit we're setting up for December, Mam,' he said. 'There are two people we need who aren't replying. And we're getting all these requests from corporate lobbies, like they're trying to influence us, you know?'

'Well, you can tell them to bugger off, can't you, bo-yo?' she said. 'Government representatives only.'

Joe wasn't sure he had the strength. He felt the corporations were circling him like vultures, piling up the pressure until he had no choice but to yield. 'They're very persistent,' he said.

'So are you,' said Grace in her 'no nonsense from you, young man' voice. 'What about the two who don't want to come? Who are they? Why are they avoiding you?'

Joe tilted the bottle higher so Yonas could extract the last few drops. 'The Chairman of the Eurasian Economic Union and the Secretary General of the South Asian Association for Regional Cooperation.' He sighed. 'It's obvious really. The guy from Kazakhstan doesn't want to offend Putin and the guy from Nepal doesn't want to offend Modi.'

'Why don't you just invite Putin and Modi, then?' she said, carefully piercing the final stem on her daisy chain to create a loop. She pulled it gently over her hair until it hung around her neck like a string of pearls. 'You've got the Chinese President and that Obama chappie, haven't you? Maneewan told me.'

Maneewan? How had *she* heard? He said, 'Wherever we can, we want individuals who represent a wider population than that of their own countries. There are many more people in South Asia than in India alone. And Russian troops occupied a corner of Ukraine in 2014 and haven't budged since. Having the Russian president here would be . . . awkward for the other guests.'

Yonas finished his bottle, ejecting it with a small, pink tongue. His eyes blinked and closed. The little body was getting heavy; Joe wondered if he'd be able to put him down without waking him.

'Pop him upright, with his head on your shoulder,' ordered Grace. 'He needs a chance to burp. Don't worry, you won't wake him.'

Joe obeyed.

'Put a cloth underneath, or you'll have sick all down your back, love. That's it.' Grace gave a brief nod of approval as he complied with her instructions. 'Sounds like you need to send Kitty to pay them a private visit. She could say it's too risky to have all the "real" important people off the planet at once. That they're being super brave and doing the world leaders a favour. She can be very persuasive.'

True. She could. Joe began to see a way forward. 'You might have something there, Mam. The representatives should report back to their own organisations afterwards, to share what they've learnt. They can start setting up those summits now.'

An enormous burp echoed round the clearing, shattering the tranquillity. Joe couldn't stop himself from laughing, but the baby didn't stir. Grace got slowly to her feet, her joints popping audibly. 'We can put him down to sleep now.' Tenderly, she unpeeled the sleeping child from Joe's chest and placed him in the pram, tucking him in under a soft, fuzzy blanket. Then she took the cloth from Joe's shoulder and dabbed at his rugby shirt. 'You don't need to get changed now, but pop it in the wash tonight or it'll smell tomorrow.'

They walked back to the farmyard together. Joe carried his shoes in one hand, enjoying the sensation of the forest floor massaging the soles of his feet. 'What if I don't manage it, Mam?' he said. 'What if Earth's authorities won't cooperate with us? Or can't? The more I learn about them, the more I realise how little power they have.' He wrinkled his nose with distaste. 'The world belongs to the big corporations now. Corporations with the same rights as people but without human morality. You can't put them in prison if they break the law. They're like vampires – they don't die and they're sucking all the life from the Earth.'

They reached the gravel path and Joe stopped, standing on one leg to pull on his socks and trainers. Concentrating on his feet, he said, 'Now they know about the *Shantivira*, they're trying to worm their way in here, too. They're too big to fight. Too . . . amorphous. It's like battling a cloud, or jelly.' He stood up straight. 'I'm frightened, Mam,' he said. 'I feel like I've walked into a bog and can't see the path to escape.'

Grace reached out and squeezed his hand. Her skin was cool and dry. 'If anyone can, then it's you and your team,' she said. 'And if you do fail, it won't be for want of trying. I am so, so proud of you.'

Wow. He couldn't remember her ever saying that before. The situation must be even worse than he'd thought.

21. WHAT DO *YOU* WANT?

HANNA

H ANNA AND HASSAN sat at the long table in the Dunia House kitchen, drinking coffee and deciding what to do with their day. More than a week of their fortnight's break had already passed in a series of blissful days – revisiting old friends, favourite restaurants and beloved beauty spots.

There was a real pleasure to holidaying somewhere you knew well. They had adventure aplenty in their everyday lives. Familiar surroundings made a vacation truly relaxing. It was a pity they'd missed Farida, but it meant they could stay in her room while she was away. They'd catch up another time.

Because, for once, Hanna had time. Minimal childcare, no more extra training shifts with Urca. Now she'd qualified, all she had to do were her *Shantivira* duty shifts. She had three whole days off each week. A luxury she was still getting used to. So far, she'd spent the extra time catching up on all the little tasks which had fallen by the wayside since Yonas' arrival: cleaning, mending, paperwork, as well as more fun projects like making the long-promised skirt for Rose.

Hanna's clever tailoring had charmed Hassan's foster

mother: the multi-coloured panels swishing and flowing vivaciously with each step. Now Hanna was considering doing one for Lucy. It was too late to start it for her birthday, but perhaps for Christmas, as a surprise? Her friend loathed clothes shopping, preferring to wear jeans whenever possible. But Hanna knew Lucy would look great in a skirt: reds, pinks and oranges, she thought, to bring out the auburn highlights in her chestnut hair.

The peace was broken by bells chiming a melody, coming through the speakers on the television. The Korean drama about a mermaid negotiating the challenges of city life in Seoul – which Mrs Park had been watching with subtitles while she chopped carrots – had been interrupted to show a map of their block. A red dot flashed on the other side of the square.

'Would you two take the garbage out?' Mrs Park asked. 'You've finished eating, haven't you?'

Hassan's chair scraped on the flagstones as he stood. 'Sure, Mrs P. No problem.'

Hanna gulped her remaining coffee and cleared the dishes while Hassan brought in bags of waste from the shed beside the back door. Together, they carried them along the corridor, across the grand hall with the curving staircase and out through the front entrance.

Other neighbours were already standing on the street with their rubbish, chatting as they waited for the bin lorry. Hanna recognised many faces from her time at Dunia House last year. She returned nods and smiles of greeting: she and Hassan were a distinctive couple and had not been forgotten.

Gabian, who owned the fish shop next door, came

FAY ABERNETHY

over to offer them each a Syenitian hand press. 'How lovely to see you both again!' he said. 'Are you staying long?'

'We're on leave,' explained Hassan, adding, 'and we missed Mrs Park's cooking.'

Gabian threw back his head and laughed. 'I can imagine.' He leaned forward conspiratorially and said in a low voice, as if imparting a state secret, 'You tell her I have some wonderful *Samaki Nahven* today. Came in this morning, super fresh. I can put some aside for her, if she likes.'

Hanna suppressed a chuckle. He hadn't changed one bit. Still trying to make a deal, even while putting out the bins. The residents at Dunia House were some of his best customers.

'I'll let her know, Gabian,' she said. 'I expect she'll call you.'

Now Hanna could hear the bells, getting louder: a pretty tune which her made think of snowflakes and icicles. They watched the lorry turn the corner and stop at the first house. The neighbours crossed the cycle track and flower beds to the roadside where the lorry waited, the workers standing by to inspect their bags for incorrectly sorted waste.

Soon it was their turn. The bells would warn cyclists to expect pedestrians on the track and slow down, but Hanna still kept a wary eye out for bikes.

'What shall we do with today?' said Hassan, when they were done. 'Another city walk? Go to the beach? Or the forest?'

Hanna took his hand and deliberated. She loved their

city walks, exploring the squares among the blocks of houses. Each one had something unique to offer. But it was such a beautiful day, she needed a view. 'Would you be up for Dragon Hill? We could take a picnic.'

'Why not? I'll be fine if we take it slow.'

THEY TOOK IT slow. They boarded the flying tram and got out at the stop for the tourist route up the sacred mountain. They plodded along the stony track with the other pilgrims, all kitted out with rucksacks, sun hats and waterproofs. It was a pleasant day, but here by the sea the weather could change in an instant.

Hanna carried the rucksack with the food and drinks. As usual, Mrs Park had done them proud; Hanna was sure they wouldn't manage everything and she'd end up carrying half of it all the way down again. Still, they wouldn't go hungry.

The track was more boring than the smaller paths Hanna had explored with Lucy and Aneira but, this way, there was no chance of getting lost. She wanted to think and talk and contemplate the glorious panorama, not worry about map-reading.

Step by step, they gained altitude. Above the treeline they could see the mountain range which separated the prosperous east coast from the less-developed west coast of Syenitia. Even at this time of year, the tops were capped with snow which glinted, mirror-bright, in the sunshine. Dragon Hill was tiny in comparison.

They were mostly silent, lost in their own private thoughts. Steady climbing didn't leave much breath for conversation. Hanna's mind returned to the thorny problem of how to spend her life with Kia, Yonas and Hassan if they weren't living in the same place. Whichever way she looked at it, it was impossible without commuting. But that wasn't a long-term solution. Just the idea of it made her feel exhausted. So what was she going to do?

They stopped for a break in a small clearing sheltered from the sea-breeze. After some *saiju* and several spring rolls, Hanna stared at the mountains and said, 'I don't know what to do for the best, Hassan. I can't see a way to make it work, if Kia goes to live on the Earth and you want to stay on the *Shantivira*.'

Hassan laid his hand on hers. 'Hanna. Look at me.' She turned away from the sterile beauty of the rocky landscape and focused on his face. The rich, dark eyes and wide mouth always ready to curve into a smile. She loved this man. But she didn't want to have to choose between him and her sister – her one known living relative, who she'd only just found again.

'Who is the single most important person in your life?'

Hanna's eyes welled with tears. Her voice came out as a croak. 'Don't make me decide between you and Kia. That's not fair.'

He flashed a grin at her. 'No, Hanna. That's not what I meant at all. It sounds to me like you're looking at the whole thing backwards. *You* are the most important person in your life. You're twisting yourself into knots thinking about what *I* want, what *Kia* wants. What do *you* want? Really? Put your feelings for Kia and me to one side and just think about that.'

They packed up their things and continued plodding

up the hill. Hanna tried to listen to her inner voice. What *did* she want? Since Kia had exploded back into her life, it was something Hanna had barely considered. She'd seen everything through the prism of her familial obligation to care for her little sister. A duty she'd been delighted to take on. A privilege.

But. Kia's life was not Hanna's life. Yonas was Kia's baby, not Hanna's. The newborn phase was over and Kia had her own ideas about how he should be brought up. Rightly so. With the *Shantivira's* crew as her support network, Kia would always be able to access the help she needed.

So. Back to the question. What *did* Hanna want? If there were no Hassan in her life, no Kia, what would she do?

The answer was obvious. Hanna wanted to stay on the *Shantivira* and fly. Nothing beat the satisfaction of feeling she and Urca had become a capable team, stopping the Mwongo probe all by themselves. More moments like that, please.

'Hassan?'

He stopped walking. 'Yes?'

'If Kia's determined to live on the planet, we'll make sure she and Yonas find a proper home with someone to look after them. Someone who isn't me. I'll see them as often as I can, but I won't commute. I want to live and work on the *Shantivira* with you.'

Hassan threw his arms around her in an all-embracing hug. 'Thank God for that,' he said, the relief clear in his voice. 'I worried you might go somewhere I couldn't follow. I'd understand, of course, but—'

Hanna silenced him with a long, loving kiss. Having set down the emotional burden she'd been carrying for months, she felt floaty-light with joy. The pieces of her confused jumble of a life were finally slotting into place.

When they came up for air, she said, 'Let's go to *Laulaahaalia* tonight. I feel like singing.'

+   +   +

THE SATURDAY AFTER they returned to the *Shantivira* was Lucy's thirtieth birthday. Lucy had started event planning the moment she'd got back from holiday, deciding on a pool party instead of holding it in the less intimate canteen. A day-time party, because the enormous, curved swimming pool was on the accommodation deck; Joe said they could have it there as long as they didn't disturb anyone on the night shift trying to sleep.

Lucy also managed to persuade Joe to let her invite Alice, her best friend from home, and her husband, Pete, for the weekend. They knew about the *Shantivira*, but it was the first time they'd been on board. They arrived with Kitty, holding hands and staring round with wide eyes, reminding Hanna of the first time she'd visited the space station. It seemed like several lifetimes ago now.

Farida was back from Indonesia. She wasn't one for swimming, so she and Hanna sat at the poolside, sipping mocktails with their feet in the water. They watched the others swimming and playing, dolphin-Kitty towing guests around by her dorsal fin.

Hassan had his fins on and was doing circuits, shoulder muscles rippling. Watching him, Hanna experienced a familiar tug of attraction. This pool was one of their special places: it was strange to share it with so many other people at once.

'Hey,' said Lucy, sitting down next to them. 'Having fun?'

'Yes thanks,' said Hanna. 'We were catching up. Farida's parents want to meet Saïd.'

'What about you, Lucy?' asked Farida. 'What's the latest?'

'Felix and I have decided to buy a place to live together!' Lucy bubbled with enthusiasm.

Farida said, 'That's exciting!' and, half-thinking about where Kia might want to settle, Hanna asked, 'Any ideas where?'

'Well, the UK or Germany, hopefully,' said Lucy. 'More likely Germany, because you can buy a flat freehold instead of leasehold.'

Hanna had no idea what freehold and leasehold meant, but didn't want to interrupt Lucy in full flow. She'd ask Hassan later.

'The real problem is Brexit.' Lucy blew air through her lips in a frustrated sigh. 'If they end freedom of movement, our plans could become impossible. I don't want to pay a mortgage on somewhere I can't live. Or somewhere Felix can't live.'

Hanna and Farida made sympathetic noises.

Lucy brightened. 'Ireland might be an option. I've never been, but Felix loved it when he went on a school trip. It's in the EU, so Felix can live there and so can UK nationals without extra paperwork.'

'That's a long way from your families,' said Farida, frowning.

'And our friends,' agreed Lucy. 'It's not ideal.'

'Maybe you should wait and see,' suggested Hanna. 'Don't rush into anything.'

Lucy nodded. 'We'll keep saving for our deposit. But I'd rather live on the planet than up here. I want my own kitchen, you know? And perhaps a garden, or a balcony.'

'What about Essoona?' said Farida.

Lucy shook her head. 'Most places there are only to rent. We want to save for our retirement. Owning property is a part of that.'

Hanna couldn't imagine looking so far ahead. Who knew what the world would look like by the time they were old? Was it a Global North thing, to think you could plan your whole future?

'Anyway,' continued Lucy in a lower voice, 'I talked to Nikolai earlier. His mum has set up a mobile lab on a ship cruising the North Pacific.'

'She should join forces with Björn,' said Farida. 'They'd learn lots from each other, working with the same power source.'

'Svetlana's operation isn't supposed to exist,' Lucy scoffed. 'Not even Joe knows about it, remember? She can't go round *collaborating* with people. Weapons development and power generation are two completely different fields.'

They were interrupted by Kia and Yonas, approaching across the pool. 'Here's Auntie Hanna!' cooed Kia, swooshing him through the water. 'Yes she *is*! Yes she *is*!' Kia lifted the dripping baby out and onto Hanna's lap. Luckily she already had her swimsuit on.

'He's getting cold. Can you dry him off and keep him

warm while I practise my swimming? His bag's behind you, under the table.'

Farida leapt to her feet and retrieved it, rummaging for a towel.

Kia watched as they swaddled Yonas in a fluffy yellow square with a hood shaped like a duck's head. 'Hey, guess what?' she said.

'What?' said Lucy.

'Grace has asked me and Yonas to go and live with her, when she goes back.'

'In *Wales*?' said Hanna, stunned. She'd never been, but she'd heard it rained all the time. More than in London, if that was possible. She couldn't imagine Kia being happy in a place like that. She remembered Joe saying even the houses were grey, to match the sky. She thought he'd been winding her up until he'd shown her pictures.

'That was kind of her,' said Farida.

'I think she's worried about being lonely,' said Kia with a rare flash of insight. 'After living up here, you know?'

'You could be right,' said Hanna.

'I'm seriously considering it,' Kia continued. 'Yonas needs to be christened and Grace has the connections at her local chapel to organise one easily. Chapel's Welsh for church,' she said in an authoritative aside to Farida.

'You don't want to have it up here?' Hanna said. 'Joe could do it. He did Samuel's funeral.'

Kia shook her head. 'I want a proper ceremony with a proper priest in a proper building.'

'Fair enough,' said Hanna. It was a reasonable wish. But *Wales*? 'Maybe you should visit first. See what it's like.'

'What about once you're settled, Kia?' asked Lucy. 'Any ideas what you want to do with your life, apart from being a mother?'

'Sure,' Kia replied without missing a beat. 'As soon as Yonas is old enough for daycare, I'm going to train as a nurse.'

Hanna goggled. A *nurse*? Where had *that* come from? And why had she never spoken about it before?

22. THE SECOND SHIPMENT
DAN, NOVEMBER 2016

A FRA SET THE *Gezi Urdina* down lightly and taxied towards the hangar. The doors were opening, like the jaws of some giant beast. There were no lights on inside. 'I don't like it, that they're using the same delivery location,' she said. 'Not clever.'

'No,' said Dan, standing behind her with his hands on her shoulders. 'I'll ask to meet somewhere else next time.'

Dan marvelled at how different he felt, compared to their last stop-off here. Still nervous, sure, but excited and optimistic too. The quality control test would be more of a formality this time. Some kind of test was fair enough when you were paying so much money.

It had been his thirty-fourth birthday a couple of weeks ago, but as they'd been en route here, they'd not done much to celebrate. Dan had given Afra an impromptu unplugged concert of all his favourite songs: like doing his old set back in *The Garden*, on Amra. All gone now, he remembered, with a tightness in his chest.

As soon as this job was over, they'd have enough funds for a proper break. A belated birthday treat. After days of discussions, they'd settled on returning to Syenitia for a month. It was expensive, sure, but it had the advantage of being safe.

Dan planned on exploring the mountains which separated the Eastern and Western oceans. He didn't know if the Syenitians were into skiing or snowboarding, but Afra had never seen snow. *He* wanted to be the one to show it to her.

The *Gezi Urdina* came to rest in the hangar. Afra left all the ship's lights on and together they watched the doors close with an echoing boom.

'Right then,' said Dan. 'Better get to work.' He hit the button to lower the ramp and turned to leave the cockpit.

'Wait!' called Afra. She stood up and put her hands on either side of his face, kissing him firmly on the lips. 'Good luck,' she said.

He kissed her back, quite thoroughly. Then he departed to meet their guests.

They also seemed more relaxed than last time. Dan assumed his best slave demeanour and led Henning and the chemist to the hold. He stood aside, staring resolutely at his boots while the chemist set up his kit.

'What's this, Sslave-Bellyn?'

Dan's head jerked up. Shit! Henning was holding his guitar, turning it over curiously in his four-fingered hands.

Why-oh-why hadn't he tidied that away? That was where he'd—

A slip of paper fell out of the sound hole and fluttered to the floor.

—hidden the Earth's coordinates for safekeeping. Kitty had given them to him when he'd broken off contact with the *Shantivira*, so he could make his own way home one day.

Henning bent to examine it and Dan leapt forward,

snatching it off the floor and tucking it into his back pocket. His heart thumped violently against his ribcage and he suppressed an urge to vomit. At least they were just numbers, not a named location. They wouldn't mean anything to Henning.

'It's my guitar, sir, a musical instrument,' he said, attempting to sound calm and deferential. 'So I can entertain my captain? May I demonstrate?' He held out his hands and the Ranglatiri passed it to him, studying him with new interest. Dan hoped his uncharacteristic reaction hadn't raised Henning's suspicions.

He put his foot on a box and strummed the opening chords to Bowie's *The Man Who Sold the World*, before starting to sing. He prayed the music would act as a distraction, preventing Henning from thinking too much about the coordinates he'd just glimpsed. Henning listened with an unnerving stillness. By the time Dan had finished, the chemist was ready with his verdict. The product was satisfactory.

'Good,' said Henning. 'I have initiated the payment. You may begin unloading when your captain informs you she has received the full amount. We will wait outsside.'

Dan bowed low as they left the room. Phew. He was glad that was over with. Now there was just the small matter of moving the cargo out pallet by pallet, then he and Afra could beat it out of here.

✦   ✦   ✦

DAN OFFLOADED THE crate from the pallet truck and wiped the sweat off his forehead. It was warmer than last time. The air was stickier. How many loads was that now? Must be at least a dozen. The chemist took it away with the forklift and Dan turned back to the ramp for the next load. A grating noise stopped him in his tracks.

He spun round and saw Henning had twisted towards the sound, too. Henning took an involuntary step backwards – as if he could sense a threat in the darkness of the hanger that Dan couldn't.

'No!' croaked Henning in Ranglatiri, raising his hands in a gesture of surrender.

Dan heard the hum of plasma guns charging, ready to fire. At the same instant, something solid poked between his shoulder blades and a voice hissed, 'Hands up, primitive, you are ssurrounded.' Several pairs of boots marched up the ramp behind him. Afra! Shit. Shit. Shit. How could he warn her?

He couldn't.

Dan's brain whirled, weighing up his chances of reaching the knife taped to his chest and using it before his assailant could pull the trigger. Non-existent. He put his hands up. A jab to his spine made him stagger forwards towards Henning.

A group of Ranglatiri in full battledress stepped into the pool of light cast by the *Gezi Urdina*. They were a head taller than Henning, and broader across the shoulders. Females. Icy dread flooded Dan's belly.

There was a yell from the darkness and the whine of the forklift accelerating in their direction. Dan's spirits lifted. The chemist was going to ram their attackers!

Almost casually, the largest Ranglatiri aimed her weapon and fired. There was a smell of hot, burnt air and the forklift stopped sharply as the chemist released the controls. His body flew out of the vehicle and landed on the edge of the illuminated area with a thud and a crunch.

Dan was still staring numbly at the smoking corpse when someone pulled down his arms and cuffed them roughly behind his back. Bellyn's survival training kicked in and he fell to his knees, trying to appear as submissive as possible.

Afra must be watching on the cameras though. Why hadn't she fired the *Gezi Urdina's* short range weapons? An explosion from inside the spacecraft answered his question. The cockpit windscreen shattered outwards and a plume of acrid smoke rose into the darkness. Dan heard Afra scream: a bellow of terror and fury, suddenly silenced. Oh God.

He was relieved when they dragged her out and dropped her next to him. Her hair was full of dust, her mouth was bleeding and they'd cuffed her wrists behind her back. But where there was life there was hope, right?

Strong hands lifted them to their feet and marched them away, into the blackness. Dan heard the grating noise again, closer this time: a small door. Outside, it was already twilight. A shadowy hulk squatted on the take-off strip – a Ranglatiri shuttle. The three prisoners were pushed up the ramp, which closed behind them with a bang. Dan's stomach lurched as the craft took off. Presumably it would be a short trip, as they remained in the loading area, the captives encircled by a white wall of menacing sentinels. The air was stale, but breathable. Dan kept his head bowed, not daring to see if there were any windows beyond his jailors. Afra did the same. She caught his eye just once: a look that said, 'This is it. It's over.' Dan couldn't disagree.

Perhaps twenty minutes had passed in silence when Dan's stomach lurched again, informing him they were about to land. The ramp lowered and they were shoved out into the docking bay of a large cruiser.

They were orbiting the planet; outside, Dan could see a waiting fleet of Ranglatiri ships. Henning stared at them and muttered, 'Which one of you bastards betrayed me?'

A Ranglatiri with an entourage approached them across the docking bay; faceless chess pieces led by a terrifying white queen. Their captors bowed low, and the leader announced, 'Prisoners, the Minister of the Interior has quesstions for you. Show respect.'

Dan fell to his knees and gazed at the ground, radiating humility in a desperate effort to survive. Henning followed suit.

Only Afra remained standing, defiant to the last.

23. A MIYAWAKI FOREST

JOE

'So?' said Rob, spreading his arms and turning on the spot with pride. 'What do you think?'

Joe eyed the scrubby wasteland: a largish square of gravel and weeds with a handful of pioneering trees and bushes, seeded from their relatives on the other side of the fence. This late in autumn, only a few orange-brown leaves still clung to their branches. Low-rise 1960s social housing flanked the plot on three sides; a mighty tower block which could have been transplanted straight from East Berlin dominated the north end.

'It's lovely,' he lied. This wasn't at all what he'd been expecting when Rob had phoned him from a public call box to suggest 'an update in person'. But this was the first opportunity they'd had to meet up since Rob had been expelled from the *Shantivira* in July. Joe had missed his company.

Rob laughed. 'No, it's not. But it will be.'

Joe pulled his motorbike jacket closer around him. The stiff breeze coming off the Firth of Forth was icy and damp at the same time, reminding him of winters in Essoona. 'How long have you been in Edinburgh?'

'We moved in with Sarah's dad this summer, after I

left the army. He's still in the house she grew up in, on the other side of Leith Links,' Rob said, gesturing vaguely to the south-east. 'The kids started at her old primary school in September. John needs more support since Sarah's mum died a while ago. We only lived down south because of my job, so it made sense to come back. Her brother lives in Canada; he's not able to help much.'

'What about Sarah's work?' said Joe. 'She's a translator, isn't she?'

'French into English,' confirmed Rob, 'specialising in pharmaceutical texts. The move's no problem for her. She's always had a mobile career, because we never knew where I'd be posted next.' He grinned. '*That's* not something I'll miss. It'll be great for the children to put down some proper roots.'

Joe watched domestic-cat-Kitty stroll along the top of the graffiti-spattered fence which surrounded the plot. 'What's your plan? Kitty said she's providing you with a basic income so you can do full-time voluntary work?'

Rob followed his gaze. 'I didn't ask her for money. When I told her I'd enjoyed working in the *Shantivira's* biomes so much, I wanted to set up an urban community garden, she offered.'

'She likes to put her dragon's hoard to good use,' said Joe, picturing Kitty's hideaway inside *Yr Wyddfa*, piled high with gold coins and other ancient treasures. Was it him, or had the heap diminished in the years he'd known her?

'But it turns out they're already doing that, over there.' Rob continued, pointing eastwards. 'I'm volunteering with them, helping plant fruit and nut trees. But I need my own project, too, you know?'

Joe nodded, curious now. His secretive wife hadn't told him anything about what Rob was planning.

'So, with Kitty's assistance, I'm now the proud owner of this tiny plot of land which, with the help of the local community, I'm going to turn into a Miyawaki forest.'

Joe blinked. 'What's one of those when it's at home?'

'A fast-growing urban micro-forest,' explained Rob earnestly. 'You prepare the soil, densely plant a load of native species, mulch it a lot, water it, and, after three years, it's self-maintaining. Sort of a mini-version of the wild zone on the *Shantivira*.'

'Bringing nature into the city?' said Joe, trying to imagine the neglected parcel of land bursting with life. It sounded like an impossible task.

'Boosting biodiversity, improving air quality, absorbing CO_2 and noise, helping manage storm water. Plus all the unquantifiable benefits to people's everyday lives.' Rob looked at the nearby tower block. 'When we're done, the neighbours will wake up to birdsong in the morning.'

Joe was still sceptical. 'And what *do* the neighbours have to say about it?'

'Early days, mate. I'll involve the local schools and take it from there. It won't work unless the community actively wants it.' He grinned. 'But if there's one thing my time in the army taught me, it's how to get people to want to do stuff.'

Joe chuckled. 'Yeah, you're good at that.' He glanced up at the surrounding buildings. 'What about planning permission? I'm sure some would rather use a central location like this to build more houses.'

'That's why Kitty and I bought the land outright: so developers can't touch it. I'll be launching a charm offensive at the City of Edinburgh Council too, of course.' Rob pushed his hands into the back pockets of his jeans. 'Legally – as far as I understand – the plot's so tiny, we don't actually need planning permission to create a forest.'

Black-cat-Kitty jumped down from the fence, crossing the gravel to rub herself against their legs.

In his head, she said, *Will you be alright if I head off?*

Sure, he replied silently. *I'll let you know when I need picking up.*

She disappeared, leaving Joe and Rob alone. Joe scuffed his boot on the ground, saying, 'Fancy a walk? It's years since I've been to Edinburgh.'

Rob smiled. 'And you're so busy and important nowadays, who knows when we'll get another chance for a chat. Come on, then.'

They left the future forest and Rob led Joe through the housing blocks to the Water of Leith. They walked along the Shore, in the direction of the docks. 'How are the preparations for your VIP visit going?' Rob asked.

'Things are finally slotting into place,' said Joe. 'We had a couple of guests who didn't want to accept our invitation for fear of offending some powerful people.' He hunched his shoulders against the wind. 'Can't blame them really, politics at that level is like opening one can of worms after another.'

'But they've agreed after all?'

'Kitty paid them each a private visit and laid it on thick, emphasising what a service they'd be doing humanity and assuring them there'd be no diplomatic repercussions for them personally. Quite the opposite. Their courage would be appreciated in the highest circles, that sort of thing.'

'With the implicit threat that she can get past their security anytime she likes?' said Rob.

Joe twitched his eyebrows in unspoken acknowledgement. 'It was Mam's idea, actually. And, to be honest, if Kitty can manage to get my mam on side, then a couple of reluctant politicians aren't much of an obstacle.'

'How's your mum getting on, living on the *Shantivira*?'

'OK, I suppose.' Joe thrust his hands deep into his jacket pockets. 'No. That's not fair. She's been brilliant. She's gone out of her way to make friends and be helpful.'

Rob gave him a sidelong glance. 'You sound surprised.'

'Well. You know we never got on. There's other stuff I never told you. Bad stuff, buried deep, but festering for years.' Joe studied the boats moored along the quayside. Rust-stained old barges rubbed shoulders with swanky floating restaurants. 'We're both still struggling to get over the damage we did to each other. This is the most time we've spent together since I joined the army. It's forced me to get to know her again, as an adult.'

They reached the docks and walked along the edge of the Albert Dock Basin, gazing at the gigantic vessels crammed with heavy duty equipment for the oil fields. Like ocean-going *Koppakuoria*, Joe thought, wondering how Björn was getting on.

They stopped briefly at the Royal Marines Memorial before rounding Whisky Quay to admire the *Royal Yacht*

Britannia through the fence. In an awed voice, Rob said, 'Imagine having your own ship and being able to go anywhere you want in the world. It must be amazing.'

'It is,' said Joe, grinning. 'In fact, why stop at the world?'

Rob spun round and laughed. 'You're a bloody lucky bastard, you know that?'

'Yeah, I know. But nothing in life is free. There's always a price.'

They turned away from the yacht and made their way around the basin to Lighthouse Park, with a spectacular view across the Forth Estuary. They stood on the breakwater and the wind buffeted Joe's body, blasting its way into his lungs. It was energising, like jumping into cold water without the inconvenience of getting wet.

'What's the latest on the kidnappers?' asked Rob.

'The driver has been charged with dangerous driving and misuse of government property,' Joe said. 'The rest has been hushed up.'

Rob pulled a face, but Joe shrugged. 'I'm not too bothered. It means Mam won't have to testify and relive the trauma. The people who should know, know. The prime minister's enquiries traced the instigators to a particular right-wing think tank which has since been shut down.'

'Really?' said Rob. 'I'm surprised they got a result so quickly.'

Joe continued walking. 'Perhaps it's a scapegoat. Those involved are still around, with their dark money and darker opinions. These think tanks are like mushrooms, linked by underground networks and popping up all over the place.' He wasn't about to tell Rob, but Delius was monitoring those individuals now. They wouldn't be pulling a stunt like that twice.

They passed some fancy modern flats, obviously expensive but devoid of character. If it weren't for the balconies, he'd have assumed they were office blocks. Given their exposed position, Joe hoped they had quality double glazing. There couldn't be many days where the wind didn't blow here. Eventually they reached the lighthouse at the other end of the breakwater and paused for a breather.

'So,' Rob asked, 'who'll represent the UK at this big meeting of yours?'

'Donald Tusk,' said Joe.

'Ha!' Rob guffawed. 'That'll go down like a lead balloon in Westminster, won't it?'

'Tough. If they'd been in control of their people, they could have had *you* there, mingling with the great and the good. Donald Tusk will represent the EU countries. The UK is still in the EU, for now. End of story.'

Rob shook his head. 'I'm kind of glad I won't be there. I don't envy you, mate. It's a can of worms, like you said. My father-in-law's furious about Brexit. He voted to stay in the UK in the Scottish Independence Referendum the year before last, because they said that was the only way for Scotland to remain in the EU. And now look.'

Joe leaned on the railing which surrounded the little lighthouse. The padlocks which visiting lovers had attached to the wire mesh, expressing the permanence of their affections, were all rusting in the salty air. 'Perfidious Albion is turning on its own people,' he murmured, contemplating the shifting water below. He raised his head and looked out to sea, saying, 'At least your father-in-law appreciates the EU. How can I get humans to understand the value of cooperation with the Galaksi Alliance – that we're stronger and safer as part of a larger group – when people like my mam believe Brexit has set the country free?'

Standing beside him, Rob gave him a sympathetic glance.

'She's a simple soul,' Joe continued. 'She sees something's wrong with how the country's run; that it doesn't serve the interests of the majority. And she's rightly angry. But she believes what she reads in the newspapers. She trusts politicians to deliver on their promises to fix things. As do many normal citizens.' He shook his head in disbelief. 'To me, that's the only explanation for the US election result.'

'That and the cult of celebrity,' Rob agreed.

Joe imitated his mother's voice. '"I've seen that Boris Johnson on the telly. He made me laugh." Is that how you get to be fucking Foreign Secretary, Rob? By making people *laugh*? What the *fuck* is going on with the world?'

Rob patted him on the shoulder. 'Calm down, mate. Getting in a tizzy won't change anything.'

'A tizzy?' Joe smiled at the word. 'Is that what you tell your kids?' He contemplated the boats in the tiny marina, the Victorian fish market – now a restaurant – and the community of Newhaven beyond, its church spire sticking up like a defiant middle finger.

'Must I buy a whole media outlet just to get my message across?' he said, frustrated. 'Or do deals with tycoons in back rooms? Because that's not who I am, Rob. I can't see that working for me.'

'No,' agreed Rob. 'You're a soldier, Joe, not a politician. So think like one. This is a campaign like any other: you have superior firepower and superior intelligence. Once the penny drops that you have the strategic advantage, the truly powerful people – not the politicians – will be beating a path to your door.'

'They already are,' said Joe glumly. 'But they all want things I can't give them.'

✦ ✦ ✦

THE FOLLOWING MONDAY was Grace's sixty-eighth birthday. Joe managed to secure a table for two at the swanky restaurant in the glass pyramid on top of the Library tower. Sometimes it was handy having the Syenitian Council leader as a brother-in-law. It was the first time he and his mother had been out alone together for—he tried to remember—it must be at least two years. And that'd only been to the Three Horseshoes Inn, near Brecon. Everything had changed since then. He was so nervous, he'd not only shaved twice that day, he'd actually put on a suit and tie.

When he picked Grace up from her cabin, it was clear she felt the same: that dressing up boosted her confidence. She wore an elegant, calf-length dress, burgundy to match her crocodile-skin handbag, with a string of pearls he'd not seen since his childhood. They'd belonged to his grandmother, he recalled. Dark tights and her sensible, arthritis-friendly shoes completed the ensemble.

'Look at us,' he said, his face crinkling into a grin.

'Aren't we smart?' He held out his elbow for Grace to take and, arms linked, they crossed the accommodation deck to the lift/teleport.

It wasn't Grace's first time in Essoona. Vadim had been showing her the sights and she'd visited various bathhouses with Chooli. But it was the first time she'd come with Joe.

In honour of the occasion he hired a transport pod, just for them. His mother gazed at the passing residential blocks; here at street-level, you got a great view of the traditional Syenitian decorative style on the facades of the lower floors.

The trams flew level with the third-floor windows, so – if you managed to get a window seat – you only saw the greenery-covered second and third storeys, and the solar panels on the two top floors.

'William Morris would've liked it here,' commented Grace.

Joe understood what she meant. The ornately carved doors and windows, adorned with flowing depictions of the natural world – flowers, plants, insects, animals – ensured no two buildings were alike.

The pod dropped them at Kirjasto Square and sped away into the traffic, platooning with the vehicle in front. Grace crossed the flagstones to the ancient *tammi* tree at the square's centre, its heavy, twisted boughs propped up with wooden supports. It had shed its leaves completely now: a clear sign winter was coming.

'Vadim said the blossom on this tree is especially beautiful,' she said, reaching up to touch the pale bark.

Joe nodded. 'It's the sacred guardian tree of Essoona.

Thousands of years old. The legend is that, as long as it lives, the city will be safe and prosper.'

'It looks on its last legs to me.'

'Well, I'm no gardener,' said Joe, smiling. 'But I reckon Kitty's sister tops it up with life energy to keep it going.'

'Rowan, isn't it?' said Grace. 'When will I get to meet her? Kitty doesn't talk about her much.'

Not out loud, thought Joe. According to Kitty's latest update, Ranglatiri council members each kept a personal slave. To maintain her cover, Rowan had to do the same. Hers was a young Ranglatiri male, utterly indoctrinated with the ruling elite's dogma. If he ever got wind of the truth about her, he'd report her to the authorities and her mission would fail. This meant she had to stay permanently in character and in costume, resulting in intense psychological strain. Kitty was desperately worried about her.

'She's not on Syenitia right now, Mam. I expect you'll meet her one day.'

'Chooli said she went away because of problems with Aldeman? I don't understand why. He's such a nice man. Lovely manners.'

'You never know what goes on in other people's marriages, do you?' said Joe, remaining discreet.

Grace pursed her lips. 'I suppose not. Well, rowans are pioneer trees. They can survive almost anywhere.'

Joe thought about his sister-in-law and what she was trying to achieve. 'Let's hope so,' he murmured.

The late afternoon sun glinted on the glossy black stone of the Library, making the tower look like an enchanted fortress topped by a flashing diamond. Due to strict planning regulations, it was the tallest building in Essoona by far. 'Come on, Mam,' he said, 'we don't want them giving our table to someone else.'

Inside, glistening white columns shaped like trees supported the high ceiling. Elaborate paintings of flora and fauna filled the spaces between the interlocking branches. Grace craned her neck, trying to take it all in. 'This is a *library*?' she exclaimed. 'It's more like a cathedral!'

'It's the planet's primary data archive, Mam. So you're spot-on, seeing as the Syenitians practically worship knowledge.' He led her to the lift and pressed the button for the top floor. As he'd hoped, Grace was favourably impressed by the restaurant. It was like the showpiece greenhouse in some botanical gardens: mature tropical trees in oversized containers gave the dining room an intimate feel, despite the dizzying height of the apex.

The Syenitian waiter helped them out of their coats and showed them to a table at the corner of the pyramid. A verdant potted shrub provided them with a degree of privacy.

'Do you think we'll get any service hidden back here?' Grace whispered, a little awestruck.

'Don't worry. They'll take good care of us. The corner tables are the most sought-after.' He turned to the windows. 'We have a dual aspect, see?'

They spent several minutes admiring the view, with Joe pointing out the local landmarks. Then they remembered their menus and Joe translated the names of dishes he thought Grace would like. They ordered and sat back as the waiter poured their drinks with a flourish. When he'd gone, Joe raised his beer glass. 'Happy birthday, Mam.'

She clinked her wine against it. 'Thank you, Joe.' She peered around at the other diners. 'How the other half live, eh?'

'Something like that.'

'Do you come here with Kitty?' Grace asked. 'On special occasions?'

Joe shook his head. 'Kitty gets bored watching me eat. Dates with Kitty involve going somewhere wild and deserted. I don't come to places like this often. It's a treat.' He took a gulp of beer. 'So, how's it going with little Yonas? Did Kia give you an answer yet?'

'About coming to Brecon?' said Grace. 'She turned me down. She's going back to Ethiopia.'

'Really?' This was news to Joe.

'She's going to live with one of your former pilots, in,' Grace frowned, trying to remember, 'Addis Ababa, is it?'

'Senai?' said Joe. As far as he knew, she was the *Shantivira's* only contact living in Ethiopia's capital.

'That's the one. She's got it all set up for January.' Grace put down her wineglass. 'Kitty's funding a nanny for Yonas so Kia can go back to school. I think Hagar inspired her. She's determined to train as a nurse.'

'A nurse?' He *was* learning things this evening.

'They have a huge shortage of healthcare staff, apparently. Kia wants to make a contribution to her country, and quite right too.'

'January? Just a couple of months.' He'd miss seeing the pair around the base.

'Yes, dear,' Grace said. 'I'll stay until the New Year to help out, then I'll head home, too. It's safe now, isn't it?'

'As safe as it'll ever be. You could go now, if you wanted.'

Grace's steel-grey eyebrows moved closer together. 'Are you trying to get rid of me?'

'No! Honestly, Mam, no.' He turned his glass round and round on the white tablecloth. 'I might have felt that way, over the summer. But I've sort of got used to having you about. I just thought . . . your garden, that's all.'

'It's nearly winter, the garden can wait. I promised Kia I wouldn't go home before she did.'

'You'll miss her, won't you?' Joe said.

Grace smiled. 'It's been lovely. Like being a grandparent.' She observed his expression and added hurriedly, 'I didn't mean . . . I know you and Kitty . . .' She shook her head, exasperated at herself. 'I'm not trying to put pressure on you. I can see you're both happy as you are. I just meant; it was nice to be needed. To have someone who *wanted* me to look after them.'

To Joe's relief, the waiter arrived with their food, placing their plates in front of them with confident precision. The intensity of the moment was broken before things got awkward.

'What did you order?' he asked. 'I've forgotten already.'

'You said it was some kind of flat fish, like a Dover sole? With baked vegetables and a fancy sauce?' Grace's eyes flashed with surprise as she examined her plate.

'*Kampelakala.* That was it. Sorry, I should have warned you, Syenitia's potato-equivalent is purple.'

'Right,' she said slowly. 'OK. And you?'

'I'm trying the Pweza's fried shrimp,' he said. 'They're

304

supplying restaurants now, from the farms they set up last year. I told you about the Pweza, didn't I?'

'Several times, yes.'

Joe bit into a shrimp and sucked out the juicy meat. That was *good*. So fresh, he could taste the sea. He wiped his chin. 'So, will you visit Kia in Addis Ababa?'

His mother heaped her fork with fish. 'Of course. April, we thought. For Yonas' birthday. Kia and Senai are planning to have him baptised on the same day, so it'll be a big celebration. She assures me they'll have plenty of food which isn't spicy.'

'That's great.' Joe tried and failed to imagine his mother participating in an Ethiopian christening ceremony. 'You've become quite the jet-setter, this last year.'

'Well. I've had to, haven't I?' she replied defensively.

What was it with them? Taking the most innocent of remarks as criticism. She did it to him; he did it to her, he understood that now. It would take years to unlearn the habit. He patted her hand. 'I meant, I'm proud of you, Mam. How you've handled . . . everything.'

Grace sipped her wine. 'Thank you. You know, Kitty says we're very alike, you and me. You might be a dead ringer for your Tad, but personality-wise we have a lot in common.' She smiled ruefully. 'That's probably why we always end up arguing.'

'He spoiled so much, for both of us.'

Grace leaned back in her seat. 'I know,' she sighed. 'But it was hard for him, being unemployed and having a woman provide for him. Being dependant on your nan for a roof over his head. That wasn't how he'd been raised. He lost all his confidence.'

Joe twirled his fork in his noodles. Not looking at his mother, he said through tight lips, 'He was a weak, violent bastard.'

'He was *my* weak, violent bastard,' Grace whispered. 'I married him for better or for worse.'

Joe knew if he said another word, their evening would be ruined. He focused carefully on eating his shrimps.

Eventually, Grace said, 'You and Kitty saved my life that day. I'd never have had the strength to kick him out myself. One of his beatings would have killed me eventually. It was just ... easier to hate you both than admit I needed your help. That hatred—well, it stopped me being a proper mam to you.'

Joe put down the tail of the shrimp he'd just eaten. 'And I hated you, for not protecting me from him. It took me decades to realise how powerless you were against him. And then there's me, his *doppelgänger*, walking about like a permanent reminder.'

Grace picked up her napkin and dabbed her eyes. 'It's not your fault, love. None of it was ever your fault. I've wasted so much time. Can you forgive me?'

'I already have. You can thank Nestor for that.'

Grace laughed, a choking sound, half cough.

'Can you forgive *me*?' Joe continued. 'For ending your marriage without your permission?'

His mother smiled through her tears. 'I already have. You can thank Kitty for that.'

It was Joe's turn to laugh. 'She has a way of wearing you down, hasn't she?' Joe stretched a hand out across the table. 'Friends, then?'

'Friends,' Grace confirmed. 'Now eat your dinner, boyo, before it gets cold.'

PART THREE

24. THE MAN WHO SOLD THE WORLD
DAN

'HAVE THEY BEEN checked for weapons?' asked the minister.

There was a flurry of activity and Dan was hauled to his feet for a full body search. His cuffed hands were lifted painfully high behind his back and he heard them remarking on his slave tattoo.

One of the guards gave a little cry of surprise as she lifted his T-shirt and uncovered the knife sheath taped to Dan's torso. She ripped it off in one swift movement, making him yell with pain as the tape took his chest hair with it. He stifled his scream quickly, resolutely studying the metal floor as the guard handed it to the minister. On Afra they found nothing.

The minister nodded, as if this was expected. She unsheathed the knife and dropped the rest to the ground before sniffing the blade. She said, 'When we located the remains of Adelharz's team, two had died of stab wounds and the traitor Bellyn's ship was misssing.' She stepped in front of Afra, who glared, unflinching, at the creature's mask. 'You knew we'd ssearch you. So you hid your weapon on your sslave. It must be very loyal.'

She spun on her heel to scrutinise the guards. 'Which

one of you incompetentss captured this primitive?' She pointed at Dan with his knife. Hesitantly, a guard raised her arm.

'Remove her mask and resstrain her.' The minister pronounced the death sentence coolly, as if performing some tiresome administrative task. For her part, the guard made no audible protest. Dan didn't dare look up to watch.

The minister turned back to Afra. 'Did you think we wouldn't notice this attempt to destroy our civilisation? Plunging male fertility, in the sspace of a few years? Isegrimma, our mighty and invincible leader, has sent me to find out what you know before sstopping your operation for good.'

She ran the tip of Dan's blade lightly across Afra's throat, drawing blood. Dan imagined her licking her lips behind the white mesh of her mask.

'Who do you work for, Ssayari? Your government? The Galakssi Alliance?'

Afra's ears waggled in amusement. 'Who do I work for? I worked for Bellyn, the best Ranglatiri I ever met. He was acting on behalf of all Ranglatiri males, who are not permitted to live freely and not treated with the respect intelligent life deserves. Your problems are home-grown, bitch.'

'Men's rights? You're telling me all this – fusss – is about *men's rights*?' The minister put her head back and laughed, a deep belly laugh which shook her whole body. 'Isegrimma will be *delighted* to hear that's all it is. Oh, Ssayari, you've made my day! *Thank you.*'

She twirled Dan's knife back and forth around her

fingers in a casual display of expertise. The minister was clearly no stranger to handling weapons. 'Now, what shall we do with you?' she said in a thoughtful tone. The blade flashed as it spun, the movement mesmerising Dan. Afra remained stiffly upright, her chin jutting boldly. If you didn't know her, you'd think she wasn't scared at all, thought Dan with pride.

'I *should* send you to Our Leader, Isegrimma,' said the minister. 'Inventing cruel and unusual deaths is a hobby of hers. And you have surely earned a nice, slow one, on display somewhere.' Her laughter was a spine-juddering bark. 'But I'm hungry and I've never tasted Ssayari before. I've heard the meat under that tough exterior is most ssucculent.'

Without warning, she plunged Dan's knife violently into Afra's stomach, slashing her open with a practised twist of the wrist. Afra emitted a single, ear-piercing scream, then folded in half and crumpled to the ground, unmoving.

Unable to stop himself, Dan howled. He fell to his knees and let his tears flow, mingling with the widening pool of Afra's blood. It didn't matter what happened now. They could do what they liked with him. He watched the light leave his lover's eyes until they stared glassily into nothingness. He touched his head to hers for a moment, then rough hands pulled him away, forcing him to stand.

The minister fingered his chin. 'I believe the sslave was genuinely attached to its mistress. Interesting.'

'Lady Luchsa, may I sspeak?' Henning addressed the minister for the first time, speaking Ranglatiri.

Still holding Dan's chin, her head whipped round.

'Speak, sspecies-traitor.'

Henning stood a little straighter. 'I have worked with the primitive for some months now. It is exceptionally loyal. It continues to follow its former masster's orders, beyond the criminal Bellyn's death. It eats no meat, making it cheap to feed. It is docile and obedient, yet sstrong and healthy. And you must admit its likeness to a Syenitian is an amusing quirk.'

Dan frowned. Was Henning trying to help him? He hadn't expected that.

'Yess,' said the minister, dropping her hand and looking Dan up and down. Regular *stakarh* training had kept him in shape and it showed. His short sleeves were tight around his biceps. 'I see it has a few more months of sservice in it. We will send it to the Mines of Kifo.'

Although he'd been expecting this as the best outcome for his current predicament, Dan's heart sank. Maybe he should do something to make them kill him right now. Surely a fast death would be preferable?

'I know where there are more of them, Ma'am.'

WHAT? Dan nearly lifted his head to stare at Henning, then remembered they didn't know he understood Ranglatiri. Better keep it that way. Pulse racing, he forced himself to remain motionless.

'Check its back pocket. You'll find a thin sstrip of white with coordinates on it. I ssuspect they are the location of its home planet.'

Luchsa motioned to a guard, who rummaged in Dan's pockets until she pulled out the paper with Kitty's curly hand-writing. The minister studied it with interest.

'I musst consult with Isegrimma,' she said, turning

away to make the call.

Next to Dan, the guard who'd had her mask removed gave a tiny sniff. How long did she have until oxygen toxicity set in, he wondered, remembering Bellyn's execution. Another hour before the fits started and she lost consciousness? Ninety minutes if she was lucky. Whose corpse would the others eat first? Hers? Or Afra's? A tear rolled down Dan's cheek as he imagined his captors tearing Afra's perfect body limb from limb.

Luchsa rejoined the group. 'These coordinatess are known to Our Leader,' she said to Henning. She gestured at the fleet waiting outside. 'Take your ships and find out what'ss there. We will be watching on a live feed to assess the local ssituation. If the primitives attack, you may retaliate. If you ssurvive and return with more like this,' she waved a hand at Dan, 'you will be permitted to live.'

Henning bowed low, 'For your glory, Ma'am. May I also donate all the profitss from my business venture to the government?'

'Your accountss have already been frozen and confisscated.' Dan suspected Luchsa was smiling as she said this. He was sure she'd just learnt these were the coordinates where their prototype frigate had disappeared without trace.

Luchsa was sending Henning and his fleet to their deaths, and the Ranglatiri leaders would be watching to see what they were up against. Armed with that knowledge, they would, in time, launch a full-scale invasion of the Earth.

And it was all *his* fault. Why hadn't he memorised those coordinates and destroyed them? How could he warn the *Shantivira*? Unless Kitty came looking for him – which he'd asked her not to – he'd no way of getting in touch. Somehow, he had to survive long enough to find a way.

A guard approached, carrying chains. By sheer effort of will, Dan managed to keep still as she fitted the shackles to his ankles. They'd kill him instantly if he showed the slightest sign of resistance. He had to stay alive, for the sake of the Earth. Someone behind him unfastened his handcuffs; he longed to stretch his stiff muscles, but instead allowed the guard to secure his hands together in front of him and link them to his feet with a yard-long length of chain.

Nobody had ever taken away his freedom of movement to this extent before. It was far more humiliating than he'd expected. And frightening. He could feel the slave mindset encroaching on his brain, threatening to steal his capacity for independent thought. He couldn't let that happen. He *must* warn the Earth what was coming. If he lost himself to fear, the Earth would be lost, too.

The whole time, he kept his eyes fixed on Afra's corpse. If only they'd stopped their operation when she'd wanted to. *He'd* persuaded her to keep going. If he hadn't, she'd still be alive. And the Ranglatiri wouldn't have made the connection between the Earth and humankind's potential for slavery.

Two guards bundled him onto a gurney and wheeled him out of the docking bay, down dimly lit corridors smelling of raw meat and cold sweat. They halted by an open door to a small chamber with a bench along one wall and a sanitary unit in the corner. No blankets, no pillows.

They shoved Dan in without ceremony. The door slammed shut behind him, vibrating the cold metal walls and plunging him into absolute darkness. A grinding noise signalled unoiled bolts sliding into position.

Alone in the pitch black, Dan slumped on the bench and wept for all he'd lost.

25. THE BCV
JOE, DECEMBER 2016

I T WAS HIS turn to speak. Joe strode to the front of the U-shaped arrangement of tables in the corner of the canteen, which they'd screened off for what he and Shakila had dubbed 'the Big Cheese Visit', or BCV for short. Fleetingly, he fingered his torc. The weight of it grounded him, reminding him why he was here and giving him courage.

Knock 'em dead, cariad.

His eyes flashed to the edge of the room where, dressed in her all-black action-woman outfit, Syenitian-Kitty stood impassively in her bodyguard pose, silent and watching. She'd kept well away from all the hand-shaking and small-talk, preferring to scan the room like the seasoned professional she was. Every so often, a visitor would glance at her uncertainly, but mostly they ignored her.

Cheers, babe, he answered. *Home turf today. Should be easier. Things are going well so far.*

She retorted, *Don't jinx it by saying so.*

He winked at her as he passed, unconcerned. The indoor guided tour had been well received, as had lunch with the senior pilots, who were also doubling up as interpreters where necessary. The crew could anticipate questions and offer satisfactory answers without revealing too much about the inner workings of the *Shantivira*.

Aldeman had arrived right on time, at the end of their meal. For security reasons, they hadn't announced his coming in advance. Confronted by a 'real alien', the guests were initially disconcerted, but relaxed as he introduced himself and explained the wider aims of the Galaksi Alliance. His urbane presence gave a new formality to the proceedings, precisely as Shakila had intended. Now he'd finished speaking, he took the seat Joe had just vacated.

They'd finally reached the true purpose of the day: laying out the road map for structural changes to the human institutions and attitudes which were destroying the planet. Joe took a deep breath. 'You have, no doubt, all come across the Syenitian histories of planets which failed to evolve sustainably.'

Solemn nods.

'I hope they scared your pants off!'

Awkward laughter.

'I mean it,' continued Joe. 'Humanity is staring down the barrel of precisely that future. We have perhaps a decade, maybe two, to change course. Then the tipping points will come, one after the other, like unstoppable dominoes. The time to act is now!'

He looked around the table, meeting the eyes of each representative in turn, and the three photojournalists who'd accompanied them.

'I know,' he said, his tone sympathetic. 'Paralysis on this runs through all governments. You don't know where to start, or what action will be most effective. Plus, you recognise the required changes will disadvantage some frightening people who will fight – ridiculously, but very possibly – to the fall of our civilisations, just to hold on to power. For them, it's a matter of pride. Everybody's death before *their* dishonour. They will never back down. They will never surrender. You understand this better than most.'

Joe took a step forward and gestured at his audience. 'Between you, you represent the majority of humans on the planet. You are, I hope, interested in achieving a stable society which does not descend into chaos at the least provocation.'

Murmurs of assent.

'So,' said Joe, 'what's the key to a stable society?' He didn't wait for an answer. It was a rhetorical question, after all. 'A stable society is a *fair* society. The Syenitian's civilisation has existed in its current form for tens of thousands of years. Do you know why?' Another rhetorical question. 'No individual Syenitian earns more than eight times the salary of the lowest-paid worker. All excess wealth is taxed and redistributed into local amenities. They follow the principle of public luxury and private sufficiency. Communities are wealthy. Not individuals. Take Aldeman, there, for example.' Joe waved a hand in the direction of his brother-in-law. 'As leader of the Galaksi Alliance, he is currently the most powerful person in the galaxy. Whole star fleets respond to his command, should he give it.' To Obama he said, 'Star fleets which make the entire US military look like a bunch of tribespeople fighting with sticks. Not meaning any offence, sir, just putting things in perspective. And yet:

Aldeman owns no property. He rents a two-bedroom flat from his local council. I suspect his annual salary is a fraction of yours.'

Aldeman leaned back in his seat, touching his fingertips together and smiling at the gasps and horrified looks from his neighbours. 'It is an exceedingly pleasant apartment. And my remuneration is sufficient for my needs. But you digress, Captain Llewellyn. Please return to your argument.'

Joe bowed his head respectfully. 'Yes, my lord. My point is, the Syenitians didn't get there the easy way. They had a monarchy, once. They've experimented with many forms of society. Complete financial equality is neither possible nor desirable in a free society, but only one which strives to avoid severe inequality will prevent upheaval in the long term. We are lucky. We can benefit from their experience and switch to what works straight away.'

He beckoned to Delius and Shakila to join him. Necks craned as the bulky Cylf stood, towering over the diminutive Shakila. 'Delius, my esteemed colleague and the space station's chief computer, has analysed Earth's economic systems. With Aldeman's support, he and Shakila have created a road map detailing the organisational changes humanity must make to avoid imminent ecosystem collapse. Before they start their presentation, I have one more thing to say.'

He paused, making sure he had his audience's full attention. 'Last year, at the UN General Assembly, we promised you enough information about shield technology and gravity generators for you to develop your own versions. In return for a regular supply of sewage.'

Timid chuckles rippled round the table.

'That agreement stands. But any future technology transfers will be linked to milestones on this road map. Failure to comply with those milestones will result in the defence service provided by the *Shantivira* being revoked.'

The chuckles turned to instant outrage.

'How dare you?'

'That's blackmail!'

'We don't need your "defence service" anyway!'

Aldeman leaned forward in his seat. 'Let me be very clear,' he said in a low voice. The protests hushed as the guests endeavoured to hear him. 'We are happy to defend your planet as long as we believe humanity is capable of evolving into a society with values matching those of the Galaksi Alliance. But my people will never share our technological advantages with a species pursuing an extractive economic agenda. We made that mistake once before, many millennia ago.'

Joe wondered what he meant. He'd have to ask about it, next time they were alone.

'Captain Llewellyn is correct,' continued Aldeman. 'Any potential technology transfers will be tied to milestones on the road map. However, let me add this. With or without additional technology transfers – if humanity finds it impossible to amend your society's direction of travel, our defence operation will cease and we will relocate the *Shantivira* to a more deserving planet. Of which there are plenty. You have one decade to start making the necessary changes. I hope that focuses your minds sufficiently.'

There was a moment of stunned silence as the dignitaries digested this.

Aldeman smiled disarmingly. 'Sticks and carrots, that is what you call this approach, is it not, Captain Llewellyn?' He caught Joe's eye and Joe responded with a small smile of encouragement. Aldeman turned back to their guests. 'He assured me it is the only way to get humans to do anything. Ladies and gentlemen, never forget, we *want* to help you. We *want* to be friends. We believe you can change – we believe you can turn things round before it is too late. So prove us right. Show us what humanity is capable of.'

DELIUS AND SHAKILA presented their road map, elaborating on the first three stages, to be implemented urgently and in parallel. One: changing the underlying legal structure of all companies away from profit maximisation to favour an equal balance of interests. Two: dismantling the international Investor-State Dispute Settlement system and cancelling its preposterous ten-year sunset clause. Three: shutting down all tax havens.

When they'd finished, the UN Secretary General regarded his fellow representatives. 'I'll say this, because I'm sure it's what everyone else is thinking. These are laudable objectives. But, in the current system, I fear we are powerless to make these changes.'

From her position by the wall, Kitty gave a derisive snort of laughter, then covered her mouth with her hand. Ban Ki-moon ignored her and ploughed on.

'You're asking us to change structures which evolved over centuries. To transform how we think about profit and growth in the space of a few years. I'm not sure humanity is capable of that.'

'We'll find out, won't we?' Joe looked around the room. 'I understand that even those with their hands on the levers of power feel trapped and helpless. You've lived within this system your whole lives. You can't imagine different ways of running things. But we're here to tell you: you have so many options, if you can only free your minds enough to examine them.'

'Change is not linear,' added Aldeman. 'Things can carry on in a steady state for millennia, then reach a tipping point in the blink of an eye. Political reality is not immutable like the laws of physics. Do not underestimate yourselves. Improve your laws, enforce them without fear or favour, and watch your world change for the better. You *can* do this. We will help you.'

Meg Taylor, the Pacific Islands representative, asked, 'What about the frightening people Captain Llewellyn mentioned earlier? The ones who will fight us if we try to make changes? They are formidable enemies. If we go down this road, I fear for the safety of my family.'

Kitty spoke for the first time. Heads whipped round to see where the sound came from. Her deep voice was almost a growl. 'It may be I must pay them a personal visit to . . . explain the situation more clearly. I can be very persuasive if necessary.' She gave a predatory leer, revealing her mayonnaise-coloured canines. The guests closest to her shrank back.

'Many centuries ago, I made a solemn oath to protect this planet. I cannot change your economic system for you, or your corporate law, but I *can* deal with individuals who obstruct our progress and threaten your loved ones' safety.'

Joe raised his eyebrows at her. *Isn't that a bit blatantly menacing, babe?*

Kitty pushed out her bottom lip. *Blatant would be swearing to hunt them down and murder them in their beds, surely? These people need to understand I'm not to be messed with, Joe. It'll save time and heartache later.*

'Let's call a spade a spade,' she continued aloud. 'On its current path, humanity's time is running out fast. Evolve your societies now or prepare for global chaos, misery and death.'

'A stark choice,' said Obama.

'But a simple one,' Joe insisted.

Aldeman stood up. 'Shakila, Delius, thank you for your presentation. I must move on to my next appointment soon, but I would appreciate a stroll and some fresh air first.' He looked along the table. 'Is it correct you have not visited the *Shantivira's* biomes?'

'They've heard about them,' said Susan. 'But they haven't seen them yet.'

Aldeman glanced at Joe. 'Saving the best until last, eh? Tropical or temperate, Director Omondi? You choose.'

'Tropical,' said Susan, not missing a beat. 'Follow us, ladies and gentlemen, you're in for a treat.'

There was a general scraping of chairs as people got up, mildly bewildered at the sudden change of activity. Joe imagined they'd assumed they'd be stuck in a meeting for hours, arguing about the impossibility or not of reconfiguring human society within the next ten years. But that wasn't the way Aldeman did things. Prior to his political career, centuries of working as a lawyer had honed his skills in knowing exactly when to close an argument. A walk among trees and fields would allow their guests to digest the new information and ask questions in a less pressured, more informal setting. They'd sown the seed. Now they had to give it time to germinate.

Kitty strode behind one of the paper screens and reappeared in her jaguar form, a shadow at Joe's side. There were a few nervous glances, but nobody commented. Her reputation preceded her nowadays. He reached down and scratched the fur between her ears.

Once they'd safely negotiated the outside hatch, Joe let Yisheng and President Xi lead the way, deep in discussion. He and Kitty brought up the rear, eavesdropping as subtly as they could.

The US President asked Aldeman if he played basketball, backtracking when he learnt every Syenitian was seven feet tall. Aldeman's only point of reference was rugby, from long association with Joe, so Obama had to explain the game. Syenitians didn't go in for ball sports at all.

THEY WERE RETURNING from the central jungle zone when Delius stopped in his tracks, tilting his head. Joe eyed him with concern.

'What is it, Delius?'

'Incoming, sir. A fleet of ships has entered the solar system and is headed this way. The electromagnetic signature suggests Ranglatiri pirates.'

Fuck. The blood drained from Joe's face as he met

Aldeman's horrified gaze. They watched their guests and pilot escorts strolling, relaxed and happy now, towards the hatch to access the space station.

Aldeman said, 'I'll cancel my appointment and look after your visitors while you deal with this.'

'Thanks,' said Joe, relieved. He asked Delius, 'How long have we got?'

'Twenty minutes? Perhaps twenty-five?'

'Sound the alarm and get to the control room as fast as you can.'

Delius did so, setting off at a run.

Aldeman took Joe's hands and squeezed them. 'Good luck,' he said.

Joe returned the pressure. 'Take good care of our guests. Maneewan should have their dinner ready by now. That'll keep them occupied for a bit. See you later, I hope.' He crouched next to Kitty and wrapped his arm around her.

Cath, *get us to the* Pride. *You start the pre-flight checks; I'll meet Delius in the control room, see what we're dealing with.*

Yes, boss, she replied.

Materialising in the living area, Kitty headed for the cockpit while Joe tore off his smart clothes and pulled on his flight suit. He didn't have time to remove his torc. He'd leave it on, for luck. The alarm was deafening, even in here. He shoved his feet into his boots and ran for the door.

Pilots were streaming to their *Tumbas* from all directions. In between the siren wails, a recording in Kawaida repeated the words, 'Emergency. Emergency. All hands, to your ships immediately.'

Joe arrived at the control room, where Delius was studying the screen. The dots showed the approaching fleet had almost reached Mars.

'Deactivate the alarm, Delius, people have got the message.'

He did so and the wailing ceased.

'That's better. What have we got? Are they Ranglatiri?'

'Without a doubt, sir. Thirty-seven pirate frigates. ETA in nine minutes.'

Joe shuddered. Had that fleet of unidentified probes they'd destroyed last year been sent by the Ranglatiri? Was this a follow-up mission to find out what had happened to them?

'Normal ships, or more indestructible ones like last time?' he asked.

'The data indicates they are unlikely to be equipped with the superior shield technology,' said Delius. 'But we will only know for sure when you fire upon them.'

Joe rubbed his face with both hands. Was he sending his whole crew out to die? In front of a bunch of world leaders? And his mother? Only time would tell. This was what they were here for. Time to get to work.

'OK.' He reached for the microphone. Trying to keep the terror out of his voice, he announced, 'This is Joe Llewellyn. You heard the alarm. Thirty-seven Ranglatiri frigates are on their way. ETA nine minutes. Those who are ready, you're cleared for immediate take-off. Rendez-vous at the usual coordinates. Any stragglers: we need every one of you. Join us as soon as you can.'

He switched from Kawaida to English. 'All visitors in

the canteen, this is your Captain speaking. A fleet of armed enemy craft is approaching. We're going out to ensure it doesn't reach the Earth.' He laughed, trying to sound cheerfully confident. 'You're about to get a live demonstration of our capabilities. Aldeman will stay with you to provide information and explanations. Remember: the *Shantivira* is cloaked. You're perfectly safe up here. Enjoy your dinner and we'll be back soon.'

Joe deliberated briefly. Then, in Welsh, he added, 'Mam, if you're listening, I've got a job for you. Knock on all the doors on the accommodation deck and send anyone you find to the canteen. Especially the kids. Get somebody to help you. People will be less frightened if they're together. If we do have to evacuate, it's better everyone's gathered in one place. But it shouldn't come to that. Aldeman and Delius are in charge. Do what they say. I love you, Mam. Ta-ra.'

He turned and patted Delius on the arm. 'Stay in touch. Good luck.'

Delius nodded solemnly. 'You too, sir.'

Joe sprinted across Docking Bay 3 and bounded up the steps to the *Pride of Essoona*. Kitty already had the engine running and the wings extended. Seconds later, they were soaring through the opening to meet whatever it was Fate had in store for them.

26. THE BATTLE
HANNA

HANNA WAITED IN position. From Urca's cockpit, she could see prickly *Tumbas* stretching in a long V, like a skein of green geese with a great dragonfly, *The Pride of Essoona*, at its apex. She'd never seen them all out together before, uncloaked. It was impressive, but unnerving. There were no reserves to call on. They were all that stood between the pirates and the Earth.

She remembered the *Shantivira's* last encounter with a single Ranglatiri frigate. Their weapons hadn't made a dent in it. Kitty had managed to stop it, but even she wouldn't be able to handle thirty-seven ships at once. Was this it? Were they all going to die and consequently let the Earth suffer the same fate as Amra? Even if they succeeded, it was probable at least some *Tumba* pilots would be killed today. People Hanna knew. Colleagues. Friends. Maybe even herself. Hanna pushed the thought away.

Her mind turned to Kia and Yonas. How long would they survive on the *Shantivira*, if the Ranglatiri won this battle? Would they be able to escape to the safety of Dunia House? She wished they'd had time to discuss a plan for the worst-case scenario. Then again, evacuating to Dunia House was the obvious thing to do, as long as Kitty was around to make the teleport work. Those on board would undoubtedly think of it and organise it in time. It was probably already in some protocol somewhere, waiting to be activated.

Joe's voice crackled in her ear piece. 'Two minutes until they're visible. Delius reckons they could be standard ships without the fancy shields, but we won't know until we fire on them. We mustn't open fire until I've spoken to the leader. Perhaps we can persuade them to turn round.'

Hanna heard Hassan scoff via their private channel. 'Ain't never gonna happen,' he said. She agreed with him, but said nothing.

'*Tumbas* 200 to 198, go and cover the ISS. *Tumbas* 197 to 195, go and cover the *Tiangong*,' continued Joe. 'Remain cloaked for now. The rest of us stay visible. If they open fire, split into your prearranged groups and return the attack. Try to surround them, stop them escaping. Everyone works in pairs. NO ONE goes off alone, do you understand?'

'Aye aye, Captain,' said Hanna, although she didn't open the channel for Joe to hear.

'Here they come,' said Joe. A row of hulking black craft appeared in front of them, each many times the size of a *Tumba*. Intimidating weaponry protruded from every possible surface. 'Look like a bunch of fuck-ugly stonefish, don't they?' he commented. 'Attempting to establish communications now.'

Joe shared the transmission with the *Tumba* pilots: a hologram of a faceless figure, dressed in white, appeared at the lower edge of Hanna's screen. Faceless because, where most life forms had features, this creature had only a convex mesh which blended into a white helmet. White armour covered its upper body; a heavy, pleated skirt hid its legs.

Joe's voice said, 'I am Joe Llewellyn. This planet is protected by the Galaksi Alliance. Leave this solar system immediately. You are outnumbered and outgunned.'

The creature laughed, an unpleasant sound halfway between a cough and a bark. 'I am Henning. I am here to tesst this planet's defences and, after we overcome them, to fill my shipss with primitives.'

He seems confident, thought Hanna. The image vanished.

'Fire at will,' said Joe, simultaneously blasting his dematerialisation beam at the lead ship's gun turrets. The V-formation fragmented as the little *Tumbas* wheeled away into their groups. Kazembi was Hanna's group leader, the others were Hassan, Aussie Ozzy, Lucy and Vadim.

'Pair up,' commanded Kazembi. 'Me and Vadim, Hassan and Ozzy, Hanna and Lucy. We're going to get behind them. Full speed. Stay together.'

Blue energy pulses from the enemy spacecraft flashed past, but they were moving too fast for them to connect. In her earpiece, Joe's voice sounded jubilant and slightly breathless. 'We've taken out the lead ship's main weapon. Focus your fire on a single point and their shields won't hold. Let's take these fuckers down, guys. I want nothing left but a smoking ruin, d'you hear? Don't let a single one escape to report back on our capabilities.'

Heartened, they dodged the enemy fire, weaving in and out of their colleagues who were going for a frontal assault. Eventually, they passed the last Ranglatiri craft in the line. 'Right,' said Kazembi. 'We start with this one and work our way along, while they're distracted from the front. Hassan and Ozzy, focus your firepower on the port turret, Hanna and Lucy, you take out the rear gun. Vadim and I will try to punch a hole in the bridge.'

Hanna and Lucy wheeled away to the back of the vessel. 'Watch out, it's moving, they've seen us,' cried Lucy.

Hanna opened fire, aiming at the point where the canon swivelled. Lucy followed suit. The gun discharged a stream of blue pulses, but couldn't match the manoeuvrability of their *Tumbas* and the shots were easy to avoid. Thanks to their years of training and flying together, Hanna and Lucy were a well-oiled team, able to anticipate each other's movements and needing only a few words to communicate complex ideas.

At last, to Hanna's relief, the turret under their demat beams glowed and disappeared. She watched her fuel gauge jump up a notch: it seemed a weapon provided more energy than an asteroid or broken-up space debris, which was all she'd dematerialised so far.

'Kaz?' she said into her headset. 'We're done. What now?'

'Come and help us with the bridge.'

With four of them aiming at the same spot, the shields failed in minutes and it was short work to breach the hull and dematerialise the ship's control centre. Hanna noticed her fuel gauge jump again, much further this time. Her stomach flipped as she understood the significance: for the first time in her life, she'd killed sentient beings. No doubt even Ranglatiri space pirates had friends and family who cared about them. She hardened her heart, remembering Amra. 'That was for Aneira, you scumbags,' she whispered. 'You're not getting anywhere *near* our planet.'

'Good,' said Kazembi as the wreck drifted away. 'On to the next. Same plan.'

Steadily, they worked their way along the line. It became easier as other groups understood what they were doing and joined them. 'This is almost fun,' said Lucy, as they dematerialised their fourth enemy weapon. 'Almost,' agreed Hanna. 'If only I wasn't so freaking terrified the whole time.'

Lucy giggled. 'Yeah. But we're awesome. I think we might win this.'

Hanna prayed she was right.

After taking out the fifth enemy craft, Hassan asked her how they were doing.

'OK,' she said. 'I thought I'd be more tired by now.'

'That's the adrenaline,' he said. 'The exhaustion will hit later. With any luck, we'll be long done by then.'

Hanna visualised them both safely back on the *Shantivira*, warm under their double duvet, dozing in each other's arms. That was an image to hold onto.

Kazembi interrupted her train of thought. 'Right,' she said in their headphones. 'On to number six. Don't get cocky.'

'Stay safe,' Hanna told Hassan, and followed Lucy to the rear of the hideous black ship. They had a routine going now: hoping to confuse the weapon by giving it multiple targets they stayed some distance apart, with Hanna at close range and Lucy further away. The gun was just beginning to glow when, over the comms link, Hanna heard Lucy scream: a terrible roar of fear and pain, ending in a choking sob.

Hanna whirled Urca around, her stomach somersaulting as she saw three Ranglatiri frigates closing in, all blasting neon pulses at the *Tumba* between them and her. Lucy.

'Help!' Hanna yelled to the rest of her group. 'They're attacking from behind! We need help!'

She returned fire, but there were too many of them. 'Lucy, we must get out of here. Come on!'

'Can't,' Lucy croaked. 'I've lost my starboard thrusters and the shields are all but gone. The control panel's on fire. I can barely breathe. Go without me, Hanna. One more hit and I'm toas—'

Another scream, more gut-wrenching than the first. Lucy's *Tumba* ignited in a brief blaze of energy before fragmenting into dark, smoking wreckage.

HANNA STARED, NUMB and unmoving, the image burnt onto her retinas. She couldn't believe it. She *wouldn't*. Not Lucy. Not after they'd been through so much together. Her best friend, apart from Farida and Hassan. She remembered how much she'd disliked Lucy when they'd first met. How she'd disapproved of her. The ridiculous assumptions they'd made about each other. She could smile about it now. It had taken a long time for their relationship to develop to the point where Hanna trusted her arch-rival with her life. To the point where she considered Lucy part of her family. And now she was gone? Just like that? Impossible.

Urca shuddered as Ranglatiri shots pelted her shields. Soon it would be Hanna's turn to die. At least it would be quick, she consoled herself. But she didn't want to. She wasn't ready. She still had too much to do with her life.

The shuddering stopped. Hanna blinked. Hassan and Ozzy's *Tumbas* had appeared beside her, drawing the deadly blue pulses away from Urca.

'Hanna!' Hassan shouted in her earpiece. '*Move!* We have to go. We can't help Lucy now. You *must* survive, Hanna. Kia and Yonas need you. *I* need you.'

Hanna returned to herself, her consciousness snapping back from wherever it had just been. 'Yes. Of course. Urca? As fast as you can.' She plunged her *Tumba* downwards, away from the line of fire and out of range. Hassan and Ozzy followed.

She pulled up at a safe distance and took a swig from her water bottle, trying to wash away the painful tightness in her throat. The hand holding the bottle was shaking, she noticed dispassionately, as if it belonged to someone else.

'You OK?' said Hassan.

'Lucy,' was all she could say, tears trickling down her cheeks.

Hassan said, 'I wish I could come in there and hug you.'

Hanna sniffed, clutching her locket. The warm oval fitted perfectly in the palm of her hand, like a pebble worn smooth by the sea. She managed to croak, 'We must tell Felix.'

'We will,' said Hassan. 'But the job's not finished yet.'

'How are your shields?' asked Ozzy.

She peered at her control panel. 'They were down to thirty per cent, but they're recharging fast.'

Hassan said, 'The others need us, Hanna. Are you able to carry on?'

Hanna blew her nose and wiped her eyes. Nothing left of the Ranglatiri but a smoking ruin, Joe had said. That sounded good to her. She sat up straight and took a deep breath.

'Yes,' she said. 'Let's go.'

27. HENNING

JOE

JOE TWISTED AND turned in his seat, weaving the *Pride of Essoona* between the Ranglatiri craft, aiming for the vessel which held their leader. The remaining space pirates were clustered in a defensive sphere around it. It must be clear they'd lost the battle, but they doggedly refused to surrender, earning Joe's grudging respect. His pilots were picking off the enemy ships one by one, in a bitter, drawn-out struggle.

But he wouldn't let the captain—what had he called himself? Henning?—off with a quick, honourable death. They must capture him and find out where he'd got his information about the Earth. Delius had discovered the lead ship was transmitting a live video feed: presumably his superiors were watching somewhere, assessing the *Shantivira's* capabilities. A deeply unsettling prospect. It was as if the pirates had been sent to a gladiator fight for the benefit of a remote audience. Gladiators were slaves. Was that why these guys weren't making a run for it? Was dying preferable to going home empty-handed?

The *Pride* wasn't as nimble as a *Tumba*, but its shields had more power. As did its weapons. All he had to do was get close enough. Kitty stood ready outside, directly above him on the dragonfly's bulbous head. If he looked up, he could see the soles of her bare feet.

OK, Joe. That'll do, she said. *Hold steady.*

I wish you were wearing a dress.

Perv, she retorted, but he could sense her amusement.

She disappeared and materialised on the enemy's hull, within the shields. Now a distant black-clad figure, apart from the pale skin of her extremities, she was almost invisible. He squinted, tracking her with his eyes as she roamed the craft's exterior, looking for a way in. Unless she'd had physical contact with someone inside, Kitty needed to see where she was going in order to teleport somewhere she'd never been. Minutes passed. He tried to think of a backup plan, in case she couldn't penetrate the ship.

Then she vanished.

Babe?

I'm in. There was a window in a hatch.

Thank God for that. *And now?* he asked.

I'm a gecko on the ceiling, headed for the bridge. Joe?

Yes?

The holds are all empty. Not like last time.

That's good, isn't it? he said. *We won't be killing inno-cent people.*

But it means they were telling the truth. They came to get slaves.

Joe clenched his teeth as he thought of Amra. Of Pwe-za. Of all the innocent people going about their lives down there on his own home planet, oblivious to the drama unfolding just outside their atmosphere. He took a big, slow breath. *They won't get them*, he replied.

No, Kitty agreed.

Joe didn't watch through her eyes. He was too busy avoiding incoming blue pulses and giving as good as he got. Next to him, a *Tumba* erupted into flames. Shit.

'Who was that?' he asked on the group channel.

'Nader,' came William's voice, cracking with emotion. There was nothing else to say.

That's three now, Joe thought. Traian. Lucy. And now Nader. A dread-weight settled in his stomach as he thought of all the families they'd have to inform. The memorial services they'd have to organise. Time to end this before he lost any more pilots. He reached out with his mind to Kitty.

Cath? *How are you doing?*

Got him. See you back on the Shantivira.

Put him in the brig. I'll be there as soon as I can. He wheeled the *Pride* out of the mêlée and made a beeline for the space station. As he did so, a flash of inspiration hit him. *Babe? You can teleport straight to the lead ship can't you, now you've been there?*

Sure, why?

Secure our prisoner, then pick up some mines from the armoury, he said. *Get back there and blow it the fuck up. We need to stop their transmissions. Who knows what the Ranglatiri government are learning about us today?*

He felt her smile. *Consider it done, boss.*

Tell me when you're ready so I can warn our lot to get to a safe distance.

When he landed in Docking Bay 3, a welcoming committee consisting of his mam and a selection of world leaders crowded round the steps the minute he lowered them. A weary-looking Aldeman stood a little way away, watching them. Over their heads, Joe shot him a glance which said, 'Can't you keep them off my back? I'm busy.'

Aldeman responded with an eloquent shrug. Joe read his expression to mean, 'Like trying to herd cats, that lot. Your mother is the worst of them.'

Joe grinned, then focused on getting past them. A photographer was snapping pictures for all she was worth. 'Everyone all right?' he said. 'Good. I'm afraid I can't update you yet. We're still in the thick of it. If you want to see some fireworks, get back to the canteen and watch from there.'

Not waiting to see if they followed his suggestion, he strode across to Delius in the control room. As he did so, Kitty made contact.

Ready, she said. *Four minutes.*

Thanks, love. He nodded a curt greeting to Delius and reached for the microphone switch. Out loud, he said in a clear, calm voice, 'All units, the lead vessel is about to blow. Disengage and retreat to a safe distance while keeping the other ships surrounded. Ten kilometres should be enough.' He eyed the display showing the mines' timer. 'You have three minutes.'

There was a chorus of 'Aye, aye, Captain's as the *Tumbas* withdrew. On the big screen, he watched them form a loose sphere around the knot of pirate frigates. Kitty materialised by his side and slipped her hand into his. 'Showtime,' she said out loud. Silently, they monitored the red digits counting down.

3

2

1

0

The image on the screen flashed white hot as the centre craft exploded, cannoning wreckage into the neighbouring vessels, spinning them off course. The group scattered and the surrounding *Tumbas* immediately moved back in for the kill, packs of them swarming over each enemy ship, continuing to disable their weapons and propulsion systems. Joe wondered how long they'd have to wait before the few craft left finally admitted defeat and surrendered.

His mind turned to the next problem: what to do with the survivors? The thought of having to keep them all on board the *Shantivira* made his skin crawl. One was bad enough. And they didn't have space for more than a dozen or so. Could they stay on their ships? Dalian would certainly want the *Koppakuoria* to tow at least one back to Syenitia to take apart and study. Damn. He sighed inwardly. They'd be stuck without a cargo ship, just when they were building a reputation for reliable aid deliveries.

He was deliberating whether they could use the *Pride* instead, despite its tiny capacity, when, as if by some prearranged signal, the remaining Ranglatiri frigates self-destructed. The force of the blasts blew back the *Tumbas* simultaneously, propelling them uncontrollably outwards and into each other. The voice feed filled with shocked screams. Next to him, Kitty gasped and almost crushed his hand in hers.

Joe's heart somersaulted. 'Everybody OK?' he said into the microphone, trying to keep the panic out of his voice. 'Report your status, starting with *Tumba* Number One.'

The shouts of alarm subsided and there was a moment of tense silence before confirmation began to come in, pilot by pilot, that nobody had been injured and damage was minimal.

'Our shields all held, Captain,' said Yisheng, who was the fleet leader in Joe's absence. 'I think they wanted to stop us capturing their craft for analysis.'

Joe nodded. 'I think you're right.' He exhaled and let his shoulders slump forward. This bitter slog of a battle was finally over. 'Right,' he said, straightening up again. 'Dematerialise the biggest chunks of wreckage, then come back for a break and something to eat. We'll all go out again after dinner to clear up the rest.'

'That could take all night, Captain.'

'I know, William,' he replied. 'But we can't risk the wreckage destroying any terrestrial satellites. It takes as long as it takes.' And that wasn't the only job left to do.

Joe turned off the microphone and said to Delius, 'How's our prisoner doing?'

'Sorry, sir, I haven't checked recently. I was focused on the battle.' Delius switched the screen to show the brig. A white figure slumped in the corner, facing the wall, a pool of coagulating claret creeping across the cell floor. Joe blinked, trying to make sense of the image. Kitty clapped her hand over her mouth in shock.

'Fuck!' Joe shouted as the penny dropped. '*Cath*, get us down there now! Delius, play back the recording. Try and work out what happened.'

He clamped his eyes shut as the falling-into-a-swimming-pool noise rushed in his ears. When he opened them again, they were in the *Shantivira's* tiny prison block.

They surveyed the same scene they'd seen on the screen upstairs, enhanced by the bitter scent of blood and desperation.

Joe asked, *Is he still alive?*

Kitty shook her head.

How did he seem, when you left him?

She wrinkled her nose. *How can you tell, with that mask?*

Good point.

Kitty said, *I remembered what Rowan told me, so I deactivated his mask communicator. He couldn't have sent any transmissions since arriving here.*

She opened the door and, stepping carefully around the lake of blood, grabbed the Ranglatiri's shoulder, pulling it round to face them. Joe stepped back in alarm: the creature had removed his mask. The chalk-white face was blank, the pink albino eyes unfocused and clouded in death. The jaw hung slack, revealing ferociously pointed teeth behind blood-stained lips. Joe flinched at the sight of it. Some predators – Kitty, for example – had an awe-inspiring beauty. Others were ugly enough to strike horror into your soul. It seemed the Ranglatiri were the latter.

The remains of the mask lay in its lap, crushed to pieces. They'd have difficultly extracting information from it. Kitty lifted Henning's sleeve and showed Joe the raw wound on his wrist. The other arm was the same.

He bit his own wrists open? said Joe, incredulous.

Looks like it. She shrugged. *Better than dying of oxygen toxicity, which is what happens without the mask.*

Faster, too, Joe said. *He really didn't want to talk to us, did he?*

I shouldn't have left him.

I asked you to, he reminded her. *Only you could plant that bomb. Even if we'd had someone else watching him, how could we have saved him, if he was determined to destroy his own life support system?*

We could've sedated him.

There was no time, Cath, he insisted. *We had to stop those transmissions from his ship. Sometimes balls get dropped when you're juggling. You were busy, the Cylfs were busy. Look at those teeth! I wouldn't risk letting any other crew member near him. He chose to die. I respect that.*

Joe's *zana* bleeped. When he pulled it out, it projected a little image of Delius. 'Would you like to see the recording now, sir?'

Joe sighed. 'Go on, then.'

The *zana* screen showed a 2D version of the scene in front of them. The white figure was pacing up and down the cell like a caged tiger. In a clear voice, Kitty said, 'You are a prisoner of the Galaksi Alliance. You will stay here until my captain has time to question you.'

The pacing stopped and Henning gripped the bars with snowy fingers. He tilted his head to one side. 'Why do you help them, Ssyenitian? These primitives are born sslaves. My people will take thiss planet, now they know it's here. We will feed off it for decades to come.'

Kitty twisted her lips into a mirthless, toothy grin. 'I respectfully disagree.' She spun away from him and teleported.

Henning froze briefly, disconcerted by her sudden disappearance. Then he turned his back to the camera and unclipped his mask. He dropped it to the floor and stamped on it with his heavy boots until the electronics within had disintegrated completely. He scooped up the bits and knelt in the corner, still determinedly facing away from the camera. He lifted one wrist to his mouth, followed by the other. Then he settled his arms in his lap and leaned against the cell wall. The whole procedure took less than two minutes.

Wow, said Joe. *He meant business.*

A dark expression crossed Kitty's face, but all she said was, *I'll take the corpse to Syenitia for dissection. We need to discover the Ranglatiris' physical weaknesses and how their empathic field works. Perhaps there's a way to block it.*

Yes. He thought rapidly. *Wait. Lay it on a slab in our sick bay first, so we can take our own photos. I can imagine our guests might want to see what we're up against, too.*

✦   ✦   ✦

JOE RETURNED TO the control room and called back the fleet. Then he stuck his head round the kitchen door. 'Maneewan?'

She came over. 'Well done, Joe. You showed those monsters that humans are a force to be reckoned with.'

He grimaced. 'We lost three pilots.'

She patted his hand. 'I know, dear. And we'll mourn them properly. But we must deal with today first.'

'Exactly,' Joe said. 'Maneewan, they're all coming back for a break and if they feel anything like me, they'll be famished. Do you think you could rustle up some—oh.' As he was speaking, a movement over her shoulder caught his eye. It was Vijay, setting down a plate piled high with *samosas.* The table's legs were practically sagging, it was so heavily laden with food. Joe grinned. 'Way ahead of me as usual, I see.'

'The curry's keeping warm for whenever you need it. If you could organise people to set up the tables, that would be helpful.'

He stood up straight and saluted. 'Yes, Ma'am,' he said, making her laugh.

Joe pushed his way through the anxious crowd in the canteen and sprang onto the window ledge to gain height. 'Listen up, everyone,' he said, speaking Kawaida to the sea of faces. His VIP guests were clustered around Aldeman. Hopefully he'd interpret for the ones who understood English. 'It's over. We won. The Earth is safe. For now.'

Cheers and applause rippled across the hall. Joe waited for it to die down. 'But today's victory came at a cost. We lost three of our own: Nader, Traian and Lucy.' There were isolated cries of shock and dismay in the audience as their closest friends received the news.

'The Ranglatiri know where we are now, and what we're capable of. We've not heard the last of them.' Joe touched the twisted gold cable around his neck. 'The crew is coming in for a break and something to eat. Our work isn't done yet. We'll have to go out again and remove the debris orbiting the Earth, before it damages something.'

He smiled, trying to radiate positive vibes. 'But that's for later. Would you please help set up the tables and bring out the food from the kitchen? We deserve a small celebration. And I'm *starving.*' He rubbed his stomach and the crowd laughed. Chatter broke out and people began to disperse.

Over their heads, Joe raised his voice and called in English, 'Honoured Earth representatives, I don't know how much you understood. To summarise: all is well. The others are coming back to eat now. If you stay out of the way, you can watch them land. Take all the pictures you want.'

He stepped down and found his mother standing in front of him, a complicated expression on her face.

'*Ti'n iawn, Mam?*' he asked.

She said nothing, just enfolded him in her arms, pressing her grey curls into the stiff fabric of his flight suit. Surprised – at her and at himself – he returned the embrace.

'My boy,' she said in Welsh, when she came up for air, smiling through her tears. 'I am so, so proud of you. You were *amazing.*'

Joe blinked. '*Diolch, Mam.* Just doing my job.'

After dinner, Aldeman stood up. 'Ladies and gentlemen, it is time for me to leave you.' There were a few shouts of 'No!' and 'Stay!' Ignoring them, Aldeman turned to where the visitors were sitting and bowed courteously, saying in English, 'It was a pleasure to meet you all. I hope you think carefully about what was said.'

He switched back to Kawaida and addressed the rest of the room, 'Before I go, will you all join me in *Laulaahaalia*? The Song of Gratitude, perhaps? I believe most of you are familiar with the words.' He glanced back at the guest representatives and added in English, 'We will sing together now. The text is less important than the act of making music together. Just sing la-la-la, or hum.'

Chairs scraped as people got up to link hands. Aldeman took the centre; Joe held his brother-in-law's left hand and allowed the human spiral to form clockwise around them. The confused world leaders remained seated until residents and crew members pulled them up, insisting they participate.

Shakila had a firm grip on the guy from Bahrain, while Yisheng and his daughter Qingqing flanked a politely smiling President Xi. Kitty was explaining the concept to Meg Taylor and the representative from Kazakhstan, and Susan was doing the same for Obama and Ban Ki-moon.

Joe glimpsed his mam and Chooli towing a bewildered Donald Tusk into the crowd, giggling like teenagers. Although she'd never experienced *Laulaahaalia*, judging from Grace's body language, she knew what was coming and couldn't wait to try it. Joe felt a stab of guilt. He should have taken her to Essoona for a sunset session long before now. After all, it was just like going to chapel, which she must have been missing all this time. He resolved to go with her at the weekend.

When everyone was in position, Aldeman started the simple melody in his pleasant, light tenor. After a few bars, Joe overlaid it with his own rich baritone, adding the baseline. Ring by ring, the rest of the coil joined in, until the canteen echoed in a harmonious crescendo. Then, loop by loop, the singers dropped out again. Eventually only Joe and Aldeman were still singing. Joe finished his part and Aldeman continued for the final bars, mirroring the start.

For a moment there was silence, then the hall filled with conversation and laughter as people shook hands with those around them. Aldeman bowed, then, without saying another word, headed for the lift which would teleport him back to Essoona.

Joe reached out silently for Kitty.

Cath?

Her eyes met his across the room. *Yes, love?*

Will you take the VIPs home? I need the Pride *for de-materialising.*

Sure, she said.

Joe scratched his chin. *We should take them to Sick Bay and show them the corpse, first.*

Yes. Kitty nodded. *And the video. Delius already put subtitles on it so they'll understand.*

✦   ✦   ✦

THE UPLIFTING EFFECT of *Laulaahaalia* evaporated quickly in the *Shantivira's* medical facility as Joe showed the Earth representatives the video of Henning's suicide. Then he lifted the sheet covering the body, triggering cries of horror and disgust from his guests. With remarkable speed, revulsion switched to fascination. They pulled out their phones and started snapping photos.

With Kitty interpreting for those who didn't speak English, Joe said, 'This is what the Earth is up against. I've seen these monsters strip entire planets bare within weeks. They enslave intelligent life and work their slaves to death in a matter of months.' He made eye contact with each of the representatives in turn, trying to impress the seriousness of the situation upon them. 'If you want our help, you'd better make those changes we talked about, and fast. Otherwise, our beautiful planet will suffer the same fate as

Pweza, Amra and many others.'

Obama said, 'But this is an immediate existential threat! Why didn't you tell us about these creatures before?'

A bitter bark of laughter escaped Joe. 'We didn't want to scare you unnecessarily. But after today, I think we're past that. Sir, the true existential threat on our planet is climate and biodiversity breakdown. We can probably hold off the Ranglatiri. The Syenitians' question is, is it worth the effort? Is humanity worth saving?'

Meg Taylor said, 'And if we can't solve our own problems, we're not, correct?'

'That's about the size of it.' Joe pursed his lips, attempting to think of a better way to explain. 'Consider the human body,' he said. 'It's a complex, interlinked ecosystem which has evolved over millennia: a precisely balanced biome of helpful bacteria and other things which keep us alive. Right?'

Nods of agreement.

'If your body's temperature rises, say, two degrees above normal, you're properly ill, sweating in bed with a fever. Three and a half degrees and your brain effectively starts to melt. Death follows soon after. That's what we're facing here, on a planetary scale.' He spread his hands wide to underline his words, willing them to understand. 'You can't stop destruction from the inside with a plasma gun, or a dematerialisation beam,' he said. 'You must deal with the root cause – fundamentally change whatever is causing the imbalances.'

Next to him, Shakila cleared her throat. 'Achieving real, lasting change is much harder than firing weapons at a defined enemy,' she said.

The visitors looked at each other and the corpse on the table, then followed Joe back to Docking Bay 3 in glum silence. When they arrived, Idriss Déby, the African Union Chairperson spoke first. 'Well, you've certainly given us plenty to think about. Now we must communicate all we've learnt to our colleagues. Will you take us home?'

Joe nodded. 'I'm afraid I can't take you back in my ship. I have to help dematerialise the wreckage before it destroys any terrestrial space stations or satellites.' He gestured at his wife. 'Kitty has kindly offered to teleport you home individually.'

A collective gasp rippled through the room. Most of the guests hadn't known about teleporting when they'd woken up that morning. Joe ignored their reaction and worked his way around the group, shaking hands, followed by Shakila.

'Thank you so much for coming. It was a pleasure to meet you,' he said. 'Any questions, you have Shakila's number. Good luck with persuading your colleagues. Stay in touch.'

When they'd finished, Kitty stepped forward. 'Who wants to go first?' she said, her eyes twinkling.

28. ON THE GOAT WALK

HANNA

HANNA PULLED THE front door of Lucy's parents' house shut behind her with a jarring bang. The moist sea air had swollen the centuries-old wood and she had to tug the brass doorknob forcefully to close it properly.

She looked up at Felix. 'Well, that was horrible. In fact, I think it was the hardest thing I've ever done,' she said.

His expression matched her own. 'Me too,' he replied. 'Can we go and sit on the Goat Walk? I'm not ready to go back to the real world yet.'

'Sure.'

They walked down The Strand, past the pretty pastel houses with their Dutch gables, to the tiny beach and the raised walkway which bordered the Exe Estuary. It was a dull winter's day in Topsham, with a damp chill that penetrated to Hanna's bones.

Felix selected a bench and they sat, looking across to the hills beyond the river, watching a train progress along the opposite shore. A few seabirds pecked the ground below them in a desultory fashion, hunting for worms in the oozing mud revealed by the outgoing tide. The scent of seaweed and saltwater filled Hanna's nostrils, reminding her of Essoona and happier days.

Felix said, 'They took the news well. Considering.'

'Hmm,' replied Hanna. 'They were very . . . in control, weren't they? I won't need to drink any more tea for a week at least. I thought they'd be more upset to hear about the death of their daughter.'

'They're English.' Felix shrugged. 'Just because they didn't cry in front of us doesn't mean they don't feel wretched. Making tea is a coping mechanism for them.' He caressed a hardy little plant growing out of crack in the stone wall behind them. 'They don't know either of us very well. I suspect they were holding back until we left.'

Hanna thought of Samuel and how she hadn't been able to restrain her floods of tears at his funeral. But that had been after she'd had time to get used to the idea of his life ending before he'd even been born.

She remembered the morning after Kitty had found them both by the Regent's Canal, one dead, the other half-dead, and taken them to the language school. Irion and Mary had been strangers to her then: she hadn't wanted to cry in front of them either. Realising this, she felt she understood Lucy's parents better. People reacted to bad news in different ways. Of course they would cry in private.

If only it had never happened. Those moments when the enemy ships had appeared behind them and opened fire on Lucy haunted Hanna's daydreams and nightmares on a merciless, inescapable loop. She relived them every time she closed her eyes. Hanna shivered. 'I keep going over it in my head, Felix,' she said. 'Could I have saved her? If we'd done things differently? We should've taken turns and switched our positions more. Spread the risk.'

'From what you told me, there was nothing you could've done, Hanna' said Felix, staring vacantly ahead. They'd had this conversation before, multiple times.

'It all happened so fast.' Hanna pressed her fingers into her eye-sockets. 'And now we've lost our Lucy.'

Felix buried his face in his hands and his shoulders shook with silent, wracking sobs. Hanna laid her arm across them and gave him what she hoped was a comforting squeeze. She contemplated the horizon, focussing on a lonely white tower on the skyline. Stinging tears welled up and the image blurred.

Felix sniffed and sat up. 'I've been keeping it together, but I just can't anymore. She's *gone*, Hanna. What am I going to do without her?'

Unstoppable tears trickled down Hanna's cheeks. She let out a wail of anguish and Felix joined in. It was a relief to allow the grief the upper hand at last. She thought of Nader, who'd been so patient with her on the awful day she'd nearly crashed her *Tumba*. And Traian, an introverted young Romanian from Hassan's year who'd sometimes entertained them with his guitar playing. She hadn't known either of them well, but now she mourned them all the same. Lives cut short. Potential extinguished. She thought of Lucy again and the gaping hole she'd left in their lives. The river flowed on impassively as she howled.

Eventually, Hanna fumbled for a tissue and blew her nose, noisily and snottily.

'Got one for me?' Felix asked, wiping his eyes on the sleeve of his padded jacket.

She handed him the packet. She jumped as, seemingly

out of nowhere, a black Labrador with a grey muzzle nudged her knee. 'Hello there,' she said, stroking its silky head. An extendable red lead attached the dog to its Barbour-jacketed owner, who hovered awkwardly nearby.

'Is everything all right?' the elderly lady asked hesitantly. 'Nelson always knows if someone's feeling down.'

Hanna sniffed, trying to smile politely. 'He's super. We're fine, thank you. A good friend of ours died last week. We were just remembering her. She loved the Goat Walk.'

'Was she local?'

Felix nodded, still unable to speak.

'You should think about organising her a memorial bench,' the dog walker said kindly. 'Then she'll always have a place here you can visit.'

Hanna beamed at the woman, blinking back the tears which were welling up all over again. 'That's a lovely idea. Thank you. We might just do that.'

'Well, if you're sure you're OK, we'll be on our way. Come along, Nelson.'

'Yes. Thank you,' said Hanna. 'Goodbye Nelson.'

'Have a nice walk,' Felix added.

They watched the figures recede and disappear around the corner. 'I thought Nelson was Kitty, for a minute,' said Hanna.

Felix grinned. 'So did I.' He stood up. 'I'm ready to go back now, if you are?'

Slowly, they returned the way they'd come. The trees behind the wall to their right were skeletal, devoid of all life. It would be a long time before she felt better. Hanna had been through the grieving process often enough to recognise that. But Lucy had died for a cause she believed in. A life she'd chosen, knowing the risks.

Something inside Hanna clicked into place. It was the life she had chosen, too. With Kia and Yonas safely in Addis, she was free to stay on the *Shantivira*, fighting side-by-side with Hassan and her friends, doing what they'd trained so hard for.

She remembered what the Ranglatiri in the video had said – '*My people will take thiss planet, now they know it's here*' – and her resolve strengthened. There would be another, bigger, battle with the Ranglatiri, she was sure of it.

And, when the storm broke, Hanna would happily suffer the same fate as Lucy, if she could stop those monsters from ever setting foot upon the Earth.

29. CHRISTMAS AT THE CATH PALUG
JOE

JOE LEANED BACK in his chair with a satisfied sigh, surreptitiously unfastening the top button of his jeans. Turkey, stuffing, roast potatoes, glazed carrots and not too many sprouts. Now *that* was a Christmas dinner. Angharad and the *Cath Palug* team had done themselves proud. Now he had a difficult decision to make: pudding or another pint? He certainly didn't have room for both.

He looked around the table. John, Rob's aging father-in-law, was trying to explain the finer points of fly fishing to Vadim. He spoke rapidly with a clipped, born-and-bred Edinburgh accent and Vadim wasn't getting one word in ten. Rob was doing his best to fill in with Kawaida, compensating for his lack of specialist vocabulary with enthusiastic gestures and rough sketches on a paper napkin.

Grace was telling Sarah about the bathhouses in Es-soona – how they were less crowded and far cheaper than their UK equivalents. Jaguar-Kitty dozed on the rug in front of the fireplace, stretched out luxuriously. And she hadn't even eaten anything. He could do with a snooze himself. A single triangular ear swivelled in their direction, monitoring the conversation at the table.

Rob and Sarah's children, seven-year-old Carys and five-year-old Jamie, were polishing off the remaining crumbs of their chocolate brownies. They'd eaten faster than the grown-ups and Joe sensed they were getting tired of sitting still.

Jamie pointed to Grace's crocodile handbag, on the floor by her chair. 'That's not *real* dragon skin, is it?' he asked.

Carys backed him up. 'Because that would be *cruel!*'

Joe smothered a chuckle. That bag had always offended him – as if it were an expression of Grace's previous hostility towards his wife. Of course, when she'd chosen it, she hadn't known about Kitty's true form. But now she did, and she was still using it. Luckily, Kitty herself found it hilarious.

Grace picked it up and showed it to the children. 'Not dragon skin. Crocodile skin. So, yes. You're right. It is cruel. I bought it more than twenty years ago, when people didn't think about that sort of thing so much. Now I have it, I feel that if I got rid of it, the poor croc would have died for nothing. So I use it, and remember to be respectful, because a living creature gave its life to make it. It's a great handbag. It'll last me forever.'

So that was her reasoning. Fair enough. 'Anyone need another drink?' Joe asked. 'My round.'

As he stood at the bar, waiting for Ianto to pull the pints, small fingers tugged at his top. Carys and Jamie gazed up at him with two pairs of Rob's brown eyes. From their expressions, they wanted something. He crouched to their level.

'What's up?' he said.

Jamie pointed at Kitty. 'Can we play with her?' he whispered shyly.

Cath? he asked privately. *That OK with you?*

Sure.

Joe showed them how to rub her tummy up and down, the way she liked it, and left them to it. He paid for the drinks and let his change clink into the collecting tin for the lifeboats. He thought of the brave men and women who went out in all weathers, their craft tossed about by the elements, doing what they could to save people. Like the *Shantivira's* crew.

His eyes moistened as he remembered last week's memorial service for the pilots they'd lost. Lucy. Traian. Nader. They'd held a tree-planting ceremony in the *Shantivira's* orchard. Not a religious service: their closest friends and relatives had written and given the eulogies, with touching little personal details which still stuck in Joe's memory.

As the families planted the trees, he'd recited Dylan Thomas' 'Do not go gentle into that good night' with a lump in his throat so thick, he was amazed he'd made it to the end of the poem without breaking down completely.

He returned to the table, blinking the tears away. Somehow, they'd stop the Ranglatiri. They had to. And he would avenge his lost crew members, from this battle and the last one. He wondered what useful intelligence Rowan had managed to gather so far on her lonely undercover mission. According to Kitty, 'Reinecka', the Ranglatiri council member, was already feared and respected, progressing up the ranks one fight-to-the-death at a time. At some point Rowan would be in a position to challenge

Isegrimma, their leader.

He pushed the dark thoughts of vengeance away and forced himself to smile as he handed out the drinks. Today was Christmas Day and, for the first time ever, he could celebrate it with both friends and family. That was something worth fighting for.

On the hearthrug, Kitty had shifted to her Syenitian form and was kneeling on the floor, talking to Carys and Jamie. They ran back to the table and accosted Sarah. 'Muuuum, can we play out with Kitty?'

Kitty stood up and crossed the room. She caught his eye and winked at him. 'Would that be OK?' she asked Sarah and Rob. 'They've got the fidgets and, to be honest, so have I. Some fresh air'll do us good. I promise to take care of them.'

Husband and wife regarded each other, reaching an agreement without needing words. Rob said, 'Sure, if you don't mind. Thanks.'

The children cheered and Kitty's face spilt into a toothy grin. 'Right then kids, wrap up extra warm. Coats, hats, gloves and scarves.'

What was she planning? She wasn't saying.

The door banged shut as they left the bar. Into the silence that followed, Grace said, 'By the way, we have an announcement to make.'

An announcement? With surprise, Joe noticed she was holding Vadim's hand. Gripping it, in fact, as if she were nervous about something. Behind them, through the window, he observed black-horse-Kitty picking her way up the steep mountainside behind the beer garden, headed in the direction of *Moel Lefn*. Two brightly coloured figures were perched upon her back.

Vadim said, 'As you know, I retire at the end of the year.'

'Yes,' said Joe, raising his glass. 'Congratulations! Here's to you, mate. I hope it's a long and happy one.'

Vadim looked at Grace. 'I hope so too,' he said, his eyes sparkling with affection.

Joe began to understand what this was all about. A broad grin spread across his face as he waited for confirmation.

'And I'll be going home in January, once Kia has gone back to Ethiopia,' said Grace. 'So Vadim's going to come and live with me. In Brecon.'

Joe stood up and pumped Vadim's hand up and down. Then he walked round the table and hugged Grace tightly, kissing her on the cheek. 'That's wonderful news!' He winked at Vadim. 'You'll be able to keep an eye on her for me. She has a terrible habit of getting into trouble!'

Vadim's laughter lines deepened into a warm smile, making his moustache bristle.

Joe said, 'I knew you two got on well, but I thought you said you were just friends?'

'We were,' replied Grace. 'We've had so much fun together, these last few months. But when you all went out to fight and I realised I might lose him as well as you— well, then I understood it was more serious.'

At the end of the table, John got unsteadily to his feet. 'There's hope for us all yet. A toast! To passion for pensioners!'

They raised their glasses. 'Passion for pensioners!' they cried, causing heads in the rest of the pub restaurant to swivel in their direction.

John sat down again, saying with a cheeky twinkle in his eye, 'I know we've only just met, Gracie, but I can see you're quite the catch. Do you have any friends you could introduce me to?'

Luckily, their dessert arrived at that moment, saving Grace from having to respond. Joe sipped his pint, a warm glow of happiness spreading outwards from his heart. Sometimes things did change for the better.

He watched the black dot outside, climbing high on the snowy hillside. It stopped moving, grew and turned red, then leapt off the mountain into the air, wings unfurled and beating steadily. The red dragon flew towards the *Cath Palug*, Carys and Jamie still on top. Their mother had her back to the window and Rob's attention was on his Christmas pudding. Joe decided to say nothing: it was probably better they learnt about this little joyride after it was safely over. That had always been Kitty's way, he realised – to ask for forgiveness rather than permission.

Happy Christmas, Joe, she said in his head, flying past the pub and out of view, headed for the deserted wilds of Eryri.

Happy Christmas, my love, he replied.

CHARACTERS, PLACES, ALIENS

Main characters in *italics*.

Afra Azu	A Sayari smuggler, captain of the *Gezi Urdina*. Love of Dan's life
Aldeman Varpushaukka	Head of the Syenitian Council, Syenitia's representative to the Galaksi Alliance, Joe's brother-in-law
Aldina	Syenitia's second city and home of the Syenitian spacecraft-building industry
Amra	Remote planet in the Elegua sector, where Rowan exiled Dan
Aneira	Hanna's Amranese friend whose life has been devastated by the destruction of her planet
Aussie Ozzy	Australian *Shantivira* pilot, Hassan's best friend
Bellyn	Afra's former Ranglatiri co-pilot and business partner
Björn	Tima Rahimi's commercial diver husband and frequent visitor to the *Shantivira*
Cephalo	Pwezan Chief Engineer
Chooli	The *Shantivira's* stores manager, a Navajo from New Mexico
Cylf	Syenitian cybernetic life forms / walking computers
Dalian	Syenitian Council member and Syenitia's defence minister

Dan Simpson	Former ISS flight engineer turned interstellar smuggler
Delius	The *Shantivira's* main computer, a Cylf
Dunia	Kawaida name for planet Earth
Dunia House	Home to the *Shantivira's* second year students during their training at the Essoona Pilots' Academy
Essoona	Administrative capital of Syenitia
Eyvindran	A Syenitian and the first captain of the *Shantivira*
Farida	Indonesian former *Shantivira* trainee, Hanna's close friend
Felix	German trainee *Shantivira* pilot. Lucy's boyfriend
Gambrinus	The *Shantivira's* backup computer, a Cylf
Gezi Urdina	Afra's blue spacecraft
Grace Llewellyn	Joe's mother
Grooka	Planet home to short green-furred aliens
Hagar	The *Shantivira's* medical officer
Hanna Abebe	Trainee *Shantivira* pilot from Ethiopia, former cleaner
Hassan Nhial	*Shantivira* pilot from South Sudan, Hanna's boyfriend
Henning	Ranglatiri space pirate and distributor of contraband contraceptives
Irion	Kawaida teacher at the Dunia School of Language in London. From Sayari, married to Mary.
Joe Llewellyn	Captain of the *Shantivira*
Jorge/Pedro Mendez	UN representative for Argentina and Nestor's friend
Kazembi	Senior *Shantivira* pilot with a talent for leadership
Kia Abebe	Hanna's younger sister

Kitty / Kitvian / Reika / Kelpie Ahmitorsdottir / Llewellyn	Ancient shape-shifting and teleporting space demon, half Syenitian, half space spirit. Red Dragon of the Britons, Guardian of Wales and wife of Joe Llewellyn
Laro	A city on the planet Amra
Lucy	English trainee *Shantivira* pilot, in Hanna's year
Malwod	Mwongo captain
Maneewan	The *Shantivira's* catering manager
Mary	Manager at the Dunia School of Language. From Yorkshire, UK
Matthew	Nestor's assistant engineer
Mhasibu	Planet home to grey-skinned aliens with three eyes, founder member of the Galaksi Alliance
Min-joon Park	Korean caretaker and gardener at Dunia House
Mwongo	Planet home to slimy aliens with a reputation for dishonesty
Nader	Senior *Shantivira* pilot from Tunisia
Nestor Evans	Leader of the Anti-Alien League and engineer extraordinaire
Nikolai Poroshkin	Russian trainee *Shantivira* pilot, in Hanna's year
Nkosi	Senior *Shantivira* pilot from Johannesburg, Kazembi's husband
Oso-Urrun	Planet at the outer edge of the galaxy, location of Bellyn's backup facility
Pride of Essoona	Joe's *Korento*-class live-aboard spacecraft
Pweza	Planet home to blue octopus aliens
Qingqing	Senior *Shantivira* pilot and Yisheng's daughter

Ranglatiri	Planet home to terrifying, marauding cannibals
Roberto	Brazilian trainee *Shantivira* pilot, in Hanna's year
Rob Morgan	Joe's friend / former NCO from the Royal Regiment of Wales
Rohini Chatterjee	First human captain of the *Shantivira*, from West Bengal
Rowan / Reinecka / Verndari Ahmitorsdottir	Kitty's twin sister, also a space demon. Married to Aldeman
Samuel Abebe	Hanna's stillborn son
Samuel Abebe	Hanna's younger brother, died of rabies in 2004
Saïd	French trainee *Shantivira* pilot, in Hanna's year
Sayari	Planet in the Sungura sector, home to silver aliens with brightly-coloured hair, founder member of the Galaksi Alliance
Shakila	Senior *Shantivira* pilot from Iraq, Joe's public relations officer
Shantivira	The Syenitian space station protecting the Earth
Song-yi Park	Korean housekeeper and cook at Dunia House
Susan Omondi	Director of the United Nations Office for Outer Space Affairs
Svetlana Poroshkin	Former *Shantivira* pilot and Nikolai Poroshkin's mother
Syenitia	Kitty's home planet, founder member of the Galaksi Alliance
Tarumbet	Planet home to orange aliens with elongated heads

Tima	Flight instructor for trainee *Shantivira* pilots, married to Björn
Urca	Hanna's *Tumba* on the *Shantivira*
Vadim	Senior *Shantivira* pilot from Armenia
Vruxil	Planet home to disreputable space-voyaging rodents
Yisheng	The *Shantivira's* second-in-command
Yonas Abebe	Kia's son / Hanna's nephew
Yonas Abebe	Hanna's dead older brother
Wadudu	Planet home to insect-like aliens with four arms
William	Senior *Shantivira* pilot from Rapid City and Joe's close friend
Westwood	

AUTHOR'S NOTE

Sharing ideas and educating ourselves are essential steps on the path to a fair and sustainable future. But there's a lot more we can do to build resilience within our communities. For example, getting to know our neighbours. Offering help. *Accepting* help. Forging genuine, enriching connections with other living, breathing humans. Learning new skills. Passing on knowledge. Becoming active citizens rather than passive consumers.

Change for the better can only come from the bottom up.

Fay Abernethy
March 2025

REFERENCES/INSPIRATION

BOOKS

Kate Raworth: Doughnut Economics, Seven Ways to Think Like a 21st-Century Economist

Jason Hickel: The Divide: A Brief Guide to Global Inequality and its Solutions

Stephanie Kelton: The Deficit Myth: Modern Monetary Theory and the Birth of the People's Economy

Jon Alexander: Citizens: Why the Key to Fixing Everything is All of Us

Paddy le Flufy: Building Tomorrow: Averting Environmental Crisis with a New Economic System

Claire Provost, Matt Kennard: Silent Coup: How Corporations Overthrew Democracy

Nelson Mandela: The Long Walk to Freedom

Eoghan Daltun: An Irish Atlantic Rainforest: A Personal Journey into the Magic of Rewilding

Kim Stanley Robinson: The Ministry of The Future

Masanobu Fukuoka: The One-Straw Revolution

Nick Hayes: Wild Service: Why Nature Needs You

Rutger Bregman: Humankind: A Hopeful History

Fork Ranger: Solving Climate Change with Food (recipes) https://forkranger.com

LINKS

Shakila's plan to reshape corporations' priorities in Chapter 8 was inspired by the Future Guardian™ model of governance, brainchild of Riversimple, a Welsh hydrogen fuel cell car company. This is a revolutionary way of structuring an organisation which complies with existing UK law. For more information, see Chapter 3 of Paddy le Flufy's book *Building Tomorrow: Averting Environmental Crisis with a New Economic System* or, for a brief summary, go to www.riversimple.com/governance.

www.planetcritical.com or on YouTube.
Fascinating, deep-dive podcasts to stop you feeling helpless about the climate crisis:

How did Grace learn Spanish so quickly? The same way I've been learning Welsh.
www.saysomethingin.com

The Miyawaki method
www.nippon.com/en/in-depth/d00789

The Miyawaki Method | Trees Outside Woodland
youtube.com/watch?v=0VizWfEIW1U

Leith Community Croft, Edinburgh
www.earth-in-common.org/leith-community-croft

Want to know more about the punk scene in Siberia?
https://daily.bandcamp.com/scene-report/yakutsk-punk-scene-list

ACKNOWLEDGEMENTS

Thank YOU, for reading this book. And extra thanks to the members of the Shantivira Readers' Club, who keep me going with their kind words and encouragement.

Thanks to Hilary, Emma, Michael and the teams at Jericho Writers and BB eBooks. Thanks to Patrick for another wonderful cover. And special thanks to Alex, for pretty much everything else.

NOT READY TO LEAVE THE SHANTIVIRA JUST YET?

Then come on over to www.fayabernethy.com and download The Man with the Dragon Tattoo – the story of how Joe joined the *Shantivira* back in 1997. For FREE!

This is an *exclusive* story. You can't buy it anywhere: you can only get hold of it by joining The Shantivira Readers' Club. In return, I'll (occasionally) update you on how the latest *Shantivira* book is coming along.

I promise to only send you emails I believe you'll find

interesting and entertaining. You can unsubscribe easily anytime. I will guard your personal data fiercely, with dragons.

If you enjoyed *First Contact, Second Chances*, then please tell other people you think might like it too. And if you could leave a little review – or even just a star rating – that would be fantastic. As a part-time indie author, my marketing budget is so tiny, it's invisible to the naked eye. This means I rely utterly on the kindness of readers like you to spread the word about the *Shantivira*.

Get it here:

Want to read more by Fay Abernethy?

THE CLEANER, THE CAT AND THE SPACE STATION

THE SHANTIVIRA BOOK ONE

There's an alien space station orbiting the Earth, secretly protecting us from invasion.
And it's recruiting humans like you to train as fighter pilots.

Since leaving Ethiopia, Hanna Abebe has survived in

London by working illegally as a cleaner. But her life unravels after a sexual assault; living rough, she loses the resulting pregnancy and very nearly her life. Help arrives and Hanna's rescuers welcome her into an unusual new family: a school for recruits to the *Shantivira*, the secret alien space station which protects the Earth. Then Hanna uncovers a traitor in their midst . . .

Lucy Cooper is horse riding on Dartmoor when a mysterious shape-shifter offers her a place on the *Shantivira's* training programme. Her instinct is to refuse, but an organisation claiming the *Shantivira's* motives are sinister persuades Lucy to become their spy . . .

Joe Llewellyn is bored. Being the captain of the *Shantivira* isn't the challenge he'd hoped. Plus, he'd like to inform the Earth about aliens, but his boss won't permit it. Then a stray asteroid hits the ISS and Joe is forced to let the cat out of the bag . . .

This heart-warming blend of fantasy and science fiction is a must-read for fans of Becky Chambers, Ursula Le Guin, Ben Aaronovitch, Douglas Adams and Doctor Who.

What readers are saying about *The Cleaner, the Cat and the Space Station:*

'A promising new series that will delight fans of Becky Chambers.'

'Great fun! Humor, pathos, and a rather different kind of storyline.'

'Fantastic sci-fi adventure . . . a wonderful romp through a believable universe.'

'Amazing . . . one of those you can't put down.'

'Highly imaginative and entertaining.'

'A gem of a book . . . a thrilling and surprising storyline.'

Get it here:

DID MY SPELLING ANNOY YOU?

Colour instead of color, realise instead of realize, grey instead of gray?

Then I'm going to go out on a limb here and assume you might be a) in the US or b) an American. Possibly both!

Currently, there's just one version of this book available and that's in the only variety of English I feel capable of writing in – British English. *Vive la différence!*

ABOUT THE AUTHOR

Twenty-five years ago, Fay Abernethy left the UK for a six-month engineering secondment in Germany, fell in love and stayed there. Brexit broke her heart.

First Contact, Second Chances is her third novel.

Printed in Great Britain
by Amazon

61738897R00221